C000227318

CIVILIZATION

BOOK TWO OF THE "DISPLACED" SERIES

STEPHEN DRAKE

THE DISPLACED SERIES

Displaced

Civilization

Dedicated to Linda and Susan; for without their help and support, this work would not have been possible.

A special thanks to K.J. Simmill and J.C. Stone, excellent authors in their own right, for all their suggestions, help, and for taking the time in their busy lives to read my work.

The Murdock family watched the pod descend, complete with smoke and fire and roar, as it cut a path through the early morning sky. Murdock, taking his position as Guardian seriously, knew he'd have to investigate and act as a liaison between human and Oomah. After it landed, some distance away, Murdock and Mei Lee herded the kids into the cave from the overlook.

"Are you going to stay here or head to the cabin?" Murdock asked Mei Lee.

"I'll head for the cabin with the kids," she answered. "Beron is going with you, isn't he?" Murdock could see the concern for him, both by the question as well as her knitted brows and the worried, questioning look on her face.

Murdock could read her expressions completely after three years together. "Yes, he is. He seems to be curious."

Mei Lee raised an eyebrow and turned to look at Murdock. "Are you serious? That would be a first!"

"Not really. He was curious about us, when we first arrived," Murdock replied.

"I just find it curious that he's curious," Mei Lee quipped.

They both chuckled a little. "All of you behave and mind

your mother," Murdock warned. The children had lined up from eldest to youngest, as was their custom whenever their father left for an extended period of time. He knelt down and kissed their foreheads individually. After which he would look at them as if to burn their images into his memory. The children knew, from long practice, that this ritual was not for their benefit, but for his. Murdock was well aware that there were no guarantees in life. Even though he was well versed in living here, he knew that any accident could be fatal and could befall anyone at any time. He knew it, Mei Lee knew it, and the children knew it.

When all the children had filed past, Mei Lee came over to say her good-byes. Murdock was still kneeling down, finishing with little Rosa Lea, when Mei Lee came over. He placed his hands on his wife's swollen belly and kissed it gently. As he did, Mei Lee smiled and stroked his head gently. As he stood, he picked her up. Her arms slid around his neck with practiced ease as her feet left the floor of the cave. They kissed, passionately, as if for the last time.

"When were you going to head back to the cabin?" Murdock asked, still holding her close, her feet well off the cave floor. *I do love holding her this way and she never complains about it*, he thought.

"I don't know. The kids need to eat first and we have to pack the cart," she replied, smiling down lovingly at Murdock.

I've done my best to make her happy and I think I've succeeded as much as anyone could. "Don't overdo it," he said sternly but lovingly. "If *they* get to be too much, let me know and I'll cut things short, if I can," he said, more for the kids' benefit than Mei Lee's, as he set her down and started gathering his gear in preparation for leaving. Mei Lee had started herding the kids down to the residential area of the cave. As she got them all going down the tunnel, she turned to see Murdock's back as he stepped off the edge of the overlook.

It didn't take long for Murdock to levitate down the side of the mountain for the two hundred feet to the valley floor. His

2

feet softly touched the ground close to Rose's tomb. He made it a personal ritual to kiss his fingers and then touch them to Rose's tomb; a symbolic kiss for one as beloved as she was. When he finished, he turned and walked toward the grounded transport pod, following the trail that paralleled the stream.

As he walked downstream, Beron walked beside him and this caused Murdock to smile. He hadn't heard his large, brown friend come up beside him. It didn't surprise him that Beron just appeared; it was a habit of his. Usually, Murdock could sense when his friend was close by. Of late, though, Beron had taken to just popping up, just as he had in the early days of their relationship. *How long had it been?* To Murdock, it seemed that Beron had always been his friend and he had always lived here. *Five years doesn't seem right, somehow. It doesn't seem to be long enough.*

"Old stuff on mind," Beron flashed after they had been walking for some time.

"Just remembering," Murdock replied with a small smile.

The telepathic communications between Murdock and Beron had improved greatly. Now, it seemed effortless to Murdock, and was more like the rapport he and Mei Lee shared. Telepathic communications between the other Oomah were improving slowly, except for the huge white bear; the name "Nanuk" seemed to pop into his head whenever he thought of him.

He had spent quite a bit of time in Alaska and Canada, back on Earth, and had picked up that name from one of the local Inuit tribes. The huge white bear had been the bane of his existence for the first couple of years, but was now ranked among his dearest friends and Murdock could communicate with him as easily as he did with Beron. He had ceased to think of the Oomah as "bears". To him, they all had individual personalities, wants, and desires and weren't that different from humans. They just looked different.

"How are young ones? Bridget?" Murdock asked his big friend.

"Growing," the answer flashed to Murdock's mind. He took it

3

as all was well with them and that was always a good thing. An angry or upset Oomah would be bad for all concerned.

"You cubs grow quick! Any age of understanding?"

"None yet."

As best as he could figure out, the "age of understanding" was that age when kids understood that their actions held consequences and could be held accountable for them. To the Oomah, that depended on the individual, but usually occurred by the age of seven. In humans, it was the age when parents quit covering for their kids' mistakes or bailing them out. On Earth, Murdock had known some thirty-year-olds that wouldn't have qualified.

The pair had walked for some time before they could see the pod in the distance.

"You sense anyone inside?" Murdock flashed as the pod grew slowly closer. He had tried and could sense nothing.

"None," Beron responded.

"You see pod that carried me land?" In the past five years, this was the first time that the subject had come up.

"Yes, two darks to know someone inside," flashed to his mind from Beron who had levitated a fish from the stream and was eating it as he walked.

Murdock was hoping the same procedures would be in operation; a two day wait, but he couldn't be sure. He had promised Beron, and Beron's father, that he would meet the new arrivals to ensure the Oomah's safety from the humans. After all, it was his responsibility as guardian. It took several more hours of walking before they had arrived at the pod.

Murdock looked at the pod in awe. It was at least seven times the size of the transport pod he had arrived in and seemed to be a lot thicker at the outer edges. As he inspected the pod, he sent his astral self to the pod he had arrived in, more for judging the distance than anything else. *This pod has set down about five miles from the first one,* he thought, *and that is entirely too close to the Oomah sanctuary, for my tastes.*

"Wrong?" Beron flashed after an extended silence.

"This too close to the Oomah," Murdock told his friend. *"Better if was further away."*

"Move," Beron flashed. He had found a comfortable spot and had lain down to watch.

"I can't move this, it's too big!"

"Have attempted?"

"No, but I know it's just too big!"

"Can move self?"

"Yes, but this is different!"

"Different because you think it!"

Murdock just looked at Beron. He could have sworn Beron shrugged. He walked around the huge pod looking up at it. Eventually, he made it back to where Beron was reclined and plopped down beside him.

"Can you move it?" he asked his huge friend after some time.

"Easy! You do."

As he sat there looking at the huge pod, Murdock could not imagine his being able to move it. *I know the pod's proximity to the Oomah is going to cause no end of trouble. I know the occupants will start being curious and start exploring. I know it has to be moved,* he thought.

"Throw doubts far, first! Clear mind!" The flashed thoughts were insistent, but not harsh.

Murdock thought his friend was right. He had decided that it couldn't be moved without attempting it and his mind went about proving him right, convincing him of the impossibility of it. As he sat next to his friend, Murdock sat cross-legged on the ground and cleared his mind. He cleared away all of his doubts and concentrated on becoming calm. When he was ready, he attempted to levitate the pod. After several hours, it remained unmoved.

"Only think object, nothing else. See it move."

Murdock resettled and made another attempt after clearing away any doubts and distractions. As he sat there, he opened his eyes just a little and saw the pod floating a few inches off the ground. As he stood, the pod dropped heavily.

"Did you help?" Murdock asked Beron as he turned to look to his friend.

"What think?" flashed to his mind as Beron got to his feet and headed off downstream. As Murdock turned to follow his friend, he noticed the pod floating a hundred yards off the ground and in front of them. Murdock, shocked at his own accomplishment, was even more so at Beron's. As he followed after his friend, he was having a hard time wrapping his mind around Beron's capabilities and their significance.

When the pair reached the vicinity of Murdock's pod, Beron allowed the levitating pod to settle gently to the ground.

"Where?" flashed to his mind from Beron.

"I thought further downstream, on the next terrace, at least."

"You do!"

Murdock walked forward a little and made his preparations. He focused as much as he could on the pod and refused to be distracted. In short order, he levitated the pod and started off downstream once more, lifting the pod above the trees. Beron followed and didn't try to communicate or distract him.

Murdock had decided to follow the stream rather than the river. He had not been that way for a long time and not for any distance. When he saw the edge of the terrace approaching, he decided to rest a bit and set the pod down gently.

"Why stop?"

"I need a little rest and some water," Murdock explained. He had noticed that it was going to be sundown soon.

"How manage edge?"

Murdock was uncertain. He thought about setting the pod down below the edge while he stayed on top of the terrace.

"Move self with object!"

Murdock was shocked. That was something he hadn't considered. If he understood, he would levitate the pod and himself over the edge of the terrace. *I have accomplished so much*

6

more than I'd ever expected today and I'm starting to be mentally fatigued, he thought.

"Excuse!" Beron chided.

Am I making excuses, he questioned. *I don't feel I am. I honestly feel fatigued, but is that, in itself, an excuse? Beron has been pushing me, goading me to push my limits. He doesn't want me to fail,* he thought. *He wants me to see what my limits are. To be aware of them and what I can actually do if the need should arise. I have to admit that levitating the pod was a lot easier than I could have imagined.* He had been levitating the pod, true enough, but it felt different somehow, than when he levitated himself. *Can I really levitate the pod and myself at the same time in a safe transition off the terrace? To be honest, I have no idea.*

Murdock finally got to his feet, levitated the pod, and started for the edge of the terrace. When he was about ten feet from the edge, he lifted himself off the ground while still moving forward and levitating the pod. A few more steps and he, and the pod, were over the edge. A few more and he started to lower himself and the pod with him at a gentle downward angle.

He didn't think about how far up he was. The thought that he was doing the impossible never entered his mind. He found that he was tired, but the fatigue seemed to help him focus on the tasks at hand. It wasn't long and he was on the ground again and the pod was still floating above him. He proceeded downstream for another mile before setting the pod back on the ground relatively close to the stream that had met his needs so long ago.

He didn't need to see Beron to feel his pride; the pride of a teacher for a gifted student. He had decided to spend the night here and located a campsite. He started a fire and as it snapped and crackled, he sat and nibbled on some smoked venison. Beron had caught another fish and was eating quietly while Murdock ate and thought about the day's accomplishments.

Right after Mei Lee saw Murdock leave the overlook ledge, she started missing him. She didn't, however, let the fact that she didn't like the periods of absence keep her from her own responsibilities. She did have three kids to care for and another close at hand. She never had to go through childbirth alone and wasn't about to think about it now. She knew her husband would be there for her, if at all possible.

After herding all three kids into the residence cave, she made sure they all had some smoked venison and plenty of water. When all the kids' needs were met, she loaded the cart for the trip home.

Even though Murdock had originally built the cabin for himself and Rose, Mei Lee still thought of it as her home. She had lived there with Murdock and Rose as their co-wife. She had delivered Chun Hua there. She had helped Rose deliver Andrew there. *I have always belonged there*, she thought. *It is my home.*

Andrew and Chun Hua were helping her with the loading as best they could. When everything was ready, she loaded all three kids onto the cart and levitated it, and herself, down the mountainside from the overlook ledge. Once on the ground, she stopped at Rose's tomb, as was her ritual whenever she passed this way, and took all three kids over to the stone tomb. As usual, she told Rose all about everything that had happened since the last time she had stopped and shown her all the children, especially her namesake. When the girls were finished, Mei Lee made an effort to explain the whole story of Rose to Andrew. She was attempting to ensure that Andrew knew all about his brave mother through repetition, if nothing else.

When they were finished at the tomb, Mei Lee levitated the front part of the cart and used her telekinetic power to pull the cart on the trek home. Chun Hua was charged with watching over capricious Rosa Lea, to ensure that she stayed on the cart. Andrew had chosen, of late, to take his job of protecting the womenfolk very seriously.

Murdock had made his son a spear that was nearly twice as

long as Andrew was high. Mei Lee had trained him in its use and now, he had decided to lead the females to the cabin. As she walked, she first felt and then saw Bridget approach.

"*Walk with you?*" Bridget flashed, politely. To Mei Lee, their politeness was one of the many endearing traits of the Oomah.

"*Yes. Happy for company,*" Mei Lee responded. She had met Beron's favorite mate a long time ago, with Rose, and they had maintained the relationship even after Rose's death.

"*Brave one,*" Bridget stated with pride, indicating Andrew with a tilt of the head in his direction.

"*Very,*" Mei Lee responded with pride in her son. *He may not be from my body, but he is, nonetheless, my son,* she thought.

"*Soon?*" Bridget asked and Mei Lee knew she meant her swollen belly.

"*Yes, soon,*" Mei Lee responded as she unconsciously felt her belly through the buckskin dress that Murdock and Rose had made for her. "*You?*" she asked Bridget.

"*Not soon,*" Bridget responded. Mei Lee knew that Bridget had several cubs and was expecting another.

They walked on for a while and Mei Lee had the impression that there was something that was bothering Bridget.

"*Wrong?*" she asked finally. Mei Lee knew Bridget was too polite to burden her, without prompting, with her concerns.

Through an onslaught of mental images, Bridget managed to communicate to Mei Lee that she was concerned with the new transport pod and its occupants. Were they friendly or murderous? Would they hunt down and kill the Oomah? To Bridget, it was chaos to her once orderly life, and she was having trouble coping with it.

"*Murdock will keep us informed,*" Mei Lee said, doing her best to calm her friend's fears and try to get Bridget to stop worrying so much about things that no one knows the answer to. "*If the situation changes, he will tell us. I am certain Murdock will do whatever necessary to protect Oomah.*" This seemed to calm Bridget significantly.

Mei Lee stopped for a quick rest to get some water and see to the kids. Bridget was watching the young humans. After a brief rest, Mei Lee was once again headed home. She had thought that Bridget would have left soon after her fears were dealt with, but she didn't, and Mei Lee was starting to suspect other motives.

"Murdock ask you watch over us?" Mei Lee asked her large friend.

"No," Bridget responded with a shocked tint to her response. Mei Lee knew the Oomah had never lied to her or Murdock. They may not offer any information, but if asked a direct question they would answer directly and truthfully, or give no answer at all.

"Beron?" Mei Lee asked. Bridget gave no answer, which to Mei Lee was an answer. *"No need you guide me home,"* Mei Lee pointed out to Bridget.

"Like you company. Like you cubs," Bridget responded excitedly.

"Like you as well," Mei Lee responded with a smile. She did like having Bridget with her on her trip home. Her speculation was that since Beron and Murdock had to be gone, Beron had asked Bridget to see to it that Mei Lee and the kids got home safely and watch over them until Murdock got back. If true, Mei Lee was thankful for it. *I don't mind taking care of the kids alone at home,* she thought, *but I don't like us out on the trail without Kevin.*

It took Mei Lee the better part of the day to get home from the caves. She and Bridget had engaged in a mental chit-chat, which Mei Lee wasn't used to and, as a general rule, had no use for. This time, however, she did it to make sure her friend knew that her presence was wanted and appreciated. Mei Lee would not have been so rude as to ignore Bridget. *I owe far too much to all the Oomah to ever be rude to any of them.*

After the cart was emptied and stored, Mei Lee herded the kids inside and bid Bridget good night. *I know Bridget is outside somewhere keeping watch,* she thought. *I find it…comforting.*

Shortly after entering the cabin, Mei Lee, with some minimal help from the two eldest, built a fire, fed everyone, and got the kids off to bed. It did take some time to accomplish, considering her condition. Once the kids were asleep, Mei Lee stripped off her buckskin dress and boots and went out to the spa for a hot bath.

She closed her eyes as the hot water gently caressed her body. The more she relaxed, the more her thoughts turned to Murdock and the circumstances that had led to them being together. She'd stayed with him, after Rose's death, because of a promise she'd made to Rose — and, to a lesser degree, to help herself in her own time of loss. Murdock and Rose had been there when Tom Collier, her husband, had died protecting Rose. She had initially lived with the couple to give herself and Chun Hua a safe place to live after she was ousted from her leadership position of the first colony. Somewhere along the line, she wasn't sure exactly when, she had fallen in love with him. Currently, she couldn't envision a life without him.

When she finished her bath, she went inside to dry off in front of the fireplace. As she stood in front of the flames, she closed her eyes and let the heat caress her, further relaxing her already abused muscles. The comforting crackle of the fire eased her further by letting her mind know that all was as it should be. Once dry, she climbed into bed and as she lay there, she found that she desperately needed Murdock's arms around her. *I always seem to sleep better when he's home*, she thought. *He makes me feel safe.*

After Murdock had eaten and drank, he lay on his side looking at the fire. He knew Beron was close by, even though he couldn't see him in the dark, the firelight having robbed him of his night vision. As he lay there, he started to get the barest inkling of a clue that there might be something that Beron wanted to ask. It was like an itch inside his mind. This was the way Beron got him to ask if there was something he wanted. A statement of that nature would grant the over-polite Oomah leave to ask what he wanted to know.

"Was there something you wanted to ask?" Murdock finally asked, capitulating. Sometimes, it was the only way to scratch that itch.

Murdock was presented with two mental images of his father. Murdock didn't understand. One image seemed to zoom out, and the view was on this planet. It looked like him standing on the edge of the terrace, just a few hours ago. The image zoomed back in on his face. The other image zoomed out showing one of the many images from his first sharing session with Beron. He recognized it as his father talking to his uncle in their home. The image zoomed back in on the face.

"Same. Why?" Beron asked pointedly. A human would have said he was rude, but the Oomah didn't mince words.

"Same...age?" Murdock speculated. This was disturbing to him as well. He had no mirror to look at his face every day, so he had no way of seeing what Beron, or anyone else, saw. As best he could figure, he now was the age his father was then, but that didn't explain why he should look so much like his father. *I know sons tend to favor their fathers, but this seems to be more, like we were identical twins,* he thought. *"Other than that, it is mystery to me."*

Beron was quiet for a long time. *"Mystery. Investigate later."* Murdock knew Beron disliked mysteries. Beron's world view was that there is always an explanation and he always needed to know what it was.

As he lay there, he decided to check with Mei Lee and tried to communicate with her telepathically. Their telepathic communication was more than just checking in to see how she was and how the kids were. There were those questions, to be sure, but that wasn't the extent of their communication. They also exchanged many of the personal things husbands exchange with wives. It was made all the more personal because of the telepathy. *What could be more personal than sharing thoughts with someone else?* They were still in telepathic contact when they both fell asleep.

Murdock awoke at sunup. He managed to get the fire going again to take the chill off as he ate and drank. Beron was still there and was having his own breakfast. As he sat and ate, Murdock was looking at the large pod more closely. *The length of the landing struts seems to be the same as the pod that brought me,* he thought. *It's roughly the same shape. I see the larger storage compartments on the underside. I wonder what surprises they hold. This pod is just bigger, bigger in circumference, thicker.* He was still marveling that he had managed to levitate something this massive and himself, at the same time.

"No sign inside, yet," Beron flashed, interrupting his thoughts.

Murdock got to his feet and decided to explore the area. Since he had never been here before, he needed to know what was around. It was well past dusk when they had arrived, and he was otherwise occupied.

Deer scat. Tuft of hair that looks like deer. Hoofprints everywhere, he thought as he wandered around. He checked the creek. *Lots of fish, but how many occupants were in this pod?* There was something nagging at his memory. Something he should remember. *Each successive pod will increase your population by a factor of ten,* the thought finally came to him. It was what the short briefing had said aboard the pod when he first woke up. *Two Hundred people,* he thought. *I'm not sure the stream can support that many. There might be enough fish for a change of diet, but not as a major food source, not for two hundred, anyway.* As he looked around, he could see the top of the terrace. With his back to the stream, looking toward the river, he could see the slightly rolling hills. Some of the hills might be able to hide an approach, but without going there, he wasn't sure.

Murdock crossed the stream and found that there were few

13

trees past the stream. There was, however, a steep cliff-face. It appeared to be lower than the terrace edge, but not by much. The little bit of exploration he'd done had disclosed no immediate or easy access to the top of the cliff.

"*Restrictions?*" Murdock flashed Beron telepathically, trying to ascertain any restrictions Beron wanted for the new humans.

"*None, this place,*" Beron responded. He did, however, send an image to Murdock that some distance up the cliff-face and away from the steam, the "dread area", as Murdock referred to it, did extend this far downstream and further.

"*Easy way up?*" Murdock asked. Even though he had failed to locate an easy path up the cliff-face, that didn't mean there wasn't one. He still had the stinging memory of his failure to locate the cleverly concealed entrance to the residential area of the cave many years ago.

"*Walk? no,*" Beron responded.

That eased Murdock's mind. He did want a way to keep an eye on the newcomers without them knowing they were being observed. He was periodically trying, but failing, to get any sign that anyone was moving inside the pod yet. Beron hadn't gotten any, either, Murdock found after checking with him. As he looked up the cliff face, he decided to levitate up to see what was up there. As he did so, with Beron close behind, he noticed how high the cliff face was and that the tops of the trees failed to reach the top of the cliff and the top of the cliff overhung the treetops of the closer trees.

As he settled lightly on the ground, he looked over the edge and could plainly see the top of the pod as well as the tops of the trees. He could not, however, see the ground by the pod's edge closest to the stream; the angle was wrong. Murdock turned from the edge and surveyed the plain. It, too, had gently rolling hills and a good number of trees in the distance. He didn't, however, see any source of water.

"*Sign inside,*" Beron told him as he continued to look around.

"*Share?*" he asked Beron as he sat on the ground. He

immediately started to feel the effects of entering the semi-dream state that facilitated the meshing of individual minds; Murdock referred to it as the "sharing state" and had shared with Beron, and others, many times in the past five years.

While in the *sharing state*, Murdock freely discussed with Beron a course of action. He needed to know what tools were at his disposal and how a ban, on being above the pod, could be enforced. Murdock had the idea of something to act as an alarm for trespassers breaching the ban. He was then introduced to the smaller black Oomah.

They looked similar to *ursus americanus*, but with some nuanced differences. Murdock did remember seeing a couple of them at the annual ceremonies, but they were less sociable, preferring to keep to themselves. They had agreed to act as an alarm system, since most of their kind wandered the entire area and were aware of all the comings and goings. They had seen Murdock levitating the pod and were quite impressed, even though he had not seen them. All Murdock needed to do was to inform them as to the extent of the boundaries and they would inform him if someone violated it. They also understood that none of their kind was to endanger themselves.

A few seconds later, as the sharing state ended, Beron informed Murdock that there was an increase in activity at the pod. Murdock could sense it as well and he set off toward the first pod landing to find a concealed place to levitate down to the level of the newly landed pod.

Upon landing, he set off toward the larger pod. As agreed, Beron would watch from the cliff above. *I'm not expecting any trouble*, he thought, *but I know it will happen eventually. Especially, as these newcomers get more comfortable with their surroundings.* He could see the first few newcomers exit the pod as he approached.

As Ben Palmer walked down the ramp of the transport pod, his mind was still swimming. The quick briefing, the meager meal, the waking up inside a transport pod; he felt he needed time to process all the facts. As he looked around in the bright light, he saw what looked to be a man walking toward him. As the man got closer, Ben could make out a few details. *I don't recognize him,* he thought, *but hell, I couldn't recognize any of the rest of the group.* He did notice, however, that he was dressed in buckskins. The man kept getting closer and Ben could make out that he was carrying something in his hand. Ben heard more people on the ramp.

"Look, someone is coming," a distinctively female voice exclaimed.

"Who is it?" a man asked.

"Is it our welcoming committee?" another man asked.

"I don't know," Ben said, shading his eyes from the bright sunlight with his hands. "Keep everyone back until we figure out who this Jasper is." Ben wasn't the leader; he was just the closest person to the approaching man, and he had been the first one out of the pod.

It wasn't long before the man stopped just outside the shadow of the pod. Ben was wary of this stranger. *He seems dangerous, somehow.*

"May I approach?" the stranger asked curtly.

"Come ahead," Ben commanded cautiously. As the stranger approached, Ben backed away to keep his distance until he could see the man clearly. "That's far enough," Ben commanded after the man had taken a dozen more steps.

"I know you have lots of questions," the stranger was saying, "and I may be able to answer some of them for you, but first you all need to stay close to the transport pod. Don't let anyone go wandering off. There is good water over there," the man indicated the stream to his right. "Once everyone is awake and aware, I'll have a few announcements to make to everyone."

"And who are you to be telling us anything?" Ben asked brusquely.

"First, I'm not *telling* you anything. I'm just...*strongly suggesting*," the stranger said. "Secondly, you're on a dangerous planet and none of you have been outside the ship longer than five minutes. I'm Murdock and I've lived here for five years. If you take my...*suggestions*, you might be able to live longer than today. But all of you are free to do as you please."

Everyone stared as Murdock turned and walked away.

2

Murdock didn't go far. He returned to his campsite and sat by the fire; watching the others while they milled about. He saw them talking among themselves and staring at him.

"Who does he think he is? Trying to tell us what to do!" he heard a few of them say. *I've been here before,* Murdock thought and chuckled to himself.

"I don't trust him!" he heard the man who had granted his request to come toward the pod. "Something inside me says he's dangerous!"

Murdock chuckled again to himself. He had removed his bow and quiver of arrows and laid them on the ground next to his spear. After drinking some more water, Murdock decided to recline on the grass.

"He doesn't look dangerous to me," he heard someone from the shadows of the pod. "He just looks anachronistic, rough, and uncivilized!"

As he lay there listening, he heard a dozen of them heading to the stream. "Where's the pump? Is there a cup? Aren't there bugs in the water? How are we supposed to get the water?" Murdock was smiling openly at what he heard.

"How's it going?" Mei Lee flashed.

"They're as ignorant as the first pod," Murdock responded, shaking his head and grinning. *"It's quite entertaining."*

"You be careful. There are a good many more of them than the first pod."

"How sweet of you to worry," Murdock responded softly and smiled, *"but these...these people, and I use the term loosely, are no threat to me. They're more of a threat to each other. From what I've seen so far, they're well on their way to total destruction."*

"How so?"

"They're all out for themselves. No teamwork. No concern for the next hour, let alone the next thirty days."

"How are we supposed to get water?" a woman asked standing a few feet from him. It had startled him that she managed to get that close without him noticing. *I'm getting too complacent,* he chided himself. *I need to be more aware.*

"There are several ways," he responded coolly, "only one of which is to suck it up by putting your face into the water."

"What? That's so...uncivilized and unsanitary. You really should have cups for visitors."

"This ain't no damned resort, lady," Murdock scolded through clenched teeth. He was quite angry at the woman's arrogance. "If you can't figure out how to get water out of the stream, there's a cliff about twenty miles that way." Murdock pointed downstream. "Go throw yourself off it before you do some real damage!"

"How rude!" She stomped off toward the pod in an obvious huff.

He sat up and looked to the sun. He judged it was late morning. He dug out a piece of the smoked venison and started nibbling. As he did so, he glanced over toward the pod and saw that most of the people were outside. As he finished the small piece he was nibbling on, Murdock took up the spear and got to his feet. He walked purposefully to the edge of the shadow of the pod.

"Attention," he yelled in his best commanding tone. "Attention. Can I have your attention?" A few people were meandering toward him. "I need to have everyone's attention for a few minutes!" More and more of them were heading toward him. "Quiet, please! I need everyone's attention!" He waited for the majority to stop talking and pay attention. They all seemed to be very slow in responding. Once it was somewhat quiet, Murdock cleared his throat.

"First, I have a couple of announcements. The boundaries are the terrace edge," he pointed upstream to the terrace, "and the cliff," he pointed to the cliff across the stream. There was a deep rumble coming from the crowd as they murmured their displeasure. "Anyone caught breaking those boundaries will be dealt with severely!"

A big man stepped forward slightly and Murdock recognized him as the one he had talked to first. "Who the hell do you think you are?" the man asked in a bellowing tone that everyone heard. "You can't tell us what to do! We go where we want! We don't answer to a petty dictator!" Several members in the crowd yelled their backing of the man's speech.

"I'm sorry," Murdock yelled back to be heard over the murmuring crowd and smiling sarcastically, "if I gave you the impression that this is a discussion or a negotiation. It isn't! Your petty dictators are in your midst right now. They just haven't made themselves known, yet, but they will, sooner or later, they always do. Let me be crystal clear. When I said dealt with severely, I meant *dead*. The only exceptions are by my orders. No one has more authority in this matter than I. You're free to utilize the land downstream from the terrace ridge. That should be sufficient for anyone!

"Second, anyone with the following skill set, come over to my left. Doctors, nurses, paramedics, or anyone with any medical training," a few started meandering over to his left. "Hunters, fishermen, outdoorsmen of any kind," a few more meandered. "Butchers, woodworkers, potters," two more started for the group that had already been called out.

"Third, you'll need to cajole, appoint, elect, or draft a spokesman, or spokespersons. I want to deal only with someone, or a group of no more than three, who speaks for everyone. That's all, for now!" Murdock turned to the few that had queued up to his left and motioned them to follow him as he walked over to his campsite.

"I want the fishermen and hunters first," he said loud enough for the small group to hear. Three men approached. "That stream has fish in it, but there may not be enough to feed everyone fish every day. That way," he pointed toward the river, "about twenty or twenty-five miles, is a river with more and bigger fish in it. The fish on this planet are very rich and will stretch further than you'd think. If you look around, there's plenty of deer sign. The animals here are a lot larger than you think they should be. You don't want to waste anything. You're going to have to brain-tan hides for clothing and other uses. Like the fish, the venison is quite rich and will go further than you'd initially expect." He handed a couple of them some of his smoked venison and they sniffed and tasted gingerly. Only one thought it was good. The other two handed theirs back. "You two are going to get mighty hungry!"

"How big are the deer?" asked the one who appreciated the venison.

"They run, roughly, the size of an elk. One of your first jobs should be to teach basic woods-craft to as many as you can. If you see any bears, go the other way. You're not to touch, harass, hunt, shoot, or molest any bears in any way at any time. To do so will exact a swift and severe retaliation. When you unload the storage bins, make sure you get a good inventory. I want to know what you have for weapons." He had stopped talking to them and taken a drink. They knew he was finished with them.

"Medical personnel?" he asked, and three people came

21

forward. "What kind of practice did you have?" he asked the first man.

"Paramedic," the man said.

"You?" Murdock went to the next person, a female.

"G.P.," she said haughtily. His eyes widened with interest.

"You?" he asked the last person, another female.

"Practical Nurse," she answered.

"We're sorely lacking in medical personnel and medical facilities, so you three are going to be worth your weight in gold, so to speak. I will personally see to it that you have housing and are fed well. I'll also get the others to contribute. When I'm finished with the rest, Doctor, I want to talk to you privately. When the storage bins are emptied, you three should take charge of any and all medical equipment and drugs. Anyone gives you any grief, you tell them to take it up with me." All three went back to the pod with a smile.

"The rest of you need to find people familiar with certain skills. All woodworkers, farmers, and potters. Anyone with those types of skills is what you need. Ignore lawyers and politicians, they're useless. When you get around to emptying the storage bins, make sure the craftsmen take charge of their tools, if any, and I want to be notified immediately." The rest left when it was evident that he was finished talking to them.

After everyone had left him, Murdock was trying to figure a way to get the doctor to the cabin to examine Mei Lee and be available when she went into labor. As he sat there, he heard the others having the discussion of selecting spokespersons. Murdock got that *déjà vu* feeling again.

It took several hours for the others to elect three spokespersons. *It shouldn't have taken that long*, he thought. *It isn't that complicated. That's what happens when you get a bunch of people together to make a decision. I knew I should have just picked three and let the rest choose from them.* Murdock had noticed that it was getting to be rather late in the day, so he invited the doctor over to his campfire while he caught, cleaned, and cooked a couple of fish. By the time they were eating, it was already quite dark.

In the course of their dinner conversation, he had found out that the doctor, Irene Harris, would first talk to the practical nurse to see if her skills, experience, and judgment were what they should be. If she were found lacking, the doctor agreed to examine his wife.

"And how were you going to pay for my services?" she asked. They had been sitting across from each other and their faces were lit by the campfire. As soon as she spoke the words, Murdock's pleasant expression turned cloudy.

"What did you have in mind?" he asked cautiously.

"Gold, silver, any precious metals, precious gems," she said in an offhand manner as she continued to eat.

Murdock said nothing for some time. He just sat there looking into the flames. "Will those things keep you warm in the winter? Will they fill your belly when you're hungry?" he asked finally. She could hardly hear his questions; he spoke so softly.

"I could buy those things with whatever passes for money here."

"Housing and food aren't worth anything then?" Murdock asked.

"They are, but they don't come close to the remuneration my skills will require. I *am* the only doctor, after all!"

Murdock sat there quietly looking at the doctor's expression. He could tell she was serious as she was looking quite pleased with herself.

"Well, then, *Doctor*, I'll be sure to remember that before you examine any of my family. Should you run across me when you're hungry, I'll be glad to remind you to pay cash!" Murdock stood his anger apparent by his expression. The Doctor stood reflexively and turned to run as he grabbed her by the back of her collar. His other hand grabbed her clothing at her Gluteus Maximus. "You have officially worn out any and all welcomes!" he said sternly through clenched teeth. Murdock then tossed her about thirty feet. He stood there watching her as she landed with a satisfying thud and seeing her get up slowly before he returned to his campfire.

After the doctor left, Murdock had some difficulty getting to sleep. *I'm tired of dealing with these people,* he thought. *I want to head home.* He had been worried about Mei Lee, as he knew she was close to delivering. He did make telepathic contact with her and maintained it until he went to sleep.

Murdock woke up the next morning at daybreak, as he usually did. He had eaten his breakfast and was waiting for some time when the others finally got around to showing signs of life. He picked up his bow, quiver, and spear and walked, with purpose, into the shadow of the transport.

"Those selected as representatives will come to my campfire as soon as possible," he commanded and then walked back to his camp to wait impatiently.

He didn't have to wait long before the practical nurse was heading his direction. Murdock watched as she approached.

"Excuse me, sir?" she asked as she stood in front of him.

"Yes?" he said sternly, impatiently, looking down at her.

"Doctor Harris told us what happened last night. I would like to apologize for her actions."

"Why are you apologizing for her?"

"She *is* a Doctor!"

"Is that an excuse?" Murdock asked bitingly. He saw the woman back up a step.

"No, sir, she's used to giving orders and having them obeyed. She's used to being in demand and being able to call the shots," the woman explained.

"So?" he responded brusquely becoming more impatient.

"I'm telling you this because there's trouble coming your way. Doctor Harris isn't used to being treated the way you treated her and has stirred up the others to do something about it."

"What do you know of her treatment?"

"I didn't see it, so I don't know what happened, but she did say that you attacked her."

Murdock started chuckling a little. "Is that what she said?"

"Yes, sir, she did."

"She considers getting a bum's rush an attack? Wonder what she considers a punch in the face?" Murdock noticed that there were three people heading toward him. "I take it you aren't part of the elected delegation."

"No, sir, I'm not. I just thought you should be warned." The woman turned to leave.

"You don't need to leave," Murdock said placing his hand gently on her shoulder to stop her retreat. "Stick around and enjoy the fun. Just stand behind me a little."

The woman moved to comply as the other three came over to him.

"What's she doing here?" Ben Palmer asked roughly. "She wasn't elected!"

Murdock stood looking at the three with a slight grin on his face. "I'd like to know who taught you your manners," Murdock asked.

"Nobody," Palmer responded dourly.

"Apparently," Murdock quipped. "Maybe someone should have!"

"You better watch yourself, mister. I'm in no mood to put up with you or your mouth," Palmer warned.

"Really?" Murdock stood there looking at Palmer with a grin. "I'm sorry if I gave you the impression that you were someone to fear or respect. That was a totally erroneous assumption on your part. I'm neither concerned with your mood or you, for that matter." Murdock stood there with a grin and head cocked a little to the left.

Palmer drew his fist back, having had enough, and stepped forward punching where Murdock was. Faster than Palmer, or anyone, could see, Murdock moved out of the way of the ineffectual punch and gave Palmer a quick tap to the back of his head as he passed, sending the bigger man sprawling to the ground.

Palmer rolled over, his face red with anger. He scrambled to his feet and rushed headlong toward Murdock, attempting to grab the man. Again, he felt the butt of the spear on the back of his head. This time he went sprawling into the stream, face first. Palmer rolled over and backed out of the water, looking at Murdock. Murdock spun the spear several times, in a figure eight pattern, left, right, and in front of himself before stopping it and striking a fighting stance. The shocked expression on Palmer's face made it apparent that he had finally realized he was vastly outmatched.

"Now then, shall we begin?" Murdock asked as he stood straight, asking calmly of the others who had stood there watching with gaping mouths. It took a few ticks before the others realized they had been spoken to.

"The people of the transport pod demand that you return them to Earth," a woman stated with a whiny voice.

Murdock looked at her. She appeared to be about five foot six with blonde hair and blue eyes. "And you are?" he asked politely.

"Phylicia Cunningham," she responded sharply, dismissively. She acted as if he should have known who she was.

"Well, Phylicia was it? I don't care what the others demand. You're all mistaken if you think I'm here to do anything for any of you. I am here to *suggest strongly* what you should be doing and give you some direction as to how to do it. If you don't want to follow my *suggestions*, that is up to you. If you want to survive, you'll do as I suggest. If not, well, it won't concern me too much to let you all starve, or worse. There are only a few things that are required of you by me. I've already stated those requirements. I called this meeting to demonstrate to you that I'm not one to be trifled with."

"All you've demonstrated is that you're a bully," Phylicia responded hotly.

"You saw that I was attacked first and did little to protect myself? What would you have me do? Stand still and let Palmer hit me?"

"We saw you attack Mister Palmer, who is unarmed, with that...that weapon," Phylicia continued.

Murdock dropped the spear. "Would you like Palmer to try again? Do you think he would fare any better?" Murdock looked to the others. He did lock his gaze on Palmer for a second. Palmer looked away as Murdock locked eyes with him. "No? Glad we got that settled. Now then, I think we should start over with introductions all 'round and let's see if we can demonstrate, for those without manners. Let's start with...you." Murdock indicated the brunette practical nurse, which offended Ms. Cunningham no end, which pleased Murdock no end.

"Annie Cooper, sir," the brunette responded with a little curtsy. The curtsy made points with Murdock. He had thought no one knew what a curtsy was.

"Ben Palmer," Palmer said when Murdock had indicated him. The little brunette walked over and slapped Palmer's upper arm. "Sir," Palmer added.

"Phylicia Cunningham, of the Cape Cod Cunninghams," Phylicia responded haughtily.

"Declan Griffen, sir," the tallish man responded with a shallow bow. Murdock's heart began pounding. *Was he related to Rose?* He tried to contain himself.

"I am Murdock," Murdock said indicating himself by touching his chest with his right palm and then extending his right arm and bowing slightly. "Now, isn't that better than fighting or making demands? But, honestly, Phyl! You need to drop the arrogance. No one cares anymore for such nonsense, at least, they shouldn't." Murdock waited for someone to say something. "Good. We all know the restrictions. Everyone should be clear on the restrictions and I'll hold you all responsible for anyone who doesn't know them. I told the outdoorsmen to leave the bears alone and so should everyone.

Don't feed them. Don't hunt them. Basically, if you see a bear, go the other way. I think that should pretty well cover everything. Do you have any questions?"

They all started to ask something at the same time, except Griffen. Murdock held up his hands until all were quiet.

"You have a question, Griffen?" Murdock asked. That brought several attempts to dominate the conversation by the others. "Everyone should open a can of *'Shut the Hell Up'* and wait your turn!" He waited for quiet before indicating Griffen.

"How many survived from the first pod?" he asked politely.

"Two, my wife and I. Next?" Murdock saw Palmer trying to be noticed. "Mister Palmer?"

"Who gave you the right to tell us what to do?" Palmer asked with venom.

"Sorry, I'm a trifle deaf in that ear. Speak louder next time. Next?" Palmer was not happy with being put off. Murdock saw Phylicia and recognized her.

"The others have demanded that you stand trial," Phylicia stated with arrogance.

"This is a time for questions, not demands. Next?" No one else had a question, or if they did, they kept it to themselves. "Glad we had this meeting. It would seem that we have worked out everything. Only one more thing remains. When I show up here again, only those I send for or the three that the rest have selected will be allowed to approach. You're all dismissed." Murdock watched as the others began leaving. He stopped Annie Cooper from leaving.

"Phylicia wasn't joking about having you stand trial," she said once the others were out of earshot. "Everyone has been asking about the first pod. It was obvious that you were on it and everyone expected to be met by most of the people. To now be told that you and your wife are all that's left," Annie shook her head slightly, "let's say it isn't going to be good."

"Why is that? They just want to hold someone responsible for the misfortunes, or stupidity, of others. I, for one, refuse to accept responsibility for other people's stupidity. I told them and they refused to listen. What more can be said?"

"There is a probability that someone on this pod is related to someone on the first pod," Annie offered. "They *are* going to want answers."

I'd say it's a certainty, Murdock thought. "Would you be interested in helping with my wife's delivery?" Murdock asked, changing the subject.

"Sure, but I don't know what I can do. You should really have the doctor look at her."

"The doctor is more concerned with lining her own pockets than caring for patients. I have no use for someone like that." Murdock made no effort to hide his disgust for Doctor Harris.

"That *is* what she said last night. She did say that you and yours would come around to her way of thinking sooner or later."

"Not likely," Murdock responded loudly. "We've gotten along for the last five years without a doctor, so we can get along without her!"

"So, what do you expect from me?" she asked after a pause.

"I expect confidentiality, professionalism, and honesty," Murdock responded somewhat calmly. "For that, I will pay for your services with food and housing."

"That seems reasonable to me," Annie said honestly.

"It didn't seem reasonable to Doctor Harris," Murdock sneered. "Everyone in this transport pod needs to realize that this is not a safe place. You can die in a second, if you aren't careful."

"Oh, I believe you," Annie responded. "I feel like we have been dropped in the middle of nowhere!"

"A word of advice, don't get involved with the political machinations that are sure to show themselves."

"What do you mean?" Annie asked innocently. "Am I not to have a political opinion?"

"You can, just keep it out of your medical practice. I'd guess that two of those three *elected officials* will do their best to consolidate their perceived power. Most people don't realize that politicians only have power because the masses turn it over to them. What the masses don't realize is that the vast majority of politicians only serve themselves."

"That seems to be a rather negative outlook," Annie said with a shocked look.

"Not negative, just realistic. If any of the others give you too much grief, just remember that they need you more than you need them. Would you ask Griffen to come to talk to me?"

"Of course," Annie said, sensing that her discussion with Murdock was at an end, for the time being. "When did you want me to look at your wife?"

"I'll be heading home early tomorrow. Be ready to leave about daybreak."

"Okay. I'll see you tomorrow, then."

Murdock watched as Annie Cooper returned to the transport pod. He figured that she would be given a very thorough interrogation by the *leaders*. He caught and cleaned a fish and sat on the ground while it cooked.

"*Rose's relative was in the pod,*" Murdock flashed to Mei Lee.

"*I didn't know Rose had any relatives,*" Mei Lee responded. "*She never said anything to me.*"

"*She told me once that she had two brothers and a sister, but I think she didn't want to think about them,*" Murdock added.

"*Probably because she resigned herself to never seeing them again,*" Mei Lee responded.

As Murdock watched over the cooking fish, and while he was telepathically communicating with Mei Lee, he saw Declan Griffen making his way to the campfire.

"Sit, sit," Murdock said while smiling at the younger man. He was taller than Murdock and, when he filled out again, would probably outweigh him by quite a bit.

"What did you want to see me about?" Griffen asked as he

sat across the fire from Murdock. "Shouldn't the other elected delegates be here?"

"No, this is something personal. I'm not trying to pry, but your last name is familiar to me."

Griffen's eyes narrowed suspiciously: "You don't look familiar to me, sir. How would my name be familiar?"

"Did you have a sister?" Murdock asked.

"Two of them, actually," Declan responded.

Murdock could see the man tense and become more suspicious.

"Was one of them named Rose?" Murdock asked as he adjusted the fish on the fire.

"Rosa Lea, but she prefers Rose. How do you know all this?"

"Sorry to say this, but I have some bad news for you. Your sister was on the first transport pod," Murdock said as quickly and as softly as he could manage. He could feel himself choking up at the thought of her.

It didn't take Declan long to add two and two together. He stood when he calculated and then recalculated and still didn't like the answer. "She's dead, then?" he asked.

"Please, sit," Murdock insisted. "Yes, she is," he said softly. "She was my wife."

Declan sat again. "How did she die?" he managed after some time.

"Murdered," Murdock said softly. "She was protecting an innocent."

"Sounds like her," Declan said sadly. Murdock could see tears starting to well in the younger man's eyes. "Is she buried somewhere that I can visit?" he asked after a long pause.

"She is entombed, yes, and I will take you to her, if you wish. She and I had a son, your nephew, Andrew." A tear ran down Murdock's cheek.

"Was she happy?" Declan asked after a few seconds.

"She often said that she was never as happy as she was here," Murdock said quietly.

"That's all anyone can ask. Which one of the people in the first pod murdered her?" Declan asked.

"A man named Whittier."

"He's dead then?"

"Very!"

"Did you kill him?"

"I wasn't close enough to do it. I would have without hesitation."

"I believe you, Murdock."

The two men sat quietly for a few minutes. Each was lost in his own thoughts and memories.

"Hungry?" Murdock asked finally, offering the younger man some of the fish. Declan took some and was absentmindedly nibbling on it while watching the flames.

Both men ate in silence. After a while, Murdock offered Declan his waterskin.

"Was that all you wanted?" Declan asked quietly after eating.

"I don't know who else might be related to someone on the first pod, so I would suggest keeping the information private." The younger man nodded that he understood. "Let me know when you're ready and I'll take you to see your sister's tomb." Again, Declan nodded.

Murdock watched as the younger man walked slowly back to the transport pod.

"What did *he* want?" Phylicia Cunningham asked Declan angrily as he slowly walked back under the shadow of the transport pod.

"It was just some personal information," Declan responded coldly.

"It must have been something bad to upset you so visibly. What did he demand of us now?" she pressed.

"He made no demands. If you don't mind, I'd prefer not to talk about it."

"Need I remind you that all three of us agreed to disclose everything that Murdock has to say, to keep the elected council informed," Phylicia responded sternly, poking her finger into his chest for emphasis.

"You don't need to remind me. I said it was personal, now leave me alone," Declan snapped back.

Phylicia stopped and stood there with her mouth open, staring at him in disbelief.

Phylicia Cunningham, of the Cape Cod Cunninghams, was not used to being put off in any way. Quite the contrary, she was used to constantly getting her way. If someone were reticent to tell her something, she'd always had her ways of getting the information she wanted. Some would have labeled her spoiled, but to Phylicia, she wasn't; rather, she was *justly rewarded*. True, she had grown up in luxury and privilege, but she deserved that. Her parents had made no demands on her for anything and never inquired what she was doing, even though they had to bail her out of jail more than a few times. Despite her *tender years* she had been well-versed in the judicial and the drug and alcohol rehabilitation systems, but had never seen the inside of a cell, thanks to the best lawyers, and judges, money could buy.

Even though they had only been revived for a couple of days, Phylicia had wasted no time in cultivating a couple of the other women who were willing to do her bidding for the pleasure of her company. Seeing one of them, she gave a predetermined signal and the young woman joined her.

"Kimberly, follow that man," she commanded.

"Declan?" the black-haired ditz asked.

"Yes, I want to know everything you can get out of him."

"How am I supposed to do that?"

Kimberly's questioning was getting on Phylicia's nerves. "I don't care. Sleep with him, if you have to," she said tensely but quietly.

Ben Palmer, seeing Phylicia whispering intently with Kimberly, came over to Phylicia.

"What are you cooking up now?" he whispered while he grabbed her wrist to keep her close.

"Declan had a meeting with Murdock," she said tensely, but quietly.

"Yeah, I knew that, so what?"

"He just returned and doesn't want to talk about it."

Palmer's left eyebrow raised in interest: "Do you want me to get the information out of him?" Palmer asked with too much enthusiasm.

"No, you brute, I've sent Kimberly to get it from him. If she fails, then I may consider you and your means as necessary. Until then, let go of me," Palmer quickly released her wrist.

"People going out to talk to Murdock privately is going to be a big problem in a hurry," Palmer said overloud.

"Keep your voice down, imbecile. I know. Did you find out what Annie Cooper and Murdock talked about?"

"No, she said nothing."

"Well, it can't be helped that this place is so open," Phylicia whispered. "We need a meeting room for the council where we can talk openly. Maybe you could come up with something?"

"I'll see what I can come up with," Palmer said with a grin.

Don't strain anything, Phylicia thought. "You do that and let me know." She continued to look around and found her other confederate, Heather Stevens, with Roy White, the paramedic. She gave a little sign and Heather came over to her.

"Did you find out anything about the meeting between Murdock and Annie Cooper?" Phylicia asked the other woman conspiratorially.

"Nothing yet," Heather said quietly.

"Well, stay close to the medicos and report to me

immediately if you hear anything." The woman nodded and returned to the side of the young man.

Phylicia continued to walk around under the transport pod. When she saw Ben Palmer again, she called him over to her.

"Did you find the storage compartments, yet?" she asked the big man when he was standing beside her.

"Not yet. They're hidden pretty good," the big man responded.

Phylicia looked to find the ramp, to orient herself, then looked up. There was an obvious panel above them.

"Is that one?" she asked sarcastically while pointing up at the panel.

"I dunno. I'll check," Palmer said. He called for a few of the smaller men to come over. He indicated the panel that Phylicia had pointed out and the men immediately found the latch and opened the panel.

"We found one of the storage compartments, sir," one of the men reported.

I'm surrounded by geniuses, Phylicia thought to herself, frustrated.

While a couple of men cleared people out from under the opened panel, others were emptying the contents of the compartment onto the ground. When one was emptied, they found another and began emptying its contents. This process continued until all the storage compartments had been opened and emptied.

"I want all this stuff inventoried, categorized, and stored in a secure place," Palmer told his workers.

They all began sorting and categorizing all the contents by use.

While Murdock had been making preparations to head home, the sun had gone down. After stoking the fire, Murdock stretched out on the soft grass to sleep a little before the long trek home.

"*Home soon?*" Beron flashed.

"*Yes, home tomorrow,*" Murdock responded. "*We having company.*" Murdock pictured the practical nurse in his mind.

"*Why?*" responded Beron.

"*Mei Lee soon have cub. Less worried if human healer looks at her.*" Murdock often did his best to explain things to Beron, who, in turn, did his best to understand his, often incomprehensible, human friends.

"*Shouldn't someone ask me if I want to be inspected?*" Mei Lee chimed into the telepathic conversation and it made Murdock smile.

"*I would feel better if the practical nurse looked at you,*" Murdock explained, trying to smooth any of his wife's ruffled feathers.

"*I thought you were bringing the doctor?*" Mei Lee asked testily.

"*The doctor needs to be re-educated. She brought her modern ideas to our backward world,*" Murdock explained.

"*I happen to like our backward world,*" Mei Lee added.

"As do I," Murdock responded.

"Show me what has been happening," Mei Lee requested.

Murdock relaxed and, with Beron's help, entered the sharing state with Mei Lee over the distance that separated them. It only took a few seconds to show Mei Lee everything that was said and done over the last couple of days. Beron, who had also been watching, added his perspective to the situation.

"You certainly have a way with people," Mei Lee good-naturedly chided her husband.

"It's a gift," he chuckled.

Murdock broke the telepathic link to his wife, leaving her chuckling, with the promise to reconnect before he went to sleep.

"Can I telepathically connect with someone specific in the pod?" Murdock asked Beron.

"Difficult. Much practice," Beron responded after a small pause.

"But it can be done?" Murdock asked, but it was more of a statement than a question. He got an affirmative from Beron.

While Murdock was thinking about the approach to connecting to Annie Cooper, he decided to astrally project himself to look around the underside of the pod. It seemed to take no effort and he was able to see and hear everything that was going on. He saw a nice-sized pile of supplies, but saw no modern weapons. *I'm most worried about firearms,* he thought. *In my opinion, firearms would destroy all the Oomah.*

The supplies did contain numerous crop seeds and starts. He did see some equipment that caused him some immediate concern. He didn't identify all the equipment, but he did recognize some metal smelting equipment. He made a vow to himself to do what he could to dissuade the manufacture of firearms.

As he continued to look around, he overheard Palmer giving orders to an underling. The man appeared to be guarding the supplies.

"We have reason to believe that Annie Cooper is planning on

leaving the pod soon for an extended period of time. We don't want that to happen. We don't want her hurt, but we don't want her to leave either," Palmer was whispering to his confederate. The man was nodding that he understood the instructions. "If these instructions aren't followed, you will be held responsible." Palmer gripped the man's trapezius muscle in the hollow between muscle and collar bone. The man's knees buckled in pain.

"Okay, I'll do it," the man said quietly through clenched teeth, in obvious pain.

"Glad we understand each other," Palmer said, clapping the man's shoulder as he walked away.

As Murdock pulled back his astral self, he was trying to figure a way out for Annie that would afford her the most leeway.

"*Before I met you, I had disturbing dreams,*" Murdock asked Beron telepathically. "*Were they from you?*"

"*You unknown element, most apologies,*" the large bear responded.

"*It's okay, I just want to know if it was you,*" Murdock pressed and received an affirmative from Beron.

"*Plan?*" Beron asked telepathically.

Murdock quickly showed Beron the conversation he had overheard. "*Human healer needs go where needed when needed without restriction. Can Palmer be made fear restricting her?*"

"*May not. Did not for you,*" Beron responded. "*Will take many participating.*"

As Ben Palmer was getting ready to sleep, Phylicia Cunningham came to see him. Everyone slept in the pod, in various corners and wherever they could. By setting several guards around the supplies, he did manage to get a little privacy, but it amounted to no more than just a few feet of separation from the others.

"Haven't found out anything on the Griffen issue," Phylicia whispered close to his ear. "Not yet, anyway." Palmer nodded. "Did you tell the guards to prevent Annie Cooper from leaving?" Phylicia asked, still whispering in his ear. Again, Palmer nodded. "Keep doing a good job and I might keep you around," Phylicia whispered as she got up to leave.

Palmer watched Phylicia leave to find her own sleeping spot. He made a mental note, as he was waiting for sleep, to see what would be involved in building houses. He needed his own private housing. He deserved it; he was an *elected delegate*. All the delegates needed their own offices and their own houses. He felt himself drifting off to sleep, thinking of Palmerville and all the buildings.

He knew he was asleep and walking dirt streets lined with log cabins. All the cabins were similar, and he could see some of the people entering them. He could see the transport pod close by as he walked. Suddenly, he couldn't breathe, and he tried to call out for help, but his voice was silent. He could see Annie Cooper trying to get to him, but she was being held under the transport pod by several guards. It didn't take long before he was lying face down on the ground looking at Annie, who was desperately trying to get to him, but still being restrained. He saw others walk by without helping him, but he couldn't see who they were. Just when he felt that he was about to die, he woke up with a start, gasping for air.

Ben Palmer was used to nightmares and knew he had just been wakened by one. What he couldn't get over was how real it felt. His chest still hurt from not breathing. That had to be from him actually holding his breath while in the dream. He rolled over and tried to go back to sleep, but fear of the dream wouldn't let him. No matter how hard he tried, he just couldn't get back to sleep. After an hour of tossing and turning, Palmer got up and went down to where the supplies were stored and guarded.

"Has Annie Cooper tried to leave?" he quietly asked the first guard he came to.

"No, sir!" the guard responded quietly.

Palmer paced the immediate area before going for a walk around the perimeter of the transport pod. As he walked, he could see the glow of Murdock's fire and could see what he thought was an outline of a man; he assumed it was Murdock. As he walked on the opposite side, he had a sudden image from his dream of the cabins and the dirt street. The shock of the flashback was enough to drop Palmer to one knee and cause his chest to ache again. When he had recovered sufficiently, he went to the guards.

"You're not to restrict any of the medicos' travels," he said to the guard captain.

"But your orders were —," the guard captain argued.

"I said no restrictions on any of the medicos," Palmer said forcefully while grabbing a fistful of the man's shirt. "Understand?"

"Um...yes, sir," the guard captain responded clearly out of fear.

"See that my orders are followed, or I'll replace you with someone who can," Palmer bellowed as he headed back inside the transport pod.

When daybreak came, Murdock had already been awake for an hour. He had built up his fire to get the morning chill off, eaten some of his smoked venison, drank plenty of water, and let the fire burn down to just smoldering coals. When he glanced over toward the transport pod, he saw Annie Cooper talking to one of the guards and then walk over to his campsite.

"Is everything okay?" Murdock asked with a slight smile when she arrived.

"Sure. The guard just wanted to know if I knew when I'd be back," she responded. "I told him I didn't know how long I would be gone and that was that. How far are we going?"

"It will take us many hours to get there," Murdock said as he dumped the remaining water of his waterskin onto the hot coals, causing a loud hissing sound and lots of steam. The steam drifted toward the transport pod obscuring the guards' view. "Close your eyes, please, and keep them closed." When he saw that she was complying, he levitated himself and Annie straight up the cliff face and a little distance back from the edge so no one could see what happened. "You can open your eyes, now."

When Annie Cooper opened her eyes, she quickly looked around and saw no transport pod.

"What happened to the transport pod?" she asked with a touch of panic in her voice.

"Magic," Murdock said with a little chuckle as he turned to lead the way toward his home.

The pair walked for, what seemed to Annie, a long time before Murdock turned toward the stream. They were already well past being seen from the transport pod. Annie had no idea where they were or what direction they were traveling. Murdock stopped at the stream to refill his waterskin and drink his fill. When he was finished, he offered the waterskin to Annie and she drank heavily as well. When she finished, she handed the waterskin back to Murdock who promptly refilled it.

"Hungry?" Murdock asked offering her some smoked venison in his open hand. Not knowing what it was, Annie gingerly picked out a piece and took a small sample bite.

"That's pretty good," she said with relish. "What is it?"

"Smoked venison," Murdock said as he popped a piece into his mouth and started chewing it. "It's good for traveling or when you just want a little something," Murdock said while chewing.

"It's quite good," Annie said while chewing. *Obviously, table manners don't apply while walking in the wild*, she thought.

Murdock suddenly leaped over the stream and was heading on. Annie looked down at the stream and hesitated for a second. She saw Murdock going on without her, so she tried to leap the stream much the way she had seen Murdock do and was surprised that she managed to get across the stream without getting her feet wet. She didn't know why. Maybe it was the exercise or the fresh air, but the leap seemed to be easier than she would have originally thought. By trotting a little, she managed to catch up to Murdock in short order.

"That was easy," she said with pride as she caught up to him.

"You may want to stop talking when out here," Murdock said to her quietly. "It's wild out here and there are plenty of creatures that would like a freshly revived, weakened human for a snack. It would be best not to advertise our presence."

It was close to midday when Phylicia finally made her rounds of the transport pod. It was nice to see the people hustling around doing whatever they were doing. It reminded her of the big cities that were now long gone, and the remembering helped to keep the slight bit of melancholy from setting in.

"Did the Cooper woman try to leave?" Phylicia asked the first guard she came to.

"No, ma'am," the guard responded, "she didn't try, she left."

"What!" Phylicia screamed in a high-pitched voice. "Who permitted that?" she asked, miffed, while looking around for Palmer.

"Mister Palmer told us, in the middle of the night, to allow the medicos to go where they will," the guard said with a straight face.

Phylicia stared at the guard while he talked and saw no sign of deception on his face. She did her best to try to smile and speak calmly and sweetly. "Okay. Could you be a dear and direct me to Mister Palmer?" She batted her eyes a little at the guard.

The guard said nothing more but did point the general direction that he had last seen Palmer.

Phylicia returned to her meandering with a smile pasted on her face. *Palmer, you son-of-a-bitch! I am going to ream you good when I find you. We had agreed to not allow Cooper to leave and you went behind my back. No one does that to me,* she thought.

Kimberly Grey and Heather Stevens saw Phylicia wandering around doing an impromptu, unhurried inspection. They both fell into line on her slightly behind and slightly to the left and right, so the three women formed a wedge as they moved through the crowd.

"Declan! How *are* you this fine morning? We really need to have a meeting about building a meeting hall, or some such," Phylicia said sweetly to Griffen when she ran across him in her search for Palmer. "Since we're here, we should work on getting things more...civilized. More organized. Let me discuss it with Palmer. We'll get back to you, okay?" Once Griffen agreed to the later discussion, she moved on.

Finally, Phylicia saw Palmer ahead of her and guided her steps, slowly but with determination, to intercept him. As she came up behind him, she hooked and entwined his right arm with her own left arm.

"Benjamin," she greeted him quietly and sweetly. "I should really slit your throat," she said emphatically but quietly while she dug her fingers into his semi-flaccid bicep, all the while maintaining her smile for the rest of the people.

"I had no choice," Ben Palmer retorted while trying, but failing, to free his arm.

"No choice?" Phylicia questioned sweetly, maintaining her smile and her grip. "Everyone has a choice and your choice was to stab me in the back."

"No, I had no choice," Palmer maintained. "I had a nightmare about the medicos being restricted and I woke up unable to breathe, so I had to let her go!" His voice was on the verge of panic.

"You let her go because of a nightmare?" Phylicia asked incredulously.

Annie became silent after his chiding. Murdock was correct and she had forgotten that she was in the wild. They walked for quite some time before Murdock stopped and knelt down. He took out the waterskin and handed it to Annie, who drank deeply. She hadn't noticed until she stopped that she had been sweating profusely. As she handed the waterskin back to Murdock, he held a finger to his lips and then pointed ahead of them. She raised herself up a little to look over a slight rise and saw a small herd of deer. To her, they looked to be a hundred yards away, but even at that distance, they were huge. She did notice that the slight breeze was in her face and that none of the deer seemed to know that they were there.

"Ready?" Murdock asked quietly. Annie nodded that she was sufficiently rested to continue on.

They both stood, scaring the deer as they did, and continued on their way. Annie noticed that Murdock maintained a good pace that would cover ground quickly. By the time she saw the river, she knew they had traveled a long distance, and this brought her to the realization that she was done in.

"I need a long rest," she told Murdock, breathlessly and quietly, as she tried to find a place to sit.

"It'd be better to walk off the fatigue," Murdock whispered to her. "If you sit, you may cramp up. It's midday so resting here for a quick lunch will be fine. See if you can find some dry wood."

As she wandered around looking for wood, she saw Murdock go to the river and spear a large fish. He seemed to make it all look easy. *He has been doing it for at least five years, dummy,* she chided herself. By the time she returned with a small load of wood, Murdock had the fish cleaned and on cooking sticks. She dropped the wood and he handed her the fish. As she watched, he expertly set the wood, kindling first, and started to use the back edge of a knife on a flint. A few sparks into something soft that he had in his pocket and the sticks were smoking. Murdock blew on the embers a few times and the sticks were supporting a flame. He took the fish from her and placed them for cooking.

"You make it all seem so easy," she said with awe.

"I have been living this way for a long time," he said with a smirk.

"Five years is a long time," she responded.

"I've been doing it a lot longer than five years," Murdock said with a chuckle, "closer to twenty years."

"You lived this way on Earth? Before coming here?" she asked in disbelief.

"Yup."

"From what I saw yesterday, you also seem to be a martial arts expert as well."

"Some would say that. I know at least one who wouldn't."

"Really? Who?"

"My sensei. Last time I saw him I was eighteen and he was eighty. At eighty he could defeat me as easily as I did Palmer."

Annie watched him intently as he tended the fish while it cooked and tended the fire. She noticed the flame was low and very hot. The fish seemed to cook in no time. "Dig in!" he said when the fish were finished. They both took out bits with their fingers and ate them, relishing every bite . Annie hadn't thought she would be as hungry as she was. More than once she saw him watching her.

"When was the last time you ate?" he asked finally.

"I don't know, maybe yesterday morning?" she said between bites of fish.

"What did you eat?" he asked suspiciously. "I happen to know that the supplies were found late yesterday afternoon and I don't recall you eating anything except the little bit of venison I gave you today." Murdock took some more fish and popped it into his mouth. "I don't appreciate being lied to," he said quietly.

Annie hung her head a little. "Sorry, I didn't want to impose on you any more than I needed to."

"I said I would feed you. Did you think I wouldn't?" he asked.

"No, I just wanted to do the job before getting paid for it," she said quietly.

"I've had enough," Murdock stated as he got to his feet and wiped his hand on his pants leg. "Eat as much as you want. It won't keep and we'll be at my home late tonight or early tomorrow. You'll need it to keep up your strength." Murdock walked over to the river and filled the waterskin and drank.

Annie ate as much as she could of the fish. Between the two of them, they managed to eat almost all of it. When she finished, she went to the river and washed her hands and mouth in the cold water. Murdock dumped the contents of the waterskin on the fire causing more steam and hiss. He refilled the waterskin and dumped the contents again on the fire. When he was sure that the fire was out, Murdock filled the waterskin again and handed it to Annie, who drank deeply.

"Are you ready to continue?" Murdock asked while he topped off the waterskin and secured it.

Annie gave a nod and the pair set out again. The pace seemed slower to Annie, but it did seem to pick up the longer they went. Before long, Annie was close to trotting just to keep up. After a few more hours, Murdock called for a rest close to a well-traveled part of the riverbank. Both were sweating profusely, and Murdock removed his shirt to let the light breeze cool him faster. Annie was watching him closely, without being

46

obvious, and noticed that he was extremely well muscled and did have a few scars to indicate the dues he had already paid. Annie had gone to the river and dipped some water with her hand and rubbed it through her hair to cool herself. While she did so, she drank some.

"Don't drink too much," Murdock warned. "You don't want the water sloshing in your belly. We do have some distance to go, yet," he said as he put his shirt back on and rehung all the gear on his person. "Could you find your way back to the transport pod from here?"

Annie looked around a little. "I think the transport pod is that way," she said pointing mostly downriver and a little away from it.

"That's pretty close," Murdock responded warily. "Now you know why I required confidentiality. Don't want to get woke up in the night with a knife in my ribs."

"I would never divulge where you live," Annie said somewhat offended. "I promised confidentiality and I keep my promises."

"That's the only reason you've made it this far," Murdock responded brusquely. Annie took the comment as a compliment to her and her professionalism.

"If someone refused to divulge to you how something was done, would you try to find out on your own?" Murdock asked with a sideways glance.

Annie frowned a bit. "If there's something that I'm not supposed to know, or you're not comfortable with me knowing, then don't tell me. If it isn't required for medical treatment, then I'm fine with not knowing," she said after a slight delay to formulate her answer.

Murdock walked over to her and, while facing her, extended his lower arms so they were parallel to the ground. "Stand on my feet and hold onto my arms," he said after he was in position. Annie complied without thinking about it. "Close your eyes and keep them closed until I tell you otherwise." Annie complied and closed her eyes. Murdock then levitated them across the river and upstream a short distance so she wouldn't know that they had crossed the river. "Okay, open your eyes and stand on the ground." Annie complied and looked around to orient herself.

Without saying anything else, Murdock indicated that she should follow, and they were off again. As it was starting to get dark, Annie was beginning to be very fatigued. She had been walking and trotting further and for a longer duration than she ever had before. She could feel some leg cramps beginning in her tortured legs and she had been breathing very hard for the last hour. Finally, she called for a stop when she could go no further.

"We're close," Murdock said as he handed her the waterskin. "Can you last another hour?"

"No, I can't," Annie responded after having a little water. "I'm done in. I'm sorry, but I can't go another step."

"You lasted longer than I thought you would, so there's no need to apologize." Murdock looked around a little, trying to judge the distance remaining. "We're at a delicate point. We're close to the house, an hour maybe, and it's getting dark. It'll get dark quickly."

"Please, stop beating all around that poor bush," Annie said trying to lighten the mood, "and just spit it out."

Murdock looked at her stoically. "There's a way to get you to the house, but it's one of those things that you shouldn't see or even know about."

"So, I should close my eyes and not peek?" she asked sarcastically.

"If I had a hood, I'd put it on you," Murdock said without smiling. Annie knew he was serious with a single look at his face. "I don't think you can keep your eyes closed for that amount of time, so let's classify it as *doctor-patient confidentiality*."

"Agreed," Annie responded enthusiastically.

Murdock began handing her the bow, quiver, spear, and waterskin. "Put them on as I had them." Annie complied as best she could. "Now, jump on my back, like a piggy-back ride." Again, she complied. Murdock shifted her weight a bit. "Hold on!" When he felt her tighten her grip on his shoulders, he started off at a slow trot and then picked up speed.

Annie had no idea how fast Murdock was traveling while carrying her. She could feel the breeze on her face, from the speed of their passage, but it was too dark to have any visible reference to judge velocity. She couldn't see any path to follow and didn't know how he knew where to step. Fifteen or twenty minutes later, Murdock stopped in the yard of a cabin and let go of her legs.

"We're here," he pronounced after she was on the ground.

The light from inside the cabin did very little to light the yard area, but it did increase a little when the door was opened.

"Come," Murdock said as he hustled Annie into the cabin. "This is Mei Lee, my wife," Murdock said beginning the introductions. "This is Annie Cooper, the nurse."

Annie made a quick glance around the cabin and then at Mei Lee. "How do you do," she said, extending her hand.

"Pregnant," Mei Lee replied with a grin as she took the other woman's hand lightly and shook it femininely. They both chuckled. "I hope my husband didn't put too much of a demand on you during the trip here? He does tend to forget that others don't possess his...gifts."

"No, the trip was strenuous but not overly so," Annie responded cordially.

"I'm sure you're very tired, anything in particular you require?" Mei Lee asked.

"I'm a little afraid to ask how you bathe. I'm in need of a bath, or something, but am not looking forward to jumping into the ice-cold river, especially at night," Annie asked sheepishly.

Mei Lee looked to Murdock, who nodded slightly. "I think we could manage something," Mei Lee stated as she motioned for Annie to follow her outside.

Both women went out the back door and Mei Lee followed a

well-worn path to the side of the cabin away from the river. Annie could feel the moisture in the air change.

"Will this suffice?" Mei Lee asked as she knelt down and dipped some of the hot water out with her hand and dumped it back into the spa.

Annie's mouth was agape in surprise. "Yes, it will do nicely," she said finally after recovering from her initial shock and surprise. "Thank you!"

"We've never had any issues with critters, so you should be okay," Mei Lee said as she turned to leave.

"How do I find the cabin again?" Annie asked nervously as she couldn't see the cabin.

"I'll come out and retrieve you," Mei Lee said comfortingly.

Annie quickly took off her clothes and slowly lowered herself into the luxurious hot water. As she settled herself and relaxed, she found herself thinking about everything that had happened since she was revived. *The trip here had been strenuous, but not overly so,* she thought. *Murdock had done plenty of things to reduce the stress of the situation. The biggest shock, so far, was finding that Murdock and his wife were pleasant and hospitable, and finding a spa this far out in the wilderness. All of it was more than anyone could possibly imagine. From what I saw at the meeting, Murdock is more than capable of handling himself and dealing with whatever threats he comes across.*

"How is your bath?" Mei Lee asked quietly.

Annie was startled and jumped a little. She hadn't heard the woman approach at all. "It's great! Do you have any soap?" she answered breathlessly.

"No, we have no need for it. We depend on game and having soap would alert the game to our presence. Besides, we prefer the natural scent."

"That makes sense," Annie answered.

"My husband needs to bathe as well. I'm not trying to rush you, just making you aware."

Annie could see that Mei Lee tended to speak quietly. She

thought it was more of a cultural thing than anything else. "I'm finished," Annie said as she got out of the spa and began dressing. When she finished dressing, Mei Lee led her back to the cabin.

"How was your bath?" Murdock asked.

"Heavenly!" Annie responded enthusiastically. "How does it work?"

"Volcanically heated rocks transfer heat to the water that comes in, continually, close to the bottom of the pool," Murdock explained. "The water overflows the pool, replacing the water that is dragged out by anyone getting out. The heat and the constant replacement keep the water clean." Murdock had gotten to his feet. "I'm going to take a bath. Mei Lee will give you some venison and get your hammock slung."

"Is this your first?" Annie asked Mei Lee after Murdock had left for his bath.

"Hardly! This is my third," Mei Lee answered as she rubbed her swollen belly.

"How many were left behind on Earth?" Annie asked innocently.

"None. I delivered them all here and they're all sleeping in the loft. The youngest is one year old and Chun Hua, my eldest, is four years old."

"Oh, so there are just the two kids here," Annie stated.

"No, I have two, three with this one. Murdock has one, a son, from his first wife."

"Did you know his first wife?" Annie asked innocently.

"Of course, Kevin knew my first husband, who died shortly after I became pregnant."

"Did Murdock know this Kevin who was your first husband?"

Mei Lee started laughing. During her laughter, Murdock walked in, still wet from his bath.

"Did I miss something entertaining?" he asked innocently.

"Did you know this Kevin who was Mei Lee's first husband?" Annie asked Murdock.

Now, it was Murdock's turn to laugh uproariously. Annie just looked from one to the other and was very confused.

"I guess I don't understand," Annie said finally in frustration.

"I think you're confused," Murdock said through chuckles. "I don't like it to be generally known, but I'm Kevin. Mei Lee's first husband was Thomas, Thomas Collier."

Annie started chuckling after she finally understood what she had said.

"I guess I did make a mistake!"

They all sat, once they had their laughter under control, and nibbled on venison that Mei Lee had set out for them.

"What did you think of the meeting with the *elected delegates*?" Murdock asked while chewing.

"It went a little better than I expected," Annie commented. "It did surprise me that Palmer would attack you as he did."

"I wasn't surprised. I knew he would," Murdock said.

"I knew Phylicia would say what she did, but how did you know Palmer would attack you?" Annie asked.

"We had a few words before the meeting when I made the announcements. He saw me as his rival. He attacked to demonstrate that he thought he was in charge."

"Well, he is, to some degree," Annie added.

"No, he isn't," Murdock stated. "I'd say Phylicia is in charge. If she isn't totally, she does tell Palmer what to do."

Annie sat back to think about what Murdock had said. All three adults sat in silence for some time.

"I'm tired and going to bed," Murdock said after a short while.

"I think we all need to turn in," Mei Lee said. She had slung a hammock for Annie while Annie was bathing and took her to it. It took Annie a few tries, but she finally figured it out and settled in. Mei Lee joined her husband in their hammock and snuggled into him.

"What do you think of her?" Murdock flashed.

"She does need to learn to listen, but she does seem to be competent," Mei Lee responded.

"I like her," Murdock responded. *"She's a lot tougher than you'd think and she's polite and well-mannered."*

4

Murdock, Mei Lee, and all the kids were awake shortly before dawn, as was their habit. Murdock and Mei Lee had decided to let Annie sleep after her extreme exertions of the previous day. Andrew and Chun Hua went about their daily chores, loading the hearth with logs and kindling, refilling waterskins, and keeping an eye on Rosa Lea. Murdock and Mei Lee had gone out to commune with their friends Beron and Bridget.

Roughly an hour after everyone else was awake, Annie, being mostly asleep, felt like she was being watched. When she opened her eyes a little, she saw a little girl of about one year in age sucking her thumb. It was obvious that she was a Euro-Asian mix. Annie didn't say anything to the youngster and the youngster said nothing. They both just looked at each other for a time.

"Mother said we should let you sleep," the little girl said clearly after removing her thumb from her mouth. "I was just checking to see if you were finished."

Annie couldn't help but smile at the little girl. "I suppose I should be," Annie said with a grin. "My name is Annie Cooper," she said as she tried to sit up.

"It would be more efficient to swing your legs over the edge of the hammock as you sit up," the child instructed matter-of-factly and without smiling back.

When she did as the child instructed it was easy to sit up. She rubbed her eyes a little to make sure she was awake. It seemed more than a little odd to have a one-year-old talk to her in that fashion.

"You must be...Rosa Lea?" Annie asked the child still smiling.

"That's what some would say," the little girl responded stoically with a suspicious sideways glance, "but who can say for certain?"

Annie heard the door open and saw Mei Lee walk in.

"Rosa! Be nice! Annie is a guest. You're such a precocious child!"

"I was being quite cordial, mother," the child said to Mei Lee, "Considering that she's a stranger to me."

Mei Lee turned toward Annie. "Please excuse her, Annie. We get so few guests that she is uncertain of what her actions should be."

"Yes, please forgive me my precociousness in my ignorance, Ms. Cooper."

"Does she always speak in that fashion?" Annie asked Mei Lee, amazed.

"Unfortunately. She's at that stage where she hears a word and then uses it as often as possible," Mei Lee explained.

"Does she know the definition of the words?" Annie asked incredulously.

"Not completely. She derives most of the meaning by the usage."

"It's because I'm a genius." pronounced little Rosa Lea very matter-of-factly as she turned circles. "Descendant of geniuses!"

STEPHEN DRAKE

"That is enough, young lady!" Murdock said sternly as he entered the cabin.

Annie saw the child immediately become silent; not in fear, but with an expression of self-satisfaction. Two other children came into the cabin.

"This is Andrew and Chun Hua," Murdock introduced with a hand on each of the children's shoulders.

"Nice to meet you," Annie said offering a hand to each in kind. Andrew bowed slightly when he took her hand and shook it. Chun Hua dipped a bit when she took her hand. Neither child blinked, nor took their eyes off Annie for a second.

Annie stood and stretched her tortured muscles. She walked outside to get a look at the cabin and surrounding area in the light of day. She squinted in the bright sunlight as she exited the cabin and stood on the covered porch off the front door. The air smelled a little damp, but not overly so. *This reminds me of brochures I've seen of...where was it? Idaho? Maybe it was Montana or could've been Alaska,* she thought as she looked around. *It's very picturesque.* "It's very nice, here," Annie said to Mei Lee, who had exited the cabin to join her outside.

"We like it," Mei Lee responded conversationally.

"How long did it take Murdock to build it?" Annie asked.

"I have no idea. I came after it was built."

"Did you know Murdock's first wife well?"

"Very, we were co-wives."

Annie looked at Mei Lee, shocked, her mouth agape. "That's terrible," she said, aghast.

"Why is it terrible?" Mei Lee asked innocently.

"Why, being forced to share a house and a husband, of course!"

Mei Lee chuckled. "You have no idea what you're talking about," she said quietly, but forcefully. She looked Annie in the eye and didn't smile or blink.

"Care to elaborate?" Annie asked snidely.

"I came for a visit, sometime after I was elected leader of the first group. I had just found out that I was pregnant, and no one was friendly to me and they all kept their distance. When I was replaced, Kevin and Rose took me in, fed me, and cared for me when I needed it the most. I wasn't forced into anything. I requested the position of co-wife. There was nothing sexual until well after Kevin's first wife was killed."

Annie was watching Mei Lee's face while she gave the information. She did see a tear start to trickle down Mei Lee's cheek before she wiped it away.

"It was very advantageous for all concerned, especially for me," Mei Lee added, knowing that Annie was watching her expression.

"I still find it to be an appalling situation," Annie said vehemently.

"If you were out here, alone and pregnant, with no idea of how to survive, I wonder what you would do?" Mei Lee quietly walked back into the cabin and closed the door behind her.

As Annie stood there, she tried to imagine herself in the same situation as Mei Lee. She could see that being pregnant would make a woman do things they wouldn't normally do.

She had classmates that found they were alone and pregnant, but they just took a pill to rectify the problem. The financially challenged women, whom she treated when they came in after their boyfriends beat them, often stayed in untenable situations simply because they had no other choice. She was wondering if that was Mei Lee's situation. It was then that Annie felt she needed to apologize to Mei Lee.

"Is there somewhere I can examine you in private?" Annie asked Mei Lee after reentering the cabin.

"We hide nothing from the children," Mei Lee said without expression.

"I'll take the older two with me," Murdock said quickly. "I need to catch some fish for lunch, and they can help."

Mei Lee started removing things from the table. "I assume you want me to lie down on a hard surface?"

Annie looked around blankly and realized the table was the only hard surface available, except for the floor. "Yes, I would," Annie said as she helped Mei Lee.

When it was cleared, Mei Lee climbed onto the table with practiced ease. "You did that quite easily," Annie commented.

"I made this table with delivering babies in mind," Mei Lee stated. "In fact, all of the kids were born on this table and I expect to deliver this one on here as well."

Annie shook the table a little and found it to be amazingly stable. "It is really well built! Would you remove your dress so we can start?"

Mei Lee sat up on the table and quickly removed the buckskin dress that Murdock and Rose had made for her. Once done, she lay back down.

"Is that a burn?" Annie asked indicating the brand on Mei Lee's upper breast while her hands expertly pressed on Mei Lee's belly.

"It's a brand, courtesy of Whittier!" Mei Lee spat.

"It looks like an *M* to me," Annie said professionally.

"No, it's definitely a *W*," Mei Lee said. "I was there, I should know!"

"Who was this 'Whittier' person?" Annie asked conversationally.

"How should I answer her questions on the first pod?" Mei Lee asked Murdock telepathically.

"Any way you want to, but I would be as vague as possible. Why is she asking questions?" her husband asked.

"She saw the brand that Whittier put on all the women."

It had been many years and Murdock had seen the brand so many times that he had stopped seeing it. Thinking about Whittier brought back all the hurt he had felt at the time of Rose's death.

"Put her off as best you can," Murdock told his wife telepathically. *"We need to discuss the possibility of sharing with her."*

It would be the only way to explain to her everything that happened before."

"He was someone on the first transport pod," Mei Lee said to Annie. "He was not a nice man."

"But would she believe what she was shown was true?" Mei Lee asked.

"You appear to be in your third trimester, about thirty-four weeks along, with a healthy baby," Annie said to her patient. "I would feel better about it all if you had been seeing a doctor regularly and there was a scale to chart your weight gain, but those things can't be helped in this situation."

Murdock smiled to himself when Mei Lee relayed the information. *"If she continues to ask questions about the first transport pod, we'll have to deal with it, but we do need to consult Beron!"* He had speared two fish and Andrew and Chun Hua helped by cleaning them, as their father and mother had taught them. When they were finished, they all headed to the cabin. By the time they had gotten to the cabin, Mei Lee was dressed and was replacing all the things that she had cleared from the table.

"You have another healthy baby on the way," Annie said to Murdock, with a smile, as he and the children entered the cabin. "At least, that's what I think considering the lack of equipment and facilities."

"That's reassuring," Murdock said.

"Did you want me to examine your children, as well?" Annie asked Murdock.

"That doesn't seem to be necessary," Murdock told her. "All of the kids seem to be healthy and well-adjusted."

"Is that your professional opinion, Doctor?" Annie asked with some smugness in her voice.

"I know them better than any stranger ever will."

"And being their parent doesn't color your opinions?"

"No, it doesn't," Mei Lee answered vehemently. She had been listening while overseeing the older children cooking lunch. "I don't think you've noticed that my husband and I have no delusions about our children. We know them as they really are."

"If that's true, then you are the first parents I've ever heard of that didn't have delusions about their kids," Annie stated emphatically with a little chuckle. "Should they be cooking like that?" she asked somewhat excitedly, concerned.

"Why shouldn't they? They know the fire is hot. Even little Rosa knows that! They'd have to do the same if they were alone in a survival situation," Murdock stated. "They're old enough and both are quite good cooks."

"But they should be protected," Annie said adamantly. "Children are our future!"

"Yes, they are," Mei Lee responded, "but to what end if they can't take care of themselves? On Earth, everyone thought children had to be protected from everything. You're a product of that mindset, as am I, to a lesser degree. Can you take care of yourself in the wild? I can, after years of living here and being taught. The rest of your group is also products of that childhood-protectionist mindset and there were how many outdoorsmen?"

"Three," Murdock answered.

"Only three, out of two hundred," Mei Lee continued. "Maybe more from our group would have survived if they had learned how to listen, how to work together, and how to take care of themselves rather than waiting for someone else to do it for them."

Murdock applauded.

Mei Lee blushed. "Sorry, but I had a strong opinion to express."

"That's the most words she's said, at one time, in years," Murdock said conspiratorially with Annie.

"I was raised to only speak when I know what I'm talking about," Mei Lee said quietly with a shrug and a sideways glance to Annie.

"But it was well said," Murdock said, praising his wife.

Annie had decided, in the future, to keep her opinions to

herself as much as possible. She had come to the realization that her views and opinions weren't relevant anymore. They pertained to a time and a place that was long gone. Now, she had to break lifelong habits that were developed with her vocation as well as those developed by growing up being overly protected by society as a whole and her parents in particular.

"Sorry," Annie said with her head down. "It would appear that a lot of self-reassessment needs to be done."

"I'm sure you'll figure it out," Murdock said with a sideways glance. "Eventually," he added after a short pause.

"You're newly arrived here," Mei Lee explained. "Once you get used to the conditions here and see what is required to survive, your attitudes will change soon enough. That's when mine changed." Mei Lee indicated that lunch was ready, and they should help themselves.

Phylicia Cunningham, Declan Griffen, and Ben Palmer had designated, and taken possession of, an area for their council meetings that was on the stream side of the transport pod and a little downstream of Murdock's campsite. Actually, it had been Phylicia and Palmer who had done the designating. Declan had just gone along with what the others wanted.

Declan Griffen had figured that his sister was dead, or worse, after the *takeover* on Earth. He had heard that bowing to the control of the *masters* was worse than death. But there was always some small thread of hope that maybe she would be alive somewhere. To find out that there was no longer a need for that small shred of hope was almost more than he could bear. Hearing that she was happy here did help some, but he felt like he had a huge dark hole through his heart.

"Declan! Did you hear what I said?" Phylicia asked in a scolding tone. "Honestly! I don't understand why you're on the council if you aren't going to participate!"

61

Griffen just looked at her. He hadn't heard much of anything since Murdock had told him about his sister.

"We need to get the workmen started on some sort of meeting house with council chambers," Phylicia repeated.

"I think it should be stone and look like the courthouses did on Earth," Palmer offered.

"Where are you going to get the stone for such an edifice?" Phylicia asked sarcastically. "It needs to be more practical. It needs to be multi-functional. If it isn't, we won't get it built and the rest of the people will protest."

"We should also need a nice table and comfortable chairs," Palmer said with relish. "We need them so we can properly contemplate what is best for the rest of the people!"

"More likely you just want a comfortable place to put your ass," Phylicia responded.

"Same thing, really," Palmer said with a shrug and a half-grin.

"We need to appoint the managers of the different groups and have them take charge of the supplies that fall under their purview," Phylicia said while pacing. "Kimberly!" she yelled after a bit more pacing. "Send Doctor Harris to us here!" she commanded after Kimberly Grey responded and presented herself.

"Yes, miss!" Kimberly responded before dashing off.

"Would you two at least *act* like the *elected council*?" Phylicia chided. "Act as if you care about what is going on and that it matters!"

It took a few minutes for Doctor Harris to present herself to the elected council. As she approached, she saw Phylicia pacing and the two men lounging, close to the stream. She walked confidently everywhere she went. After all, she was a doctor, and the only doctor on this desolate planet. As she closed the distance on the three council members, she saw Phylicia turn toward her.

"Doctor Harris! Welcome," she said with a lilting voice, smiling. "We have all come to the conclusion that you would be perfectly suited to be the Minister of Health!" Phylicia saw the doctor stand a little straighter with pride and smirk a little with superiority. "Your duties will be to take charge of all medical supplies and see to it that they're secured. Also, you are to bring suggestions to the council for improving the health and well-being of all the transport pod's inhabitants. You will, of course, be addressed as Minister or Doctor, whichever you prefer. What do you say?"

"Can I sleep on your proposition?" Doctor Harris asked as she turned away from Phylicia.

"No, you can't. You answer now, or we make the offer to someone else," Phylicia commanded harshly. *She needs to be clear on the pecking order*, Phylicia thought.

Doctor Harris paced around a little.

"Going," Phylicia said loudly.

Doctor Harris still appeared to be thinking about it.

"Going," Phylicia repeated louder.

"I'll accept," the doctor said.

"Good! Now, has —," Phylicia started snapping her fingers and straining to remember a name.

"Annie Cooper?" Palmer offered.

"— Annie Cooper. Has she returned yet?" Phylicia asked.

"Not yet," Doctor Harris responded.

"When she does, bring her here immediately," Phylicia demanded. "She has information we are going to need!"

"When were you going to return me?" Annie asked Murdock as they ate their lunch.

"Tomorrow morning would be best," Murdock responded while taking another bit of fish.

"Will you be coming back before I deliver?" Mei Lee asked quietly.

"That's up to your husband," Annie responded. "I'm willing if he's willing to come to get me. Hopefully, I'll be in better shape and won't slow him down as much."

"You do know that you'll be interrogated when you return?" Murdock asked Annie while he chewed.

"I'm sure Annie will maintain the doctor-patient confidentiality," Mei Lee offered.

"Doctor-patient confidentiality is a legal term and no longer applies here," Murdock stated flatly.

"I did take an oath," Annie said defensively.

"And who is going to enforce that oath?" Murdock asked. "What would be our recourse if you violated it? How would we know if you did violate it? From a practical perspective, all oaths are out the window."

"Then why did you bring me here?" Annie asked.

Murdock chuckled a little. "I needed to know that my wife and baby were okay. You don't know exactly where we are, but I think you could find your way back, if you had to."

"Then what made you chuckle?" Annie asked.

"You were there when I gave the others the boundaries. I think you know that I would not hesitate to enforce those boundaries," Murdock said. "Or am I mistaken?" he asked her with a hard, deadly serious look on his face.

"You're not mistaken," Annie answered with conviction.

"The others all think that I will hesitate to enforce those restrictions," Murdock said as he leaned back and allowed his face to soften somewhat, become sad.

Mei Lee turned Annie toward her. "You must convince them that he was serious when he set the boundaries," she whispered urgently. "He will kill anyone — everyone that violates the boundaries."

Annie could see the deep concern in Mei Lee's eyes as she spoke so urgently. "Knowing what I do of Murdock, the others cannot stand against him. They would be foolish to try. There is no need to be frightened of them," Annie said urgently trying to console Mei Lee.

"You don't understand," Mei Lee said looking at Annie pleadingly. "I don't fear them. I fear what that level of carnage would do to *him*," she said indicating Murdock.

"Is there no way of dissuading Murdock from that course of action?" Annie asked.

"Based on what you know of him, what would you say the chances of anyone persuading him to relent?" Mei Lee asked.

Annie had to admit that it would be "slim to none" on the chances Murdock could be dissuaded. All three adults sat quietly thinking. Annie knew that Murdock was, most likely, correct on the interrogation upon her return, and she wasn't looking forward to that prospect. She had no idea what means they would use to get information from her. She had a thought pass briefly through her mind; something about wishing she could just forget everything she has seen and done.

"You know they will put her through the wringer," Murdock flashed to his wife. *"They are going to make her life hell until she gives up all information."*

"Yes, probably so," Mei Lee responded. *"Is there anything that can be done to minimize the damage?"*

"Unknown. I could consult Beron and get his take on the situation," Murdock offered.

"Look at her. She is scared about what is coming when she returns," Mei Lee said. *"If we could, I'd keep her."*

"I know you would," Murdock responded. *"You'd do it, though,*

to spare her the trials that are coming. That would not be any benefit to her. She needs to know her own limits for herself."

"I know you're right, but it's hard to let her go through it all."

Murdock had gotten up, gathered his supplies for arrow making, and went out on the deck by the front door. As he worked on increasing his arrow count, he communicated with Beron on the situation with Annie and what was to come with the newcomers. Murdock knew that by placing restrictions on where the others could go, most wouldn't risk the repercussions, but he also knew that a few would. He knew that all it would take is one to cross the boundaries and then not be willing to face the consequences of their actions for apocalyptic events to occur.

First, they would disregard what Murdock had told them about the boundaries, especially if punishment isn't immediate. It won't matter if Murdock follows through with his threats or not, they will eventually kill one of the Oomah. *When that happens*, he thought, *that'll be all she wrote. Game over.*

After discussing it with Beron telepathically, while he worked on arrows, Murdock thought he had come up with a workable plan to try to salvage the lives on the transport. As he was picking up his supplies, he telepathically relayed his plan to Mei Lee, so she could mull it all over and give him her assessment when they went to bed.

"Better get lots of rest tonight," Murdock told Annie as they all sat around the table eating their evening meal. "We'll be leaving early."

"I'll try to be ready when you are," Annie replied. "I guess I should say my good-byes to the kids before I go to bed."

"They get up when we do," Mei Lee responded stoically and with a shrug. "You can do as you please, though."

"There are always plenty of things to do and plenty to learn," Murdock added, "so we don't tolerate layabouts." He chuckled when all the kids made their complaining noises.

Sometime later, after the kids had gone to bed and after

Annie had said her good-byes to them, Annie decided to avail herself of Murdock's spa. Mei Lee led her to the spa while Murdock put more logs on the fire and waited for Mei Lee to return.

"What did you think of the plan?" Murdock asked his wife telepathically when she had returned.

"It won't spare her the inquisition she'll be facing when she returns to the transport pod," Mei Lee responded. *"No one will believe her."*

They both sat in silence watching the flames in the hearth until Mei Lee went out to retrieve Annie. Murdock had decided that he needed a good long soak before bed. He waited in the cabin until Annie was dressed and inside before he and Mei Lee got into the spa for a long soak. By the time Murdock and Mei Lee reentered the cabin, Annie was fast asleep. They both got into their hammock and drifted off to sleep, cuddled together as they always did.

As she was starting to wake up, Annie could feel grass beneath her hands. She wasn't cold, just a little chilled. As she sat up, she opened her eyes and looked around. She seemed to be a little disoriented. To her, things weren't as they should be.

"G'Morning. Sleep well?" Murdock asked as she looked around.

"Yes, I did. Thanks." Annie was still a little chilled and moved closer to the fire to get warm. She looked up at the sky and judged it to be about mid-morning.

"I was beginning to wonder if you were ever going to wake up," Murdock said as he handed her a waterskin. Annie took the waterskin and, after taking a long pull on it, handed it back. "You look a little puzzled. Is everything alright?" he asked as he rehung the waterskin on his side by putting one arm and head through the long strap.

"I'm confused," Annie said questioningly. "It's like

something is out of place. I don't know. Maybe it's just me." She stretched forward to try to get her hands warmed. Murdock hunkered down beside her to tend the fish. "Where are we?" she asked finally after looking around a little more.

"We are about two miles from the transport pod," Murdock said as he pointed a direction. "The pod is that way."

Annie looked at him suspiciously. "When did we get here? I remember leaving the transport pod area, but I don't remember anything after that."

"The fish is done," Murdock said as he handed her some. "Eat up while it's hot. We need to have a discussion about your memory. You know as well as I do that the others are going to try to get information out of you about me and mine," Murdock explained while eating. "For our safety, your memories of the past couple of days have been blocked."

One of the guards saw Annie Cooper and Murdock approach. He immediately sent word to Minister Harris and to Phylicia Cunningham of their approach. By the time Murdock and Annie got to the perimeter of the transport pod, they were facing Doctor Harris, Phylicia, and two guards.

"It's about time you got back," Doctor Harris said sternly to Annie.

"That is far enough, Murdock!" Phylicia commanded. The two guards moved to block Murdock's progress. Murdock stopped, leaning on his spear. "What is it you want?" Phylicia asked with as much disdain as she could muster.

"I'm looking for Declan Griffen. Can you direct me?" Murdock asked Phylicia with more than a touch of condescension.

"Declan Griffen is a member of the elected council and I think he has better things to do than to talk to the likes of you," Phylicia responded pompously to Murdock. "Take her to the council area for debriefing and wait for me there," Phylicia commanded the doctor as she started to walk away.

"Was that a yes or a no?" Murdock insisted as he stepped a little forward to stop Phylicia's retreat. One of the guards pushed Murdock's shoulder, roughly, to stop his advance. Before either guard could react, Murdock hooked the guard with the butt end of his spear and smacked him on the side of the head, knocking him to the ground. The other guard rushed head-long toward Murdock. His attack was just as easily stopped. "These two may need your services, Doctor," Murdock said as he stepped over the downed guards, both were holding their heads and moaning loudly.

"What is the meaning of this attack?" Phylicia demanded with all the pomposity she could muster.

"Hey, Declan! Declan Griffen," Murdock started yelling as he walked further under the transport pod and among the inhabitants.

"You stop where you are," Phylicia yelled as she stood in front of Murdock trying to block his way.

"Declan Griffen! Are you around?" Murdock continued to yell after unceremoniously shoving Phylicia aside.

"You stop where you are," Phylicia repeated loudly as she, once again, stood in front of Murdock trying to block his way.

Murdock looked down at her with contempt. "Lady, and I use the term loosely, get out of my way, or you'll be finding yourself on your ass!"

Phylicia swung at his face ineffectually. Murdock ducked under it and pushed her arm on past, throwing her off balance, sending her stumbling; barely able to keep her footing. At that point, Declan Griffen came running over to Murdock.

"What is it?" Declan asked rather impatiently. "What is it you wanted?"

"A word, if you don't mind," Murdock said roughly. "Let's go outside the shadow of the pod, though!" He turned and walked back the way he had come with Declan in tow. Once outside the shadow of the pod, Declan was waiting for Murdock to stop, but he showed no interest in stopping. Murdock walked on for another hundred yards before he turned on Declan. "Have you given any further thought about paying your respects to your sister?" he asked looking around Declan to see if anyone else was going to be nosy.

"I have and I would like to see where she is buried," Declan said quietly.

"Entombed," Murdock corrected.

"Entombed," agreed Declan. "I would also like to hear about her life here."

"When did you want to leave?" Murdock asked. "We can do it now or in a month. It makes no difference to me."

"Next month would be better than now," Declan responded after a little thought.

"Okay. I'll be back in a month to get Annie Cooper and I can just as easily take you with us."

"What do you need her for?" Declan asked.

"That, youngster, is none of your concern." Murdock could see that Declan took offense at his comment. "You should respect a man's privacy. If I wanted you to know, I would've told you!"

"I am a duly elected member—," Declan started his hot response.

"Don't let that position go to your head. By the looks of things, your tenure is extremely limited!"

"What's that supposed to mean?" Declan asked in a surly tone.

"You cross Phylicia what's her name and you'll be gone!"

"Cunningham. What do you mean by gone?"

"You'll be voted out or dead, maybe both, the latter being most likely and probably by accident." Murdock could see that Declan was thinking along the same lines. "Let me guess. Palmer volunteered and Phylicia said she really didn't want to be on the council, but she would if that is what the people really wanted. You were selected." From the shocked look on Declan's face,

Murdock knew he was right. "Now, Phylicia pretty much runs things and acts like you and Palmer aren't needed?"

"Not quite, but it is getting close to that," Declan said in awe. "How did you know?"

"In our group, we had one of those," Murdock explained with disdain. "Our group was significantly smaller, so he just took over and became a dictator."

"What happened to him?" Declan asked skeptically.

"He died, but not before he killed just about everyone else."

"I take it he was the one that murdered Rose?"

"Yes, he was. Anyway, to get back on subject, your group is larger and will probably require the appearance of more than a single person to run things, but the true nature will be a dictatorship. Be wary of the *appearance* of diffusing power."

"I will. You, on the other hand, need to stop being so violent toward everyone in our group."

"Your *group* needs to learn some common courtesy. I defend myself, but I'm the problem? I don't think so!"

"Well, something needs to be set up so you can get the attention of the person you want to talk to. We have to feel secure, though, too."

"I guess it's me!" Murdock said as if he ignored what Declan had just said. "For as long as I can remember I've always disliked being grabbed, groped, or touched by people I didn't grant leave to do so and I don't recognize anyone's authority to do so whenever they feel like it. Call me crazy because I refuse to be one of *the flock!*"

Murdock turned back the way he had come. Declan watched him until he was out of sight before returning to the pod. Murdock had given him plenty to contemplate. He would have to watch Phylicia more closely, but he was afraid that her consolidation of power had already gone far enough that it would be difficult to take it away from her, and he doubted that she would just give it up.

5

After Doctor Harris had examined the guards and determined their injuries to be minor, she escorted Annie Cooper to the area designated by the council. She heard Phylicia behind her, mumbling complaints about Murdock under her breath.

"Well, it appears the prodigal returns!" Ben Palmer said once they reached the area.

Doctor Harris indicated where Annie should sit.

"Well, my dear," Phylicia started once she'd gotten control of her emotions. "You were certainly gone for a while. Where did you go?"

"I have no idea," Annie answered honestly. She saw Phylicia turn quickly toward her and glare.

"You were gone for three days and you have no idea where you went?" Phylicia asked. "Very well, since you don't know where you went, tell us who you saw."

"I have no idea what has happened to me since the time I left here," Annie replied. "I don't know where I went or who I saw."

"She's lying," Palmer said hotly. "She's covering for Murdock!"

"Why would she do that?" Doctor Harris asked Palmer. "She

doesn't owe him anything. She hasn't known him long enough to throw all of her training down the drain!" The statement was more a warning than a defense; a warning to Annie.

"Did Murdock do anything to you?" Phylicia asked Annie.

"He said he removed all memories of the past three days from my brain," Annie replied cooperatively.

"That would be impossible," Doctor Harris said heatedly. "No one can remove memories!"

"No one? Or do you mean *you* can't?" Annie asked the doctor pointedly.

"It would be impossible without the use of drugs," the doctor replied adamantly. "And the drugs would only block the memories after the fact!"

"Well, he gave me no drugs that I'm aware of," Annie retorted. "You, Doctor Harris, can look for injection sites, once we have privacy," Annie said after seeing the leer in Palmer's eye.

"Did Murdock give you any messages that were to be delivered to us?" Phylicia asked slyly.

"None whatsoever," Annie replied.

Phylicia paced around the area without saying anything for a few minutes. "Okay, we're done. I would just ask that if you remember anything, please come tell me immediately and please stick close to the pod for the next few days."

"You can't be serious," Palmer raged, finally getting to his feet.

"Annie, you can go, but I want you two to stay," Phylicia said to Doctor Harris and Palmer. Harris and Palmer knew enough to keep quiet until Annie was out of earshot.

"She was lying," Palmer raged again once Annie was gone. "She was covering for that bastard Murdock!"

"I don't think she was," Phylicia said softly, almost as if she were talking to herself. "I think Murdock knew we'd question her, and he didn't want us to know anything. He seems to be very clever, more than we gave him credit for. Against my orders, Annie managed to get out of the pod area," she looked at Palmer, who blushed. "I'm still wondering how she pulled that off. And now, Annie is returned with no clue as to where she's been or who she's seen." She was walking around thinking. "Was that true what you said about removing memories?" she asked Doctor Harris.

"Have you ever had a surgery that required you to be unconscious?" Harris asked Phylicia. "If a patient," she continued after Phylicia indicated the negative, "requires a surgery where they have to be unconscious, they can be given a benzodiazepine combined with Fentanyl so that the patient doesn't remember the surgery once it's over, as an example."

"Do you think Murdock would have access to any drugs like that?" Phylicia asked Harris.

"If he does, we're going to need them. From what I've been able to inventory, there are no drugs of that nature, in our supplies," Harris explained.

"Interesting," Phylicia said contemplatively. "I think you should inspect her for injection sites, though I doubt you'll find any," Phylicia told Doctor Harris. "I want you," she said to Palmer, "to put a couple of good men to follow her for the next few days! I don't want her leaving! Understand? I don't want to be informed that you let her escape again!" She took pride in Palmer's bright-red face.

～

"So, how did it go?" Mei Lee asked her husband telepathically.

"About what I expected," Murdock responded. He had contacted Mei Lee when he reached a point downriver from the current pod site.

"That bad, huh?"

Murdock communicated to Mei Lee all that had happened when he tried to get someone to get Declan so he could talk to him.

"You know me. I don't tolerate being shoved, pushed, or grabbed. I just react." he explained.

"Add to that, your people skills are sadly lacking," Mei Lee chided.

"I know," Murdock replied. *"I keep hoping that some of the people I meet would show a little more respect. You'd think they would realize that I have survived here for five years and they have just arrived and know nothing."*

"But they are coming from Earth and their last memories were of a place where they knew all the rules. They don't know the rules here and they don't know that most everything they had learned means little or nothing here. You have to give them time to adjust."

"Do I? I hope the wildlife here gives them a chance to adjust." Murdock was getting a little petulant. He had always felt that he should have *taken care of* Whittier at his first opportunity. If he had, maybe Rose would still be alive. *But you know that isn't in your nature,* he thought, *but maybe it should be.* Murdock dismissed the thoughts as stemming from his extreme frustration with people in general.

"Did you get to talk to Rose's brother?" Mei Lee asked after a long pause, changing the subject.

"Yes, he said next month would be better."

"So, what's your plan?"

"My plan is to get home as soon as possible. I will look for an acceptable spot to locate Annie's house, though."

"I think you need to discuss it with Annie before you do any building. It will be her house, so she needs to have a hand in the designing of it."

"Point taken, but I can still look for a good spot to put it."

A few days after Annie Cooper's return, the task of building the meeting hall and council chamber fell to Declan. He knew nothing about building anything, but he did do the leg work to get those who did, prepared for the undertaking. They spent the better part of a day trying to decide where to build it and which way windows and doors should face. After all that was settled, Declan sent for Phylicia and Palmer to get their approval on the project.

"How big is it going to be?" Phylicia asked after Declan finished explaining his thoughts and plans.

"How big do you want it to be?" Declan asked with a shrug.

"I'd say a square one thousand feet on a side," Palmer chimed in. Both Declan and Phylicia looked at him in disbelief.

"Would you be serious?" Phylicia snapped back at Palmer.

"I am serious," Palmer replied. "It should be a grand building!"

"Okay, then, be practical. It will probably be the first human building on this planet!" Phylicia corrected.

"I think it should be at least three stories tall!" Palmer added after Phylicia corrected him.

"I'd say two stories, at the most with the upper story as the council's quarters," Phylicia stated giving Palmer a warning look. "I do want it big enough to allow everyone enough room inside for colony meetings and such."

"I'll check with the contractor to see what it will involve. I am assuming that there should be a fireplace for heat and cooking should an emergency arise?" Declan asked Phylicia.

"Of course," Phylicia responded. "It should also have plenty of storage space for wood, water, and extra food. How long will it take to build?"

"I'll have to check with the contractor on completion time and get back to you. I assume you will give the project top priority?" Declan asked.

"I would like it done yesterday!" Palmer commanded.

"That will be fine, Declan, but I am thinking that it would be better on the other side of the transport pod. If it is as tall as I think it will be, we could use its height to extend our sight toward the river and toward the *forbidden* ridges." Phylicia had been wandering around picturing it all in her mind. She could see the advantage of it being a little further away from the stream if it gave them a longer vision range. "Did you find any farmers in this crowd?" Phylicia asked Declan as an afterthought.

"I did find a few farmers as well as a few builders. The same for metal workers, cabinet makers, butchers, and masons," Declan informed her. "The majority of the people have no special skill."

"We only need one of each skillset so the others should all work under the ones with the most experience," Phylicia explained. "Use the unskilled for anything that calls for brute strength. They will be the ones that are expendable. We're also going to need paper and writing utensils, so get on that as well."

"Why don't you, or Palmer, deal with some of that?" Declan asked. He felt like she was trying to bury him under all the tasks that needed to be done.

Phylicia led Declan aside to talk privately. "Surely you don't expect me to do those sorts of things! And Palmer is useless," Phylicia responded conspiratorially. "You heard him yourself! He has no practical ideas or suggestions!"

"Then why is he on the council?" Declan asked.

"He's on the council because the *little people* want him on it. What that means for you and me is we have to get everything done. All we can hope for is enough people see how impotent he is and get rid of him," Phylicia said as she walked away with a sad look on her face.

After her back was turned to Declan, the smallest hint of a smile danced briefly across her face. *These fools have no clue,* she thought. She already had control of Palmer, for the most part, and was gaining control of Declan. *Soon, I'll have complete control over the council. Then I'll control everyone!*

~

Declan understood that the conference was over when Phylicia turned her back and walked away. He was feeling overwhelmed with all the tasks that were being assigned to him. Somewhere deep inside, he was thankful that he was being kept busy. He didn't want to think about his sister and the work helped somewhat, during the day. He knew he would have to figure out what he was going to do. He knew nothing of farming or anything else that would be productive to the colony. He didn't have the skills or the experience to even begin to take care of his needs in a wild environment. He had trouble in the *civilized world* before the takeover. If it wouldn't have been for Rose, he had no idea where he would be now; probably in a prison or dead.

After locating the contractor and discussing the changes to the originally planned construction, Declan talked to a few of the farmers and hunters. He managed to get them to agree to cooperate somewhat. The hunters agreed to take one or two of the farmers with them when they go out hunting. The farmers were looking for some wild varieties of wheat or rice. The hunters had no idea what the grains looked like standing in a field. The farmers were willing to go looking on their own, but Phylicia had decreed that no one be out wandering around alone. The hunters, having finally decided to try to locate the river and bring back some of the larger fish, thought the farmers could help carry back any fish they managed to catch.

After the hunters left with a couple of farmers, Declan spent the rest of the day asking around if anyone knew anything about making paper or writing utensils of any kind. After asking everyone, and having no luck, Declan had another discussion with the contractor about locating a stand of trees. The contractor wanted to look up on the ridge that overlooked the stream. Declan, trying to abide by Murdock's rules emphatically declined. Instead, he instructed the contractor to start with the trees that lined the stream, but the contractor was also given orders not to clear-cut the stream bank.

By the end of the day, Declan was exhausted. He had managed to get the *meeting hall* project started, the hunters had returned with plenty of fish for everyone and the farmers managed to find what appeared to be a kind of barley growing wild close to the river; they weren't positive and further investigation was needed, but it was promising. As it was getting dark, he collected his ration of fish, built a fire by the stream, and got the fish cooking before he could relax and get off his feet.

"May I join you?" Phylicia asked as he was tending the cooking fish and not paying attention to his surroundings.

"Of course," he responded quickly with a forced smile. "The fish isn't finished, but you can join me when it is."

"I've eaten," she said declining the invitation tersely. "I just wanted to get to know you better. You do seem to be quite a proficient manager, even if you are a bit too introspective. Have you always been this quiet or did it come on you since you talked to Murdock?"

"I prefer to keep to myself," Declan responded while tending the fish.

"I've noticed that. Tell me about you?" she asked slyly. "Any brothers or sisters?"

"If I did, you would be the last person I'd tell anything to," Declan said coldly without looking at Phylicia. As soon as she had asked the question, Declan heard Murdock's words of warning again inside his mind. Since his last talk with Murdock, Declan had been watching Phylicia closely and could see that she was clearly taking over all leadership of the colony. As he picked at the cooked fish and nibbled some, he thought he was still on the council just to stay on the inside and know what was going on. Otherwise, he had no good reason to remain.

"That is no way to talk to a lady," Phylicia retorted with mock petulance.

IF there were a lady present, I wouldn't, Declan thought. *Maybe it would be better not to antagonize her needlessly.* "I'm wise to your taking over leadership of the colony." He could see Phylicia start to protest. "I'm not opposed to that. I don't want it and Palmer getting it would be a huge mistake. I'm content in my current position." Declan could see Phylicia relax.

"So, I take it that you support me in this *enterprise*?" Phylicia asked.

"No, you can't make that assumption."

Phylicia looked stricken which transformed into a tense anger that Declan could see clearly. "I'm sorry, what *can* I count on from you?" she asked tensely.

"First, you don't assume anything, not with me. Second, I won't oppose you openly and will continue to try to do as you ask. Third, I will be free to leave when I choose and return when I choose."

"Is that *all*?" Phylicia asked impatiently.

"That's all. I am not your friend or your ally, so don't make the mistake of thinking that," Declan warned.

"And if I don't agree?" Phylicia asked cautiously.

"I'll make sure that everyone knows what you've been up to and what you're planning."

"That would be a mistake." Phylicia grinned slyly. "Most of the people wouldn't care and the rest would support me. That threat is an empty one. Repeat it again, and you'll...disappear!"

Ben Palmer was standing under the shadow of the transport and surreptitiously observing Phylicia talking to Declan. She had said to not disturb them during the conversation in such a way that Palmer knew he had better restrain himself. He had been leaning on the landing skid closest to the pair's conversation waiting for her to finish. Kimberly Grey and Heather Stevens were also waiting close by Palmer, but he could tell that they weren't comfortable being around him. If he moved closer to the two women, they would stop their conversation and move away casually.

Palmer could tell that Phylicia was upset when she came walking back toward him. She didn't slow down as he and the two women stepped toward her, trying to get her attention. She held up her hand in a stopping motion and kept walking. Palmer and the two women fell into line behind her, following her. She didn't stop until she was inside the meeting hall, or rather, where it would be. The contractor had scratched out where the walls would be and Phylicia led her little entourage inside the scribed marks. With a look, she put the women on hold.

"What do you want?" Phylicia asked Palmer gruffly.

"What did Declan want?" Palmer asked.

"Nothing. I wanted to talk to him, not the other way around." Palmer was getting on Phylicia's nerves and she was intentionally being snappy with him to get the point across, not that Palmer ever took a hint.

"Well, what did you want to talk to him about?" Palmer asked sheepishly. "We did say that the council would be open with each other."

"That was so *I* would know what is going on," Phylicia snapped harshly. "You wouldn't know what to do with any information."

"Do I need to work him over a little for upsetting you?" Palmer asked with too much relish.

"You *upset* me far more than Declan does. Are you going to go work yourself over?" she asked sarcastically. "Why don't you leave me alone so I can think? I'm really not in the mood to deal with you!"

Palmer was dumbstruck, and it took several seconds for her words to sink in, and for him to do as Phylicia requested. Once he had left, the women got together for their scheming and planning.

It was some time after Phylicia stormed off that Kimberly Grey came over to the area that Declan was using to relax.

"Mind if I join you?" she asked seductively.

"Suit yourself," Declan said absentmindedly. He was lost in his own thoughts. Murdock's words of warning were running through his consciousness and refused to stop. He thought he had figured a way out for himself. *To hell with everyone else. What have all these people done for me? There are none that I would classify as friends, and none think of me as a friend. I know that situation could change, and I had decided to include any would-be friends in my deal with Phylicia. The rest can fend for themselves.*

Kimberly had come over and sat close to him on the ground. After sitting with her legs under her and leaning on her hand, she patted her lap, indicating that Declan could put his head in her lap. Declan thought the offer might prove interesting, so he complied.

"What did Phylicia want?" Kimberly asked softly while gently rubbing Declan's chest.

"Council stuff," Declan said as he selected a blade of grass to stick in his mouth before reclining once more in Kimberly's lap. "Nothing that should concern you," he said around the blade of grass. He had eaten his fill of the fish and was actually enjoying Kimberly's ministrations.

"If it concerns you, it concerns me, Declan," Kimberly said softly. She had unbuttoned a couple of buttons on his shirt and was gently using her fingernails on his bare chest. "Besides, she was talking to you for so long! I was starting to think you preferred her company to mine."

"You don't need to worry about that," Declan said with eyes closed and a smirk on his face. "Phylicia isn't my type. All my dealings with her are strictly of a business nature!" He was starting to really relax under Kimberly's skilled hands.

"You seemed to be upset, the other day," Kimberly said after a long pause in the conversation. She could feel Declan relaxing more all the time. "You know, when you had the chat with Murdock? What was it all about?"

"Just personal stuff."

"Did you know him before coming here?"

"No, never met him before in my life."

"Then how personal could it be, if you never knew him before coming here?"

"You seem to be inordinately interested in my business," Declan said without opening his eyes.

"You act like you are hiding something. I'm trying to let you know that you can tell me." Kimberly's ministrations had lowered to Declan's stomach and she had managed to get his shirt completely unbuttoned.

"Can I? I thought you spied for Phylicia?" Declan asked point blank.

"That's what she thinks," Kimberley defended. "I hear lots of things that I don't tell Phylicia."

"Really? Tell me three things that you haven't told Phylicia."

Kimberly's hands had not stopped at all during their conversation and hadn't stopped even though she was trying to think.

"That's what I thought," Declan chuckled after a couple of minutes had come and gone and Kimberly hadn't offered anything to back up her statement. "Now, you know why I keep my own counsel."

"Phylicia thinks I am wasting my time with you. If you give me something that I can give her, maybe she'll let me stay with you. Otherwise, she'll assign me to someone else."

"If she's bought you, then so be it. If you can't be your own person, then you can't be with me." He moved away from Kimberly a little and saw that she had gotten to her feet and left. Declan had been enjoying her company and it bothered him a little to see her leave. "Oh, well. Better luck next time!" he said aloud to himself. "I'm in trouble, now. I've taken to talking to myself out loud." He chuckled as he shook his head.

~

Murdock had decided to forgo searching for a site for Annie's cabin for the peace and quiet of home and family. He had managed to get home just after dark after his talk with Declan. The kids greeted him with hugs and Mei Lee gave him a big hug after he was sitting at the table.

"Did you find a site?" Mei Lee asked as she set some meat in front of her husband.

"Didn't look," Murdock responded around a bite of meat. "I'll find one after I figure out a few things."

"Like what?" Mei Lee asked as she sat gingerly beside him at the table.

"I'm thinking it should be close to the transport pod, but I have some, shall we say *unique*, building techniques that I don't want the others on the pod to know about. I've been thinking of building it in one location and then moving it where I decide to put it, but that in itself would cause even more questions."

"Sounds like a real conundrum."

"I thought about building it close to the river, but I think Annie would want to be closer to the pod."

"Why don't you wait and ask Annie what she'd like?"

"I wanted to get it done so we can start laying up venison and fish for winter."

"You have plenty of time for that. You always seem to finish early and we always have plenty."

"It will be enough time, unless we end up with some unwanted guests."

Mei Lee nodded, indicating that she understood what he meant. "There is that possibility."

They spent the rest of the waking hours in silence; both

adults had been thinking of the coming winter and the all too probable problems with the newcomers.

Over the twenty-one days since Annie's return, the *meeting hall* project had progressed minorly. The first-floor walls were two or three courses short of where they needed to be and there were issues with splitting the logs lengthwise for flooring, but they were getting worked out. Declan was having problems with the contractor wanting to get the logs from a closer source. The contractor would spend two days getting the logs to the site and the next day building. The manpower needed was insufficient to the task as everyone on the project had to first cut and limb the trees needed, then spend the better part of a day rolling the logs to the building site.

The contractor spent a lot of time arguing with Declan over crossing the boundaries. He complained that he had to go further downstream to find trees in sufficient quantities and size to continue the project. The further away from the building site, the longer it would take to get the materials, which, in turn, pushed out the completion date.

Declan, being pressured by Phylicia and Palmer, was starting to consider the idea. He could feel his resolve being weakened with every day that passed. In addition to the contractor's complaints, he also heard all the complaints from the people about the food and the lack of facilities. He tried directing them to the other members of the council. But, since he was the only one that would listen and try to resolve the issues, they constantly returned to him for redress. This felt, to him, like he was being pressured to provide for the others. Most days, he felt as if he were being *nibbled to death by ducks*.

Feeling the need to get away, Declan had decided to join the contractor. Both men were across the stream, looking up at the cliff above. They had just engaged in another of their innumerable arguments about the warning that Murdock had given. The contractor didn't believe anyone had the right to stop him from doing anything and had sent one of the workmen assigned to him and his project, up the cliff face. Declan was holding his breath while the man climbed to the top and looked over the edge at them. The workman sat on the ground, anchoring one end, and had tossed a length of rope down to the rest who proceeded to climb to the top of the cliff. Declan had been the last one to climb the rope.

The contractor had been surveying the new ground from where he stood, while everyone else climbed up. Once everyone was on top of the cliff, the contractor took the lead as they headed away from the transport pod. Declan, who had decided to stay close to the edge, was watching the workmen. The men had gone about fifty yards when they all dropped. He had called out to them, but no one moved. He couldn't tell if they were alive or dead. It was then that panic began to set in. He knew they all should have heeded Murdock's warnings and now all the men were dead, he was sure, and he was stuck on the cliff with no way to get down.

Five hours later, Declan was still stuck on the edge of the cliff and, from his vantage point, had seen no signs of life from any of the workmen or the contractor. It was starting to get late in the day, and he had no water or food. He was sitting on the ground at the edge of the cliff looking down, trying to get up the nerve to slide down.

"Didn't you believe me?" Murdock said close behind him.

The sound scared Declan into starting to slide over the edge, but Murdock had grabbed him to prevent it.

"I told them to heed your warning," he said in his own defense, with a hint of both panic and relief in his voice. He looked surreptitiously over to the others, afraid to ask their condition.

"It looks to me that all of you ignored me," Murdock said sternly. He had been standing and glaring, accusingly, at Declan with his arms crossed over his chest.

"I tried to tell them not to defy you, but they wouldn't listen," Declan pleaded. He saw Murdock look over the edge of the cliff and then back to him.

"It certainly looks like it," Murdock said sarcastically. "If you tried and failed, then what are *you* doing up here?"

"Honestly, I couldn't tell you," Declan stated flatly, quietly. "I knew it was wrong, but I was curious as to what the others would find. And I didn't want the razzing for being the only one that wouldn't climb up."

Murdock looked at Declan for a few seconds before turning and walking toward the fallen men.

"Don't go there! They just dropped," Declan yelled, panic edging his voice.

Murdock ignored Declan's warning. He walked up to the first two men he came to, picked them up by their belts, and carried them like they were luggage. He set down the first two ten feet from the edge of the cliff. "You going to help?" he asked Declan with some impatience.

Declan watched as Murdock walked over to the others again and picked up two more and carried them back to be placed with the first two. He then started walking gingerly to the others and tried to pick up two as Murdock had. Try as he might, he couldn't. He did manage to drag them one at a time to the ones that Murdock had carried. "Are they dead?" he finally asked Murdock.

"No, just unconscious," Murdock responded. "They may have been better off dead, though."

"How long will they be unconscious?" Declan asked with a puzzled look on his face. "What did you mean by they might be better off dead?"

"Look at them," Murdock snapped. "They're dreaming and it doesn't look like its anything pleasant. I have no idea how long they will be out. The longer they are unconscious, the worse off they're going to be."

Declan looked down at the men. They were all twitching and whimpering and Declan felt pity for them. The workmen were just following the contractor and now they all had to pay for it.

"So, who's the Einstein that came up with the idea to defy my order?" Murdock asked while he sat by the edge and had some water.

"The contractor needed to get materials for the meeting hall, and this was closer than walking to the river," Declan explained while eying Murdock's waterskin. "The rest were just following along."

"Do you pity them?" Murdock asked in disbelief.

"Yes," Declan said flatly with a shrug. "They were just following someone that had authority over them."

"Did you tell them not to come up here?" Murdock asked with a sideways glance.

"The contractor and I have been arguing about it for quite some time, days," Declan told Murdock in a matter-of-fact way.

"So, by your own admission, they all knew they shouldn't be up here," Murdock stated. "What should their punishment be?" he asked after a short pause.

"What?" Declan asked in disbelief.

"Should I toss them over the cliff?" Murdock asked. "Should I slit their throats and leave them here? Either? Both? Something else?"

Declan looked at Murdock in shock. "Surely, you're not serious!"

"Life and death decisions have to be made every day," Murdock said heatedly, "so, I'd get used to it, if I were you. The decisions have to be made by someone. If you won't, then someone else will. And you will regret the result." Murdock started walking toward the men and started to pull his twelve-inch machete.

"What are you going to do?" Declan shouted.

Murdock stopped and looked back at Declan. "Are you saying that you want to make the decision?" he asked offering Declan the machete.

Declan looked down at his feet. "I can't make a decision like that. That would be cold-blooded murder."

Murdock, holding the machete by the handle started tapping the side of his head with the flat of the blade. "You know, I never really understood that. Murder is something done in the heat of the moment, with passion, so how can it be cold-blooded? Wouldn't *hot-blooded murder* be more accurate?"

Murdock's question seemed sincere, to Declan, so he was unsure if it was rhetorical or if Murdock actually expected an answer.

"And then there's the question of what to do with you," Murdock stated gravely.

Declan blanched at the thought of what his punishment should be. That aspect had slipped his mind, initially. Now, he was more than a little concerned about his own situation. As he watched, he saw Murdock advancing on the unconscious men again. "If you must punish someone, punish me," Declan blurted out. "Let them live." He had surprised himself with the statement.

Murdock stopped and turned to look at Declan squarely. "You would sacrifice yourself for the likes of these?" he asked indicating the unconscious men.

"Yes," Declan responded quietly and thoughtfully, "if I must. I was responsible to see the project finished."

"Accepted," Murdock said quietly. "What's to stop me from taking out the punishment of their defiance on you and then doing the same to the rest after you're gone?"

"I don't think you would do that," Declan responded quietly.

"What makes you think that?" Murdock asked suspiciously.

"Whatever else you are, Murdock, you do seem to be honorable. Retaliating against the others once you have dispatched me would be dishonorable."

Murdock looked at Declan skeptically. "I have a job for you. I want you to go down and get outfitted for traveling."

"But what about them?" Declan asked indicating the others who were still unconscious.

"I'll deal with them. You don't need to worry about it. You do need to worry about following my instructions to the letter," Murdock said sternly. "You'll need a waterskin and a knife, preferably one like this," Murdock continued indicating his twelve-inch machete. He looked at Declan, who nodded in acknowledgment of the instructions so far. "Then I want you to collect Annie Cooper, outfit her, and escort her to the river. Go that way," Murdock indicated a direction that was toward the river and a little downstream at an angle.

"But it's going to be dark soon," Declan protested. "How are we to find our way in the dark? Besides, Phylicia won't allow it."

"You'll figure it out," Murdock said roughly. "What Phylicia allows is of no concern to me. You'll do it or these men are forfeit."

Declan chuckled nervously. "Just that simple?"

"Just that simple!"

"And how shall I get down? I had a rope to climb up, but that isn't possible now," Declan asked.

Murdock had collected the rope and tied one end to the feet of three of the unconscious men. He then threw the rest of the rope over the cliff. "I'll meet you by the river. Since it is getting dark, you should have no trouble finding my camp." Murdock said as Declan started down the rope.

6

"When he is out of sight, I'll levitate the others down to the ground. You can do what you need to wake them after I leave to go to the river," Murdock flashed to Beron. Beron sent a very pleasing sensation to his mind. *I don't know what they're going through and I'm not sure I want to know,* he thought. Murdock's mind was suddenly flooded with a scene of being hung from a cliff in a lightning storm and slowly slipping. Another scene was of hanging over a pit of wolves and being lowered slowly. Another was of facing a pack of angry bears with lots of growling, snorting, teeth, and claws. Another was dreaming of being on a very narrow cliff with high winds blowing every direction and having no way down and nothing to hang on to. All the scenes made him shiver. *"That is what they're experiencing?"* he asked after the scenes faded. He got an affirmative feeling from his huge friend. *"Glad I'm your friend."*

It didn't take Declan long to descend the rope and get to the underside of the transport pod. He immediately started searching for Annie Cooper. As he looked, he procured a waterskin and a twelve-inch machete from the stockpile of tools and supplies. No one questioned him as he was on the council. Finally, he spotted Annie Cooper heading to the upstream side of the position where most of the people used to get drinking water. He knelt down and filled his waterskin close to her.

"We need to go somewhere," he said quietly as he didn't want anyone else to hear.

"Why would I go anywhere with you?" Annie responded angrily and louder than Declan found comfortable.

"Keep it down," he said through clenched teeth. "Someone has requested our presence."

"Who would that be?" she asked quieter but still too loud.

"Murdock has requested that we meet him," Declan said after an exasperated exhale.

"Who is he that he thinks he can request anything from me?" Annie asked curtly.

Declan stood after his waterskin was filled and capped. "Look, people's lives are at stake. You don't believe me, then that is your decision, but I'm going!"

"Where did you say you were going?" Phylicia asked from behind Declan, causing him to jump perceptibly.

"Murdock has requested me and Annie to meet him," Declan said as he turned to face Phylicia.

"Oh, okay. If there truly are lives at stake, by all means, you should go," Phylicia responded in all seriousness and indicating that she had overheard most of what Declan had said to Annie. "There are lives at stake!"

Declan stood there looking at her in shock.

"Okay, Declan, where are we going?" Annie asked after being outfitted as Declan was instructed.

"Just follow me," Declan said as he started off in the direction Murdock had indicated.

As Declan and Annie started toward the river, Phylicia directed a couple of her security people to surreptitiously follow Declan and Annie. Their instructions were to follow and report back. They hadn't gone far from the transport pod when it became quite dark. More than once, during their walk, Declan would stop and look around. He felt like he was being followed, but he saw nothing. Declan and Annie both stumbled a few times in the darkness, but neither lost their feet. Two hours after setting out, Declan called for a brief rest. He took a swallow of water from his waterskin and Annie did the same.

"Six people are quieter than you two," Murdock said in the darkness; so softly that neither was certain that they had heard him or were just imagining it.

Annie Cooper physically jumped back and let out a tiny yelp. Declan stumbled back and fell to the ground.

"Where did you come from?" Declan finally asked with difficulty catching his breath.

"I've been around," Murdock responded.

Being dark, Declan couldn't see it, but he could hear the grin on Murdock's face in his tone.

"Who are you to make requests of me?" Annie asked warily.

"My kids want their mother may," Murdock spoke the coded phrase as an answer.

Annie seemed to get disoriented momentarily. "Murdock," she said with great excitement.

"Oh, so, now you know who he is?" Declan chided.

"Just a little precaution," Annie explained, "in case Phylicia or Palmer decided to torture me."

"I don't get it," Declan said, confused.

"It's called a post-hypnotic suggestion," Annie tried to explain. "I only had a very dim idea of who Murdock was, but I wasn't able to say what I did remember. The rest of my memory was blocked off. It took hearing the key phrase to allow me to remember everything."

"You do know that Phylicia sent guards to follow you," Murdock said matter-of-factly.

Declan jumped back and faced the way they had just come. "Are they still out there?"

Those cat-like reflexes, Murdock thought. "Sort of," he said. "They were *taken care of* an hour back."

"He probably killed them," Declan stated.

"Bullshit," Annie chided. "If that's what you think, then you don't know Murdock at all."

"He threatened to kill a dozen men I was working with when they violated his edict," Declan responded greatly piqued.

"You really should learn to control your passions," Murdock warned quietly. "They could very well be your undoing."

"I find that hard to believe," Annie stated scornfully. "The Murdock I know would have to have a very good reason for doing such a thing. More reason than just a show of force for defiance."

"We need to table this discussion, for now," Murdock stated. "We need to get moving," he said as he turned and started walking toward the river.

They had queued up with Murdock leading, Annie in the middle, and Declan bringing up the rear. After a couple of hours, Murdock called for a halt.

"How much further are we going before stopping for the night, Murdock?" Annie asked. "I'm exhausted."

"I thought we'd walk all night," Murdock said sarcastically.

"Very funny," Annie chided. "Now, can I have a serious answer?"

"I was thinking of stopping shortly after we cross the river," Murdock said matter-of-factly. "We *are* a little ahead of schedule, since Declan did such a good job sneaking you out of camp."

"Phylicia came up behind me and overheard," Declan justified immediately after the perceived ridicule. "I guess I underestimated her."

"I saw her coming up behind you, but I couldn't say anything to tip you off," Annie explained. "Since I didn't remember anything, seeing her was no threat to me. Say what you will, Phylicia is no dummy."

"Let's move on," Murdock stated.

About an hour later, they reached the river. Murdock had intentionally led the pair further downriver than he had initially indicated to Declan. Annie, at Murdock's request, started working on getting a fire started. Declan helped by gathering what wood he could find. Murdock went to the river and quickly caught and cleaned two fish. It wasn't long before they were all three sitting around the fire waiting for the fish to cook.

"How are you two holding up?" Murdock asked. "How much longer can you go?"

"I can't go any further. You seem to be in a bit of a rush," Annie observed, "how come?"

"Mei Lee will be delivering soon," Murdock stated.

"Has it been a month already?" Annie asked.

"It's been twenty-four days, roughly," Murdock answered.

"I'm done in as well." Declan chimed in testily, even though no one asked. "You certainly aren't one for small talk, Murdock," Declan observed. "Most people would like more information than you usually offer."

"I say what I need to, when I need to," Murdock responded as he looked into the flames.

Everyone sat quietly waiting for the fish to cook. When it was finished, they all ate their fill. After eating, Annie and Declan tried to get comfortable on the ground while Murdock had the first watch.

When Declan awoke, it was morning, but he was not lying on the ground by the river. He was under a man-made roof, which caused him to sit up with a start and immediately fall out of the hammock he was lying in. Hitting the floor, he was surprised to find it was wood. He was expecting compacted dirt.

"Are you okay?" Annie asked poking her head inside his sleeping area.

"How did we get here?" Declan asked, confused. "Where is *here*?"

"We're inside Murdock's cabin," Annie informed him, "and I have no idea how we got here."

"You seem to be lacking perplexity with the fact that we went to sleep in one area and are now somewhere else without any memory of how we got here, how long it took, or how we are going to get back," Declan said with a scolding tone.

"I, for one, know where we are and have a very rough idea of where the transport pod is," Annie responded coldly. "I have no questions as to how we got here. I don't need to know everything to be able to accept something. I can accept that we are here, now, safe and cozy. Why should I care as to the means of transportation? What difference would it make if we arrived by elephant caravan or wagon?"

"I'm not like you," Declan snapped back.

"Obviously! Why don't you come out? Calm yourself, first, and I'll introduce you. I would caution you to be civil to these nice people," Annie chided as she turned and left his presence.

When Declan finally parted the hide, he saw that the hide was for his privacy. It was all that separated him from the main room of the cabin. There were several people in the main room, the majority being children, and all sporting a knife of some kind. Annie introduced him around to everyone.

"You are brother to my mother?" young Andrew asked suspiciously, his hand on the hilt of his knife, when Declan was presented to him.

"Who is your mother?" Declan asked innocently.

"Rosa Lea Griffen bore me and nurtured me, until she died," Andrew responded coldly. "Mei Lee raised me and is now my mother."

"I guess that makes me your uncle, then," Declan said with a shrug and a grin as he stuck out his empty hand to the youngster.

"Until I have more data on the subject, I have no choice but accept what you say as a given," Andrew responded while staring at the proffered hand.

"Shake his hand, Andrew!" Mei Lee interjected. "Sorry, Declan. The children tend to be off-putting to strangers."

Andrew took his offered hand, but Declan could see the suspicion in the child as a palpable thing.

"I'd count your fingers, Declan," Murdock interjected with a chuckle, as he entered the cabin just as the handshake was ending. "Sit, Declan," Murdock said indicating the table where Annie and Mei Lee were already sitting. "Take all the waterskins and refill them," Murdock said to Andrew and Chun Hua, who took up all the waterskins and headed to the river.

"I can see my father in Andrew," Declan said as the two children left the cabin, "and Rose as well."

"He's lucky. He favors his mother," Murdock quipped. Mei Lee good-naturedly slapped his upper arm.

"Nice place you have here," Declan said as he looked critically around the room. "How long did it take you to build it?"

"It took as long as it took," Murdock answered. "There weren't any watches or calendars."

"How did we get here?" Declan asked with more than a little anger.

"Pachyderm parade," Murdock said sarcastically. "Does it really matter?"

"It does to me," Declan said, his anger swelling. "I don't like being shanghaied or feeling like I have been."

"You haven't been shanghaied," Murdock responded, anger tinging his voice. "I brought you here to meet your nephew and to visit your sister's tomb. After that is done, I'll be more than happy to return you to your own little corner of heaven."

No one said anything for quite some time. Mei Lee first looked to Murdock and Annie first looked to Declan. After a few seconds, they each switched who they were looking at. Both women had been shocked at the level of anger that had developed so quickly between the two men.

"Wow! The testosterone sure is thick in here," Annie said finally. "I think I need some fresh air. Why don't you two take it outside?"

Murdock, finding wisdom in Annie's suggestion, beckoned Declan to come outside the cabin with him. Both men were angry, but Declan was by far the angrier of the two. He decided to join Murdock outside, to spare the women and children his anger.

"What's your problem?" Murdock asked after he and Declan had walked out of earshot of the cabin.

"I have a problem with anyone who hides things from me, especially if they are a killer!" Declan said heatedly.

"I'm at a loss. In what way have I offended you?" Murdock asked trying to calm Declan.

"You killed those workmen." Declan accused.

"You saw that they were still alive for yourself, so I'm curious what you have for proof?"

"I have no proof, yet. When I get back, I plan on publicly accusing you!"

"You won't have any proof," Murdock said with a small grin. "The men that you and I moved to the edge of the cliff are as alive as you are!"

"You shanghaied Annie and me, for what purpose, I have no idea!"

"If you ask Annie, she'll deny being shanghaied. The purpose of her being here is to help my wife deliver a baby, not that you need to know. You have not been shanghaied. You were simply transported in the most efficient way available."

"What was the means of that transportation?" Declan asked, his voice full of disdain.

"That information is on a need to know basis and, frankly, you don't need to know," Murdock answered calmly. "So, that is something else you can't prove. Anything else?"

Declan stood glaring at Murdock, his hands clenching and un-clenching rhythmically. Murdock could see that there was something else behind his anger.

"You killed her!" Declan finally blurted out.

"Whom have I killed, in your opinion?" Murdock asked quietly. He had closed his eyes dreading what he knew was coming.

"Rose! You killed her!" Declan accused hotly.

"I didn't kill her, Declan," Murdock said quietly. "I would have given anything if I could have taken her place."

"If she wouldn't have been with you, she'd still be alive," Declan accused as he started crying openly.

"If she wouldn't have been with me, she would have been dead long before she finally died," Murdock tried to explain. "They tried to kill her within thirty days of our arrival."

"And how are you going to prove that?" Declan asked with venom.

"You'll have to take my word for it," Murdock said quietly. "Or you could talk to Mei Lee."

"I should ask your current wife about my sister? I already know she would lie for you! So, that would be a useless exercise!"

"If that is how you feel about it, then I will take you to your sister's tomb and then return you to the transport pod." Murdock got up and went back into the cabin, leaving Declan outside alone.

"What's going on?" Annie asked Murdock as he entered the door.

"I'm taking Declan to visit his sister's tomb and then I'm taking him back to the transport pod," Murdock said coldly as he collected his and Declan's waterskins and rest of his gear. "I'll be back as soon as I can. I need you to stay with Mei Lee and the kids."

"I will," Annie said quietly.

When Murdock had exited the cabin, he saw where Declan

was now unconscious. He levitated Declan and strode out toward Rose's tomb.

"Can you give him the information we discussed?" Murdock flashed.

"Certainly," Beron responded.

"He doesn't need to know about the Oomah," Murdock said. *"He also doesn't need to know my position with you."*

As soon as Murdock had entered the cabin, Declan felt very fatigued. He sat on a log and closed his eyes; he felt like he couldn't keep his eyes open another second. As he closed his eyes, he could feel himself falling over, but it felt like slow motion. He had time to hope he wouldn't be hurt when he hit the ground and braced for the collision with the hard surface. The collision never came, or if it did, Declan was unaware of it.

He felt like he was floating, but was unable to control any movement. He could see his sister following a few men into trees. He could see Murdock talking to the men, from a distance away. He then saw one of the men threaten Rose with a knife. Apparently, some time passed, and he then saw one of the men hit his sister from behind rendering her unconscious. He couldn't hear what was being said, but he saw clearly the man who knocked Rose out. He didn't see Murdock around anywhere, but he did see the men tie her to a tree and leave her naked, bleeding and beaten. The scene tore at his heart, but he couldn't move or yell or do anything.

He then saw, as if watching through some night vision contraption, Murdock finding Rose and tending her injuries. He saw Murdock care for Rose over some course of time. He didn't know if it was days or weeks, but he did see how Murdock genuinely cared for his sister. He saw Murdock teaching her to shoot a bow. He saw Rose filling waterskins by a stream. He could see that Murdock was looking around and both were talking. Suddenly, he heard his sister in a clear voice say, "I was just thinking that I have never been this happy, that I can remember." To Declan, she looked very happy and it made his heart happy to hear her voice say so.

He saw a thin man being beaten and tied and a very thin Mei Lee being beaten. He saw his sister shoot one of the men with an arrow and saw her and Murdock deal with the two thugs that were beating the couple. He could see that Murdock trusted Rose by the fact that he had his back to her when she was armed. It filled his heart with pride to see his sister standing up to apparent bullies.

He saw an unarmed Murdock take on the two armed bullies and defeat them. He could see Rose behind the fray with arrows ready. He saw the thin man jump in front of Rose and get hit with a knife in the throat.

He saw Murdock, Rose, and Mei Lee working together on making something with skins inside the cabin. All three seemed to be a team and all looked very happy. It was then that he noticed that Mei Lee and Rose were both pregnant and Rose seemed to be further along than Mei Lee. He saw Mei Lee help Rose deliver and then he got to see Rose help Mei Lee deliver. He also saw the three adults work together to care for each other and the two kids.

He saw Rose getting cold weather gear on and trudging through the snow to a stockade. He saw her tied to the stockade wall. He saw her escape and hitting someone with all her weight, and he saw the knife enter her. It was then that he heard Rose's voice again saying, "I love you both! I wanted to thank you both for loving me the way you have. I have never felt so loved, wanted, needed as I have with the two of you! Love each other to the hilt, just as the two of you have loved me. I want you both to remember that no one took my life, I gave it freely!" Declan wished he could cry aloud. He knew he had just heard his sister's last words.

⁓

Declan finally woke up. When he did, he was lying on the grass and he could see Murdock standing in front of what looked like a granite tomb. As he stood, he felt his cheeks and found they were damp, even though the grass was dry. As he got to his feet and approached the tomb, he saw the plaque and read it to himself. *"Rosa Lea Murdock. Beloved wife, friend, mother. She saved us all."*

When he looked at Murdock, Declan could see the tears on his cheek.

"Did she have words carved into her back and chest?" Declan asked.

"Yes, she did," Murdock said quietly. "Why do you ask?"

"I don't know how you managed it, but I think I saw glimpses into Rose's life," Declan said quietly, "and her death."

"I did nothing to allow you to see things like that," Murdock said as he turned and walked away a little distance to wait for Declan.

"I take it she liked this place?" Declan asked as he joined Murdock after ten minutes of communing with the spirit of his sister.

"It was her favorite place," Murdock said coldly.

"When you return me, will my memory be wiped?" Declan asked quietly.

"Yes, it will," Murdock informed him.

"I would like to retain the memory of what I was shown about Rose, and of this spot," Declan requested quietly.

"I have no control over what you will be allowed to remember," Murdock told him, "but I'll see what can be done. Are you ready to go back to the transport pod?"

"Not quite yet," Declan said. "I understand that you have been transporting me, somehow, to keep me from seeing things I shouldn't. I was shown how much you meant to Rose, both you and Mei Lee. I could see that she was very happy with you and that you did your best to keep her safe. I just wanted you to know that I appreciate it."

"Being safe all your life, isn't a good thing. It's better to step out, take a chance, to stand for something, even if it isn't safe. Rose understood that. I didn't do anything for you or your appreciation." Murdock corrected, rather harshly. "I did it for her, because it was easy to do things for her."

"Be that as it may, I still appreciate what you did to make her life a happy one." As Declan took one more look at Rose's tomb, he felt himself drifting off to sleep again.

Shortly after Murdock had levitated the dozen workmen over the cliff and into a hidden spot by the stream, their nightmares stopped. By the time Declan, Annie, and Murdock were sitting around their fire by the river, they awoke and found their way to the transport pod. They were all extremely nervous and despite being late at night, were unable to go to sleep. It appeared, to some, that they were afraid to sleep. A few hours before sunup, the two guards that Phylicia had tasked with following Declan and Annie Cooper, returned to camp.

Phylicia was awakened at her normal time and was informed that the work crew that had gone out with Declan had returned sometime in the night, and so had the guards she had dispatched to follow Declan and party. After giving orders that someone bring her water and something to eat, she sent for Heather Stevens, Kimberly Grey, and Doctor Harris. They arrived shortly after she started her breakfast and were shown in immediately upon arrival.

"Have Declan and Annie Cooper returned?" Phylicia asked as she took another bite of fish.

"No, they haven't," all three women said as one.

"Heather, go tell Palmer to join us," Phylicia ordered.

"When and if Declan and Annie return, we need to keep a

much closer eye on them," Phylicia ordered after Heather left to comply with her instructions.

The remaining two women nodded that they understood the instructions. "When Palmer gets here, I want you two to retrieve the workmen that had returned in the night, and the guards. I want to talk to the guards first, after Doctor Harris' assessment, and then I want her to assess the workmen." Phylicia leaned forward toward Doctor Harris. "I want your report right after and you're to keep your findings confidential. You're not to discuss anything you find with anyone, even the ones you examine. Understood?" Phylicia dismissed the two women with a wave of her hand as Palmer presented himself.

"Have you heard?" Phylicia asked Palmer, obviously irked.

"I have heard about the workmen returning," Palmer responded. "Has something else happened that I didn't know about?"

"When Declan and the Cooper woman left, I told a couple of my guards to follow them, discreetly. They returned just before sunup and are being examined by Harris. They'll be here when she's finished," Phylicia said. "Do you know anything about why Murdock would want Declan?" she asked as she paced.

"I haven't heard anything that would indicate a reason," Palmer responded.

"There has to be a reason why Murdock and Declan have been so amicable." Phylicia continued her pacing. "To us, Murdock has been dictatorial, short-tempered, and arrogant, but he seems to be softer toward Declan," Phylicia said aloud to herself, as if Palmer wasn't there. It was then that the guards were shown in. "What happened to following Declan and Annie Cooper discreetly?" Phylicia asked the guards as she stood looking at them. She was as imposing as she could manage, considering her size and sex.

"We were following them," one of the guards responded. The other had obviously chosen him as spokesman. "We could hardly see them, but we could hear them. We saw nothing and heard nothing that would indicate someone else was there."

"So, what happened?" Phylicia asked, impatient with them.

"We don't know," the guard responded. "It was like hitting a wall. One second we were following them, the next, it was close to sunup and we were lying where we once stood."

"Did you try trailing them?" Phylicia asked.

"No, we didn't," the guard answered sheepishly. "We don't know how."

Phylicia abruptly dismissed the guards with an angry gesture. "You're useless," she shouted at their back.

"What do you make of it?" Palmer asked. He had remained quiet while the guards were present.

"I don't know! We don't have enough information to even form an opinion, yet," Phylicia said angrily.

While they were waiting on Doctor Harris to finish examining the workmen, Palmer looked around the smallish room. A fortnight prior, Phylicia had commandeered one of the rooms in the transport pod for her own personal use. It served as her sleeping quarters as well as a place to hold private meetings. It had nothing in it to indicate that it was anything other than an empty room. No chairs, a table, a proper bed, or embellishments of any kind. The only thing that made it hers was the fact that she was in it.

Doctor Harris finally reported to Phylicia and Palmer.

"What did you find in your examinations of the workmen and guards?" Phylicia asked impatiently.

"Physically, nothing," Doctor Harris said with a look of perplexity. "However, the workmen seem to be having nightmares."

"Nightmares?" Phylicia asked exasperated, glancing at Palmer.

"They seem to be suffering from some sort of flashback. It appears to be close to P.T.S.D. Post Traumatic Stress Disorder,"

Doctor Harris added seeing Phylicia's questioning look. "That's all that I can find, with these primitive conditions and tools."

"Did they say what happened?" Phylicia asked.

"All they said was that they had climbed up the cliff on the other side of the stream. They took a few steps and then they woke not far from the stream, but on this side of the cliff," Harris tried to explain. "They had no explanation for how they got off the cliff."

"Murdock did say that the cliff was off-limits," Palmer added.

"If you don't have anything useful to add, Palmer, keep your mouth shut," Phylicia snapped. The more she thought about it, the more irate she became. The more irate she got, the more she thought of the reason why she was irate. "Get out! Both of you," she screamed. She was apoplectic.

7

When Declan awoke, he was alone. When he stood, he found that he still had his twelve-inch machete and his waterskin. When he scanned the distance, he could see the transport pod. When he turned around, he saw that he was at the base of the cliff that lay upstream from the transport pod. He could see the stream off to his right, a fair distance away. He tried to ascertain what time of day it was and guessed that it was mid-morning, but had no idea what day it was or how long he had been gone. Without much thought, he started off toward the transport pod by the most direct course.

As he walked, he remembered what was shown to him of his sister's life, visiting her tomb, and surprisingly, Murdock's family. He hadn't actually accepted the fact that he was also part of Murdock's family. He had been told that Murdock and Rose were married, but he hadn't seen the usual trappings to indicate that it was so. He saw no wedding ring on Murdock, no marriage license, and he wasn't invited to the wedding, so, to him, it was just something that couldn't be independently verified and was thus subject to interpretation.

The closer he got to the transport pod, the more concerned he became, he knew he would be questioned extensively by

Phylicia or her goons. He hadn't, as yet, decided what to tell them about where he went and why. With each step he took, the closer he was getting to having to make a decision. Should he tell Phylicia and Palmer what Annie was doing and why she was needed? He had no idea when she would return, if ever.

The more steps he took, the more he remembered Rose. She was the eldest and saw to it her siblings were taken care of when their parents had been working so many jobs to provide for them. Now, she was gone, and he would never be able to express his gratitude for all she had done for him when he was growing up.

After all the years of being so close to Rose, he had thought he knew what type of man she would have married. Granted, her options were extremely limited, but he never would have considered someone like Murdock. The more he thought about it, and remembered what was shown to him, he was starting to reconsider his opinion. From what he was shown, Murdock gave Rose a chance to live and gave hope to Mei Lee when everyone around her had given nothing but pain and suffering.

It struck him, finally, that he couldn't explain how he was shown what his sister's life had been. How was it accomplished? For that matter, how was he transported without a cart or wagon? He saw none at the tomb. How was he made unconscious at Murdock's command? What made the workmen unconscious? Murdock wasn't around then, at least, not that he knew about. How were the individuals that were told to follow him and Annie dealt with? His first inclination was that Murdock had killed them, but he said he hadn't killed the workmen and Annie knew that Murdock hadn't killed the ones following them. So, how was it done? The workmen appeared to be asleep and so was he, but how? Without some explanation, he dare not bring up anything to Phylicia or Palmer else they would think he'd lost what little sense he had.

As he entered the camp, under the transport pod, Declan had decided not to mention anything about where he was or why. He could have, but the only person that he would consider family would be hurt. He had seen how visibly upset Murdock had been at Rose's tomb. For Rose and Andrew, Declan decided what little he did know, he would keep to himself.

Declan hadn't gotten very far before Phylicia's guards stopped him and instructed him to follow them. In short order, he was in front of Phylicia and Palmer.

"Nice to see you, Declan," Phylicia said with a mock smile. "Would you mind telling me where you were and what you were doing?"

"As a matter of fact, I would," Declan responded coolly. "My business is my business."

Palmer had gotten to his feet and crossed the space between them surprisingly fast. Declan was knocked to the ground by the bigger man with the back of his hand. "You better answer up, Mister," he warned angrily.

"Ben! Ben! Declan is one of us! He wouldn't consider being rude to us, would you, Declan?" Phylicia asked sarcastically. "You'll tell us what we want to know, sooner or later." Phylicia motioned for the guards, who tied his arms to his side and stood him back up. "One more time, Declan. Where did you and Annie go?"

Declan could taste his own blood where his lip met his teeth. "To Murdock's cabin," he said as Palmer made a move toward him. *I don't know anything, so why not tell them what I know*, he thought. *Rose would understand*, he told himself.

"Where is this cabin?" Phylicia asked with a hypnotic tone.

"I have no idea," Declan responded truthfully.

"How did you get there?" Phylicia asked, again with her hypnotic tone.

"I have no idea," Declan answered again.

Palmer slapped him with an open hand, again. The strike was sufficient for Declan to see stars. "Answer the question!"

"I answered truthfully," Declan answered back hotly. "I was unconscious most of the time."

Palmer backhanded him again, knocking him to the ground. Declan was starting to feel woozy.

"Now, Ben, don't be so anxious to inflict pain on poor Declan," Phylicia mocked. "Who was at this cabin?" she asked Declan softly.

"Murdock, Murdock's wife, their kids, and Annie," Declan said weakly.

"Do these people have names?" Phylicia asked sweetly.

"Probably," Declan responded. Palmer promptly punched him in the solar plexus, leaving him gasping for air. The guards held him upright.

"As you can see," Phylicia said with a false sadness, "I have trouble controlling Ben. He really seems to enjoy inflicting pain and he really doesn't like wise-ass answers. What was the purpose of your visit to Murdock's cabin?" Phylicia asked silkily as she paced back and forth in front of him.

"To visit my sister's tomb," Declan managed to get the words out between the gasps for air.

"You had a sister here? I didn't know that!" Phylicia said with some surprise. "Why didn't I know that, Declan?"

"Because I didn't tell you," Declan managed to say.

"I know that," Phylicia said impatiently, "but why didn't you tell me?"

"You didn't ask. Besides, I only recently found it out myself," Declan said somewhat easier. Palmer had gotten behind him and punched him in the right kidney. Declan's knees buckled and the pain was excruciating, so much so that he passed out.

"Get Harris in here," Phylicia demanded of the guards. She then turned to Palmer. "If you've killed him, I'll put you in his place!"

Doctor Harris rushed in and started to tend the bloody mass that was Declan as best she could.

"Just bring him around," Phylicia ordered Doctor Harris. "We have a lot more questions for him!"

Doctor Harris looked up at Phylicia and could see the sadistic pleasure on her face in seeing Declan in pain. When she looked to Palmer's face, she could see his eyes widen when he inhaled and slightly close when he exhaled, showing signs so intense, it almost appeared as sexual pleasure, in his ferocious punishment. "He won't be answering anything for a while," she said to the pair. "He'll be lucky if you didn't rupture something."

Even though Declan knew he was unconscious, he knew he was still alive. His mind had disassociated itself from his body a few moments after the final blow. It seemed he was floating above his body. He could see Doctor Harris tending him, but couldn't hear what was being said. He could, however, hear his sister's voice in his head.

"Maybe it would have been better if you would have stayed with Murdock," he heard her say. "People in power seem to want to hurt others for the benefit of the powerful. The man who killed me was the same way."

"James Whittier!" he heard himself say.

Phylicia, waiting for Harris to finish tending Declan's wounds heard him say a name that she hadn't heard in a long time. She did her best to show no sign of recognition at hearing a name that was the same as her second cousin. "What did he say?" Phylicia asked Harris.

"Some name. He's delirious," Doctor Harris said.

How could Declan know the name of my cousin? Phylicia asked herself. "Tend to Declan as best you can," she instructed Doctor Harris. "If he regains consciousness, I want to be informed immediately!" Doctor Harris nodded acknowledgment as the guards were carrying Declan out of her quarters. Until she'd heard his name, Phylicia hadn't thought of James W. Whittier, III for many years. Her second cousin, the son of her mother's cousin, had been groomed by his father to take his place in politics. She had briefly worked for his campaign for Mayor when she was still in prep school and because of the experience, had always looked up to him.

After everyone had left her quarters, Phylicia started running the facts she knew of Murdock in her mind. She knew that he and his wife were the only survivors of the first pod. Everyone else had died. For Declan to know the name of her second cousin, meant he had to have heard it somewhere. Murdock's camp being the only place he could have heard it. Declan's sister had been on the first transport pod and had done something worthy of being placed in a tomb versus just being put into a hole in the ground. *Murdock, the murderer, killed my cousin!* The thought hammered through her brain. She figured that James had been on the first pod and had run afoul of Murdock. *Murdock, the murderer, killed my cousin!* It was then that she decided to make Murdock and all his family pay. *This is vendetta!* She gave the guards instructions to keep Declan from disappearing. She ensured her instructions would be followed by telling them their lives would be forfeit as the price for failure.

The next day, Declan was better, but was still bedridden and conscious only part of the time.

"What did Murdock tell you about your sister's death?" Phylicia asked sweetly and quietly once everyone had left her alone with him.

"He said...she was killed...by a man called...Whittier," Declan managed weakly.

"Was that James W. Whittier, III?" she asked sweetly, hypnotically, "if you know," offhandedly.

"I think...that was...the name," Declan said. "How...did you...know?"

"You told us when you were delirious. I would like you to listen and consider," Phylicia said in her best hypnotic tone. "James W. Whittier, III was my distaff second cousin. I knew him quite well! Back home, he was a kindly man who was a Mayor of a smallish town. I know, for a fact, that he wouldn't — couldn't — hurt anyone or anything. To say that he had hurt someone is something very hard for me to believe. Does Murdock strike you as someone whom your sister would consider being with? Since no one else survived, who is to say what really happened? Who would argue if Murdock secretly did away with everyone else?"

"No, not...true," Declan said emphatically as he tried to shake his head to emphasize his negative answer.

"I wasn't there," Phylicia continued hypnotically. "Neither were you, so who is to say? He could have lied to you and you'd never know!"

As soon as Phylicia started talking, there was a sweet voice in Declan's head, which sounded like his sister, saying, "*she is lying*", and it kept repeating with every sentence Phylicia spoke. The pain from his injuries was intense, but he did what he could to hang onto the sweet voice in his head.

"Did he show you any diaries, journals, logs, or any other written record?" Phylicia continued, even though she could tell that Declan was drifting off again. "My cousin was an avid keeper of a daily journal. He never let a day pass without making an entry," Phylicia was impressed with herself. Even she was starting to believe her statements. Even though Declan had lost consciousness again, Phylicia stayed with him, holding his hand, and repeating her arguments.

When Declan was unconscious, he seemed to be able to see his older sister in his mind. He could hear her talking to him as well. He also knew that someone, probably Phylicia, was holding his hand, but he could do nothing to acknowledge or pull away from it. He couldn't hear Phylicia because he was concentrating on what his sister was saying. She told him how happy she had been with Murdock. Repeatedly, she told him about the troubles caused by Whittier. It was sweet, in his opinion, to hear his sister's voice, even if it was repetitive.

It was late in the day, the same day that Declan entered the camp at the transport pod, when Murdock reached his cabin. As he entered, he noticed that the children were already sleeping and Annie was looking at Mei Lee, concern plastered on her face.

"Are you okay, Mei?" he asked as he closed to door.

"I think she will deliver soon," Annie said, her voice composed and soothing.

"Is there anything you need?" Murdock asked, his tone showing his deep concern.

"Not right now," Annie answered.

"Did Declan get back to the transport pod okay?" Mei Lee asked.

"I got him close enough for him to make it on his own," Murdock said. "You don't need to worry about that, right now. He can take care of himself."

Mei Lee smiled at him, and he smiled as he squeezed her hand lovingly.

A few hours later, a new baby boy, Huo Jin James Murdock, had arrived. Mei Lee named him after her father and Murdock, wishing to keep his wife happy, went along with her decision, but gave him his father's middle name. After mother and son were sleeping peacefully, and Murdock and Annie had cleaned up the table they had used for the delivery, they went outside the cabin and sat on the deck.

"How are you holding up?" Murdock asked Annie.

"I'm really tired," Annie responded, "also, very satisfied! That is the part of my profession that makes it all worthwhile."

"When did you want to head back?" Murdock asked.

"In a couple of days, if you don't mind," Annie said. "If it wasn't for the lack of those with my skills, I wouldn't go back. It seems that I am far more relaxed here than at the transport pod. The political maneuvering gets tiresome after a while."

"You never said where you wanted your cabin," Murdock said.

"At this point, I have no idea where I want it. If I knew how to fend for myself in the wild, I'd stay away from the transport pod and most of the people there. It's becoming oppressive there and you never know who you can trust."

Murdock chuckled and nodded his head. "I know what you mean," he said. "It's one of the reasons why I live away from the rest."

"You certainly have made a good life for yourself and your family here," Annie said as she looked around at the trees and the river. "You co-exist with this environment and you train your children to do the same. The others only wish to exploit it."

"There are things that would make it a little easier," Murdock stated. "Paper, fresh vegetables, glass, and some steel smelting would make things better."

"Yes, they probably would," Annie said as she nodded, "but with those also comes firearms, clear-cutting forests, planetary pollution, and a host of other consequences. Even though I couldn't consciously access my memories of you and your family while I waited to be returned here, I was still able to think and to see what was transpiring. Phylicia and Palmer are trying to set up a dictatorship, you know."

"I know," Murdock responded quietly. "I saw it with the first transport pod. Everyone insisted on electing someone to lead them and tell them what to do. I guess they thought it would give them a sense of normality here. I tried to tell them that they would be better off without the political machinations."

"What happened with Declan?" Annie asked.

"I took him to his sister's tomb," Murdock said. "He was given some idea of what her life here was like."

"Did that help him?" Annie asked.

"It might, someday," Murdock said. "As a favor, that he requested, Declan was allowed to remember what he learned here. It can't hurt us, and it may comfort him. I don't think Phylicia and company will let him enjoy his memories, though."

As Murdock was holding his son, a few hours after his birth, Beron was giving him an update on Declan's condition and treatment at the transport pod. Bridget, who had developed a very close relationship with Rose, was doing what she could to comfort him in the mental image of Rose. She had argued that if she didn't try to help, Declan would quickly succumb to the torture. Beron, knowing Declan's weakness of will, had agreed to the attempt to give him emotional support. Murdock was not overly concerned with Declan's predicament.

"Why not concerned about Dee Clan?" flashed to Murdock's mind. *"Situation dire."*

"You and Bridget showed him what happened with first ship," Murdock responded while he cuddled his newborn son. *"He chose to return. He could have stayed."*

"You made him welcome?" flashed to Murdock's mind and he had picked up on Beron's thoughts betraying his skepticism.

Murdock didn't answer immediately. Instead, he reflected, with contrition, on what little interaction he did have with Declan. *"Maybe not as well as I should have,"* he finally replied. No one else said anything further, however, Murdock's mind couldn't leave it alone. It wasn't long before he returned Huo Jin to Mei Lee and went outside the cabin to think and to plan. When a plan, of sorts, had formed, Murdock discussed it telepathically with Beron and Mei Lee. After the deliberations, Murdock had resolved to rescue his brother-in-law.

"I need you to stay with Mei Lee," Murdock said to Annie after he had made his decision. "The older kids will help as best they can. They know the daily routine."

"Where are you going?" Annie asked.

"I need to rescue Declan," Murdock replied. "I believe he is being tortured by Phylicia and Palmer." As an afterthought, he thought, *I need to do it for Rose.*

"I don't know how you would know that," Annie stated, "but if it's true, then you're going to need me along to tend him."

"I need you to look after Mei Lee," Murdock insisted strongly.

"I need to go where I'm needed —" Annie responded adamantly.

"— and that is here," Murdock said, interrupting her with his insistence.

"I'm going," Annie insisted loudly.

"Why can't she go?" Mei Lee flashed.

"I need to travel quickly, and she doesn't need to know how that's done," Murdock replied to his wife. *"Besides, I worry about you and the kids."*

"Oh, pooh, I've had kids before. We'll be fine. Transport her the way you transported Declan," Mei Lee suggested. *"She needs to see the condition Declan is in, once he has been delivered into your hands."*

"If you go, you have to agree to be transported the same way you were transported here, and you have to agree to do as I say!" Murdock said emphatically to Annie.

"Done," Annie answered quickly, almost too quickly for Murdock's liking.

Under Beron's assurances that no one could get more than a few feet on the cabin side of the ridge, Murdock decided against having Annie unconscious. He knew it would take a whole day just to get into the area, but they would be better prepared when they were closer to the transport pod. His plan was to spend the night on top of the ridge, where they were protected and had nothing to worry about from the humans. Early the next morning, after packing the cart and outfitting Annie, in a minor fashion, they left the cabin for the second pod.

Early in the morning, on the day that Murdock and Annie left Murdock's cabin, Phylicia and Palmer were having a private meeting.

"You're an imbecile," Phylicia yelled at Palmer. "You almost killed Declan!"

"All he had to do was to answer the questions asked," Palmer replied calmly, arms crossed across his large chest. "Besides, why do we need a Doctor who is out of practice? I just gave Harris someone to hone her skills on," he said with a sadistic smile.

"Since Declan and that Annie woman are the only ones to have seen Murdock's cabin and family, they have become of some worth to my plan," Phylicia said aloud, more to herself than to Palmer.

"What plan?" Palmer asked, "You have my attention."

"We have to stop people from having contact with Murdock," she tried to explain. "They need to stop relying on him for anything and to rely on us for everything. As soon as Declan is able, I'm planning to try Murdock for murder, in absentia."

"Don't you need to hold him first?" Palmer asked with a blank look.

"You really are a moron," she said calmly. "What did you do before coming here?"

"Head Guard at F.E.M.A. camp region six, Amarillo. Why?" he asked somewhat defensively.

"So, that's where you learned your interrogation techniques! I thought I recognized them. They had the flavor of *government goon*. We don't need to have him in custody to try him for murder. In fact, it would be less complicated if he wasn't in custody," Phylicia said more to herself than Palmer.

"You know, they say you're crazy when you talk to yourself," Palmer said while he observed her pacing, another habit she'd picked up.

"I'm not talking to myself, just ordering my thoughts," Phylicia responded without looking at Palmer. "You should try it sometime, but then I guess you'd have to have more than one thought, at any given time, to sort them, wouldn't you?"

Palmer's anger was growing and Phylicia could see it as plain as day.

"You have no reason to talk to me that way," he said sternly.

"Oh, calm down," Phylicia exclaimed haughtily. "You do have your uses, limited though they may be, and you will remain where you are as long as you are of use. Harm me in any way, however, and you will find yourself in a very different... position. If you're more than a one trick pony, prove it to me!"

"What's that supposed to mean," Palmer raged.

Phylicia, shaking her head in disbelief, left Palmer to go check on Declan. She saw Doctor Harris upon entering the small room she had set up as a recovery room.

"How is he today?" Phylicia asked as she entered the room.

"He is improving and will continue to improve, as long as he's not subjected to any more brutality any time soon," Doctor Harris warned. Phylicia took it that she was referring to what she witnessed at Declan's interrogation.

"Not to worry, Doctor. We have decided on a different tack. We need Declan up and about, somewhat. He needs to give testimony, so he at least needs to be ambulatory," Phylicia instructed as she walked past her to Declan's side.

Declan flinched a little when he saw it was Phylicia and began looking for Palmer.

"Relax, Declan," Phylicia said in a hypnotic, soothing tone. "Palmer isn't here and won't come here. I have guards to ensure that you'll remain safe from him. Have you given any thought to what I was saying about Murdock?"

"Yes, and I don't agree," Declan responded heatedly. "Murdock is quite capable of killing, he is a hunter after all, but I refuse to believe he would murder someone!"

"And what makes you think he isn't?" Phylicia asked coyly. "Did he leave you in the middle of nowhere to fend for yourself without a means of defending yourself?"

"He left me in walking distance of the pod, and I did have a knife."

"Ah, but do you know how to use it?" she asked sweetly. "What good is it if you don't know how to use it? What would you call someone who knew someone needed help and refused to help and that someone died from that need?" she continued with her siren's song. She waited for Declan to think of an answer. "I'm sure my poor cousin begged for Murdock's help, and yet it was refused," she continued when no answer came, "for if Murdock hadn't refused, my cousin would still be here," she said with a touch of false sadness, "as would the rest of the occupants of the first pod."

Declan heard Phylicia's words, but he also heard his sister's voice inside his head, *Be strong! Help is on the way!* He much preferred his sister's voice to Phylicia's prattle. "How do you know your cousin asked for help?" he finally asked weakly. "You weren't there. Maybe Murdock offered his help and it was refused? That wouldn't make Murdock a murderer. Undesirable, maybe, but not a murderer!"

"Let me see your proof of that and I'll believe it. Do you have any proof?" Phylicia asked.

"I have about as much proof as you to make your points," Declan responded with some vigor. "All we have is speculation. Speculation, and hatred!"

"What hatred are you talking about?" Phylicia looked shocked. "Sure, this little colony has its minor disagreements, but we all get along and most of the time, people are nice to one another."

Declan touched his badly bruised and swollen face gingerly. "Yeah, I see kindness just flowing in rivers around here," he responded sarcastically.

"You have to allow for some differences in a group this large, but the majority are nice and get along just fine," Phylicia defended. "You said that Murdock helped you get down from the cliff?" Declan nodded. "He never said what happened to the others after you left him on the cliff?"

"He said they were fine," Declan responded warily, "when I asked him later."

"Have you seen any of those workmen or the contractor since?" she asked innocently.

"No, I haven't. Why do you ask?" Declan asked with skepticism.

"No one has seen them since. It's been only four days, but I'm not hopeful," she said with a touch of sadness. "You get better and do as Doctor Harris says and you'll be up and about in no time," Phylicia said as she left.

Since the *recovery room* was at the end of the passageway, the guards were stationed in the passageway to stop anyone that didn't belong before they got to the room. She left instructions that they were to assist Doctor Harris and prevent Palmer from entering. She also instructed them that they were not to mention the workmen or the guards that followed them and they were not to allow Declan out of the *recovery room* without getting her permission, only her permission.

~

The trip from the cabin to the transport pod was uneventful. Annie would walk as much as she could and ride, on the cart, when she found she could no longer keep up.

"Are you expecting trouble at the transport pod?" Annie asked quietly during one of the many rest stops they took on the trip.

"I always *expect* trouble," Murdock responded flatly as he drank and had a few bits of smoked venison.

"That seems to be a rather negative attitude," she quietly chided as she had some of her own venison.

"If I expect trouble and there is none, I get to be pleasantly surprised," Murdock responded. "That outcome is far better than the reverse. Expecting trouble has kept me alive more times than you can imagine, but the important part is that I'm ready for it."

Once they were on their way again, Annie had plenty to think about. She, like Murdock, was also expecting trouble when they got to the transport pod. She knew them far better than Murdock did, and she had to agree that trouble was most likely. She wasn't used to trouble, at least not the kind that was coming. She had never considered her life as sheltered, but she had never seen violence first-hand. She always had to deal with the aftermath, and, to her, that was bad enough. She wasn't sure what her reactions would be. Would she turn and run when it all started, or would she stand beside Murdock come what may? As the miles clicked by, since their last stop, she was no closer to an answer than she was when she first started her introspection. She found herself hoping against hope that violence wouldn't be necessary so she wouldn't find out that when the chips were down, she ran.

Murdock stopped again at the point where he was going to levitate the cart, himself, and Annie over the river. With her along and conscious, he was unable to use his speed capabilities. He wasn't to the point of trusting her enough with that information about himself.

"Have you come to any conclusions?" he asked as he drank deeply.

"What do you mean?" Annie asked. She was more than a little shocked that her cogitations were so obvious.

"Well, you have been thinking on something pretty hard. I could almost hear the gears grinding in your head."

"I don't know how I'll react to the violence," she said quietly as she hung her head. "I don't want to disappoint you or desert you when you need me. I've never seen the type of violence I think is coming."

Murdock stood in front of her and used his finger to raise her face to look at his eyes directly. "You'll respond the way you'll respond, according to your strengths. I said I expect trouble, but I don't fret over it. Fretting over it all day will ruin a nice day for yourself, and you'll be no closer to the answer than you would by not fretting. As far as disappointing me, I doubt you could. You did an excellent job helping Mei Lee deliver my son and for that, I'll be forever grateful. You're old enough to know that there is a first time for everything, for everyone."

8

It was close to midday when the relief guard found Phylicia doing her daily rounds under the transport pod. She was told that Doctor Harris had requested that Declan be allowed to get to his feet and go outside the pod for a short time.

"Find out where the twelve workmen are and the two guards that failed me. Tell them to make themselves scarce while Declan is outside," she instructed the guard.

"What are you up to now?" Palmer asked quietly almost in her ear.

"What are you doing?" Phylicia asked gruffly, somewhat startled. "Stalking me?"

"Just looking after my own interests," Palmer stated quietly, calmly. "Since I can't get answers from you then I'll get them anywhere I can."

Phylicia turned to face Palmer quickly. "Benjamin! You act like you don't trust me," she said with a pouting look on her face. "If I felt that you didn't trust me, I just don't think I could bear it!" It was then that Palmer felt a sharp point in the area of his left kidney. Phylicia stepped toward him, bathed in superiority. She was glad that the guard had returned when he did and acted to protect her. "You really should be a lot more careful, Benjamin," she said slowly and so quietly that Palmer barely heard her words.

"We are supposed to be on the same side," Palmer said through clenched teeth and felt the knife tip press a little harder.

"You will know, what I want you to know, when I want you to know it," Phylicia said with arrogance. "As a warning, for your own health, I wouldn't go looking for something that you shouldn't know." With that, she made a little wave off sign with her right hand and Palmer felt the knifepoint pressure lessen. Palmer didn't bother to look to see who it was. He knew it was one of Phylicia's guards. He walked away.

Once Palmer was gone, the guard reported that Declan was being escorted out of the pod and that all she had commanded had been done.

"What was your name again?" Phylicia asked sweetly.

"Preston Freeman, ma'am," the guard answered militarily.

"That was quick thinking, Preston. Thank you for your assistance. I'm sure you'd make an excellent personal guard." Phylicia saw that the recognition had made Freeman stand taller than he already was with pride. "I want you to stay close enough to assist me again, but not so close as to hear what I say. Can I trust you to be invisible to me and to keep anything heard to yourself?" Phylicia asked the six-foot-three, blond guard.

"Yes, ma'am, you can count on me," he responded.

Phylicia turned and continued her daily stroll around the underside of the transport pod.

"Are they ready?" she asked when she had suddenly stopped at the area used by the woodworkers. After seeing Murdock's proficiency with his spear, she had the woodworkers make staffs for all of the guards.

"We have a dozen staffs finished," the head of the wood-worker shop told her. "We're working on modifying some to be able to hold a twelve-inch machete, should one be required." He handed her one of the staffs and she inspected it carefully. It appeared to be a little less than seven feet long, with a two-inch diameter which had been well-smoothed and shaped.

Phylicia turned and tossed it quickly to Freeman, who was in his guard position. He deftly caught it, with one hand, in the middle of the staff. "What do you think, Preston?" she asked the guard.

Freeman inspected it and felt the heft of it. He felt the smoothness and let it slide through his hand before holding it at one end and sighting down the wooden shaft. "It will do, for the shorter guards," he offered. "I prefer something a little longer, but this should do," he said as he handed it back to Phylicia and then returned to his position, out of earshot.

"Make one for Preston, to his specifications," Phylicia said to the man who had handed the staff to her. "Have one of your men distribute the rest to the existing guards. Do you have anyone who knows how to use one?" she asked as she tossed the staff back to Preston.

"No, ma'am, we only make them," the man said with a slight bow and with the proper deference to her position.

With that, she left and was walking toward the, as yet, unfinished meeting hall and motioned for Preston to advance.

"You know how to use that?" she asked quietly once he was closer to her.

"I did have pugil stick training in the military. It isn't too hard to be used effectively, especially if the other person is unarmed, ma'am," he answered.

"I ordered one to be made to your specifications, but use that one, for now. In your off hours, I want you to find out who knows the most about using the staff and have them train all of the guards in its use. I don't want them to look like fools when they try to use them. At some point, some or all of the guards will probably have to defend us against Murdock, and from what I've witnessed, he's quite proficient."

At the end of the day, Phylicia went to visit Declan again. It filled her with confidence seeing the guards with the new staffs.

It always pleased her to have her orders obeyed. After a short, quiet conversation with Doctor Harris, Phylicia entered the *recovery room* cheerfully.

"How are you, Declan?" she asked with just the right amount of cheer in her voice to show that she was glad he was better.

"Feeling better," Declan answered warily. "At least I don't quite feel like I was hit by a truck!" A short pause. "Not quite a truck. Maybe a car," he said sarcastically.

"Is everyone seeing to your needs?" Phylicia asked full of concern.

"I suppose," Declan responded suspiciously.

"I'm not trying to take advantage of your condition, but have you given any more thought to what I said?" she asked finally. Declan had been waiting for her to get back to Murdock's trial.

"As a matter of fact, I have," he said being rather cold.

"And?"

"Why is it you hid the twelve people on the work crew and the two guards from me?" he asked watching her closely. He could see her blanch.

"Where would you get such an idea?" Phylicia asked as she turned her back on him. "Who would tell you something like that?"

"You did!"

"I don't recall saying any such thing!" she said as innocently as she could manage.

"I've been watching you when you come to visit and your *concern* for my health. I can tell when you're lying," Declan said hotly.

With her back to him, she started working herself up for a good cry. She used tears with her parents and anyone else they would work on and felt that now would be a good time to work on Declan's sympathies.

"I've been the only one who has protected you from Palmer," she said tearfully. She suddenly turned to face him so that he could see her tears.

"You're the one that caused it all in the first place! Your crocodile tears mean nothing!" He saw her tears stop suddenly.

"Fine, you're on your own. Guards," she yelled and waited for them to enter. "Take this malingerer out of here. Toss him in the stream for all I care," she ordered.

"He isn't going anywhere," Doctor Harris said sternly as the guards were starting to lay hands on Declan. "He'll be able to leave in two days, not before!"

"He'll leave now," Phylicia said approaching Doctor Harris menacingly.

"If you remove him, you better hope you don't need my services," Doctor Harris warned. Phylicia could see that she was serious. "The same thing applies if Palmer comes in!"

After requesting Annie keep her eyes closed, Murdock levitated the cart, with Annie on it, and himself over the river and downriver a fair distance before allowing her to reopen them. When they had reached the spot where he had intended to spend the night, Murdock got a fire going and Annie prepared some raw venison to cook on the fire. While it cooked, Murdock unloaded the tanned hides he had brought for them to sleep on and cover themselves.

"Tomorrow is going to be an early morning," Murdock said as he ate.

"What's your plan?" Annie asked after swallowing the bite she had been chewing.

"If the hunters come to the river to fish for everyone, I'll send at least one back to get Phylicia to meet me away from the pod for a palaver. If they aren't there, then we'll head toward the pod and, if we have to, build a fire in sight of it. I will get their attention one way or another."

"So, you're not going to force them to give us Declan?" Annie asked as Murdock chewed.

"I'll give them a chance to give him to us willingly if that's what you're asking. However, we aren't leaving without him!"

"Is there anything that you're afraid of?" she asked in astonishment.

"I fear the unknown," Murdock finally responded after some thought. "If someone says they fear nothing, they're either a fool or lying. Fear is natural and normal. It's how you deal with the fear, that's what counts. Courage, or the lack of it, is what you do in the face of fear."

They finished eating in silence and then prepared to sleep. Annie, being exhausted fell asleep right away.

"*Is it possible?*" Murdock asked Beron telepathically.

"*Yes. Will be ready,*" the response came.

After a short telepathic conversation with Mei Lee, Murdock fell asleep.

"I hope your friends show up soon," Irene Harris said quietly to Declan after Phylicia and the guards left. "I don't know how much longer I can put them off."

"They're already quite close," Declan responded confidently.

"How do you know?" the doctor asked.

"That's what my sister told me," Declan said more to himself than to the doctor.

"Really? And where is she?" Doctor Harris asked.

"She's dead," Declan said calmly.

Wonderful, I've jeopardized everything for someone who talks to the dead, or worse, to the voices in his head, Doctor Harris thought as her heart sunk. "Does she talk to you?" she asked.

"All the time," Declan said matter-of-factly.

Doctor Harris was wishing she had followed her own advice and kept her nose out of things that she didn't understand.

◆

Murdock woke Annie a couple of hours before sunup. As Annie was becoming more mentally aware of her surroundings, she noticed that her current location was not where she went to sleep. They were still by the river, but she could see the outline of the ridge in the gloom of the early morning hours. It was disconcerting, but Annie had resolved that she didn't have to know everything about Murdock or his ways of accomplishing what he needed to.

"Any sign of the hunters?" she asked as she hunkered down to warm herself and take off the morning chill.

"Not yet," Murdock responded as he tended the fire and turned the chunks of venison. "They have been doing most of their fishing downriver a hundred feet. We should be able to see them approach long before they get here."

"And if we don't?" Annie asked as she drank deeply from her waterskin.

"If they don't show up by the time we're ready to move on, we'll head toward the pod," Murdock responded as he continued to tend the cooking meat.

"Don't you get tired of just meat?" Annie asked.

"What do you mean?" Murdock raised his eyes to look at her.

"There are other things," Annie quipped, "like vegetables."

"It would be nice, but I have only been able to find a few wild onions," Murdock explained. "If you feel the need, just pull some of that grass and wash it off. I think you'll find it surprisingly sweet. Just make sure you get grass and not weeds."

"Very funny," Annie chided.

"You think I'm teasing?" Murdock asked with some surprise as he handed her a piece of the cooked venison.

Annie didn't say anything, she just watched Murdock while she decided if he was teasing her or not.

"Have you given any thought as to where you want to live?" Murdock asked. "You are more than welcome to stay with Mei Lee and me, until I get your house built."

"What would I do to contribute?" Annie asked. "I don't have the skills to take care of myself, and I don't want to be a burden on you and Mei Lee."

"I doubt you would be a burden," Murdock responded. "You could learn to take care of yourself. You have learned a few things already, how to build a fire and where to get water. That's more than the majority of the others know how to do."

"There's also the issue of being alone," Annie said quietly. "By not returning, I won't have the chance to maybe meet someone. I'm not saying I'm in the market, but I would like to keep my options open."

"That could be a problem," Murdock agreed. "You could always wait until the next transport pod."

"Five years?" Annie exclaimed. "You want me to wait another five years?"

"Why don't we table the discussion, for now," Murdock suggested as he was looking downriver and apparently saw something. "We are going to have company soon. You stay here. I want to intercept them before they get to the river." Murdock took off downriver at a trot.

While he was gone, Annie finished eating and began to break camp. She rolled up the hides they had used to sleep on and made everything in the cart secure. She dumped the remainder of the water from her waterskin onto the fire, which made a loud hiss and a big cloud of steam and smoke. She then walked over to the river to refill her waterskin. Just as she was finishing, she heard more hiss from the fire. She turned to see Murdock walking toward the river.

"How did it go?" Annie asked as Murdock knelt down to fill his waterskin.

"I had to do some convincing, but they saw it my way," Murdock explained. "I sent them all back to the transport pod and told them to send everyone on their council out to meet me somewhere between the pod and the river."

"Do you think they'll comply?" Annie asked.

"They'll pass on the message, but I doubt the council will show," Murdock speculated. "I'll be surprised if they do."

As they headed toward the transport pod, Annie had remained quiet. She could feel the showdown coming and it made her uncomfortable. Murdock was quiet and was constantly scanning the horizon while he pulled the cart. When he was close enough to see the transport pod in the distance, Murdock stopped.

"Aren't you concerned about someone trying to come in behind us?" Annie asked as she stood leaning heavily on the cart facing the transport pod. "All they would have to do is circle around and you'd never see them coming."

"The ones who try will likely be the lucky ones," Murdock answered with a smirk. "We have nothing to fear in that event."

"How will you know they aren't going to show?" Annie asked. "Did you give them some sort of a time limit?"

"Certainly," Murdock answered matter-of-factly. "They have until midday."

Annie looked up at the sky to try to determine how much longer they would have to wait, but didn't know enough to read the sun's position.

"About three hours," Murdock said answering her unasked question. As he stood there, he took off most of the weapons and other equipment he didn't feel he would need in a confrontation. When he was finished, he stood loose, but ready, constantly scanning the distance for a sign of movement.

～

Phylicia had just awakened and was going through her daily routine when Freeman knocked on the bulkhead outside her quarters in the pod. Heather Stevens, who had been assisting her in dressing, answered the knock and then quickly showed the big guard in.

"What is it?" Phylicia asked impatiently.

"Ma'am, Murdock has come," Preston Freeman exclaimed excitedly after he had bowed. "He wants the entire council to meet him out toward the river!"

Everyone in the room watched with bated breath to see how Phylicia would react.

"I don't care what he wants," Phylicia boomed finally. "He can wait out there until hell freezes over!" Phylicia started stomping around the room, and everyone knew she was highly agitated.

"He is only going to wait until midday, Ma'am," Preston stated.

"And then what?" Phylicia asked sarcastically. "Is he going to attack us? One against two hundred? I don't think he would be that foolish! Have you told Palmer?"

"No, Ma'am. I came straight here to tell you," Freeman responded.

"Go get Palmer and bring him here. It will give me a chance to finish dressing," Phylicia commanded. She liked giving orders and seeing them carried out. She also liked the subservience of underlings. She didn't have to wait long for Palmer.

"What are we going to do about this?" Palmer asked excitedly. He seemed to be trembling.

"I'm not going to submit to the whims of a terrorist," Phylicia said, irritated. "Murdock thinks he can just show up and everyone else is to stop what they're doing and come when called. He *is*, sadly, mistaken!"

"So, what're we going to do?" Palmer asked again.

"I want you and all the guards to go out and deal with Murdock," Phylicia commanded after very little thought.

"Me?" Palmer squealed. "Why me?"

"Don't you want to redeem yourself for Murdock humiliating you?" Phylicia asked mockingly. "I would have thought you would, but you don't have to, if you're afraid." She was looking coldly at Palmer when she asked the question and could see him break out in a sweat just from the thought of facing Murdock. "You aren't afraid of Murdock are you, Palmer?" she asked when Palmer didn't respond.

"I'll take care of it!" Palmer said, gruffly, after he seemed to pull himself together and gather his strength. He was planning as he and Freeman left Phylicia's presence.

When Palmer and Freeman reached the bottom of the pod's ramp, Freeman trotted off in search of the guards. It didn't take long to gather them all together. Palmer had detoured to the woodworker and gotten a staff for himself and was feeling fairly confident. All the guards were armed with a twelve-inch machete and a wooden staff, just as he was. As they marched out to meet Murdock, Palmer had arranged the guards in a line in front of him.

Phylicia, Heather Stevens, and Kimberly Grey had emerged from the pod in time to see them all march off. Phylicia was hoping that Murdock would take care of some dirty work for her. She had been trying to figure a way for Palmer to have an *accident*. *Now, it appears, the accident has found him,* she thought.

Murdock, who was standing on the pod side of the cart, saw a dozen men coming long before Annie did. Annie, who was leaning on the cart on the river side, was talking to Murdock and was being very nonchalant.

"We're going to have company soon," Murdock informed Annie, interrupting her.

"How many?" Annie asked distressed.

"At least twelve. When they get closer, I'll go out to meet them. I want a little distance between you and them," Murdock explained calmly. He could see Annie licking her lips nervously and was close to hyperventilating.

"What are you going to do?" Annie asked nervously. "There are so many!"

"First, you need to calm yourself," Murdock said to Annie in a soothing voice. "I'm not overly concerned with the numbers. I doubt they have been training together as a team and so they will, or can be made to, get in each other's way. When they realize it, they'll only come in pairs." Murdock chuckled to himself a little. "I'm not going to let them get that far, though."

"Is Declan with them?" Annie asked.

"No, he isn't," Murdock answered. "Neither is Phylicia. I did see Palmer, though. I guess I'm supposed to help Phylicia by getting rid of Palmer for her."

"How do you know?" Annie asked skeptically.

"It's the way she thinks," Murdock explained. "If he gets killed out here, I look more like a monster and she can play on everyone's sympathy and her hands remain clean." Murdock was starting to loosen up in expectation of a violent confrontation. He twirled his spear a few times forward and back.

As she watched, Annie was becoming more confident in his skills. She could see that he was more adept than she had previously thought. She was, however, doubtful that his skills would be enough to overcome so many.

Ben Palmer, Preston Freeman, and the other eleven guards had been traveling at a trot since they had left the transport pod. Palmer, being more out of shape than the others, was starting to feel his legs cramp and he was getting winded.

"Let's take a break," Palmer yelled at Freeman, with some difficulty.

"You seem to be out of shape for this," Freeman chuckled. "We aren't stopping," he added gruffly. "You can suck it up or you can drop out. I don't care which!"

"What good does it do if we're too tired to fight once we get there?" Palmer asked. Freeman seemed to accept Palmer's logic and called for everyone to walk more leisurely. Palmer was glad for the reprieve.

"When we get close to Murdock," Freeman was saying to the other guards, "I want the four closest to run up and attack him. Keep him busy while the rest of us surround him." Four of the taller guards, who were outdistancing the rest easily, nodded their acknowledgment of the instructions.

"What's your hurry?" Palmer asked testily. "I've had a run in with Murdock and with this many guards we'll have no problem handling him!"

"I wish I had your confidence," Freeman said. "Maybe we should all hang back and let you handle Murdock?" he asked while looking askance at the older man.

Palmer remained silent.

As Annie watched the men approach, she saw four break ranks from the rest and rush headlong toward Murdock, who had moved out twenty yards or so from the cart. As the four ran up to Murdock, they were yelling. Suddenly, there was a flurry of activity. Murdock seemed to be a blur, as he countered all of their attacks and was back at the cart in short order. All four had their advance stop abruptly and were lying on their backs.

Seeing the four guards drop suddenly caused Freeman to call a halt for the remaining guards. "What is this, Murdock?" he asked mockingly. "Are you so afraid of us that you have to hide behind some strange barrier?"

"What barrier?" Murdock asked offhandedly. "You try to attack me, twelve to one, and you decide I must have done something because your plan failed. Do you think I fear you? You're more deluded than I'd originally thought!"

"We are guards for the council members," Freeman responded hotly. "We are tasked with protecting them from the likes of you!"

"Really? Were you there to protect Declan from Palmer?" Murdock asked in all seriousness. "Or is it more accurate to say that you protect Phylicia from everyone else?" Murdock waited and could see his words were getting to Freeman and were causing the other guards to question what they were really doing. "Is that more accurate, lapdog?" Murdock continued after a short pause.

"What's the meaning of your trespass into our territory?" Palmer boomed out as he pushed his way toward Murdock.

"I've come to get Declan," Murdock stated. "He will be brought here so I can ascertain, for myself, his condition and his wishes."

"You're in no position to be making demands," Palmer replied with derision as he looked around to the other guards.

"I have more standing than you think," Murdock said calmly. "It's your territory because I gave it to you! Are you going to force me to retrieve him myself?"

Freeman was livid. "You'll have to get past me for that to happen!" he blurted out.

"You present no challenge to me," Murdock responded calmly.

Freeman rushed forward yelling. He raised his staff and swung it wildly at Murdock's head. Murdock ducked under the staff and hit Freeman in the solar plexus with the butt end of his spear, which stopped Freeman's advance. He then smacked Freeman's wrists with two quick strikes and then hooked the staff. The staff flew up into the air and landed close to the cart. Freeman was on his knees trying to catch his breath.

While Murdock's back was turned, Palmer had taken the opportunity to start his own attack on Murdock. As he advanced, he didn't see Murdock's foot rising to meet him. The kick caught him in the chest and Palmer hit the ground hard, flat on his back. The impact caused him to hit his head and Murdock figured he was seeing stars.

"Anyone else?" Murdock asked as he looked to the other guards. None of the guards moved. Murdock did hear Freeman start to draw his machete. Murdock struck Freeman's hand with his spear's butt end. "I would think better of that, if I were you," he warned. Freeman immediately let go of the hilt of his machete. "If you insist on provoking me, I'll respond, and you won't like it!" he said to everyone there. When he looked at the rest of the guard troop, he saw them all starting to run back the way they had come. He chuckled to himself as he walked around the other six would-be attackers disarming them.

As Murdock walked back to the cart, his arms loaded with staffs and machetes, Annie ran up to help by taking the weapons from him. He was finishing loading up Annie's arms with the weapons when he suddenly kicked behind him. Annie heard the exhalations of Freeman, who had recovered enough to try to attack Murdock again. After Annie had the weapons, Murdock picked up some short thongs of leather from the cart. As Freeman was lolling on the ground trying to recover his breath again, Murdock secured his hands behind him. He then went to Palmer and secured his hands the same way. The four guards who had been stopped and had been unconscious were starting to come around.

"Any of you want to be secured like Palmer and his buddy?" Murdock asked them generally. Those that were aware declined. "I would gather up your friends and head back to the transport pod, if I were you," he said sternly. All of the guards decided to take his advice and left for the pod without further comment.

Murdock drank deeply from his waterskin when he returned to the cart.

"What are you going to do to us?" Palmer asked humbled, hanging his head.

"I'm going to return Phylicia's lapdogs to her," Murdock said calmly to both men. "The condition they're in when we get there depends on them. If they behave, they'll not be harmed further."

Palmer nodded, knowing he had been thoroughly defeated. Freeman glared at Murdock.

"You have something to say?" Murdock asked Freeman, sternly, after he walked around to face the man.

"This is humiliating," Freeman yelled. "Let me go and I'll make you pay! I'm not as easy to defeat as Palmer!"

"I don't know," Murdock started as he stood over the bigger man, "I didn't have much trouble before. And how, exactly, are you going to make me pay?"

"You'll find out soon enough!" Freeman spat.

"So, you're saying I had better kill you now and save myself the trouble of doing it later?" Murdock asked seriously. He saw the man blanch when Freeman saw Murdock tapping the hilt of his machete. "If that is what you really want, I can accommodate you!"

"Cut my bonds and give me a machete and I'll show you," Freeman spat back, "unless you're a coward!"

"Why in the world would I do something like that?" Murdock asked with a menacing grin. "I should just slit your throat and be done with you."

"That would be unfair," Freeman said coldly and still glaring.

"Unfair?" Murdock asked in his best mocking manner. "This is reality! It's been my experience that life isn't fair! Is it fair that you were sent to attack me with twelve and a half men?"

"I was given a job to do and I mean to do it," Freeman spat back.

Murdock went to the cart and retrieved a twelve-inch machete. He then walked over to Freeman, who was still sitting on the ground. He walked behind him and pulled his own machete and cut the bonds holding him. He then stuck the machete in the ground in front of Freeman as Freeman was rubbing his wrists.

"If you feel you must, let's dance," Murdock said with a menacing grin. "Be advised," Murdock continued as Freeman was reaching for the machete, "I'll give no quarter! I'll take your life! So, if you feel your job is worth dying for, then go for it!" Murdock then backed out of the man's reach, machete held at the ready; between the cart and the man sitting on the ground.

Annie blanched when Murdock had cut the bigger man's bonds. She hadn't been in a situation like this, so she had no idea what was going to happen. She did know that there was nothing she could do to stop it.

Murdock could see the big man think about what he was doing and what was going to happen. Freeman thought for a very long time before getting to his feet. He then bent down to retrieve the machete and placed it back in its sheath.

"After careful consideration, I find the task I was given is not worth dying for," Freeman stated calmly with his hands away from the machete at his right side.

Murdock raised his eyebrows in surprise. "That's probably the smartest thing you could do," Murdock stated coolly. "I have no desire to take your life, or anyone's, for that matter. I will kill, only if I must." Murdock continued to watch the big man for any sign that he was being duplicitous.

"I can see that, now," Freeman responded with a small

contrite smile. "I was led to believe that you were not worthy of respect. I'm glad I found out otherwise." He started walking toward Murdock with his open, empty right hand out.

Murdock skeptically took the offered hand. Once the grip was started, he could feel Freeman squeezing his hand. He responded in kind. It was then that he saw the big man's left hand start to strike him in the face. Murdock stepped to the side and used his left hand to dislocate the big man's elbow with a swift strike of his palm.

Freeman dropped to the ground writhing in pain, holding his elbow as he did so.

Murdock walked over and disarmed Freeman again.

9

P almer had seen the confrontation and was skeptical of the success of Freeman's duplicitous, and impromptu, attack. It did enforce the idea that he should cooperate.

Annie, who had seen the entire confrontation, thought that Murdock was very restrained and didn't do anything untoward. She thought that Murdock did goad Palmer and the other bigger man, but under the circumstances, he had given them plenty of leeway to avoid injury.

"Do you want me to tend him?" Annie asked as Murdock walked over to the cart.

"No, leave him," Murdock said roughly. "The Doctor can take care of him, should Phylicia feel that he is worthy of treatment. He walked over to Palmer, after putting the machete in the cart. When he got to him, he roughly stood him up. "If I cut your bonds, are you going to be stupid like him?" he asked indicating Freeman. "He is going to need your help to get back to the pod."

"Why should I help him?" Palmer asked.

"How about because it's the right thing to do," Murdock said impatiently. "Stop being such an ass!"

Palmer nodded and Murdock cut his bonds. Palmer went

over to Freeman and started helping him toward the transport pod.

Once everyone from the pod had vacated the area, Murdock and Annie started toward the transport pod.

"Aren't you pushing it by going to the transport pod?" Annie asked as she walked alongside the cart.

"Not really," Murdock responded. "The rest aren't keen on fighting me for Phylicia. Any that might be, will have second thoughts after seeing everyone that was sent out come back with their tails between their legs. Not to mention one with a dislocation. Besides, we aren't going to the transport pod. We'll be just close enough to gall Phylicia."

"And what will stop her from gathering everyone and stampede over us while we sleep?" Annie asked concerned. She saw Murdock chuckle to himself.

"They're all going to be too busy to rush us in the middle of the night," Murdock said, signaling that he just had the last word on the subject.

When the pair had traveled about a mile from the site of the confrontation, Murdock spotted a few men in the distance. They didn't seem to be getting closer or retreating and they seemed to be just milling around. It was unexpected so Murdock was cautious. As they traveled, Murdock kept an eye on the men. It wasn't long before the distance between the men and Murdock was such that they had seen Murdock and were waving and yelling. Murdock could see there were only six men and decided to leave Annie with the cart and approach them alone.

"One of you can approach," Murdock commanded the men when he was close enough to see that they were part of the guard troop. As he watched them closely, he saw one approach him and he was totally unarmed.

"Sir, a word?" the man asked once he was close enough. Murdock nodded. "We left because of some of the things you were saying. You were correct in that we spend all our time guarding Phylicia and keeping the rest away from her. None of us have a desire to be guards, but we were chosen, and it seemed to be a nice job for a while."

"So, what is it you want from me?" Murdock asked warily.

"None of us know how to hunt or fish or do anything that might help us to survive," the man said. "We thought that if we asked, you might be willing to teach us. We don't want to go back to the transport pod."

"Do you have waterskins and machetes?" Murdock asked.

"Yes, we have a couple of skins between the six of us," the ex-guard answered.

"Go over to your mates and wait," Murdock told him. "I need to think about it."

Murdock watched as the man walked back to the others. After he was some distance away from him, Murdock turned to head back to the cart.

"What did they want and who are they?" Annie asked while watching the men in the distance.

"They're disgruntled guards who have no clue on how to survive," Murdock told her. "They want me to teach them."

"You're going to teach them, aren't you?" Annie asked.

"I haven't decided, yet," Murdock said warily. He had decided to conference telepathically with Beron and Mei Lee before he could make a decision. He knew he didn't trust the men and wanted Beron, or one of the Oomah to watch them. Beron had agreed and had advised that he wait until the next day to make a decision. Mei Lee had concurred with Beron.

After his telepathic conference, Murdock walked back to give his answer to the ex-guards. As he approached, the same man came out to get his answer.

"I haven't decided, yet," Murdock explained. "However, I have business at the transport pod that might be of interest to you. I would, however, stay at least two hundred yards away from the pod."

"So, do we travel with you?" the ex-guard asked.

"No, you can travel on your own," Murdock said in all

seriousness. "After the duplicitous behavior of the Head Guard, I'm not quite ready to trust guards." He paused briefly. "No offense."

"None taken," the ex-guard responded. "Under the circumstances, who could blame you? Okay, we'll keep our distance and tag along." The man turned and walked back to his cohorts and Murdock returned to the cart.

Heather Stevens had been watching for the guards return from the safety of the transport pod's shadow. When she saw the first few guards coming toward the pod in the distance, she ran to report to Phylicia. Phylicia, Kimberly, and Heather had gotten to the unfinished community building just as the first guards were entering the camp. Heather was instructed to have the guards report to Phylicia at the community building and did as she was told.

"So, tell me all the little details," Phylicia commanded of the five guards. Each of the guards looked to one another and none were eager to speak. "What happened to Freeman?" Phylicia demanded.

"He attacked Murdock and lost as did Palmer," one of the guards said after he managed to gather some courage.

"They're both dead then?" Phylicia asked, slowly speaking the words.

"We're uncertain of their fate," the guard answered.

Heather Stevens ran over to Phylicia and reported that she could see two more coming, but they were moving slow. Phylicia sent her back to monitor their progress and to direct them to her at the community building.

"You're dismissed," Phylicia told the guards, "but you're to wait over here until these last two are present and they report." It was becoming difficult for her to keep her temper in check. *It was just a simple thing,* she thought, *I don't think it was anything hard. All I wanted was Murdock dead. Why can't anyone accomplish such a simple task?* She had gotten to her feet and was starting to pace across the length of the incomplete building. Everyone present watched her closely and could feel her anger.

It took the better part of an hour for the two to reach a point where Heather could see who it was. Once it was determined, she reported to Phylicia their identity.

"You'll be pleased to know," Phylicia addressed the guards, "that Palmer and Freeman are alive. They'll be here shortly. Apparently, Freeman was injured." She resumed her pacing.

It took quite some time for Palmer and Freeman to reach the community building and report to Phylicia, as they were directed by Heather.

"What happened?" Phylicia asked as she continued her pacing.

"We attacked, initially, with four of the guards, but they were stopped by Murdock," Freeman reported while he cradled his dislocated arm. He saw Phylicia make a rolling motion with her hand and arm that he took as a command to continue. "Both Palmer and I tried to talk to Murdock, to get him to drop his guard, and when I thought it appropriate, I attacked and was defeated. Palmer attacked, when he thought it was appropriate, and it also failed."

Phylicia said nothing for some time and everyone could feel her anger. "What happened with the guards?" she finally asked.

"They ran instead of attacking," Freeman responded matter-of-factly.

That statement caused her to stop pacing, but she didn't face them. "Are the ones who ran here?" she asked roughly.

"One is, yes," Freeman responded.

"Where are the rest of the guards?" Phylicia asked as if she just noticed that there was some missing.

"I have no idea," Freeman told her. "I don't think it would have mattered, though. Murdock is half the size of Palmer and neither Palmer nor I stood a chance."

"Where is Murdock now?" Phylicia asked mockingly. No one answered and all was silent for quite some time.

"I think he might be over there!" one of the guards said as he stood and pointed back the way all of them had come.

Phylicia turned to look and noticed that the sun had gone down and it was starting to get dark. In the distance, she could see a fire. It wasn't a large fire, but it was clearly visible. She gave orders that Doctor Harris should attend Freeman's arm and the guards should stay and keep a close watch. She made sure they understood that she didn't want Murdock in the camp.

As it got darker, more of the people went off to find a place to sleep. It wasn't long before everyone was asleep.

Murdock looked over at Annie and saw that she was asleep. *"Can Bridget get Declan to walk out of the camp?"* he asked Beron who had made himself visible.

"She will do best," Beron responded telepathically.

"Is everyone asleep?" Murdock asked.

"All. Dreams of plots and plannings are progressing," Beron responded.

Declan thought he was dreaming when he looked across the room and thought he saw Rose standing there. "You must get up and walk out of the camp, Declan," Declan heard her say. "No one will stop you. They're all sleeping." As he watched, he saw her walk across the room and out the door. Declan got to his feet, after some effort, and followed Rose. In the passageway, he saw the guards sleeping. He could see by their twitching that they must be dreaming, and he had no desire to know what those dreams entailed. He could see Rose at the end of the passageway beckoning him to follow. He was doing the best he could to keep

147

2

up, but the vision of his sister seemed to move faster, not to lose him, but to direct him. It wasn't long before he was down the ramp and was walking across the underside of the transport pod. He looked around as he walked and noticed that everyone was sleeping and dreaming. To Declan, it all seemed surreal. He felt like he was walking in a dream.

Murdock noticed Beron disappear as Declan started to approach the fire where he was waiting. He had already prepared the cart for transport and Annie was also asleep close to the fire. When Declan was only thirty yards from the fire, he seemed to fall asleep and Murdock levitated him before he could fall to the ground. Once Declan was lying on the cart and was covered with deer hides, Annie was awakened.

"We're ready to leave," Murdock told her. He could see that she was disoriented.

"We have to get Declan," Annie protested.

"Look on the cart," Murdock said as he dowsed the fire with the water in their waterskins.

"I should check him before we move him," Annie again protested sleepily.

"We need to get him somewhere safe," Murdock insisted. "Besides, it's too dark to see much of anything."

Once Murdock had lifted the front of the cart, Annie obediently got on to ride. It was far too dark for her to see where she was walking, and she was too tired to try to keep up with Murdock. Before they had gone very far, Annie was asleep once more and Murdock decided to utilize his special skills. Dawn would be in a couple of hours and he wanted to be on the ridge and at the river by then.

When dawn came and Annie was starting to stir, they were at the river and atop the ridge. Murdock had started a fire, caught a couple of fish, and had them cleaned and half-cooked before she awoke. Once she was awake, she went to the river to fill the waterskins. By the time she returned, it was light enough for her to see Declan's injuries.

When she uncovered the still unconscious Declan, she furrowed her brow at the sight of the bruises on the side of his face. They had turned a deep purple and were still very swollen. She touched his arm gently and Declan started to wake.

"Where am I?" he asked weakly and drowsily.

"You're safe, now," Annie said reassuringly.

About the time that Murdock, with Declan and Annie asleep on the cart, had reached the river on top of the ridge, the others were starting to awaken. As they did, they all had a nasty scowl on their face. No one had slept well. They all had fallen asleep wherever they happened to be and had slept in whatever position they landed. Quite a few had slept outside the transport pod.

When Phylicia awoke, she found that she was in the doorway to her quarters. When she got to her feet and looked around, none of her guards could be seen and neither Kimberly nor Heather were anywhere in sight either. She was not in a good mood, and it was just the start of the day. As she proceeded to exit the transport pod, she saw no one else inside, which was highly unusual. When she got to the top of the ramp and was about to exit the pod, she could hear some very loud discussions.

"Why should we bow down to the likes of Palmer and Phylicia!" a man was saying with considerable passion. "They'll sell us out the first chance they get! They've lied to us continually!"

Phylicia had heard it all as she made her way toward the unfinished common building, where the ruckus was originating. She was confused and tried to push her way past a person on the outskirts of the crowd. As she did, the woman turned to say something surly and noticed who it was that had tried to push past her.

"Here! She's here!" the woman screamed at the top of her lungs. "Grab her!" someone else yelled.

A couple of burly men laid hands on her and Phylicia was wishing for her guards. The men roughly escorted her to the center of the unfinished common building. In the center with her were Palmer, Heather Stevens, Preston Freeman, Kimberly Grey, and Doctor Harris.

"Hang them," someone yelled from the middle of the crowd. "Banish them," someone else yelled from the other side of the crowd.

"What's the meaning of this?" Phylicia yelled back angrily at the surly crowd. "I demand you release us!"

"You have no standing to demand anything," someone yelled back at her, and there were several agreeing yells throughout the crowd.

"Since you can't decide what to do with us," Phylicia yelled, without anger and just to be heard, with a smile, "maybe you should confine us to the transport pod until you decide." She could see several in the crowd agreeing with her. She was sorely lacking in information. She had no idea why everyone was so angry with her and the rest of her troop. She needed to confer with the others.

After some discussion, it was agreed that Phylicia, Palmer, et al, would be confined in the transport pod until more discussion and some consensus could be arrived at on their fate. Once inside the pod, Phylicia called everyone into her room. Freeman was stationed at her door to warn them of others coming.

"What the hell happened?" Phylicia asked angrily. "Why is everyone so angry? What set them all off?"

"Did you sleep well last night?" Doctor Harris asked her.

"What does that have to do with anything?" Phylicia responded heatedly.

150

"No one got any restful sleep," Freeman said testily from his position at the door.

"Apparently," Doctor Harris continued, "Murdock had something to do with it. Declan is gone and everyone has turned against us. From what I understand, everyone had information about any conversations you've had since you arrived here."

"That's impossible," Phylicia responded after she got over her initial shock. "There are no recording devices on this planet!" In her mind, she was running through all conversations that she could recall, to try to figure out what was said and how damning it could be.

"I know," Doctor Harris continued, "I have no theories as to how it was accomplished, but the fact is it was. We now have a full-blown insurgency on our hands!"

"Did someone tell you all that?" Phylicia asked Doctor Harris.

"It's what I managed to piece together from all the bits and pieces of conversations that I overheard while I was waiting in the center of the common building," Doctor Harris said.

Phylicia paced the room without looking, or talking, to anyone. The precipitation of recent events left her without a plan and that was disturbing to her. She had been spending an inordinate amount of time planning everything and now all of it was of no use. If she wasn't so tired, she would have been irate.

Freeman, from his position at the door, could hear nothing from outside the pod. He thought about moving toward the ramp, to see if he could hear anything, but decided that he wanted to be included in the planning of their futures. The side of his face still hurt from the position he had come to rest in last night. The log had been very rough and, once he was aware of it, was uncomfortable enough to wake him. His dislocated elbow was giving him some distress even though Doctor Harris had reset it.

Doctor Harris was used to not sleeping well. It was part of her profession and had become a part of her. She didn't like what she was seeing in her confined companions. There was a lot of anger in all of them, but Phylicia and Freeman had the worst of it. She didn't like being incarcerated with this group and found it insulting to be included in their ranks, but she didn't have a choice. Those that incarcerated them were not in the mood to listen to her complaints about being associated with these people. Now, she kept to herself and was hoping Declan would be well taken care of.

Murdock had spent part of the morning in telepathic communication with Beron and had been informed that he should wait a day before heading home. When he asked Beron why he should wait, he didn't get an answer, but he would have sworn that Beron had chuckled, if such a thing was possible telepathically. While the fish he caught were cooking, he was watching Annie as she spent the morning tending to Declan, making sure he had plenty of water. Once the fish were cooked, she made sure Declan had enough to eat. While Murdock ate, he was looking toward the large transport pod. It was large enough to see from his vantage point by anyone with normal vision.

"We're going to have company," Murdock said aloud to Annie and Declan.

Annie, being surprised by Murdock breaking his silence, had come over and tried to see what Murdock had seen by shading her eyes. "Do you know who they are or what they want?" she asked after failing to see anything of interest.

"It looks like the six guards that had accompanied us to the pod last night, but I'll know more when they get closer," Murdock responded. "How is Declan?"

"He'll survive," Annie said with concern. "They really beat him badly. I'm surprised he lived this long!"

"Only Palmer beat him," Murdock corrected. "His survival is a testament to the treatment he received from Doctor Harris. Has he said anything about his treatment?"

"Yes," Annie replied. "He said that Doctor Harris did what she could to ensure that no one would beat him and bought him a couple of days when Phylicia wanted him thrown out of the pod."

"Her basic human decency finally showed itself," Murdock responded with a chuckle. "It took her long enough."

When they were getting hungry and thirsty, Phylicia sent Preston Freeman to scout the ramp. They hadn't heard anyone or seen anyone since they were incarcerated.

"Everyone is gone," he reported shortly after leaving.

"Where did they all go?" Phylicia asked in disbelief.

"I have no idea," Preston responded. "We can leave the pod now, though, and I would suggest we take turns guarding the ramp."

"Is there anything to eat?" Heather asked.

It didn't take them long to exit the transport pod and start to scour for food and water and anything else they thought they might need. Palmer, who had spent hours watching the hunters harvest a fish or two from the nearby stream, decided he'd try his hand at it.

"Where are all the supplies?" Phylicia asked as she looked around the underside of the pod. "They took everything and left us nothing!"

Preston had been looking through the rubble that was left behind and managed to find a few things. "They left us some things," he corrected. "It isn't what we had before, but they did leave us a few things."

"They took all the important stuff," Phylicia argued. "Did they leave us any weapons or waterskins?"

"They left a few twelve-inch machetes and a couple of waterskins," Doctor Harris said as she came over to Phylicia. "They did, however, take all of the medical supplies."

Phylicia walked over to the ramp and sat on it heavily. "We're doomed," she said hanging her head. "We might as well kill each other off and shorten the suffering!"

"If that's what you really think," Preston said angrily, "then go for a walk! That way!" he indicated the direction downstream. "If you're going to give up, then we don't need you!"

Heather and Kimberly had come over to console Phylicia as best they could. "Why don't you pick on someone your own size?" Heather asked angrily. "I'm sure you can find something else to do and quit picking on poor Phylicia." She patted Phylicia's hand to comfort her. "It'll be okay," she whispered to Phylicia. "We'll all stick together and get through this."

Preston walked off in a huff knowing he couldn't count on those three women for anything. He could see that they were going to consume resources without contributing to the gathering of those resources. As he walked over to the stream, he saw Palmer splashing water and getting himself soaking wet. He was obviously trying to catch a fish and only had a rudimentary idea of how to accomplish it. *He knows more than me,* he thought with a chuckle to himself.

Murdock had gone down to the river below the ridge. He left Declan and Annie above so they would be safe until he judged if the six ex-guards, that were approaching, were a threat to them. He had left enough fish for Annie and Declan before coming off the ridge, and Annie knew enough to gather wood and get more water. He wanted Declan to rest and get plenty to eat and drink to build up his strength.

While he waited, he got a small fire going and found a place that might be a good place to ford the river. As he looked out across the river, he saw that both banks were low. The river was wide and slow-moving, at this point. He guessed the river was only about four feet deep in the middle.

The ex-guards, seeing the fire, headed toward it. It wasn't long before they saw Murdock waiting for them.

"Nice to see you here!" the ex-guard said with a smile. "I take it that you being here means you're willing to teach us?"

Murdock had been watching them approach and stood ready to retaliate at the first sign of aggression. "That is what it means," he said as they walked up. "I'll teach you as long as you want to learn. If I get the idea that you don't want to learn, I'm done. Understand?"

"Yes, sir, we do," the ex-guard responded seriously, but seemed excited. "I, for one, am ready to get started. I'm Bass Heartly, by the way," the man said as he held out his hand to shake with Murdock.

Murdock just looked at the offered hand and decided against shaking it. "I don't shake hands, as a general rule," he informed the man. "Last time I did, I ended up dislocating the other person's elbow. Hope you understand." He saw Bass withdraw the offered hand. "Before we get started, I would like to know what happened at the transport pod."

Bass proceeded to tell Murdock about the rebellion against Phylicia, Palmer, and their supporters. He told him about them being seized and put inside the pod while everyone grabbed something, and they all left.

"So, where are the rest?" Murdock asked finally.

"Halfway here there was a big discussion," Bass explained. "Most didn't want to have anything to do with you, so they split off and went downriver. Those that want to learn from you are on their way here."

"How many?" Murdock asked reticently.

"Forty-four more are on their way here," Bass responded.

"I'm not going to teach that many," Murdock said adamantly. "I'll teach one or two and they can teach the rest. What tools do you have?"

"We don't have any and we don't know what tools the others brought with them," Bass said much chagrined.

Not having any tools, Murdock decided to teach Bass, and two others, how to build a fire. He spent a little time telling and then showing them what was entailed in fire-building and how to recognize flint. When he decided to let them try their hand, Murdock took the other three and showed them how to catch fish in the river. It wasn't long before Murdock had all six men busy doing something constructive. When the three that were catching fish had succeeded in catching three fish, Murdock showed them how to clean them and then he showed all of the men how to cook the fish. As the men ate, Murdock returned to the ridge where he had left Declan and Annie.

"How's he doing?" Murdock asked Annie. He had glanced at Declan and had noticed that he was sleeping again.

"He's going to be okay, I think," Annie reported. "What's going on down there?" she asked indicating the men below.

"They're the ex-guards that changed sides at the confrontation," Murdock explained. "They're the start of a larger group. I guess there are another forty-four coming. Just about everyone decided to call it quits with Phylicia and crew."

"Really," Annie replied excitedly. "Where are they going to settle? Anywhere close by?"

"I was thinking about across the river," Murdock said. "It's well sheltered and has a lot of trees for building. More importantly, they won't have to cross the river for anything. There is plenty of game over there and they can fish the river as they need to."

"I was thinking that they could settle up here," Annie

suggested. "They wouldn't have anything to fear from Phylicia and her cohorts and they would be a lot closer for us to visit."

Murdock looked at her sadly. "There is a lot you don't understand. To be up here, I have to trust them, and I don't. I'm going back down to tell the six that are there to hold everyone until I get back. Then we'll leave to get you two to the cabin. I'll feel better with Declan being as comfortable as possible."

Annie nodded agreement as he made his way back down from the ridge.

When he was approaching the six ex-guards, they all got to their feet as if startled.

"We didn't hear you coming," Bass said apologetically.

"You should always have someone standing guard," Murdock chastised. "There are plenty of animals that are quieter than I am. I was thinking of having you go across the river."

"Any particular reason why?" Bass asked.

"There's plenty of game over there as well as trees," Murdock explained. "It's sheltered and has plenty of resources for building shelter. You'd still have the river for water and to fish, but the river would act as a natural barrier for those who might want to attack. They couldn't sneak up on you without you knowing."

Bass thought about what he had heard and decided that Murdock would know better than any of them would. "How do we get over there?" he asked after a long pause.

"Wade across, but do so slowly and in pairs," Murdock told him. "That way you won't kick up much mud from the bottom. Kicking up mud is a good way to give away your position. If you can get everyone over there and get them semi-organized, you'd be more prepared. I need to go, but will be back in two days with tools you may need."

"It'll be done," Bass replied confidently.

When Murdock returned to Annie, Declan, and the cart, he was glad to see that Annie had it all packed and was ready to go. Without many words, Murdock picked up the cart and started off toward his cabin. He hadn't gone very far before Declan fell asleep once again.

"He is sleeping a lot," Murdock mentioned to Annie, who was walking by his side. "Is it normal?"

"He's had a lot of trauma," Annie responded. "He's not had good food or rest since he left us. Add to that, they nearly beat him to death. His body wants and needs all the rest he can get for the next few days."

Murdock nodded that he understood and remained quiet.

"Where's the pod that you came in?" Annie asked after several miles.

"Why?" Murdock asked suspiciously.

"You obviously don't use it and I was thinking that maybe it would work for me as a clinic and residence," Annie explained innocently.

"That is out of the question," Murdock responded ominously.

"I was just asking," Annie said apologetically. "You don't need to bite my head off!"

"Sorry, but it's a sore subject with me," Murdock said, "And lots of open wounds."

They traveled quietly until they got to the river crossing. Annie got on the cart and checked to make sure Declan was still sleeping. Since she was already used to the routine, she closed her eyes and kept them closed until Murdock told her otherwise. When Murdock stopped for water and a little rest, she got off the cart to walk.

"Are you going back to help those few that came to you for instruction?" she asked after taking a long drink from her waterskin.

"Yes, I am," Murdock responded quietly. "After I rest some and play with my kids."

"Do you need me to go along?" Annie asked.

"No, I think you need to rest and take care of Declan," Murdock said.

It wasn't long before they were on their way again. The rest of the trip went quietly as both Annie and Murdock were thinking of the cabin and those that would be glad to see them.

10

J eff Carter was leading the parade of one hundred fifty souls away from the transport pod. He had chosen a diagonal course that would take them toward the river and downstream from the pod. He had been one of the hunters, under Phylicia, but now was leading those that chose to strike out on their own and live free of Phylicia and Palmer.

Carter had met Murdock when he first came to the pod, but he wasn't sure he could trust him. Phylicia and Palmer had left a bad taste in his mouth and he had decided to leave some time ago. What he hadn't planned on was "The Night of Revelations", as he called it, and leading this many people into the unknown. He had heard Murdock's warning and the restrictions on where they could go, and he chose to obey it. He'd heard rumors of what had happened to the work crew that had ignored the warning, and how they were still paying for their disobedience, and he wanted no part of it.

Carter wasn't thrilled with the numbers that chose to follow him. He had to constantly keep an eye on the stragglers and the pace was maddeningly slow. As he looked behind him, he could see them strung out for over a mile. It didn't help that they had to carry so much of the supplies, and he found himself wishing he had a wagon drawn by horses or even oxen. That would be a big help. *What good comes from wishing,* he thought. Being pragmatic, he didn't like delving into the realm of *wishful thinking*. If he wanted to go to that realm, all he had to do was to associate more with his charges. They seemed to be living in an entirely different world from his.

It has taken most of the day and we aren't more than ten miles from the pod, Carter thought. He guessed that they would be at the river by the next day sometime, probably by late in the day. Even though he had been a hunter, he had managed to slip away from the other hunters and had explored the land downriver from the pod. He had found the ridge and saw the place where the river went over the ridge to the valley below. He had no idea how far the river went, but he did have an unyielding desire to find out. At the river, they would have all the water they could want and all the fish they could eat. He knew they were far enough from the transport pod that the risk of being found by Phylicia or Palmer was minimal, as his estimation of the ten that were left behind was that they were all basically lazy. It was something, however, that he didn't want to trust to chance. *The further from the pod, the better our chances*, he thought.

"Circle up! Make camp!" he called out since it was close to sundown. He walked back along the line of people goading some and encouraging others to make all haste to the campsite.

Of the six ex-guards, Vernon Parker was the most skilled in fire building, but still had difficulty with catching fish. Because of his fire building skills, Bass had decided to leave him on the pod side of the river while the rest went ahead to scout some of the area across the river. Being the restless kind, Vernon spent his time waiting by pacing and by trying to catch something to eat after the other five had crossed the river and disappeared. His instructions were clear. He was to wait until the rest of the forty-four arrived and then lead them across the river and keep going. The other five ex-guards would meet up with them.

After leaving Vernon behind, Bass and the other four ex-guards walked straight away from the river. As they walked, they all commented on the number of trees and the high grass in the clearings. Bass, who was leading, was looking ahead and caught glimpses of mountains. He had no idea how far they were, but figured that they may find a cave for a temporary housing somewhere as they went toward the mountains. As they walked, they were all talking and joking and didn't see any game at all. After walking about three miles, the mountains didn't look any closer to Bass and, after a short break, the five men turned back toward the river.

When they were about a mile from the river, they ran into the forty-four, who had found a clearing that they liked and had started to make preparations to camp there. Once Bass had found Vernon, they all reported to Elizabeth Reyes, who had been leading the forty-four on their trek.

"From what we've seen so far, this side of the river goes for more than three miles when you go straight away from the river," Bass reported. "I could see mountains in the distance, but they must be many miles away. There also appears to be lots of trees."

"Did you see any game?" Reyes asked.

"We didn't see any, but that doesn't mean there isn't any," Bass responded.

"Did Murdock agree to give us a hand?" Reyes asked after some thought.

"Yes, he did," Bass responded. "He should be back in a couple of days. He didn't say anything about going up the ridge," Bass pointed in the direction of the ridge upriver, "but I would recommend that we observe his restrictions. He gave no indication that we had any special dispensation. He did show us how to build a fire and how to fish and said we should train the rest."

"You've done well," Reyes said. "What was your name?"

"Sebastian Heartly, ma'am," Bass responded, "but most people just call me Bass."

"Well, Bass, I want you and your fellows to show the others how to make a fire, when you have time, and to explore the area," Reyes said. "We do need to know this area as well as possible, so if you can find some way to make a map, then do so. I have to check to see what human resources we have just to be able to start building shelter."

"Murdock did ask what tools we had and said he would bring some tools when he returns," Bass added.

"That's good to know, but I'll be delegating the building to those better qualified," Reyes said with a smile.

Since Bass couldn't think of anything else to report, he bowed and went looking for his fellows to give them the news about what Reyes wanted them to do. He found a couple of them working on a crude lean-to while the rest were gathering wood for a fire. As Bass watched, he saw some of the others copying the ex-guards building the lean-to. He had gathered the waterskins from his fellows and took them to the river to get them filled. While he was there, he managed to catch a couple of fish before he refilled the waterskins.

By the time he had returned, the lean-to was completed, and Vernon had gotten a fire going. After cleaning the fish, Bass started cooking them, as Murdock had shown him. While the fish were cooking, he could see some of the others milling around trying to make some sort of a camp for themselves. After eating, and sharing what he couldn't eat with his fellows, he made up a mental watch list and settled in to get some sleep before his watch.

When they reached the cabin, Murdock and Annie managed to get Declan settled into a hammock in an area that was divided by hides to give him some privacy. Annie stayed with him, to make sure he was comfortable, for a short time before joining Murdock, Mei Lee, and all the kids at the table for some freshly cooked venison.

"Will Declan be okay?" Mei Lee asked in her quiet way after they had finished eating.

"He should be, but it will take time," Annie responded while she ate.

"You look tired, Annie," Mei Lee said.

"I am, a little," Annie admitted. "Would it be possible to use your spa?"

"I think we all need to utilize it," Mei Lee said pointedly.

"You two can go first," Annie said blushing. "I just want to stretch out and relax."

"You can join us, or not, as you please," Mei Lee stated as she got up and took Murdock's hand. She stood in reach of Annie and held out her other hand. Annie took it, after thinking about it for a second. Mei Lee started pulling the two toward the back door and the spa.

It was quite dark when the three got undressed and slipped into the hot water. Each made their own noises of pleasure as the water caressed them.

"Kevin, when do you go to teach the others?" Mei Lee asked after soaking for some time.

"In a day or two," Murdock responded with his eyes closed, enjoying the hot water. "I want to check our stores for venison and will take another deer, if needed. I'm sure they'll need some venison as well."

"How long will you be gone?" Mei Lee asked quietly.

"Not long," Murdock answered. "No more than a couple of days. They need some training, but I'm not going to do it for them. They'll have to learn some things on their own."

"Should I go with you?" Annie asked sheepishly.

"We'll see," Murdock said. "You'll be taking care of Declan and he needs to be well enough to stay here unattended. Mei Lee has enough to do already."

"Just so you know," Annie said, "I would like to go, but I'm not going to fight you on it. I'm more tired than I thought and could use the rest."

When they were finished with their bath, Annie checked on Declan while Murdock and Mei Lee went to bed. After making sure he didn't need anything, Annie went to bed soon after. They all fell asleep quickly.

While she slept, Annie was made aware of the history of the first transport pod. She was not, however, made aware of Murdock's capabilities or of the Oomah. She heard all the conversations and saw all the political machinations. She also saw all the consequences of those machinations.

When Bass was awakened for his watch, he noticed that it was quite dark, and he could smell dampness in the air. He didn't know if the dampness was rain or from the river, but it caused a chill that went through him. After building up the fire a little and getting closer to it, he was, after a short time, warmed. As he looked out over the rest of the company, he could see a fog roll in from the river and settle between the trees. It seemed to give the area an eerie view in the dark. He had noticed that one tarp was being used to cover what supplies they had and was being used by Reyes as her quarters. At each fire was one person on guard, keeping watch.

Several hours after Bass assumed his watch, he noticed it was starting to rain lightly. He put some more wood on the fire and placed logs in such a way as to use the fire to keep them dry. He was wishing he had a slicker or a poncho as he hunched closer to the fire to try to keep as much rain off as possible. He would periodically walk around the area of their lean-to to collect more wood and to listen for anything that sounded strange, not that he knew what to listen for as everything was strange to him. After a couple more hours, or what he thought was a couple more hours, he woke up his relief and then went back to the lean-to to try to sleep again.

The next morning, despite the rain that was still falling, Bass and his fellows were tasked to explore the area more thoroughly than they had initially. They were to look for caves that could be used to shelter the troop. Reyes knew enough to want someplace defensible and someplace that they could be safe, and she felt confident that Sebastian, and his fellows, could find such a place, if it existed. After breakfast, the six men gathered waterskins and twelve-inch machetes and set off upriver. It didn't take them long to get to the ridge at which point they turned away from the river.

They did their best to follow the ridge, looking for caves that would have an opening large enough to accommodate humans and still be small enough to be easily defended. The trees obscured the base of the ridge in many places and forced the men to investigate more closely. After traveling five miles from the river, they did find a box canyon that had an opening wide enough for several men to enter standing shoulder to shoulder. The canyon itself was quite large and, by Bass' estimation, would hold all fifty members of the group very nicely. There was even a small freshwater stream that fell from the ridge above in a small waterfall, into a small pool with the overflow trailing out through the center of the opening. When he tasted the water, Bass found that it was pure and cold.

Since he found this canyon, he needed to be able to find it again, so he sent one of his men to place stakes to the canyon. He was to go dead away from the ridge driving stakes periodically until he was out of the trees. From there, he was to return and catch up to them, as the rest were going on away from the river following the ridge. Even though they explored further, Bass doubted they would find something as well suited as the box canyon.

The five men walked away from the river for the rest of the day and found nothing. None of the men thought to bring anything to eat, as they had expected to find another river or stream with fish. All were getting hungry and all were looking for small game, but no game was found. Bass had called a halt and the men tried to find a large tree to make camp under. All of them were done in, but they did set a guard mount and the rest did their best to sleep and ignore their grumbling stomachs.

It had taken Palmer most of a day to catch a couple of fish. He was soaked to the bone and the stream was muddy, but he did manage it. It was only enough for a couple of them, so Preston Freeman took the other four guards to the river to harvest enough for everyone. Only one of the guards knew the way to the river, but the rest followed and kept a sharp eye out for the deserters and other threats. No one saw any sign that one hundred and ninety people went through the area, which was disturbing to Freeman. To him, it made no sense that there was no sign. It was then that he realized just how much he didn't know about living out in the wild. He had no idea how to fish, hunt, or even get a fire started.

Once they'd reached the river, Freeman was watching intently and asking questions as one of the guards caught fish and threw them onto the bank. He watched as one of the other guards cleaned the fish. He even did one himself, with instruction. After several fish were caught and cleaned, and after all the waterskins were filled, they all walked back to the transport pod.

~

Irene Harris was out walking around the transport pod trying to get things straight in her mind. Five of the men had gone to the river and it made the transport pod area seem deserted, which she was enjoying. She hadn't figured out how everyone knew Phylicia's plans or how everyone had passed out, which allowed Declan to escape. Secretly, she was glad that Declan had escaped. Seeing the trauma inflicted on him by Palmer had appalled her. She had no idea that people could be so cruel. She had done her required time in ERs, back on Earth, but it hadn't connected that most of the injuries she had treated were caused by the violence of another person. She hadn't thought of herself as being sheltered, but, now, she wasn't so sure.

"Have you figured out what you're going to do about regaining our medical supplies?" Phylicia asked Harris, having come up behind her while she was lost in her reverie.

"No, I haven't," Harris responded quietly. "What am I supposed to do about it?" Harris said with a shrug. She could see that her answer peeved Phylicia greatly.

"Well," Phylicia started finally, "you could retrieve what we had, or you can replace them all. Does that give you a clue on what to do about it?" she asked sharply.

"I can't replace most of what we lost," Harris tried to explain. "That would require some very sophisticated manufacturing techniques. The bandages will have to be manufactured here, if we can find the materials and acquire the skills to weave them. And we won't mention the autoclave needed for sterilization of scalpels, clamps, and retractors."

"So, what are you going to do about getting it all back?" Phylicia asked again, apparently still angry that the deserters had stolen all their medical equipment.

"Like I said, what am I supposed to do about it?" Harris asked with a shocked look on her face.

"You *are* the Minister of Health," Phylicia said testily. "You're responsible for all the medical supplies that we brought with us as well as their replacement. Did you think your title was just ceremonial?" she asked flippantly. "Do you think that I'm not going to hold you responsible for the supplies being stolen?"

"There was nothing I could have done about it, and you know it," Harris snapped angrily. "I was locked in the transport pod, just as you were!"

"That's not my problem," Phylicia replied in like anger. "You should have foreseen the theft and taken steps to preserve our possession of the supplies!"

Harris said nothing. She saw no point in arguing with someone intent on blaming others for their own shortcomings. She felt that no one could have foreseen the events that had occurred. She did, however, hold Phylicia partially responsible for fostering a climate that precipitated the events. *If she hadn't insisted on trying to rule everyone and everything as a monarch, the events wouldn't have happened the way they did*, she thought.

"I would suggest, strongly," Phylicia said after seeing that Harris wasn't going to argue with her, "that you find a way to retrieve the medical supplies!"

Harris watched as Phylicia left and found her thoughts focusing on those that had escaped. She was contemplating leaving, if she knew the way to Declan and Annie and could survive in the wilds of this strange planet. Murdock's words to her, about food and shelter not having value to her, hit home stingingly. She wished Murdock had taken her with him. It was becoming apparent to her that most anywhere would be better than her current situation.

Jeffrey Carter, leading one hundred fifty people away from the pod, had managed to get everyone to the river at the top of the plateau on which the pod had rested. While the stragglers were still coming toward the river, he was standing on the edge of the plateau looking downriver. Below him was a wide valley that seemed to have fewer trees than the current plateau. As he gazed across the river and then upriver, he had come to the conclusion that the trees were thinning more downriver. He had only the observations he could make from his current position, but it didn't make him feel any better about proceeding further downriver. He had decided that they had gone far enough for one day and gave word to make camp.

Everyone was doing what they could, individually, to make camp while the stragglers were still coming in. This group had most of the supplies that were stored under the transport pod. He was glad that they had the only medical person left and all the medical supplies. His group also had half of the woodworkers and most of the smelters. It did disturb him that the split of the sexes wasn't even, which he knew would cause problems later. He had vowed to not be the person in charge when that issue became a problem. It was going to be a headache for someone, though.

Since his group had most of the tarpaulins, he gave orders to erect them to keep the supplies and the people out of the weather. He had already selected one person to build the initial fire that all the others would use to light their own and saw that the man was doing his job getting the first fire going. Others were gathering fish from the river to feed everyone and still others filled the waterskins. As he walked around the encampment, he was pleased to see everyone active and doing something to further the rest of the group. His meanderings finally ended at the plateau edge and the river once more.

As Carter was looking across the river, he could see some deer grazing. He had hoped for an easy crossing of the river, but couldn't see one. The river was running very swiftly at this point in its voyage to who knows where, with high banks on both sides. He found himself wishing for his trusty Winchester rifle from home, and then chastised himself once more for indulging in such trivial pursuits as wishful thinking.

~

Murdock showed up at the first camp, at the base of the ridge, two days after he had left Bass and the other ex-guards. As he walked around, Elizabeth Reyes rushed to join him.

"We've been waiting for you," she said excitedly, after the briefest of introductions. "Most of us are anxious to get things started, but don't know what to do first. I did send out scouts to see if they can locate a suitable permanent camp, but they haven't returned, yet."

"When do you expect them?" Murdock asked while strolling around the camp.

"They should be back any time now," Reyes told him.

"In the meantime," Murdock responded, "you need to show me what you have for tools then call a meeting of all your artisans."

Reyes nodded and led him to the tool storage area. Murdock started looking through the tools and found that they had more tools than he did and there were sledges and drifts for metal working as well as some tools for doing precise work with wood and metal.

"Shall we call the meeting of artisans?" Murdock asked after his inspection of the tools.

Reyes agreed and led the way back to the tarpaulin-covered area she was using as her quarters. Once there she sent someone to round up the different artisans and deliver them to Reyes' tent. It didn't take long to get the artisans gathered and Murdock started outlining what he felt each one should be doing. After some time, he wound down and called for questions.

There weren't too many questions. Most of them dealt with making money.

"You're all under a different paradigm, now," Murdock started to explain. "There is no money here and little need for it, at this time. You should all be working together to better each other. As an example, if I wanted someone here to make me two

171

dozen arrows and he needed leather to make a coat, it would not be out of line to charge me the leather for the arrows. It would work for food as well. All you need is just a simple barter system." As he explained he could see everyone nodding that they understood. With that, the meeting ended.

As the meeting was breaking up, Bass Heartly, and his small troop, returned. After getting something to eat and drink, Bass reported their findings to Reyes. When Reyes heard about the box canyon, she sent for Murdock.

"My scouts have returned," she said once Murdock was there and they could talk. "They report that they have found a box canyon that might be usable as a more permanent camp. Would you mind looking at it and giving me your thoughts on it?"

"I wouldn't mind at all," Murdock said. "I'm ready to leave when they are."

Bass followed Murdock out of the tent and they both started off toward the canyon. It took Bass some time to find the stakes and then follow them to the ridge. As the two men stood outside the canyon, Murdock looked up and then looked first left, then right. He didn't say anything as they entered the canyon and Murdock inspected the pool and the ground around the overflow. When he finished, he pronounced that it could be made to be defensible, with a little work, and would be a good place to live. With his pronouncement, Murdock saw Bass light up with pride. Murdock led the way back to the camp and, as a result, they were back in less time. Both men reported their findings to Reyes.

"I would like to see it for myself," Reyes said cautiously. "Would you both show it to me?"

"You do know," Murdock asked Reyes as they walked, "you are going to need men to hunt deer? And those deer will supply you with the clothes that you obviously need?"

"Yes, I know," Reyes responded. "We will require your skills for tanning the hides, however. What is that?" she asked indicating the small bits of meat he was munching on as they walked.

"Venison," Murdock said, handing her some and then offering some to Bass.

"It has a smoky taste," Reyes commented after tasting it, "Not at all like I remember venison tasting."

"That's because it is smoked," Murdock informed her.

Reyes stopped short and stared at Murdock.

"What?" Murdock asked not knowing why she stopped.

"Remarkable!" Reyes responded in awe. "Next you'll be telling me you have smoked salmon as well."

"I'll bring you some the next time I come," Murdock responded soberly.

After Freeman and the four guards returned with enough fish for everyone, they all gathered around the fire for the cooking. Phylicia, Heather, and Kimberly chose to sit away from the rest while they waited for the fish to cook. Irene Harris sat closer to the fire, but was careful not to get in the way of the men. Palmer, who had already eaten the fish he had caught, sauntered over to her and was entirely too close to suit her. Everyone waited quietly while the fish cooked. When the fish were cooked, Freeman and the four guards helped themselves first and went off to eat by themselves. Heather came over to the fire and got enough for Phylicia, Kimberly, and herself. Only after everyone else had gotten their share did Irene take her portion.

"You know," Palmer said quietly to Irene Harris, sitting close to her, "it appears your choices have dwindled greatly. You may want to consider being nicer to me."

"And why would I do that?" Irene asked as she nibbled on her portion of fish. She did her best not to look at Palmer directly. After seeing his cruelty, the sight of the man made her ill.

"Just by counting," Palmer started while he looked around to see who could hear, "there're more men than women. Here, you females are going to need a nice, strong man to take care of you."

"When you find one, let me know," Irene quipped while continuing to eat. She wasn't trying to be arrogant. She just wanted Palmer to leave her alone. When she finally looked at him, she could see how red his face was. "You really should try to control your anger. What are you going to do if you have a heart attack?"

"If I do, you'll have to take care of me," Palmer stated, leering at her. "That's what doctors do, ain't it?"

"You don't know as much as you think you do," Irene said flatly. "I could always be slow to react or nick the wrong thing. Things happen and you just never know when." It was then that she made up her mind to try to find one of the other groups or Murdock. She didn't know how or when, she just knew she had to get away from these people.

At sunset, they all went inside the transport pod and tried to find a comfortable corner to spend the night. Phylicia, and her entourage, retired to her old quarters. Irene Harris retired to the space that was used, until recently, as a recovery room. Freeman and the guards slept in the main compartment, the same compartment as the ramp. Palmer had dawdled when the rest were retiring. He had seen Harris go to the recovery room and he had looked around to be sure that he wasn't observed. Once sure he wasn't seen, he slipped down the passageway.

"If I were you, Palmer, I'd leave now," Harris warned from the darkened room before Palmer could get to the doorway. She was wishing she had a door that locked, but very few of the compartments even had doors, let alone locks. As she listened intently, she could not hear anyone moving in the passageway. Harris found a small area under a table that was attached to the wall. Since the lighting seemed to be directly tied into the solar panels on the top of the pod and were only on during sunlight, it would be hard for anyone, who didn't know the compartment, to find her.

At some point, Harris must have fallen asleep because the next thing she knew, she was being dragged out from under the table by her ankle. Once she was aware of what was happening, she kicked hard, several times, with her free foot. Only one connected and it raised a howl from her attacker. It was then that she felt a fist hit her face. The first one made her see stars. She remembered nothing after the second one.

11

S hortly after Murdock had left, Declan had gotten up to walk around a little on his own. He hadn't gotten far before Annie showed up.

"Are you okay?" she asked. "I don't want you to overdo and injure yourself further."

"You need to give me some space," Declan snapped at her. "If I overdo then I overdo and will deal with it," he said, looking at her. He could see that his words hurt her and that was not what he intended.

"If that's what you want," Annie said roughly and returned quickly to the cabin. She could feel the tears starting and she didn't want to give him the satisfaction of seeing her cry.

Declan had wanted to get away to think and evaluate his situation. He did appreciate Annie and her concern, but he didn't need her help every second of every day. *That was good,* he thought. *You didn't need to be so rough. She was just trying to help, and you should appreciate the fact that she's been there for you. You wouldn't talk to Rose that way so why would you talk to Annie that way?* Since he couldn't answer his own questions, he decided to walk further away from the cabin. He wanted to sit by the river and just think.

When he found a place, he managed to sit, with difficulty, on the bank. His legs were stretched out in front of him and his back was against a smooth rock. He closed his eyes and concentrated on the sound of the river. It seemed to calm him a little and he managed to clear his mind somewhat. His thoughts seemed to roam around to all of his concerns, of their own accord, instead of focusing on any one of them. He was angry, he decided, at Palmer for the beating, at Murdock for allowing his sister to die, and at the beings that sent him here in the first place. He was here without skills and dependent on someone else, just like he was back on Earth with his sister. He had been dependent on her and hated himself for it. *I should have been stronger, more independent, more self-assured.*

"Declan," he heard behind him, "we need to talk!" It was Mei Lee, but he didn't want to talk to her either and didn't even bother to open his eyes or look at her when she spoke.

"I'm not in the mood," he snapped at her. It was then he felt hands grab him and lift him off the ground.

"We are going to talk!" Mei Lee said angrily.

When he opened his eyes, he saw little Mei Lee holding him off the ground.

"I don't much care what your mood is. I'm going to talk and you're going to listen!" she insisted as she shook him back and forth a few times.

"Alright," he yelled contritely. "Just put me down!" That was when his posterior met the grass, unceremoniously.

"You may be Rose's brother, but you have no right to talk to anyone the way you talked to Annie." Mei Lee was angry at Declan and made sure he could see it on her face. "I loved your sister and would do anything for her, but I refuse to put up with a spoiled little boy that dresses like a man. For as long as you stay here, you'll talk and treat everyone with the proper decorum and civility. You may be family, but Annie is a guest, an honored guest and you *will* be respectful!"

Declan was sitting on the ground where he was

uneceremoniously dropped, watching this little oriental woman, with one fist on her hip and shaking the index finger of her other hand, at him, scolding him. It reminded Declan of Rose. So much so that he was in shock. Many times, Rose had scolded him in exactly the same way with the same body position and using the same exact words.

"You don't understand," he said with a pouting tone when the shock wore off somewhat.

"You're mistaken if you think this is a conversation," Mei Lee continued. "There are rules everyone has to follow, and you will follow them. It's called common courtesy. If you have problems you need to work out, do so, but you will be courteous to everyone in my house!" Mei Lee turned and stormed back to the cabin.

It took Declan a second or two to get his wits about him and get off the ground. Mei Lee's outburst had surprised him. He had thought that she was so subservient that her scolding him, or anyone, was totally out of character. He had seen her deal with the children, as brash as they were, and never need to raise her voice. He was suspecting that he had grossly underestimated her. He slowly made his way back to the cabin and knocked on the door.

"What do you want?" Mei Lee asked gruffly once she opened the door. Even though the door was open, she barred the way.

"I wish to apologize," Declan started with as much contrition as he could muster, "to you for my rudeness." He saw her eyes narrow as she looked at him skeptically.

"I neither need nor want your apology," Mei Lee said gruffly. "Deeds show your contriteness, not words. However, you do have to apologize to Annie!"

"Is she willing to come to the door so I can?" he asked, looking down.

"Not at the present time," Mei Lee stated flatly as she shut the door.

Declan stood there, mouth agape, not knowing what to do

next. It took him a second or two to realize that the only thing he could do was to wait, so he sat on the steps with his back to the door and tried not to engage in self-pity.

Annie, having heard the conversation at the door, got up from the table to go to the door.

"Where are you going?" Mei Lee asked sharply.

"I want to go talk to him and get this settled," Annie explained quietly.

"Let him stew," Mei Lee commanded sternly, but quietly. "He needs to learn and giving in to him too quickly will only teach him that he can do what he wants with little consequence." Then louder, so Declan could hear, "If it was up to me, I'd leave him out there all night!"

Declan was not sitting outside more than a couple hours when Annie opened the door.

"You wanted to talk to me?" Annie asked, standing with the door at her back and facing Declan with arms crossed. She was trying to look as stern as she could, but wasn't sure she could keep it up for long.

Declan stood and faced her. "I had no right to talk to you the way I did," he said contritely. "I know I hurt your feelings and that was not my intent. I'm sorry for treating you so badly."

Annie stood there, looking sternly at him. "I wasn't trying to crowd you," she explained quietly. "I was concerned about your condition. I couldn't understand why you would say anything hurtful to me."

"I was angry and just wanted to be left alone awhile," Declan tried to explain contritely, looking down at the ground.

"You should try to talk to someone about your anger issues," Annie said calmly, still looking stern.

"Who do I have to talk to?" Declan asked whiningly.

"You could talk to yourself," Annie suggested, "or you can talk to Murdock. That is, pretty much, all the options you have, at this point. I know I don't want to hear it, and I'm certain that Mei Lee doesn't want to hear it either."

"I can't talk to Murdock," Declan declared. "He has something to do with some of my anger!"

"What could he possibly have done to make you angry?" Mei Lee asked from the door, which she had opened quietly.

It shocked Declan into looking at her as he debated with himself if he should tell her or not.

"Well?" Mei Lee asked gruffly. "If you have a complaint about my husband, you can either tell me or take it up with him, when he returns!"

"It makes me angry to think that Murdock didn't do enough to keep Rose safe," Declan finally blurted.

Hearing it, Mei Lee was taken aback. "How did you come to that conclusion?" she asked finally.

"If he'd taken better care of her, she'd still be alive," Declan blurted again. The thought made him angry and he didn't know why.

"It sounds to me that you put your sister on a pedestal," Mei Lee stated.

Declan hadn't thought that he had, but it was possible and said so.

"Your sister was her own woman," Mei Lee explained. "She wouldn't have stood for anyone putting her on a pedestal. She wanted to be an equal and that is the way Kevin treated her. I never saw him treat her otherwise. She went out that night because she was more qualified than I and Kevin needed help."

Annie felt like she was intruding on a private family matter, but didn't know what to do to excuse herself. As she looked, she could see the tears start in Mei Lee's eyes.

Declan could see the tears as well.

"If there were something I could do to bring her back, I would," Mei Lee said adamantly. "I'm sure Kevin would say the same. We did all we could to care for Rose, but we didn't smother her or put her on a pedestal. We treated her as an equal. You're upset because you didn't get the chance to see her again.

You need to let it go!" Mei Lee went back inside the cabin and shut the door.

When it was almost dark, Annie and Declan entered the cabin and began the nightly routine. No one said anything else about Rose.

When Murdock, Bass Heartly, and Liz Reyes got to the box canyon, Reyes started looking around and asking questions about fortifying the entrance and food availability. Murdock spent several hours answering her questions. Bass remained quiet and learned more than he thought he could just by listening and thinking about the concerns. When the trio finished their inspection, they all headed back to the main body.

When they were about halfway back, Murdock called for a halt and unslung his bow. As he did so, he put a finger to his lips indicating to the other two that they should be quiet. After nocking an arrow and stepping forward a couple of steps, Murdock pulled back his bow. As he did so, Reyes heard the bow creak slightly when he got to full draw. After a brief pause, Murdock let the arrow fly and then stood still watching where it went. When he was satisfied, he slung the bow and they all started off again.

"What were you shooting at?" Reyes asked, whispering.

"You two didn't see the deer?" Murdock asked without whispering.

"What deer?" Bass asked as he tried to look past the other two.

"It was about one hundred yards that way," Murdock said pointing the way he had shot.

"Where is it now?" Reyes asked, looking the way Murdock had indicated.

"It ran off and should be close to bleeding out by the time we find it," Murdock explained. "I'm a little surprised we saw one."

"Why is that?" Reyes asked.

"To be blunt," Murdock responded, "you two make enough noise to scare off most game long before you get to see it."

Neither Bass nor Reyes took offense at the criticism and Bass was chastised.

"Sorry," Bass said.

"Don't worry about it," Murdock said offhandedly. "It takes practice, a lot of practice, to get good at being quiet."

"Shouldn't we hurry and find it before it gets too far away?" Reyes asked.

"No, you can't chase the deer here," Murdock explained. "They're the size of an elk and would easily trot faster than you can run. That one isn't going anywhere."

"Why not?" Reyes asked.

Murdock pulled out an arrow and, after finding a wide leaf, pushed the arrow through the leaf. After replacing the arrow in his quiver, he showed them both the hole left by the arrowhead. Reyes and Bass saw clearly the one-and-one-half-inch hole.

"If I hit the deer in a vital area," he explained, "it is now bleeding internally. Shortly, it will just get tired and go to sleep and not wake up. I'm sure it knows it was hit with something, but it has no idea that it is bleeding out. If you were to chase it, it could go miles before it would bleed out and you may never find it. The object is to *harvest* an animal, not chase it all over creation. To have something to eat and the hide, you have to be able to find it easily. Otherwise, what's the point?"

"It would seem that we have a lot to learn," Reyes commented soberly when Murdock had finished.

Bass nodded agreement.

It didn't take Murdock long to find the downed animal and gut it.

"I need to get my cart," Murdock said after taking a drink. He handed Bass his spear. "You two stand guard over our prize. I won't be gone long. If wolves show up, let them have the intestines, but you should guard the meat and hide with your life."

Bass nodded that he understood the instructions. Reyes pulled her twelve-inch machete and stood guard over the carcass. Both watched, with some trepidation, as Murdock went over the next rolling hill and disappeared.

"Was he serious about us guarding the carcass with our lives?" Bass asked a short time after Murdock disappeared.

"I don't know him very well," Reyes responded, "but something tells me he is always serious."

"I think I understand that an animal of this size means life for more of us," Bass speculated. "There does appear to be quite a bit of meat."

"And the hide is almost big enough to make a coat!" Reyes observed. "Did you see the arrow?"

"Yes, it's broken," Bass responded. "I did notice that he kept the arrowhead."

They both decided to be quiet and to walk around the carcass so that one was always opposite the other in the small clearing. For about a half-hour they circled and then they both heard several low growls from the trees. They seemed to be surrounded. It was starting to get close to sundown, so they couldn't see too far into the trees. The more they circled, the longer the shadows grew, and the louder the growls became. Bass was starting to sweat, from the stress of the expected attack, but managed to keep his wits about him. Reyes asked for and got Bass' twelve-inch machete and seemed braver with one in each hand.

After the sun went down, the gloom started to settle in faster than Bass and Reyes expected. Bass saw one of the wolves emerge slowly from the trees. It was keeping its head down, but Bass could see it was larger than a Shetland pony, but his focus was drawn to the flashing white teeth. Bass and Reyes had stopped circling the carcass, so Bass was facing the advancing wolf. *Murdock will be back soon,* he thought, and it eased his nerves a little. From Reyes' vantage point, she could see one or two wolves darting among the trees, but they didn't show themselves.

Bass lowered the spear to menace the approaching wolf and had decided to advance a little toward it and it gave ground.

"Easy, Bass," Reyes said in a low voice and as calmly as she could. "Don't get too far away. Let it come to you and be ready for the rest to attack, should you take out that one."

The sound of Reyes' voice calmed Bass' nerves. He and the advancing wolf locked gazes and neither blinked.

Reyes had a wolf advancing on her as well. She tried to not focus on its size or the large teeth.

Bass saw the wolf tense and knew it would spring soon. It was then that he heard something whiz past his ear and strike the wolf in the eye. The wolf howled in pain and scared the others into giving up, for the present, the carcass. As the wolf was thrashing and howling, Bass ran forward and stabbed it a few times with the spear. By the time it had quit moving, Murdock was at the deer carcass with the cart.

"Come help," Murdock commanded. "We need to be gone before the rest recover their courage."

Murdock grabbed the deer carcass at the head. Bass and Reyes dropped their weapons and quickly came to help load the carcass. Once it was loaded, Murdock picked up the spear and tossed it to Bass, Reyes retrieved the two machetes, replacing one to her scabbard and handing the other to Bass, who returned it to his scabbard. Murdock, in the meantime, quickly gutted the wolf, picked it up, and put it on the cart.

"Keep your eyes open and keep up!" Murdock commanded as he picked up the front of the cart and headed off toward the box canyon.

"Why are we going back this way?" Reyes asked as she trotted to try to keep up with Murdock's pace.

"We need the water to wash out the carcasses," Murdock said tensely. "Not to mention that it is closer and easier to defend. Make no mistake. The rest of the pack will be following us!" Murdock increased his speed.

Bass and Reyes had to increase their pace to keep up with Murdock and, not being used to the exertions, were unable to ask anything further due to being winded.

"You two run ahead and get a fire started close to the entrance of the canyon," Murdock commanded after a short while of forcing the other two to travel faster than they had intended.

Reyes and Bass did as they were told and ran ahead. They both found it easier going than the fast trot they had been doing, as they were able to stretch out their stride. It didn't take them long to get to the canyon. Once there, both gathered the kindling and Bass started lighting it. While Bass blew on the embers, to get them to catch the kindling, Reyes gathered bigger pieces of downed limbs. She put a couple of the smaller ones on the fire and returned to gather more. By the time she had returned with the second load of wood, Murdock came trotting past her and Bass and into the canyon. It was then that Bass and Reyes could hear the wolves in the trees. Just outside the circle of light the fire had created.

After parking the cart close to the end of the canyon, by the waterfall, he walked back to the fire, bow at the ready.

"Bass, help Reyes gather more wood!" Murdock commanded once he reached the fire. "I'll cover you both! Take a brand with you!" Murdock moved between the fire and the trees and watched intently as the other two darted amongst the trees in the dark trying to find more wood. Once they both returned, each with a load of wood, he retreated to have the fire between him and the trees. "I'm impressed," Murdock said as he re-slung his bow. "You two know how to take orders. Those that give orders should be able to take them as well."

"I, for one, was very glad to see you when the wolves were about to attack!" Reyes said excitedly.

"So was I!" Bass said emphatically. "I was startled, a little, when that arrow came whizzing past my head. That was a hell of a shot!"

"Either of you know how to skin an animal?" Murdock asked, ignoring the compliments. Both shook their heads to indicate the negative. "Bass, you stand guard this side of the fire!" Bass nodded that he understood and grabbed up the spear before taking up his position.

"What do you want me to do?" Reyes asked.

"You're going to help me skin out these two," Murdock said indicating the two carcasses. "This is going to get messy," Murdock said as he took off his leather shirt. "You may want to remove your shirt to prevent it from becoming permanently bloodstained," he suggested to Reyes.

Reyes blushed and hesitated a little before she complied. She was expecting the two men to stare at her, being as well-endowed as she was, but was relieved, and puzzled, when they didn't.

It took some time to skin the two carcasses. Reyes did the wolf, copying Murdock's movements and taking his instructions. When Murdock was about half finished, he told Bass to find a few sticks and called him over to take a couple of pieces of the venison from him after he washed them in the falling water. When Bass came to take the chunks of meat from Murdock, he was instructed on the cooking. When Murdock and Reyes had finished skinning the animals, they both washed off the blood that covered them in the cold water of the falls and put their shirts on, before walking over to the rather large fire to eat.

"Why did you harvest the wolf?" Reyes asked between bites.

"I was hoping that the wolves wouldn't have attacked," Murdock explained between his own bites of the hot meat. "Since I had to kill it, I wasn't going to leave the hide. I don't particularly like wolf meat, but I will eat it, if pressed to it. You're going to need all the hides you can get. Come winter, you're going to wish you had a lot more!"

"It gets cold, then?" Bass asked while he ate and watched.

"Very," Murdock responded emphatically.

"Are we going back to the main camp tonight?" Reyes asked.

"I would say we make camp here tonight," Murdock said. "If you insist, we can, but it will be like coming here. Being pursued the entire way. I could find my way, but you two would get lost and become easy prey for the wolves."

The carcasses were packed on the cart, covered with their hides, before the three started to settle in for the night. Murdock was retrieving the hides he used to sleep on, while the other two were talking by the fire. As he turned toward the fire, he saw the opening of a cave. By the position, Murdock could see that it was hidden because of the rocks and the way the light hit the inside of the canyon. When he investigated, he found the entry was large enough to accommodate the loaded cart.

After retrieving a brand from the fire, Murdock inspected the interior of the cave. The floor raised two feet in the first six feet of the cave and was spacious enough to hold the cart and all three of the humans and enough wood to last quite some time. The ceiling was ten feet off the highest point of the floor. There appeared to be no other chambers off the main one. Murdock wasn't so sure, but decided to leave it at that. He exited the cave, put the cart inside it, and then signaled the other two to bring wood and get the fire transferred inside the cave opening.

"Where did this come from?" Reyes asked as she wandered around the interior in awe.

"This wasn't here before," Bass insisted as he wandered around.

"It had to be. The exterior rock tends to mask things, depending on the lighting and the angle," Murdock explained.

It didn't take them long to take advantage of the cave and the protection it provided. Murdock took the watch while Reyes and Bass found a place to sleep and snuggled under the warm hides Murdock had provided. Once he was assured the others were asleep, Murdock communed with Beron telepathically to get an update on the rest of the newcomers' situations.

When Irene Harris finally woke up, she refrained from moving quickly. She was very sore, mostly her face. She gingerly touched it and found it to be very swollen. She did notice that it was still night, or she thought so. Her eyes seemed to be open, but she could see nothing. As she lay there, she tried to mentally assess her condition. Her body felt bruised and sore in places it shouldn't. When she touched her chest, she found that her clothes had been placed over her, rather than her wearing them, which is what she last remembered. She continued to examine herself as best she could and found that her breasts were sore, and her inner thighs were badly bruised.

As she slowly got to her feet and tried to dress, she discovered that she was bruised worse than she initially thought. As she dressed, she realized that her shirt was missing a button or two, but her jeans were intact. Her undergarments, however, didn't fare as well. They were nothing more than scraps of cloth, well beyond her ability to repair. With great difficulty, she managed, eventually, to get her shoes on and walk very slowly out of her compartment and head for the ramp.

She could feel the coolness as she descended the ramp and it felt good, to her. She slowly looked around to see if anyone else was about, but, to her relief, saw no one. She headed for the stream, needing the cold water to help reduce the swelling, but it was a long slow process. By the time she had reached the stream, she found herself wishing Annie Cooper was there. She was competent and knowledgeable and would have consoled her when her emotions finally caught up with her.

As she dipped the cold water with her hands and splashed her face, she tried to remember what had happened to her. She didn't know who attacked her, but she did remember landing at least one kick. After her face felt better and her head had cleared some, she decided to soak the rest of her bruises. After undressing, she slowly lowered herself into the cold water and felt the relief she was seeking for her bruises. As she made her way out of the water, she became aware that it would soon be sunup, and she needed to get dressed as soon as possible. She wanted no one to see all of her bruises. It was bad enough that she couldn't hide the ones on her face. She'd never been overly vain, but she now wished to not be seen by anyone.

Sunup found her almost to the ridge, as sore and battered as she was. She thought she had been angling toward the river. She had brought nothing with her: no water, no food, no weapons. *I'm extremely vulnerable to animal attacks,* she thought. *Why not? I've already survived one animal attack, why not another,* she answered in her thoughts. It was then that she dropped to her knees and started wailing loudly. She gave no concern about being heard. It took her the better part of an hour to calm down enough to continue her painfully slow trek toward the river.

12

M urdock, who wasn't sleeping, but was in a meditative state, had his awareness awakened by low growls outside the cave. When he looked out the entrance, he could see that it was still dark, and he did see a few dark shadows pass by just outside the circle of light from the small fire close to the entrance. He automatically sent his astral self to reconnoiter the box canyon outside the protection of the cave.

His astral self's vision turned the dark into shades of grey, much like his own natural night vision. He could clearly see a dozen wolves vying for a more dominant position in a possible ambush of those inside the cave. They all stayed outside the circle of light that came from the cave entrance. With little mental effort, he levitated the would-be attackers straight up to the ridge above the box canyon and tossed them away from the edge. The ridge above was at least fifty feet above the floor of the canyon, so he knew it would take them some time to return, if at all.

Murdock stood to stretch his muscles, took some water, and then checked on his two companions. He walked so quietly that they were not disturbed by his nocturnal wanderings. Both Reyes and Bass were sleeping soundly. He had planned to wake

Bass shortly to take the watch so he could get some sleep, being as exhausted as he was, but seeing them both sleeping so soundly, he felt regret at waking either of them. He finally woke Bass as gently as he could, so he wouldn't wake Reyes, and both men walked over to the entrance and the fire.

"Stay inside the cave," Murdock said quietly as he handed Bass the spear. "Keep the fire going and stay awake. I did hear wolves outside, so stay alert." Murdock walked over to the spot where Bass had been sleeping only moments before and settled into sleep. To him, he had no more closed his eyes and Bass was waking him. He knew he hadn't been sleeping soundly, that was reserved for home. As he turned over, he could see that it was almost sunup.

After getting to his feet and stretching the sleep out of his muscles, Murdock headed out to the waterfall. Once there, he splashed the cold water on his face and neck and ran his wet hands through his hair. He dumped out his waterskin, refilled it with fresh cold water, drank his fill, and then refilled it. The sun was coming up, and he looked around for any sign of the wolves. He saw them at the top of the ridge, but they couldn't get down inside the box canyon.

"Fixated, aren't you?" he asked quietly while looking up.

Murdock spent some time gathering more wood. He was hungry and knew Reyes and Bass would probably be just as hungry. After gathering more wood than they would need, he headed back to the cave. Once he entered the cave, he dumped the load of wood close to the fire. He noticed that Reyes was making use of the falls and Bass was faithfully standing guard. Murdock cut off some of the meat and got it started cooking.

"You want to make use of the falls?" Murdock asked Bass as he hunkered down to tend the fire and the cooking meat.

"Yes, I would, as a matter of fact," Bass replied good-naturedly as he handed the spear to Murdock and headed out of the cave.

"Good morning," Elizabeth Reyes said cheerfully as she

entered the cave. "I slept very well. Why didn't you wake me to take a turn guarding?"

"Bass and I handled it, and I didn't want to disturb you," Murdock explained.

Reyes and Murdock discussed the process of moving everything to the box canyon and getting things set up while the meat cooked. Once Bass returned, with more wood, he joined in the discussion. When the meat was finished, the discussion continued while they all ate.

While Murdock was listening to Reyes and Bass argue back and forth, he was presented with a mental picture of a female meandering along the base of the ridge. She appeared to be in some distress and would periodically drop to her knees and cover her face.

"There's a problem," Mei Lee communicated with him telepathically. "I sent you the image that Bridget sent me. I don't know how you want to handle it."

"Is Declan sufficiently healed to stay with you without you needing to nursemaid him?" Murdock asked telepathically. "I would like Annie to come to me at the base of the ridge by the river, but not if she's needed there."

"I would like to come instead of Annie," Mei Lee explained telepathically. "I need to get away awhile."

"Clear it with Annie, first, and Declan, of course," Murdock told his wife. "If it is something that requires medical treatment, it can be dealt with once we are at home. You will be okay on your own?"

"I doubt we are ever alone," Mei Lee expressed, "but I should be."

"I will be leaving soon to assess the situation," Murdock told his wife. "Something has come up that requires my attention," he said to Reyes and Bass. "I'm going to need my cart, so the meat should be okay here, on the rock floor, as long as someone stays to guard it. Elizabeth would be my choice, as Bass knows the way to the encampment and back again. I'll be back as soon as I can."

"Anything you need, just let us know," Reyes told him.

"Just stand guard and don't go too far from the entrance until some of the others are here. Keep the spear. It will help you to deter any wolves that come your way."

Murdock and Bass unloaded the cart and Murdock pulled it quickly over the fire that had died down after their breakfast. He left his waterskin, since Reyes didn't have one and had requested Mei Lee bring an extra with her. Before long, Murdock was well on his way toward the river following the ridge. At the river, he paused long enough to be certain that he wouldn't be seen before levitating himself and the cart to the other side. Once across he proceeded to follow the ridge. An hour before midday, he came upon a female form that was kneeling, holding her head in her hands, and wailing bitterly. Murdock dropped the cart handles and went to her to see what the problem was.

"Here, now," Murdock said gently, but firmly. "What's the problem?" He gently took her wrists and the female fought back, slapping him hard and trying to run toward the river. The brief glimpse he managed to get of her face made him wince. "Doctor Harris?" he asked gently. "You're okay, now. No need to fight or run." As he advanced toward her, she ran a few steps before stopping. Since she wouldn't let him get close to her, he hunkered down and decided to wait for Mei Lee. *"I think it is Doctor Harris,"* he told his wife telepathically.

"You think? You don't know?" Mei Lee asked.

"She has been badly beaten and it is hard to recognize her from the brief glimpse I managed to get of her face," Murdock explained. *"Where are you?"*

"At the main crossing," Mei Lee replied. *"I just crossed the river. I should be there soon."*

"Beron, can you, or one of the Oomah, calm her down?" Murdock asked his large friend. *"I don't want her to hurt herself."* Since he was still watching her during the conversations, he saw that she suddenly collapsed.

Murdock pulled the cart over to the unconscious form and

gently levitated her onto the cart and covered her with a deer hide. He then continued toward the river. Mei Lee had gotten to the river first, but he was within fifty feet.

"What did you do to her?" Mei Lee asked as she gently inspected the bruises while the female was still on the cart.

"I didn't do anything to her," Murdock stated. "I asked Beron to calm her down."

"Well," Mei Lee started with a smirk, "she certainly is calm, now!"

"How bad is she?" Murdock asked concerned.

"Pretty bad," Mei Lee said. "It reminds me of someone else almost as badly beaten, many years ago," she said in a melancholy tone.

"Do we take her home, so Annie can look after her?" Murdock asked softly while looking at Doctor Harris.

"Let's tend her here for a bit," Mei Lee said softly. "She looks like she needs some water and something to eat. I'd like to see if she will eat before we go too much further." Doctor Harris was starting to stir. "It's okay," Mei Lee said to her gently. "We won't hurt you. We're trying to help."

Since Mei Lee's voice seemed to have a calming effect on Doctor Harris, Murdock let his wife tend her and he walked a short distance downstream and got a fire started. He then got some of the fresh venison cooking for the three of them. He then went back and pulled the cart closer to the fire. While the meat was cooking, Mei Lee did what she could to get some water into the doctor. Harris drank greedily from the waterskin.

"Can you tell me what happened?" Mei Lee asked the doctor as gently as she could as she retrieved the waterskin. Doctor Harris just shook her head and tried not to look at Mei Lee. "Can you tell me who beat you?" Mei Lee asked.

"Palmer, I think," Doctor Harris said weakly not meeting Mei Lee's eyes, "but I can't be sure. It was dark and I did kick whoever it was, but that is all I know."

Doctor Harris' voice lacked any vitality and hearing it tore at

Mei Lee's heart. She gave her a reassuring pat on the hand and stood there trying to be a comfort. Mei Lee had relayed what Harris had told her to Murdock telepathically and was not surprised at the anger that came from her husband's mind.

When the meat had finished cooking, Murdock took some to the two women. As he returned to the fire, he saw four men coming toward them. They were some distance away and Murdock warned his wife. The closer they got to Murdock, the more he was certain of their identity. He saw Preston Freeman clearly and the others with him looked to be the guards that had first attacked him. While he waited, Murdock had a piece of meat and was eating it as he watched the men approach.

"What the hell are you doing in our territory," Freeman asked when he got closer to Murdock, the cart, and the two women. He had stopped twenty feet away and the other four men stopped behind him.

"Rendering assistance," Murdock said as he cut a bite of meat and popped it in his mouth. "Not that it's any of your business!"

"Assistance? Who needs assistance?" Freeman asked. "All I see is a slope bitch and you!"

"Your mother must be proud of the crap that comes out of your mouth," Murdock responded angrily, his blood boiling at the racial slur to his wife. "You need to keep a civil tongue in your head before it ends up in your pocket!"

"That looks to be a nice cart," Freeman taunted. "I'm sure we can put it to good use!"

"That's not likely to happen," Murdock said with a chuckle.

"So, who are you assisting?" Freeman asked. "I don't think you understood the first time I asked!"

"Rape victim," Murdock responded curtly.

"That's a serious charge," Freeman responded with a look of surprise. "I hope you can prove it. Who's the victim?"

"Doctor Harris," Murdock said hotly.

"Really?" Freeman asked with surprise. "We were looking for

her. We think she wandered off in the night. We'll take her off your hands, now!"

"No," Harris screamed from the cart. Mei Lee was hard pressed to get her to stop struggling.

"It sounds to me like she doesn't want to go with you," Murdock said flatly while staring at Freeman.

"I don't think you understand," Freeman yelled. "She *is* coming with us, as is the cart and that slope bitch as —"

Murdock was on Freeman in a flash, knocking him to the ground. He had his twelve-inch machete at Freeman's throat. The other three men hadn't seen Murdock move. They had been waiting for the prearranged signal to fan out and take Murdock, but his attack had stunned them all into inaction.

"If you want to keep that tongue of yours, apologize to my wife," Murdock said low and menacing with his machete at Freeman's throat.

"You don't —" Freeman started before Murdock hit him in the head with the machete handle, knocking him out.

"I'd stay right there, if I were you," Mei Lee yelled. The other three men, being shocked at the turn of events, had stepped forward to help Freeman. When they looked up, they saw Mei Lee holding her bow at full draw.

Murdock had rolled forward and used the momentum to get to his feet. He was now standing in the midst of the three men. All were shocked and didn't know what to do. They did, however, step back a couple of steps. When they did, Murdock noticed one of them limp a little. Murdock grabbed the man by the wrist and jerked his hands up.

"Well, what do you know," Murdock said with a mock smile. "This one limps and has abrasions on his knuckles!"

"That don't mean nothin'," the man yelled adamantly.

"Did you enjoy raping a woman who couldn't fight back?" Murdock asked rhetorically. "Do you get off on beating women?"

One of the men reached for Murdock and then suddenly had

a hole through his hand. He grabbed it and started running around screaming, spouting blood everywhere. One of the two remaining men tried to grab the one screaming so he could see if something could be done to stop the bleeding.

Through all the chaos, Murdock maintained his hold on the man with the abraded knuckles. "You gonna answer me?" he said shaking the man.

"Hey, what's the big deal?" the remaining man asked. He had been holding onto the man with the hole in his hand. "It's not like it is illegal or anything!"

"Really?" Murdock asked incredulously. "I suppose you helped him? Did you hold her down while the two of you took turns?"

"Um, no," the man said reluctantly. "I just don't see what the big deal is."

"Tell me that when your wife, or daughter, is raped by some moron," Murdock responded heatedly. He reached into one of his pockets and produced a small length of leather that was about two inches wide and tossed it to the man. "Wrap his hand with that and then get the hell out of here!"

The man caught the piece of leather and did as he was told. "Both of us?" he asked when the wrapping was done.

"Yes! Get out of here before I change my mind," Murdock yelled. He watched as the two men headed back the way they'd come. When they were a hundred yards away, Murdock pulled some thongs of leather from another pocket and tied the man with the limp, hands behind him and dragged him back closer to the cart and then tied him securely to a tree. He then went back to retrieve Freeman, who was just starting to come around. Murdock tied his hands as well and walked him back to the tree that the man with a limp was tied to and tied Freeman to it as well.

"What are you going to do with those two?" Mei Lee flashed.

"I haven't decided, yet," Murdock responded. *"I'm tired of dealing with rapists and I can't abide a racist. Add to that, he needs to*

learn to keep a civil tongue. I was actually enjoying a little time alone with my wife and then these morons ruined it for me!"

"We have the one that raped you," Mei Lee told Doctor Harris calmly. "He's tied and can't hurt you." She could see the news upset Harris. "What would you like to see happen to him?" she asked.

"You better turn us loose," Freeman yelled.

"I'm only going to say this once," Murdock said to him roughly. "Shut up or I will silence you myself. You have disrespected my wife and me, so I wouldn't press my luck any further, if I were you!"

"I demand you release us," Freeman said loudly. "You have no —" he was suddenly screaming in excruciating pain as Murdock squeezed the elbow he had previously dislocated.

"You're in no position to demand anything," Murdock said sternly. "What are your names?"

"Nels Osterlund," the one that limped said quietly.

"Preston Freeman," Freeman spat in defiance.

"Tell me something, Nels," Murdock leaned down to talk conspiratorially, "did you get off on raping the doctor?" Nels didn't answer. "Oh, come on. You can tell me. There's no one here but us chickens!" Osterlund remained silent.

"You can't prove that charge," Freeman spat. He was then screaming again as Murdock squeezed his elbow.

"I really don't know what I should do with you two," Murdock said after releasing Freeman's elbow and his screams subsided. "I thought about slitting your throats and be done with you, but that would be too quick. You two need to suffer!"

Jeff Carter had managed to lead the group to the first cliff-face they came to downriver from the landing pod, negotiate the cliff-face, and get the entire group down to the next lower valley with no mishaps. Then, he decided to go exploring and left Emily Brooks in charge.

Emily Brooks was scared. She'd been appointed to take over responsibility for the one hundred fifty of their group. She had no expertise with managing herself, let alone over a hundred others. The thought of it caused her dread. The thought of addressing so many made her shake all over and want to hide. Since they had arrived here, she was trying to get along with a few people, but Keith Rogers was the easiest to talk to. The two had hit it off right away and she was so happy when he agreed to be her *second in command* once she was appointed. She was certain that he wouldn't steer her wrong and would be a good sounding board.

They both were standing by the river watching Carter's back retreating steadily downriver.

"Okay, Boss," Keith said cheerfully. "What do you want us to do first?"

"I haven't a clue," Emily responded, her voice trembling as it usually did when she was stressed. "I would think that a more permanent camp would be nice, so would food."

"I'll tell you what," Keith said reassuringly, "I'll get with our woodworkers and hunters and see what they would suggest and get back to you."

"That'll be fine," Emily responded with more calm. Keith had a way of putting her at ease and she enjoyed having him as an adviser. They had been standing downriver from the rest and Keith had left at a fast trot to find those he needed to talk to. This had left her standing there, exposed, feeling as if everyone were watching her and being overly critical. *Calm yourself, Em,* she thought. *No need to get all worked up. Keith can be trusted. He'll make things okay.* As she walked back to the crowd, they all were looking at her expectantly. "Make camp here while I figure out what to do next," she said to the crowd and everyone started making camp. Wood was gathered, fires were lit, and fish were caught and cooked. She had marveled at how smoothly it all went.

Emily had no idea what she should be doing, so she went about gathering water, the same task she had since they left the transport pod. When she returned from the river with waterskins filled, everyone was looking at her strangely. Emily read it as them being unsure of her, probably as unsure as she was of herself. While she delivered the waterskins around, Keith had come up to her.

"What are you doing?" Keith asked. "You're in charge now. You don't need to carry water!"

"I know," Emily responded, "but it gives me something to do and I enjoy it. Do you want to discuss it while I finish or after?"

Keith chuckled to himself a little. "I'll be a little downriver. Come there and we can have our discussion." He left to find a spot that was far enough that they wouldn't be overheard. He had to admit that she didn't know anything about being a manager, but she did wonderfully, winning the hearts of the people. *All our leaders could take lessons from Emily. Most leaders quit worrying about those that gave them the job. Not Emily.* As she came walking up, he thought she'd do well as a politician, with the proper guidance.

"What did you find out?" Emily asked breathlessly.

"First, the woodworkers recommend we cross the river. They say the resources needed are lacking on this side. Second, the hunters have been hearing complaints about having fish all the time. They suggest harvesting a couple of deer, but that raises another issue. To harvest deer, they need ranged weapons of some kind. That would mean more resources for the woodworkers."

"Okay, what about you?" Emily asked. "What would you suggest?"

"Hmm, that is a tough one," Keith said after a short pause to think about it. "I would say do all of it," he finally said. "The woodworkers are correct. There aren't enough resources to build anything on this side of the river. Finding resources for buildings is sure to allow the craftsmen to find the materials they need for ranged weapons."

"I don't understand — *ranged weapons?*" Emily asked shyly.

"Spears, bows and arrows, crossbows are all ranged weapons," Keith explained. "A weapon made to be used effectively at a distance."

"Oh. What do you think about building a bridge over the river?" Emily asked.

"Our efforts, in my opinion, need to be focused on shelter and food gathering," Keith expressed. "A bridge would be nice, but just isn't a priority, at this point."

"I was asking because of the farmers and Jeff Carter," Emily explained. "The farmers would use it to get to their fields and Carter would know where we went. Besides, I'm not one for walking with wet shoes."

"How about we put up an arrow, or a sign, to indicate where we crossed the river," Keith said. "I'm not keen on walking through deep water either, and your suggestion has merit, but a sign, at this point, would be better."

"Okay, then," Emily said. "Send some hunters and woodworkers to investigate the other side of the river. You know, find a usable site for a more permanent camp."

"Already done," Keith responded. "Some fish should be finished cooking soon, I'll get us some and come back."

"I prefer to get my own, thanks," Emily said with humility.

"But you're in charge," Keith pleaded. "No one would think anything of it!"

"I would," Emily countered. "I prefer to get my own and after everyone else have theirs!"

Keith stood there, looking exasperated, while the arguments ran through his head. Emily wasn't what most would call a beauty, physically, not at six-foot-four and over two hundred sixty pounds. She was a large woman, bigger than quite a few of the men and built like a truck, but that didn't seem to matter. She had a very pleasant and sweet disposition and she was always neat and clean and kept her long brown hair in a tight bun. What impressed him most was her unpretentiousness. Anyone else, in her position, would have played it for all it was worth, but not Emily. She didn't want to rule, she preferred to serve. *I think this group would be best served by making Emily the permanent leader, not just a stand-in until Carter gets back,* he thought as he made his way through the crowd. *Carter didn't care. He left us to fend for ourselves when we could have used his expertise.* Keith knew that everyone would have access to Emily, should they need to complain or ask her for something. *Yes, Emily is exactly what we need.* He had decided to actively lobby the others for Emily to be the permanent leader.

With Freeman and Osterlund secured to a tree, Murdock had sought and found a small branch and was whittling it. It wasn't but an eighth of an inch in diameter, when the bark was removed, but it seemed stout enough for his purposes.

"What are your plans for those two?" Mei Lee asked. She had come up to her husband quietly and had been watching over his shoulder.

"Did Doctor Harris make a decision?" he asked without turning his attention from his task.

"She has told us all she knows of her attack. She can't be absolutely sure that Osterlund is the one that attacked her. Until she is absolutely certain, she refuses to exact any revenge," Mei Lee said quietly.

"How is she doing otherwise?" Murdock asked.

"She's very fragile, emotionally," Mei Lee responded. "She keeps asking for Annie. Do you think it wise to take her home?"

"Not particularly," Murdock responded and then blowing on the little whittling project. "I had thought of taking her to the group I have been helping, but they are far from being able to take care of someone in her fragile condition. Maybe, though, that is exactly what she needs. They all seem to be people of good nature and their tasks would allow her to work through her trauma, keep her busy."

"I would like to meet them, before making a decision as to where she should go," Mei Lee said quietly.

Murdock nodded agreement as he replaced his six-inch knife in his boot sheath. He walked over to Preston Freeman holding the foot-long stick he had removed the bark from and had sharpened one end to a fine point.

"Remember me telling you to keep a civil tongue in your head?" he asked Freeman. "Consider this a gentle reminder!"

Murdock grabbed Freeman's nose and pinched it off. When Freeman opened his mouth to breath, Murdock grabbed his tongue, vise-like, between thumb and forefinger and pulled it out. Freeman tried to pull his tongue free by moving his head from side to side. During his struggles, Murdock pushed the sharpened end of the stick through Freeman's tongue and kept pushing until there was an equal distance from either end to his tongue. Freeman was struggling and screaming in pain. The length of the stick kept him from retracting his tongue or closing his mouth. During the process, Osterlund looked away, sickened.

"Now, what do I do with you?" Murdock asked rhetorically with a menacing grin.

Osterlund looked panic-stricken as he struggled against his bonds to no avail. "I didn't rape her," he screamed as he struggled.

"Can you explain your injuries?" Murdock asked calmly. "They are consistent with Doctor Harris' account. She said she kicked more than once, but did connect with one and you limp. Your knuckles look like you've been in a fight, but you have no marks on your face. Doctor Harris has been beaten quite badly.

The facts seem to be in her favor. If you have an alternate explanation, I'm all ears."

"I don't have to answer to you," Osterlund responded hotly, turning away from Murdock's gaze.

"Intractability would not be in your best interest, at this point," Murdock said sternly, moving closer to Osterlund's face. "Maybe I need to make another," Murdock's eyes flitted to Freeman, "shall we call it a *reminder,* for you and your *offending member.*" Murdock had a sadistic grin plastered on his face.

"Stop it," Mei Lee yelled. "Kevin, stop it, now!"

Murdock's face softened at the sound of his wife's voice and he retreated from Osterlund. He returned to the cart and donned his bow and quiver of arrows.

"Where are you going?" Mei Lee asked imperatively.

"Just taking out the trash," Murdock said quietly, but sarcastically.

"Where?" flashed to Murdock's mind from Mei Lee.

"Where the rest of the trash is located," Murdock responded verbally as he picked up a length of rope.

"Promise me that these two will arrive alive," Mei Lee communicated. *"You have never lied to me, so, promise,"* she said after getting no response.

"The condition they arrive in is totally up to them," Murdock told her aloud. "I can't promise that they won't stumble and break their fool necks, but I won't be the cause." He bent down to give his wife a quick peck before turning back to the captives. "Do I leave in the *reminder?*" Murdock saw Freeman shake his head to indicate the negative. "You've seen that it's better to be civil, then?" Freeman nodded frantically. Murdock grasped the stick and pulled it out of Freeman's tongue. "You will be reminded, by the pain and the swelling for a few days," he said to Freeman who had withdrawn his tongue and showed signs of some relief. "In case you're wondering, I don't like racial slurs, especially if they are directed at my wife, and I don't like rudeness. You should take this," Murdock held up the stick and waggled it, "as a warning!"

Murdock cut both men loose from the tree and directed them to walk toward the transport pod. Osterlund and Freeman looked behind them periodically as they traveled. Murdock was always thirty yards behind with an arrow nocked. Neither man had the inclination to try to attack Murdock on the trip to the transport pod. Osterlund was sure that Murdock would shoot him, if he tried, and Freeman was in too much pain to think about it. Both had become resigned to whatever Murdock had in mind for them. Both were certain that they would never reach the pod.

Eventually, they both topped a rolling hill and could see the transport pod. Their hearts lightened some at the sight of it. The closer they got to the pod the closer Murdock was behind them. When they were one hundred yards from the pod, they could see Phylicia come out to meet them with her entourage.

"You have a lot of nerve coming here after what you did," Phylicia yelled at Murdock when they were thirty yards from the pod.

"I rescued Doctor Harris, after one, or more, of your men, raped her," Murdock snapped back.

"I suppose you have proof of that allegation?" Phylicia asked heatedly.

"Not the kind of proof that you mean," Murdock replied just as heatedly. "Since your men are so rapacious, so much so that they tried to rob me of my property, none of them are allowed to be more than two miles from the pod. If I find them further than that, their lives are forfeit. Someone like you killed seventeen people from the first pod and took my wife's life. I refuse to allow that to happen again!"

"You have no right to limit us that way," Phylicia retorted

angrily. "We will go where we wish. We don't recognize that you have any authority to do anything!"

"Keep pushing me and you will be treated like any other rabid animal. A word to the wise should be sufficient, but it seldom is!" With that, Murdock turned and left for the river.

13

Once Murdock returned to the river from the transport pod, he found the doctor sleeping soundly on the cart. It took no time to levitate the cart over the river and all three were on their way to the box canyon. As they approached the canyon, they were stopped by one of the men. Murdock requested to see Elizabeth Reyes. The guard barred them while another went to get Reyes. Murdock had been silent since his return from the transport pod and Mei Lee didn't like it.

They didn't have to wait long for Reyes to show up.

"Elizabeth, this is my wife Mei Lee," Murdock introduced.

"Liz, please," Reyes said extending her hand with a warm smile.

"I'm pleased to meet you," Mei Lee said quietly to the taller woman. *She looks like she could whip her weight in bobcats*, Mei Lee thought. *Tough, but still warm.*

"We have a situation," Murdock started. "It seems Doctor Harris has been attacked. Are you organized enough to have someone look after her for a couple of days?"

"Things are hectic, here, as you would imagine, but I think I can do it," Reyes said. "Who attacked her?"

"We don't know," Murdock responded. "It was one, or more, of the men at the transport pod. I found her wandering around not far from the river."

"We'll put her in the cave," Reyes said as she led the way.

As they walked, Reyes was engaging in small talk with Mei Lee. Murdock was looking around and was pleased to see that his suggestions for securing the canyon were being taken seriously. He had suggested building two buildings on either side of the canyon entrance with a heavy, solid gate between the buildings. As they passed, he could see that they had started laying a course of logs for one of the buildings.

"What are your plans for the doctor?" Reyes asked which brought Murdock's attention back to Reyes.

"Annie is at our cabin caring for our kids and Declan, at the present time," Murdock explained. "Since Harris has been asking for her, I was going to go home and bring her back here, to care for Harris."

"I'm sorry, who is Declan?" Reyes asked.

"He was one of the appointed council members at the transport pod," Murdock explained.

"Don't think I ever met him," Reyes said, "but, be that as it may, you can bring Annie or anyone else you want. You are an honored guest!"

"I thank you," Murdock said humbly. "If they fit in, they may want to stay. For all I know, Declan may want to join your little group." He saw Reyes get a puzzled look.

"Annie Cooper and Doctor Harris are more than welcome," Reyes started, "we welcome medical people, but it would depend on what skills Declan has as to him being allowed to join us. Do you know what skills he has?"

"Not at the present time," Murdock said. "Have you talked to your woodworkers about ranged weapons? You'll need them to take a deer."

"I have and they wanted me to ask you if they could look at

your bow and an arrow," Reyes said. "They probably have a thousand questions for you."

"Next time," Murdock said. "It is getting late in the day and we need to head for home."

"I understand. You know where the cave is," Reyes stated. "Just make her comfortable anywhere."

Murdock left Mei Lee to distract Reyes long enough to get Harris unloaded and settled. He had no more gotten her settled on one of the deer hides, when Bass came in, looking for Murdock. Murdock immediately sent him to get Reyes and Bass complied. When Reyes entered, Murdock tried to explain that Harris was sensitive to males being anywhere close to her, or that is what he'd surmised. He had placed Harris on the sand, but quite some distance from the entrance of the cave. He bid Reyes good-bye and said he would be back in a couple of days. He picked up Mei Lee outside the cave and the couple headed for home. As soon as they were beyond the camp and were sure that they wouldn't be seen, Murdock applied his gifts. Despite the fact that it was dark by the time they reached the river, they were home in a couple of hours.

As darkness was falling, Ben Palmer had gone outside the shadow of the pod and headed for the stream. Shortly after he left the pod, Nels Osterlund exited the pod and seemed to be following him. Palmer stopped by a tree that grew next to the stream. He could see no one around.

"Nice evening isn't it?" Palmer asked as Osterlund came up behind him.

Osterlund grabbed Palmer and banged his back against the tree.

"What the hell were you doing?" Osterlund asked tensely, but quietly. "You almost got me killed!"

"You didn't get killed, did you?" Palmer asked rhetorically. He had put his hands on top of Osterlund's where they held him. "You need to calm down. If someone else hears, you will be killed!"

"At least you'll be dead with me, you sick bastard," Osterlund raged while shaking his captive.

"I'm sick?" Palmer asked with feigned innocence. "You're the one that beat that poor woman half to death. I wonder what Murdock would do, should he find out," Palmer chuckled sadistically. "I'm sure he wouldn't be too pleased with you!"

"You're the one that raped her," Osterlund retorted. "I'm sure Murdock would be interested in that little tidbit!"

"So, there you have it," Palmer said conspiratorially, "our fates are locked together."

"But Murdock was going to kill me for raping Harris," Osterlund raged through clenched teeth. "For something I didn't do!"

"You were part of it, like it or not. What do they call it — *accessory after the fact*?" Palmer grinned wickedly.

"I should kill you myself!" Osterlund raged.

"You could, but who would say you had no part in the rape?" Palmer questioned. "You would be hunted mercilessly for the rape and my murder! If you want that, then go ahead." Palmer grinned.

Several seconds passed without anyone moving as Osterlund was lost in thought about his options and their repercussions. Finally, Osterlund released Palmer.

"That's better," Palmer said conspiratorially. "We have little to fear, as long as we keep our stories straight. Since Freeman had his ass handed to him *again*, not to mention Jax Hornsby. Who shot him, by the way?"

"Murdock's wife," Osterlund said with disgust. "She's a damn good shot. She managed to shoot Hornsby as he was moving to grab Murdock."

"Fascinating, at what distance?" Palmer asked.

"Maybe thirty yards," Osterlund responded.

"As I was saying, with Freeman doubting himself and Hornsby out of commission for a while, there are few to oppose us," Palmer suggested.

"There is Ted Wagner," Osterlund reminded.

"He's insignificant," Palmer said with derision. "He'll join us, or he'll die!"

"Why not banish him?" Osterlund asked.

"And let him tell everyone else what happened?" Palmer asked incredulously. "There is one thing I have managed to learn in my life. You have to control the information to control the people. Those outside will have no information about anything here that isn't under our control!"

"What about the women?" Osterlund asked.

"They will be, shall we say, *well appreciated*," Palmer let out a restrained chuckle.

As Murdock and Mei Lee entered their cabin, they saw Annie sitting at the table with her head on her arms, sleeping. Mei Lee gently woke her as Murdock got something to eat for Mei Lee and himself. While the meat was cooking, Murdock took several swallows of water before handing the waterskin to Mei Lee.

"What happened?" Annie asked as she stretched and yawned.

"Doctor Harris was beaten and raped," Mei Lee said quietly. "She doesn't know who did it, though."

"That's awful," Annie said, shaken by the news. "Is she here?" she asked as she got up to look outside.

"No, we left her with the small group I've been helping," Murdock said, taking another drink.

"She's fine, but she was asking for you," Mei Lee said as she took the waterskin from Murdock and drank.

"When do we leave?" Annie asked stoically.

"How is Declan? Is he mending enough that he doesn't need to be tended?" Murdock asked.

"He's better off than Harris," Annie responded. "He has some psychological issues, but that is something he'll have to work through on his own. Physically, he should take it easy for a while yet, but he should be okay. Now, when do we leave?"

"Who's going where?" Declan asked sleepily as he staggered into the main room.

"You aren't going anywhere," Murdock said adamantly as he tended the cooking meat.

"Harris was raped," Annie told Declan.

Declan acted like he was physically struck and staggered to sit. "When? Who?" he asked taken aback.

Murdock and Mei Lee seeing Declan's reaction were surprised and were at a loss to explain it. "Why are you so concerned?" Murdock finally asked Declan.

"She was nice to me after I was beaten and did what she could to protect me when I was unable to protect myself," Declan responded.

"Doctor Harris has requested Annie to tend her and Kevin is going to take her after he rests," Mei Lee explained.

"I'm going, too," Declan said adamantly.

"And what can you do for her?" Annie asked incredulously.

"I can fetch water or food that both of you are going to need," Declan said to Annie. "I can be handy if you need help with anything!"

Declan's attitude raised the eyebrows of the other three adults.

"I don't think so," Annie said stubbornly. "I appreciate the offer, but no."

"I agree with Annie," Mei Lee said quietly. "Doctor Harris is very fragile, psychologically, and is sensitive to a male's presence."

"She doesn't need to see me," Declan countered. "I must help. I don't need your permission to go!"

"That's true," Murdock said, "you don't. But you will need the permission of the leader of those that are caring for her now. To get that, I'm going to have to vouch for you."

Murdock's statement seemed to take the wind out of Declan's sails. He sat heavily at the table and looked sideways at Murdock.

"I owe her," Declan said to Murdock. "I owe as much to her as I do to you!"

Murdock handed some of the meat to Mei Lee and took a few bites. "Okay, he goes," he said after swallowing what he was chewing, "but if you give anyone grief, I'll deal with you. And you won't enjoy it!"

As night was falling, Emily Brooks had finally found a soft place to lie down. She was wishing for something to cover herself as the mornings were a little damp and cold. As she was getting comfortable, Keith Rogers came over to her.

"Are you okay?" he asked hunkering down.

"Why wouldn't I be?" Emily asked him.

"Well, you are out here by yourself," Keith explained. "Why don't you sleep under the tarp covering the supplies? It would be warmer and drier if it rains again."

"I like the fresh air," she said as she turned over, her back to Keith. "Let someone else sleep under the tarp."

"You have no fire and nothing to cover yourself," Keith argued. "I don't want you to get sick. That just wouldn't do!"

"I don't need a fire," Emily shrugged. "Why should you care if I get sick? Wouldn't that put you closer to being in charge?"

"Probably, if that was my goal," Keith said softly. "It isn't. I'm concerned because I care about you. I have before you were in charge."

"That's true, you have," Emily said softly.

"Besides, being out away from the fire, you are a perfect target for any beasties that may be about," Keith explained.

Emily slapped the ground in frustration and turned to face him. "If you're so concerned, why don't you protect me?" she asked.

Keith's mouth was agape. He was not expecting her to suggest that. "I have no weapon and no skill with one if I had it," he said, shocked.

"Well, then, I'll rely on my bones to choke anything that eats me," Emily said as she rolled away from Keith. "Where are you sleeping?" she asked after a brief pause.

"I haven't located a spot yet," Keith answered. "I was waiting to see where you were going to sleep."

"Well, pull up some turf," Emily said patting the ground behind her. "With two of us, it would increase the chances of beasties choking on our bones." She chuckled a little.

Keith gingerly lay next to her and rolled over so his back was against hers. After lying that way a few minutes, Emily rolled over to face his back.

"I'm no beauty queen, or some skinny wench, but I'm warm to cuddle with," she said, good-naturedly, as she snuggled closer; her arm across his hip.

It was about an hour before dawn when Murdock awakened Declan and Annie. Mei Lee had some meat cooking and Murdock had filled three waterskins. The children were still asleep as the pair entered the main room. Both were sluggish, in their movements, from the foreshortened night.

"Eat up," Murdock said as Mei Lee gave them each a chunk of venison. "We need to hit the road soon. I would like to be there before the first snowfall."

Annie looked at him through heavy eyelids. Declan chewed

on a piece of meat as he looked sideways at Murdock with a scowl.

"Annie needs to go, but you, Declan, can go back to bed," Murdock stated.

In short order, Murdock had the cart loaded and was kissing his wife good-bye as Annie and Declan went out to the cart. They both got on the cart and sat patiently.

"I think I should ride and you two pull me," he said stoically as he walked up to the cart.

"Seriously?" Declan asked incredulously. "It's too early for jokes, Murdock!"

"Who's joking?" Murdock asked. "You felt you needed to go. How badly did you want to go? Was it bad enough to pull the cart?"

"Fine," Declan said with some anger as he got down from the cart and picked up on the handles.

Murdock didn't climb aboard the cart, but he did stop Annie from dismounting. As they walked away from the cabin, Murdock was walking alongside.

"You really need to get a horse," Declan said after they had gone a short distance.

"When you see one, let me know. I've been here for five years and have yet to see one." Murdock responded. "How long can you pull the cart?" he asked after a short pause.

"I have no idea," Declan snapped. "I don't see why I have to pull the cart!"

"You felt you had to go," Murdock stated. "Can you hunt or fish? Are your eyes better than mine to spot problems or threats before we get to them?"

"No," Declan said with a touch of surliness.

"Then your best contribution is to pull the cart," Murdock explained. "Everyone has to contribute something, even if it is just a strong back. When you acquire some useful skills, then you may be spared the more brutish tasks."

"How can I acquire skills doing things like this?" Declan asked.

"If you want something, you have to ask someone, who has the skill you want to learn. You have to show that you really want to learn," Murdock explained.

"Did my sister have to pull the cart?" Declan asked with a surly tone.

"No, she didn't. We didn't have the cart back then," Murdock stated. "Your sister did help me harvest and drag quite a few deer to our shelter. Whenever we went anywhere, she listened and watched. She asked questions if she didn't understand."

"So, what do you want from me?" Declan asked with a surly tone. "You want me to beg you to teach me?"

"Honestly, you're like a horse that was injured and unable to care for itself. I fed you and saw to your needs while you were recovering and now, I require you to work. Do you think that's wrong?"

"I am not a horse," Declan shouted.

"Really? Looks to me like maybe you are," Murdock retorted. "If you want to quit working like a horse, show me you want more. Do as I ask, cheerfully, and you may find that you've learned more than you think!"

Annie had been lying on the cart listening to Declan and Murdock's conversation. *He's giving you good advice*, she thought. *Listen and learn.* She had found Declan to be moody, brooding, and argumentative most of the time. He seemed to be angry about everything as well.

"It reminds me of something my martial arts master told me once," Murdock continued, not caring if Declan was listening.

"There was a young boy who had sought out monks to teach him to fight. They had him slap a table all day, every day. After three years, the boy went home. 'What have you learned?' his mother asked. The boy, being ashamed, hung his head. 'They just have me slap a table.' 'Show me,' his father said. The boy promptly slapped the table and reduced it to splinters."

"Is that supposed to mean something?" Declan asked angrily.

"Nope, just passing the time," Murdock said.

Annie groaned to herself in exasperation.

Emily Brooks woke up before first light. Sometime during the night, she had rolled to face away from Keith. She awakened to find that he was still asleep with his arm around her, holding her tight. His body was curved to match hers and was as close as he could possibly get. The two together had managed to keep warm most of the night and Emily slept more soundly than she had since coming to this planet. She shifted her position, so she was on her back. She wasn't trying to disturb Keith, she was, however, enjoying the moment of closeness. She didn't think she loved Keith Rogers, but there was much to be said for two people being close, in a non-sexual way, when they needed it. She needed it last night and was thankful her offer wasn't rejected. She had been tired of sleeping alone ever since she'd gotten to know Keith.

Shortly after Emily woke, Keith was aware of her. He wasn't awake, but he wasn't sound asleep either. He was aware of her softness and the heat of her body and it felt wonderful. When she rolled over onto her back, he was aware that he didn't want her to move away. He was comfortable and wasn't ready to wake up. As he became more aware, he noticed that he was caressing a female belly. It wasn't a hard, ab defined belly like so many females strive for, but it was a soft, rounded belly that made him feel good in the caressing. As he was caressing, he felt himself snuggle closer.

It took Keith until first light to wake up. As he did, he stretched his legs and arched his back where he lay, not wanting to move his arm. It was then that he became aware of someone lightly caressing his forehead.

"I'm sorry, Emily," Keith said quietly. "I didn't mean to do anything you didn't like."

"You didn't," Emily said with a soft smile. "I haven't slept that well since we got here, and I was enjoying your caresses. It felt...nice!"

"I just didn't want you to think I was taking advantage of you," Keith explained, embarrassed.

"You didn't do anything untoward," Emily said as she got to her feet. "Not that I was aware of, anyway." She smiled softly at him.

"I mean, I did enjoy sleeping with you and would like to do so again," Keith said awkwardly. "I'll go see if there is anything to eat, yet." Keith left, but haltingly.

Emily watched him walk toward the tarp and the fire that was maintained all night long. *That was very nice,* she thought. *I wish he were a few inches taller, though.* Thinking about his height made her chuckle a little. Being the tallest woman on the planet was not going to be an easy thing to overcome. There were some men taller than Keith, but she found his personality very attractive. He had managed to put her at ease from the first time they talked. She was very self-conscious of her height and her weight. She didn't think she was fat, but she wasn't one of those petite gym-bunnies either.

As she got to her feet and walked around a little to loosen her muscles, Emily remembered when she first put her arm over his hip, the previous night. Her hand had absentmindedly gone to his stomach and had lingered there. She remembered feeling his stomach and leg muscles. To look at him, Keith didn't seem to be very massive, but from what she felt, he was well-muscled. Maybe not a bodybuilder, but that type turned her off anyway. *For all of his faults or shortcomings, Keith makes me feel…comfortable.*

"There was some fish," Keith said, handing her some from behind her. He had noticed that her hair was mussed.

"Thanks," Emily said as she took the fish from him. "Have the scouts returned, yet?"

"Not yet," Keith said, slowly regaining his composure. "I'm hoping for a favorable report, though." He noticed it was taking him a while to get back to his comfort zone; his *all business* attitude. *One night and you fall to pieces,* he chastised himself mentally.

"Can you do me a favor?" Emily asked quietly.

"I can try," Keith said. "What favor?"

"I need to take a bath in the river," Emily started quickly lest she lose her nerve, "since it is the only water around. Would you keep the others away while I bathe?"

"Sure, not a problem," Keith responded quickly. "I'll keep the men away while you bathe."

"You don't understand," Emily said quietly. "I mean all of them, females, too."

"But why?" Keith asked innocently.

"To be honest, the others make me…self-conscious," Emily said adamantly and quietly.

"Okay, Emily," Keith said, embarrassed, "anything you need. It isn't a problem."

Emily had gotten up and was walking to a little pool she had spotted the day before. It was a place in the river where the water flowed back into itself and wasn't fast moving. As she walked, Keith followed while eating his breakfast. Once Emily had finished hers, she started to take down her hair. She ran her fingers through it to straighten it out as much as possible. Keith could see that it was long, flowing, and a rich chestnut color. When they had arrived at the spot, Keith noticed that the bank was two feet higher than the little bit of sand and rock that formed a very small beach.

"Don't look," Emily said as she started down the bank.

"I'll stay up here and keep the others away," Keith reassured her, his back to her.

"Damn!" he heard her say shortly after going down the bank.

"What's wrong?" he asked without turning around, panicked.

"Nothing, the water is damned cold, though," she said from the water.

As he heard some splashing sounds, he saw one of the scouts coming toward him. "Scout coming, I'll get rid of him," Keith said over his shoulder and he walked toward the scout. The scout tried to give him a report, but Keith sent him back and told him to give the report in a couple of hours. The scout shrugged and returned to the camp. As he was returning to the bank, he saw Emily climbing up, dressed and trying to comb out her hair with her fingers.

"You should consider leaving your hair down," Keith said walking over to her. "Just pull it back into a gather at your neck."

"I'll think about it," she said with a smile. "It's your turn!"

"What?" he said in shock. He hadn't planned on bathing.

"Get your skinny ass into the water," she said slowly and emphatically. "You'll find it invigorating!"

"I really wasn't planning—," he protested.

"Please, take a bath," Emily asked quietly. "I know it will make you feel better."

Keith hadn't intended on bathing, but the way she asked and the way she pleaded with her eyes, he found himself complying before he knew it. *This is crazy*, he thought as he got undressed and stepped quickly into the water. "Damn!" he shouted without thinking about it. It was then that he heard Emily chuckling up on the bank.

By midday and in spite of massive amounts of complaints, Murdock, Declan, and Annie had arrived at Reyes' camp. This time, the person who stopped them, showed them right to the cave where Doctor Harris was located. Annie didn't wait. She immediately entered the cave and, after shooing the others out, found Doctor Harris.

"Murdock," Liz Reyes greeted. She had exited the cave right after Annie had entered. "And who is this?" she asked indicating Declan.

"This is Declan," Murdock said. "Declan, this is Elizabeth Reyes."

"Liz, please," Reyes said sticking her hand out with a broad smile.

"Declan Griffen," Declan said gruffly as he took her hand and shook it "How is Doctor Harris?" he asked.

"She's fine," Reyes said to both men. "She's had a hard time of it, but she should pull through."

"Good," Murdock said. "How are things progressing?"

"Fine, we're making a start of a long process," Reyes explained cheerfully. "If you have time, our woodworker would like to talk to you about your spear and bow."

"Lead on," Murdock said with a smile.

Declan was hanging back, unsure if he should stay or go with Murdock. While he was looking toward the cave, he felt someone grab him by the collar of his shirt and dragged him a few steps. "Pay attention," Murdock sternly whispered.

"Hey," Declan protested. Then he saw it was Murdock dragging him and figured his protests would accomplish nothing. He resigned himself to following Murdock and quietly observing the others in the camp and Murdock.

Declan was bored listening to Murdock and the woodworker discuss the finer points of knapping spearheads and arrowheads. He was looking around at a flurry of activity. Not far away, he could see a large group of men building something that looked like a cabin close to the opening of the canyon. As he continued to watch, part of his mind was listening to Murdock and the woodworker. They were now discussing arrow lengths and draw lengths. It was then that he noticed that there were a couple of men on several ropes that went around the logs. They were pulling the logs up a few diagonally placed smaller logs that acted as a ramp, to get them placed. As he watched, he could relate. He was feeling like a beast of burden after having to pull the cart from Murdock's cabin.

After a couple of hours, Murdock and the woodworker were going out into the trees to look for suitable materials for bows. As the woodworker was getting ready to go, Murdock took Declan off to the side.

"You should be paying attention," Murdock chastised.

"I have no interest in anything you're discussing," Declan said with disdain. "To me, it's just so much gibberish."

"Where the hell do you think you are?" Murdock asked angrily. "This is the frontier. There are millions of things that you need to learn. I don't expect you to learn them overnight, but I do expect you to learn something."

Declan was looking around while Murdock was talking. He wanted to give the impression that he had no interest in what was being said, and he succeeded.

"Is there anything going on here that interests you?" Murdock finally asked in frustration.

"Not particularly," Declan answered in an offhand manner.

"Does eating interest you?" Murdock asked finally.

"I suppose it does," Declan answered with a yawn. "When can I see Doctor Harris?"

Murdock exhaled loudly, in his frustration. "Go to the cave, but Annie has the say-so if you'll be allowed to see her." The woodworker was ready, and Murdock turned to leave without Declan.

This pleased Declan, having gotten his way again. He wandered around the camp watching all the comings and goings. Eventually, he arrived at the cave and was stopped by a largish man with a staff. Declan recognized him as one of the guards from the transport pod.

"What do you want here?" the man asked gruffly.

"Murdock said I could see Doctor Harris," Declan said. He saw the man turn toward the entrance and talk to another guard inside the cave and then he turned back to face Declan. Declan tried to step past the guard and was barred.

"You have to wait," the guard stated roughly.

"Do you know who I am?" Declan asked, indignant at being stopped.

"Yes, I know who you are," the guard answered with a contemptuous tone.

"Then I demand to see Doctor Harris," Declan yelled as he tried again to push past the guard. The guard pushed Declan backward, roughly. Declan tripped over his own feet and fell to the ground. "I protest this maltreatment," Declan raged.

"What's the problem here," Elizabeth Reyes demanded as she exited the cave.

"Your guards are being abusive," Declan said getting to his feet and trying to dust himself off.

Declan saw the guard whisper to Reyes and Reyes nodding.

"First of all," Reyes started after the guard finished, "everyone here knows who you are, but, because of Murdock, we are, um…restraining ourselves. If you wouldn't have been with Murdock, you wouldn't have been allowed this far into the camp."

"Now you just—," Declan started yelling, but Reyes held up her hand in a stopping motion.

"Secondly, Doctor Harris is a patient of Annie Cooper's and, as such, Annie Cooper has the final say as to visitors. Anyone wishing to see Doctor Harris, while she is here, must wait to be admitted. Forcing the issue could lead to being denied admittance...permanently."

"I know Annie Cooper, probably better than you do," Declan raged. "You tell her I'm here!"

"Ms. Cooper has been informed that you're here to see Doctor Harris," Reyes responded, trying to be patient with Declan, but quickly losing her restraint. "You must wait until Ms. Cooper grants you admittance!"

"This is outrageous," Declan yelled. "Annie! Annie! They won't let me in," he yelled, hopefully, loud enough for Annie to hear.

"If you don't quiet down," Reyes said loud enough to be heard over Declan's yelling, "you will be removed from the area!"

"What's going on here?" Annie asked impatiently as she came from the cave entrance and walked up to Declan. The question was being directed at Declan.

"They won't let me in," Declan whined.

"I know," Annie said impatiently. "I'm the one that refused you admittance!"

"What?" Declan asked sheepishly.

"Doctor Harris is not able to see male visitors at this time," Annie said to Declan sternly. "You pitching your little fit isn't helping my patient. You are, therefore, banned until such time as you prove to me that you can behave yourself." Annie turned suddenly and went back into the cave.

Declan was dumbfounded. He stood there, his mouth agape, looking at the guard and at Reyes, who were smiling. He didn't hear them say so, but he knew it was an 'I told you so'.

"Mister Parker," Reyes started, "Would you escort Declan outside the canyon? And inform the guard there that he is not to be admitted into the canyon until I countermand the order."

"With pleasure, Ma'am," the guard said with a grin.

Parker grabbed Declan by the back of his shirt and lifted. Declan's shirt was almost pulled above his head as he was unceremoniously shoved toward the entrance of the canyon. At the entrance, Declan was shoved, and fell into the dirt. He rolled over to see Parker talking to another man, obviously a guard for he carried the same type of staff. The other guard was nodding that he understood his instructions.

Declan had decided not to push his luck any further. *You just wait until Murdock gets here,* he thought. *You're all going to be sorry.*

Murdock had just finished helping the woodworker gather materials for making bows and had deposited his load of wood and flint where he had found the woodworker. After bidding farewell to the woodworker, he went looking for Declan. He didn't have to look far. He found him sitting just outside the canyon entrance.

"Did you get to see Doctor Harris?" Murdock asked as he walked up to Declan.

"No," Declan said with a pouting tone.

"Why not?" Murdock asked, suspecting the answer.

"Because they banned me," Declan complained.

"Really?" Murdock asked, incredulous. "And why were you banned?"

"Because they stopped me at the cave and wouldn't let me see her," Declan complained loudly.

"Are you going to tell me what happened, or do I go ask Reyes?" Murdock asked. He was getting tired of Declan only giving an account in a way that portrayed him in the light of innocence. Declan said nothing more, but had decided to sit and pout. Murdock proceeded to the cave entrance and was stopped by the guard. He made a request to see Reyes and was admitted to the cave to see her. He listened intently while Reyes filled him in on the reasons for banning Declan from the canyon and why he was not granted admittance to see Doctor Harris.

When Reyes was finished, Murdock expressed his apologies for subjecting them to Declan and requested to see Annie.

"How is she?" Murdock asked when Annie appeared.

"She's fragile, emotionally," Annie answered. "Physically, she is less fragile, but it was very traumatic. She may recover, physically, in a fortnight, but emotionally," Annie shook her head, "who knows!"

"Can I see her?" he asked.

"No, you can't," Annie said. "She is too sensitive to a male's presence and I don't want her subjected to more trauma."

With that, Murdock thanked Annie for her time and informed her that he would be leaving soon, for home. He thanked Reyes for her patience and her restraint and apologized again for inflicting them with Declan. He quickly walked out of the canyon. He collected his cart and Declan and they left the camp with Murdock pulling the cart.

"We're just going to leave then?" Declan complained. "I didn't get to see Doctor Harris!"

Murdock stopped suddenly. "Yes, we're leaving," Murdock explained trying to keep his temper. "You have worn out our welcome. Pitching a fit, like a spoiled child, damaged your cause. I asked to see Doctor Harris and was denied. I was denied by Annie, just like you were. You were brought with the hope that you would take an interest in making yourself useful, but that has gone by the wayside." Declan tried to interrupt, but Murdock refused to let him. "This is a hard place. You either are just as hard or you're dead. You don't like anything, so maybe it is better that you go off on your own!"

"But I don't know how to survive!" Declan pleaded.

"You don't know because you think you're owed an existence. I have given you plenty of opportunities to try to learn something, anything. But you refuse to learn anything, so I'm at a point that I'm not going to try. From this point on, you want to know something, prove to me you want it!"

"I don't need you," Declan fired back after a few seconds of silence. "No one can stop me from seeing Doctor Harris. No one can stop me from going where I will and doing what I want." Declan sat on a downed limb and crossed his arms angrily, his back to Murdock.

Murdock looked at him for a second. "Good luck with that!" he said as he continued on toward home. Declan was too busy pouting to see that he was alone.

14

M urdock had stopped, once he reached the top of the ridge, and made camp. He did so to calm himself before going home and to try to reconcile his actions with what he knew Rose would have wanted. After getting a fire started, he started some venison cooking. As he tended the meat, he communicated, telepathically, to Mei Lee, the developments concerning Declan, Annie, and Doctor Harris.

"What are you going to do about Declan?" Mei Lee flashed.

"I'm not sure there is anything that can be done," Murdock responded. *"He has some strange ideas about his personal conduct and how he interrelates with others. He doesn't want to learn to do anything and complains when asked to help out."*

"Turning him out to fend for himself may not be the correct course, though," Mei Lee responded. *"He probably won't last long on his own."*

"Is it up to me to watch over everyone?" Murdock asked rhetorically. *"I have been giving advice to whoever wants it, but I have not told anyone what to do. Is there some reason I should give Declan special consideration? He hasn't shown us any consideration!"*

"The only reason I can think of is, how are you going to feel if

something bad happens?" Mei Lee asked poignantly. *"Can you live with that?"*

Murdock broke communication with his wife after exchanging the normal household pleasantries and started to eat. While he ate, his mind was going over all the issues with Declan and his responses to him. He had come to the conclusion that Declan knew how to push him and did so just to show he could. He theorized that Declan was doing everything he could to push people away, as if he felt he was unworthy to be liked. Add to that, he had some definite issues concerning Rose.

As he was finishing his meal, Murdock saw Beron and Bridget walking toward him and it immediately lightened his mood. Both Oomah levitated a fish from the river and started eating a short distance from Murdock's fire. Murdock didn't question his friends until after they had finished eating. To him, it would have been rude to do so. Once they were finished, Beron and Murdock entered the sharing state with Bridget standing guard.

Once in the sharing state, Murdock was shown, via mental pictures, glimpses into what was happening with the rest of the newcomers. He saw the direction and heard some of what their plans were. The scene changed focus to Declan, who was wandering around and, in Murdock's opinion, feeling sorry for himself. Again, the focus changed to the transport pod. He clearly saw and heard the conversation between Palmer and Osterlund and each one's part in the rape and assault of Doctor Harris along with their future plans for those at the transport pod. Finally, the focus changed again to a small group of men heading downriver. Murdock got the impression that they were quite some distance away.

"Is it possible to prevent Declan from falling to wolves?" Murdock asked his friend. It put his mind at ease when he received an affirmative answer.

~

After the scouts had returned and a favorable report given, Emily Brooks passed the word to prepare for the move. There was some resistance to moving across the river by a third of the people present. Emily, not wanting to force anyone into anything, asked that those with specialized skills be willing to teach others those skills. Once agreements were finalized, they divided into a group of fifty that insisted on proceeding further downriver, with the remaining one hundred crossing the river.

Fording the river was accomplished without incident and Emily experienced some sadness at seeing the group split. It wasn't something she wanted. She was thankful, however, that Roy White, the only medical person in the group that left the transport pod, had elected to stay with the majority.

"It'll be okay," Keith Rogers told Emily as they both watched the small group proceed downriver. "As it turns out, we're doing pretty well, as far as keeping skilled people," he said trying to cheer her up. It had taken a lot of convincing to keep Emily from taking the split as a statement against her personally.

"I know," Emily said quietly as a tear started to fall. "I was beginning to think of everyone as family, and now it has split up."

Emily had been standing in a low spot, which allowed Keith to be tall enough to put his arm around her to comfort her. "Don't take it so personally," he said into her hair as he pulled her close. "They said they were only going about thirty miles further downriver. Most of them were supporters of Carter."

Emily nodded as she held back the majority of the tears and wiped away the tears that had started.

"I say good riddance," Keith said in an upbeat tone. He had been lobbying the others to make Emily the permanent leader and Carter's supporters were giving considerable resistance to the idea. Now, it would be easier.

Emily tried to find the scouts. Everyone was regrouping after fording the river and it made it difficult to find them in the chaos. Keith had been following Emily, trying to find a moment to move up beside her.

Emily and Keith had been told, by the scouts, that there was a very large cave under the ridge they had descended a couple of days prior. They said it was located within two miles of the river with plenty of trees close by. They had failed to determine how large it was, as they had no torches. They all had decided to investigate further as it would give everyone immediate shelter. Once Emily found the scouts, she gave the word for everyone else to follow as best they could while the scouts led the way.

For the next few hours, there was a long line of people, who were just following the person in front of them, snaking across the open plain toward the trees and then through the trees. It didn't take the scouts long to find the cave opening. As Emily and Keith watched the scouts trying to climb up to the entrance, they were also looking at the surroundings. The cave entrance was ten feet above the ground and the trees grew to within two feet of the ridge base.

"That is going to be hard to climb and difficult to get most of the supplies in there," Emily said as her attention returned to the cave entrance and the scouts scrambling up to it.

"It should be fine, once we get a ramp, or something, built," Keith replied shading his eyes as he followed the scouts climbing.

As they watched, one of the scouts had reached the entrance to the cave and had lowered a rope to assist the others. Keith, being third up, had walked up, grabbed the rope, and started to climb, while the scouts anchored the other end. It didn't take long for the two scouts and Keith to get to the entrance. Keith tossed down the rope.

"Come on, Emily," Keith shouted down from the entrance.

Emily walked up and took the rope. She was looking up the face skeptically as she pulled on it to assure herself that it was anchored and would hold her. She felt it give a bit and she imagined three men straining to hold her weight. With apprehension, Emily followed the same path as the smaller men and, in short order, gained the cave entrance.

After she lowered the rope, Emily stood in the entrance looking out. She could see nothing except the trees that were straight across from it. The cave entrance itself was eight feet by four feet and had a one-foot ledge outside the entrance and she could see the floor raise a foot one-foot inside, forming a two-foot ledge at the entrance. The men were getting a fire started to create some brands so they could assess the size and shape of the cave.

"Keith, would you go down and tell the rest to wait and ask the woodworkers to come up, please?" Emily asked quietly, after seeing Keith was not doing anything to aid in the fire building. "I would like them to work out an easier way up, especially for the supplies."

Keith nodded and started down the rope while Emily was anchoring it. As she waited for Keith to return, the men got a fire going and it lit up the inside of the cave. As she stood there waiting, she could see the ceiling at least fifteen feet above them. The room they were standing in seemed to be very large with a flat, semi-level rock floor. It was then that Keith returned and climbed up the rope. Once he was up, he helped anchor as the other two men climbed up.

"See if you can figure an easier way up," Emily told the two men once they were inside the cave. "If nothing else, this cave will work for storage, but only if we can figure out an easier, safer, more secure way up."

Small logs were passed around to be used as torches to those that were exploring the cave. As they walked around the walls, they came to dozens of smaller rooms off the main room, on all walls except the entrance wall. Each of the smaller rooms looked to be able to hold three or four people comfortably. At the back of the cave, they came to a wide tunnel that led down in a sweeping spiral curve. As all four walked down the tunnel, the scouts had their machetes out and ready. To Emily, it seemed that the tunnel dropped about eight feet in three hundred sixty degrees of the curve. At the bottom, they had to jump down from about two feet into another huge room, wider and deeper than the one above, with a ten-foot ceiling.

As they investigated the lower room, they found dozens of the smaller rooms off the main room on three of the walls. Opposite the tunnel down, off to the left, as they faced the wall with no rooms, they found another tunnel, a straight one that dropped two feet with another two-foot ledge they had to jump down. The room at the end of the small tunnel had four pools of water going across the room. The main pool was fed by a stream of water, coming from the back of the cave, and was located high up on the wall. Emily could see one of the pools steaming and stuck her hand in each pool. She found that each pool, from the hot one, got cooler the closer they got to the stream that fed them. The stream itself was not as cold as the river, but wasn't significantly warmer either. As they all looked, they could see the runoff from one pool went into the next pool. The runoff from the hot one disappeared into the floor in a steady stream. The floor of the room was level, smooth, and dry rock. All of the investigators were dumbfounded.

"This can't be natural," one of the scouts whispered in disbelief.

"Who cares?" Emily said with relish. "I don't think we could build anything close to this, not anytime soon, anyway. We're going to need a couple of sets of steps, though," she said as she climbed back up the small tunnel. They all backtracked all the way to the main room. "Tell everyone that this is it," Emily said excitedly to Keith and the scouts. As she approached the entrance, she signaled the woodworkers. "What have you come up with?" she asked the taller one.

"Well, Ma'am," the tall one started, "would you mind a series of ramps?"

"What?" Emily asked confused.

"We can't build a single ramp from the ground up to the

entrance," he started to explain. "It would have to be very long to get to this height at a comfortable incline. The only way to use a ramp would be to do so in several smaller ones ending in a small bridge from the entrance straight across to those trees. That would take a long time to accomplish, even with all the manpower we have, but would be easier to defend and use."

"What can you do quickly to get people up here and all the supplies?" she asked.

"I suppose we could make a long ladder and drag the supplies up," he said after giving it some thought. "We have the manpower and it will be difficult to pull things up."

"Do so, because, gentlemen, we're going to make this our home," Emily told them, smiling as she clapped the closest one on the shoulder nearly buckling his knees.

It had taken Declan quite some time to realize that he was all alone. He had been too busy pouting to hear Murdock leave, not that he heard Murdock when he moved anyway. "The man is a damned ghost," Declan said quietly to himself. "How is it possible for anyone to move that quietly?" He wasn't happy with Reyes or Annie Cooper. He had wanted desperately to see Doctor Harris and took it as a personal affront when he was denied. He didn't like the guards that didn't grant him access after he had been on the council. "When I was on the council, Reyes was nothing. Who does she think she is?" he said aloud to himself.

He sat thinking for quite some time. He had ceased talking to himself out loud as he fumed. While he sat there, he heard a strange noise coming toward him from the river. As he sat, hoping that whatever it was would make a quick ending to him, he saw a doe come haltingly toward him. He sat mesmerized by the animal and was not thinking anything, lest the animal sensed his thoughts and run off. As he watched, he saw it graze cautiously, constantly watching him. More than once, Declan found that he had stopped breathing and gasped for air. On one of those gasps, the doe heard him and bounded off. As he sat watching, Declan found that his anger and frustration had left him, as if the doe had taken it from him.

As he sat there, he had no idea how he was going to survive, but that didn't seem to matter much. He felt calmer than he had been in a very long time and figured something would come up. He was trying to figure out where he could go. *The transport pod is out. Everyone there had assaulted and raped Doctor Harris or allowed it and had beaten him nearly to death. I could try for Murdock's cabin. I do have a general idea of where it is, but doubt my apologies would be accepted.* He thought of returning to the camp where Annie and Doctor Harris were, but they had kicked him out and he was unsure what would await him, should he return. He had no idea where the rest of the newcomers had gone. He thought he had overheard Murdock and Mei Lee discussing it and seemed to remember something about going downriver.

He jumped when he heard someone talking and coming in his direction. It was then that he noticed it was close to sunset and he hadn't eaten anything for many hours. Not having a weapon, Declan had decided to hide until they, whoever *they* were, had gone past. While he was hidden, he watched to see who was coming. He heard them pass downriver a few yards. He recognized their voices as those from the box canyon. He figured they were on their way to catch some fish. He followed the three men with as much stealth as he could manage. All three were competing with each other to see who could catch the most. As they caught them, they threw them onto the grass, quite some distance from the water to prevent them from escaping. One was thrown within arm's length of Declan, where he was hiding in the high grass. He stealthily took the fish and crept back to the relative safety of the trees. Once there, he got to his feet and quickly moved upriver a few hundred yards.

Looking around, he found a rock that appeared to be sharp

and about the size of his fist. He tried to pick it up, but couldn't budge it. He found another, smoother rock and managed to pick it up. Then he slammed it onto the sharp rock and managed to chip off a good-sized piece. He used the sharp rock to gut the fish and used his fingers to dig out the meat. He thought he was going to vomit, if he had something in his stomach to spew, thinking about eating it raw. Since he had no knowledge of building a fire, he had little choice. As he was choking down the raw fish, he heard the men leave the river and head for the canyon. It was sundown by the time he finished eating as much of the fish as he could.

He left the remains of his meal and headed toward the river. He found that he was in need of water. He made it to the river and started drinking. As darkness fell, and being reinvigorated, he realized he had no cover and no way to make a fire. He decided to head downriver, immediately. The other newcomers, the ones that may be in that direction, were his only chance to survive, if he could beg a place with them, but first, he had to find them.

When everyone woke up, they went about their regular routine. Palmer and Osterlund had taken to wearing a twelve-inch machete, just in case they ran across Murdock. Preston Freeman, being testy at his defeat at the hands of Murdock for a second time, spent most of his time pushing people out of his way or yelling at someone. This morning, as he knelt down to get some water on his face, he felt the point of a machete in his back.

"It would seem that things have been reversed," Palmer whispered in his ear from behind.

"You're making a big mistake," Freeman fumed quietly. "My men will eat you alive!"

"Really?" Palmer asked as he backed away.

Feeling the machete withdraw, Freeman stood and faced

Palmer. He saw that Alvin Jones, Ted Wagner, Jackson Hornsby, and Nels Osterlund were standing behind Palmer. All of them were armed.

"It would seem that your men are now my men," Palmer gloated absentmindedly tapping his left hand with the machete.

"I'll kill you for this," Freeman fumed through clenched teeth.

"I don't think that will happen anytime soon," Palmer said as he walked up to Freeman and grabbed his right elbow. Freeman dropped to his knees. "Still sore, I see," Palmer gloated with a smile. "As I see it, you can take orders from me, or I can take you out there, somewhere, and slit your throat!"

"How do you expect to get away with this?" Freeman asked trying to buy some time.

"It seems," Palmer started as he paced back and forth, "the men respect anyone who can provide an opportunity to better their situation. They are mine, bought and paid for. They'll see what I want them to see, not that it really matters." Palmer was grinning at Freeman.

Freeman was frantically trying to figure a way out. "Will you allow me a weapon to defend myself?" he asked finally.

Palmer started laughing openly. "Why in the world would I do something so colossally stupid?" he chuckled.

"Because it would be honorable to face me, like a man," Freeman said with venom.

"I'm facing you now," Palmer said with a grin. "What have I done that would give you the impression that I'm *honorable*?"

Phylicia, who had just awakened and accompanied by Heather and Kimberly, had just walked out of the pod, and saw the congregation. "What goes on here!" she shouted.

"Oh, nothing much," Palmer said grinning, "just a coop!"

"He means 'a coup'," Wagner corrected.

Phylicia gasped when the meaning of the words sunk in.

"Let's take him for a walk," Palmer suggested.

Ted Wagner and Alvin Jones grasped Freeman's upper arms

and led him off toward the ridge. The rest of the men followed. Once Freeman was two hundred yards from the pod, they all stopped.

"Are you going to turn me loose?" Freeman asked skeptically.

"Why would I do that?" Palmer asked. "I turn you loose, and then I have to worry about you…forever. I prefer to not worry," Palmer said with a wry grin. He had been spinning the twelve-inch machete on its handle in his hand while he paced. With one smooth movement, he stopped the machete from spinning and thrust it upwards, just under Freeman's sternum and all the way to the hilt. Those present thought the movement had fluidity, a gracefulness, which was surprising, given Palmer's size.

Freeman felt it initially as just a sharp blow to the solar plexus, then he felt the blade as it entered and pierced through his lung and nicked the right ventricle, with his spine stopping the blade. His expression changed to one of fearful, shocked amazement. He slowly dropped to his knees on the hard ground, but didn't feel it. Within seconds of him hitting the ground with his knees, Freeman was dead, having bled into his thoracic cavity and the ground.

Once Freeman was gone, Palmer gave orders for his clothes to be removed, cleaned, and stored for later use. The men complied. As Palmer was walking back toward the transport pod, he stopped by the creek to clean off his hands and his machete. Once he was finished, he replaced the machete to its scabbard at his hip and then washed the blood from his hands.

"What did you do to Freeman?" Phylicia asked in a shrill voice, her entourage not far behind.

"First of all, I only answer your question because it suits me to do so," Palmer said smugly. "Second, you better get used to no one jumping when you snap your fingers. You're no longer in charge. So, I would suggest all you bitches get used to the way things are, because they're unlikely to change. Lastly, trying to leave will result in you being hunted down and, if you do it too many times, killed!"

"How dare you—" Phylicia started, incensed. She was cut off by Palmer backhanding her across the mouth.

Heather and Kimberly launched an attack on Palmer, who deftly backhanded them as well.

"Did you think I was joking?" Palmer yelled at the now sobbing females. "You should have a clue by now, so go fill the waterskins!"

None of the females moved to comply. They all just stared at Palmer, in disbelief.

"Mister Jones," Palmer said finally staring at the women with a grin. "If my order isn't carried out in the next thirty seconds, kill Kimberly! Thirty seconds after that, kill Heather!"

Alvin Jones came forward with his machete drawn, his face expressionless.

Suspecting that Palmer was serious, Phylicia gave a signal to Heather that she should go fill the waterskins.

"Where are you going?" Palmer boomed. "I told Phylicia to go and she is running out of time!" He stood there looking at Phylicia with a grin.

Phylicia finally got to her feet and started collecting the waterskins and took them to the creek to fill them. She had been beaten, for now, and knew she had no choice but to bide her time and wait for an opportunity to present itself.

Declan walked all night. He was unaccustomed to being out in the dark and was frightened. He realized that he was at the mercy of any animal that happened to come along and he had no weapon to defend himself. He did stumble and fall a few times before he figured out where to put his feet. His fear helped him to walk as quietly as he could and had helped him to stop talking out loud to himself.

It was close to sunup when he reached the top of the ridge that overlooked the river below. He had seen signs across the river that someone had camped close to it. As soon as it was light enough, Declan climbed down the ridge face. It did take him some time to pick a way down, but he finally made it without any major incidents. As he reached the base of the ridge, he drank deeply from the river and then rested from his exertions. He had no idea how much further downriver the others had gone or how much further he had yet to go. As he rested, he fell asleep under a tree.

Declan was awakened by someone tapping his chest with a wooden staff.

"Hey, you," a man's voice said, "Wake up!"

It took Declan's brain a little while to become aware and open his eyes. When he did, he saw several men surrounding him. Each had one of the wooden staffs that Phylicia had contracted for. "What do you want?" Declan managed sleepily.

"Hey, I know you," one of the men, the tall one with brown hair, said excitedly. "You're the one that Murdock kidnapped!"

Declan looked sideways at the man. He didn't recognize him, but didn't know if he should keep his mouth shut or correct the man.

"What are you doing here?" a bigger man, with blond hair, asked roughly.

"I was sleeping, until you woke me," Declan answered back, the fog in his brain dissipating quickly.

"He isn't one of them that went with Carter," another man, the short man with brown hair, stated flatly.

"What's your name?" the blond demanded.

"Declan Griffen," Declan answered, "and you are?"

"Clem Adams," the tall, thin man with brown hair answered.

"Cliff Reed," the short, heavy man with brown hair said.

"Gary Carpenter," the heavy blond answered. "Now that all the introductions are out of the way, what the hell are you doing in our territory?" Carpenter bellowed.

"I was looking for those that headed this way," Declan said flatly.

"I'd say you found some," Carpenter said heatedly. "But for what purpose do you look for us?"

"I'm no threat to you," Declan pleaded. "I was hoping to join your group."

"He has nothing," Cliff Reed said. He had been looking the area over, looking for signs of others or weapons.

"You're out here without a weapon?" Carpenter asked derisively. "How dumb can you get?" All three men laughed heartily.

Declan kept his head and said nothing, but he did notice that each of the men had a twelve-inch machete as well as the wooden staff.

"We don't decide who joins us," Carpenter said finally when they all had finished laughing. "You can, however, follow us back to our camp to beg a place with our leader, or you can go on downriver."

"I'll follow you," Declan answered quickly.

The four men turned and marched deeper into the woods with Declan surrounded by the other three. He doubted he could have gotten past them, if he wanted to. They all were more muscled than he was, and it bothered him. Being on the council and doing no manual labor had taken its toll on him physically. After walking a little under two miles, the three men stopped.

"Clem, you go get Keith," Carpenter ordered. "Cliff and I will hold him here." Clem nodded and trotted off away from the river. "You better make yourself comfortable. You could be here a while," Carpenter told Declan as he found a log to sit on.

Declan had decided to sit and not talk unless they questioned him, but neither of the men asked him anything. As he sat there, Declan could hear distant sounds of chopping and dropping trees in the direction Clem had trotted off. It wasn't long before a blond man had come down the path, and Carpenter got to his feet and met him some distance from Declan. They seemed to be talking, but Declan couldn't hear what was being said.

"Mister Griffen," the man said after his short conversation with Carpenter. "I'm Keith Rogers," Rogers said as he stuck out his hand.

"Declan, please," Declan said as he took Rogers' hand and shook it.

"Okay, Declan," Rogers said after the proper amount of time had been taken in their greeting. "What brings you out this far?"

"I was hoping to join your group," Declan said.

"Really," Rogers said with a shocked look on his face. "Aren't you related to Murdock? I seem to recall you being his brother-in-law."

"Yes, I am," Declan answered. "Does that preclude me from seeking others to live with?"

"Oh, no," Rogers said, "you can live anywhere you want, as long as the others want you. We have a bit of an issue. You were on the council and there are many here that will remember that. The council, and their abuses, will not be easily forgotten. I'm not sure the others would accept you."

"Yes," Declan started, "I was on the council, but I had no say in their policies. That was all Phylicia and Palmer. In fact, in the end, I was almost beaten to death by Palmer."

"I did hear something about that," Rogers stated. "I doubt the others will accept that distinction. They won't trust you and some may try to kill you, because they equate the council as all three of you and their betrayal was by *the council*. Wouldn't you be better off with Murdock?"

"It's true that Murdock is my brother-in-law and he did rescue me from Palmer and Phylicia. However, that doesn't necessarily mean I agree with *his* methods or attitudes either."

Rogers looked at Declan for a long time without saying anything. "I would like to be able to trust you," he said finally, "but I have other people to think about. Their safety and security are my concerns."

"Would it be possible to work my way into your group?" Declan asked after seeing the direction the conversation was going.

"That *might* be possible," Rogers said thoughtfully after a short pause. "I couldn't, of course, guarantee anything. In our group, everyone has a say in what affects everyone. And our security measures are not in place. You wouldn't be allowed to come close to the camp until we decide we can trust you. Would that be acceptable?"

"It would, as long as I can get a little help with fire making and some sort of shelter. As your men can attest, I have no tools or weapons," Declan countered.

"And if I refuse?" Rogers asked.

Declan remained silent for some time. He had no idea what to do or where he would go, should these people refuse him. "Frankly, Mister Rogers," Declan said finally, "I have no idea where I'd go or what I'd do. I lack the skills to make a fire and have no tools or weapons of any kind. I'll probably starve or freeze."

Rogers thought about the situation for a moment. "Declan, go with these men and help with the collection of fish from the river. For your help, you will be fed. I need to take this situation to others for a decision. I can't make a unilateral decision like this. I hope you understand?"

"I understand," Declan said in a low voice.

As he walked away, Rogers signaled Carpenter to follow him. The two men walked some distance away to talk. Declan watched the two men during their conversation. When it was finished, Carpenter came toward Declan followed by Adams and Reed.

"Let's go, Declan," Carpenter said as they all walked past Declan.

Adams, Reed, and Carpenter did the catching of the fish while Declan, with a borrowed machete, was cleaning them, after he was shown how. Once they had enough for the others, they all headed back. When they had reached the point where Declan had talked to Rogers, they all stopped.

"You stay here, Declan," Carpenter said. "We'll bring you back some of the fish after it's cooked."

"And if you don't come back?" Declan asked.

Carpenter looked at him derisively. "You'll just have to trust us. If you want something to eat, you'll wait here. You're not to follow us or get any closer to our camp. If you do, we'll know that you can't be trusted and we'll be free to kill you or, at least, banish you."

Declan sat and waited while the others carried off all the fish. He was hot and sweaty and smelled like fish. He had managed to wash off his hands, but he wanted a bath and something to eat. He thought about trying to make some sort of shelter, but had no idea of how to go about it or what materials to use. As he sat thinking about the situation, he had come to the conclusion that Carpenter was right. He had no choice but to trust them. He had sought them out and tried to get Rogers to let him into their group. He couldn't fault Rogers for being careful. They had all traveled together and had gotten to know each other. Rogers was obviously high up in the decision making. As he was sitting, thinking, he saw a rather large woman coming toward him. He had no idea how tall she was, but at this distance, she appeared to be close to his height. *Damn, she's an amazon,* Declan thought. *She could snap most of the men in half!*

"Hello, I'm Emily," she said sweetly once she was close enough. She appeared to be carrying something wrapped in a leaf. "I brought you some fish," she said handing Declan the bundle.

"Thanks," Declan said as he took the package from Emily. He

hunkered down and carefully removed the leaf. Inside was quite a bit of the fish, already cooked. "Would you like some?" Declan offered.

"No, thanks," Emily responded. "That's yours. From what Keith Rogers said, you earned it."

15

"Is someone going to show me how to get a fire started?" Declan asked Emily as he ate.

"I don't know anything about that," Emily answered softly. She found a spot to sit and watch Declan eat. "Would you mind if we chat while you eat?" she asked.

"I don't mind," Declan said. He had come to the conclusion that cooked fish was better than raw and the company wasn't bad either.

"I hear you're related to Murdock, why didn't you go to him for help," Emily asked sweetly, "if you don't mind me asking?"

Declan looked at her while he ate. She didn't seem to be asking just to pry. He got the impression that she was actually curious. "I don't know if I should tell you," he said self-consciously. "It's kind of embarrassing."

"You can tell me," Emily answered sweetly. "I won't tell anyone." Declan believed her immediately.

"Truth is," Declan started haltingly, "it's my fault. I was acting immaturely, and Murdock called me on it."

"What happened?" Emily asked.

"I was acting like a spoiled child," Declan said finally after he had finished eating. "I embarrassed Murdock to others."

"Why would you do that?" Emily asked.

"I don't know what you've been told," Declan started, "but I used to be on the council. When I came back from visiting my sister's tomb, Palmer beat me. Doctor Harris took care of me, and when she was raped and beaten, I was very concerned and very angry. I said a bunch of sh—um, stuff I didn't mean." Declan's head had been bowing as he talked.

Emily didn't say anything for a long time. "Would you like some water?" she asked finally offering Declan a waterskin.

"Thanks," Declan said as he took the waterskin. He drank deeply from it and then handed it back to Emily.

"Who were you mad at?" Emily asked softly as she rehung the waterskin across her chest.

"Honestly, I don't know," Declan said softly. "I thought I might have been angry with Murdock or those that refused to let me see Doctor Harris. Just saying that makes me angry. Saying I'm angry with myself doesn't seem to cover it either. Maybe it's some combination of the two, but I'm not sure."

"You seem to be calmer, now," Emily observed, "why is that?"

Declan told the woman about the doe and how it had mesmerized him and how, when it ran away, it seemed to take a lot of his anger with it. He told her about stealing the fish and eating it raw the day before. They hadn't talked long, but Declan found that it was easy to be open with Emily.

"I need to get back before they send out a search party," Emily said sweetly after they had talked for about thirty minutes. "I did enjoy talking to you, though."

"I enjoyed talking to you as well," Declan said and found that he meant it. "You're very easy to talk to."

"I've been told that before," Emily said with a chuckle. "I'm sure someone will come out to help you. Hope I get to talk to you again... sometime soon!" Emily waved as she left.

Declan sat where he had eaten and somehow felt better after the conversation with Emily. He didn't seem to feel so dejected.

As he got to his feet, he wandered around looking under the trees for a soft spot to sleep. He had picked one with a lot of low hanging branches. As he lay down on the ground under the tree, he looked and could see little of the surroundings and was reassured that it would be hard to observe him. As he was finishing his selection, he saw Carpenter coming his way.

"Go gather some firewood," Carpenter told him, "and bring it over here."

Declan did as he was told and deposited the firewood close to his chosen sleeping spot.

"Now, pay attention," Carpenter said gruffly as he demonstrated how to make a fire. "I was told to give you this," Carpenter said as he stood to leave. He handed Declan a scabbard with a twelve-inch machete in it. "The rules remain the same. You're not to approach the camp. The machete is a loan. If you leave, leave it behind!" Carpenter left; back the way he had come.

For the next month, Murdock spent his time harvesting deer, tanning hides, fishing, gathering wood, and enjoying his family. He had long since come to the conclusion that this was the happiest he'd been since Rose died. More importantly, he was content. When he harvested deer, he took the two older children with him. It was a means to further their education and to spend time with them.

Mei Lee spent the time with the two younger children while repairing leather and getting cold weather clothing made for the older kids. Mei Lee felt that her life was very full. She had a husband that she loved and who returned that love. She had four children who, though trying at times, made her feel fulfilled. There were some things that would have made her life more comfortable, but they also would have unduly complicated her life and she flourished in a less complex lifestyle.

Murdock and Mei Lee trained the older children in martial arts, knife fighting, and the staff. Once in a while, Murdock and Mei Lee would spar. The children were excited to see them spar and marveled at the expertise of their parents. When they sparred, Murdock tried not to use his enhanced abilities. He wanted Mei Lee to feel like she had a chance of scoring on him.

After a particularly hard work out, Mei Lee collapsed on the soft grass, laughing. The family had been slightly downriver on an ad hoc picnic. Their laughter had been interrupted by Beron, Bridget, and their youngest cub.

"Doing?" Beron inquired telepathically of Murdock and Mei Lee. The Oomah, though they watched over the younger humans, tended to ignore them when it came to communication.

"Just relaxing," Murdock tried to explain. His mind was filled with confusion from the two adult Oomah.

"Much activity for relaxing," Beron responded.

"It's a human thing," Murdock tried to explain. *"It's more a change in daily activity that helps us relax."*

"Stay close," Murdock said aloud to the children who were playing with the cub under the watchful eye of Bridget and Mei Lee.

"Is this a social visit?" Murdock asked his large friend. He got both an affirmative and a negative.

"Elder passing soon," Beron responded and Murdock could tell that it bothered his friend emotionally.

"How soon?" Murdock asked after expressing sadness. He liked the old Oomah and knew he would miss him at the next spring gathering. Unbidden, memories of his own father's passing came to him and saddened him.

"Before long sleep," Beron responded reservedly.

Murdock knew, from his years of interaction with the Oomah, that there was something else on Beron's mind. The bears thought it was rude to ask for anything, especially from the humans, but were not opposed to accepting an offer.

"If there is something that you require of me, I will do it, if I can," Murdock offered solemnly.

"You express curiosity for our kind. Would like if you attend passing rite," Beron stated.

Murdock knew the bear creatures were immensely old, but hadn't given much thought to their rites, particularly when one of them passes. He had always felt that the Elder Oomah would be around long after he was gone.

"Shells wear out and need to replace," Beron responded mentally.

"Is it for my mate as well?" Murdock asked.

"Rite not for females to witness, but can attend after," Beron responded.

In the month since he left Murdock, Declan worked. He helped with anything that needed to be done without complaint. He still was an outcast, and therefore was not allowed to see or enter the camp. He wasn't even allowed in the immediate area of the camp. It bothered him some, but not enough to cause him to leave. He managed to build a shelter for himself under a large tree. He used existing boughs and any tree limbs he managed to cut using a hatchet that was loaned to him. The few members of the camp that had interaction with him had gone out of their way to make sure he understood that he owed them for everything, which bothered him.

"Hello in the camp," Emily Brooks called out as she neared his campsite. She had been to his camp several times and had become quite a good friend.

"Hi, Em," Declan answered back. He was tending to the fish he was cooking for himself. "You're just in time for dinner!"

"I'm not intruding, then?" Emily asked. She knew she wasn't, but still felt the need to ask.

"Not at all," Declan responded with a smile. "You know you're the only one to visit me."

"Is that a problem?" Emily asked as she found a place to sit on the ground close to the fire.

"It would be more of a problem if you stopped," Declan responded grinning at her.

"There's been talk about you," Emily said guardedly. "The people you have been working with have said good things about you."

"Really," Declan responded and shrugged. "I'm not doing anything to gain favor. I'm helping to be of some use and the guys have taught me a few things in return."

"Well, there's been talk about allowing you into the camp, making you one of us," Emily said. "Is that something you'd be interested in?"

Declan looked at her with a questioning look. "Honestly, I don't know. I've been out here so long I'm not sure I'd know how to act. Is it something that others vote on?"

"Our leader listens to all the people you have been helping, but the leader makes the final decision," Emily informed him.

"So, I can be voted out as well?" Declan asked. "I'm not sure I'd like to live with that, knowing that someone gets upset with me for something and I get voted out."

"It doesn't work that way," Emily tried to explain. "Once you're in, you're in. Issues derived from the interaction of people, in close proximity, are settled in other ways."

"Let me think about it," Declan said as he handed Emily some of the cooked fish.

Emily accepted the fish and picked at it for a while.

"Is there something else?" Declan asked between bites after a long silence.

"If you accept, I hope we will remain friends," Emily said with a touch of sadness in her voice.

"We'll always be friends," Declan said with a grin. "Will I meet your leader?" he asked after a short pause.

"I'm certain of it," Emily said, perking up a little and starting to eat.

"I suppose I would, considering the small number of people in your camp," Declan said around bites of the fish. As he looked at Emily, he got the feeling that there was more to it. "What is it you're not telling me?" he asked finally.

"I'm the leader," Emily said quietly after a long pause.

Declan was shocked and had to fight back the feeling of being deceived. Emily hadn't given him any reason to distrust her.

"How much of what I told you did you tell the others?" he asked somewhat petulantly.

"I told them nothing," Emily said quietly. "I assumed our conversations were confidential and have kept it to myself. As the leader, I couldn't allow someone untrustworthy into the camp and had to rely on my own assessment of your motives."

"What did the others say?" Declan asked in a surly tone.

"They said you were weak, and they didn't want you around," Emily answered meekly, "then they got to know you and you changed their minds."

"And you?" Declan asked warily.

"I had no preconceptions," Emily stated. "I didn't know you and you never did anything to me when you were on the council. That first night I brought you something to eat, I needed to know more about you. I got to know you and we became friends and I wish that friendship to continue."

Declan looked at her and could see that she was being honest with him. He thought about all that had transpired over the last month and finally smiled at her.

"When you've finished eating, we can leave for your camp," Declan said with a smile.

"Are we still friends?" Emily asked, concerned.

"Is our friendship contingent on entry into your camp?" Declan asked.

Emily hung her head a little. "No, you're welcome even if you can't forgive me for keeping some things from you."

"I meant what I said, Em," Declan answered. "We're friends. I understand that you had the others to think about and did what you had to."

Emily brightened significantly and ate the fish heartily. Declan had already finished his and was dumping water on the fire.

"Is it far to the camp?" he asked as he stirred the coals to make sure they were out.

"Not far," Emily said finishing her portion of the fish. "Less than a mile, I think."

It didn't take Emily and Declan long to get close to the encampment. As they approached, a guard stopped them. After Emily identified herself, they were allowed to pass. It was dusk, but Declan could see a series of ladders and suspension bridges directing them to a cave entrance in the side of the ridge. They were stopped only once more as they approached the base of the first ladder. Again, Emily was identified and allowed to pass, with no regard given to Declan.

As the pair climbed toward the cave entrance, Declan could hear wood creaking and ropes tightening. They passed two more guards, but weren't challenged. As the pair crossed a heavy wooden bridge to the cave, two guards appeared from either side of the entrance. Once they were satisfied that it was Emily, the pair stepped off the bridge into the huge cave. Declan could see a few fires and noticed the smoke went to the ceiling and passed out the entrance. Emily led Declan to the rear of the main room. As they walked, Declan saw all the smaller rooms off the main. At the back of the cave, Emily took Declan's hand as she started down a smaller tunnel.

"This tunnel gets a little treacherous, so watch your step," Emily cautioned Declan as they started down.

Declan heard her, but was trying to take in as much of what he was seeing as he could. At the bottom of the smaller tunnel, Emily stopped, and both carefully stepped down on a wooden step, which surprised Declan. As the pair walked the length of the room, Declan was glancing around at the smaller rooms, trying to not look inside them. At the end of the room, they turned again and down another small tunnel.

"Where did all this come from?" Declan asked as they entered the bathing room, as Emily called it.

"We found it," Emily stated. "We added the wooden steps and the wooden bridge, but the rest is pretty much the way we found it."

Declan walked over to the first good sized pool and put his fingers into it and found it to contain hot water.

"I brought you here, first, so you can take a bath," Emily said quietly, "that being one of the stipulations to your joining us."

"What are you saying?" Declan asked good-naturedly with a little chuckle.

"I'm saying you need a bath," Emily responded in kind.

"You mean, now?" Declan asked looking around for some privacy, but found none.

"Yes, now," Emily said with mock sternness.

"I'd love to," Declan said, "but I need a little privacy."

"Why? Are you hiding something?" Emily asked playfully. "Besides, I need a bath, too."

Emily started disrobing. Declan turned his back to her and started disrobing. He was trying to hurry so he could get into the water before Emily. He managed to enter the water first and heard Emily enter right behind him. Once in the water, he moved across the pool from her.

"What's wrong?" Emily asked. "Are you shy?"

"Somewhat," Declan responded self-consciously. "I don't want to presume on our friendship."

"Don't worry about it," Emily said dismissively. "I'm usually shy as well, but not with you. It's rare to find the baths empty so you'll have to get over it, I did...somewhat. While we are on the subject, you'll be sleeping in my chambers for the time being. Are you okay with that?"

"That's something I hadn't anticipated. Are there no other rooms available?" Declan asked as he felt his face flush.

"None, all the rooms are taken by various combinations of people. Privacy is at a premium," Emily informed him. "Usually, all the people bunking together get permission from all those involved on a daily basis. You could spend one night with two or three people and the next night be sleeping with a whole new set. Who you sleep with doesn't seem to matter around here. Most people just sleep in the same room."

"So, do I need to get permission from someone else to spend the night with you?" Declan asked. He saw Emily get pensive.

"Just me," Emily stated. "My second-in-command was sleeping with me for a few nights, but has found others to bunk with." As they talked, Emily had moved closer to Declan and noticed that he didn't move away. "There are times that I need to cuddle, and no one is available," she said quietly.

"I don't want to intrude on you or take advantage of the situation," Declan tried to assure her.

"I understand," Emily stated flatly. "Now, come over here and wash my back and I'll return the favor," she said as she turned her back to him.

Declan said nothing and moved closer to wash her back. When he was finished, he turned around and she washed his back. When they were done, Emily had moved closer and both were quiet, reveling in the soothing hot water. She did notice that Declan didn't move away from her. When they were finished bathing, they both got out and dressed.

"Where do you sleep?" Declan asked as they climbed up from the "bathing room".

"I'll show you," Emily said quietly. As they entered the main room, Emily took the lead once more and led him to the room closest to the wall across from the tunnel to the "bathing room". "This is it!" she said cheerfully. "Not much furniture, yet, but it's out of the weather." She was trying to be as cheerful as she could.

"I am a little tired. Would you mind if I went to sleep?" Declan asked quietly.

"I don't mind. Do you want company, or would you rather go to sleep alone?" Emily asked. "I can always join you after you're asleep."

"I have trouble sleeping in strange places," Declan started after briefly thinking about it. "I think I'd be more comfortable if you joined me. I am, after all, very comfortable with you." He saw Emily's expression lighten as he spoke.

Declan found a spot on the floor and lay down. He moved around a bit to get as comfortable as possible on the bare stone floor. Emily got on the floor next to him, laying her head in the hollow of his shoulder. Her back was against him. Declan placed his free hand on her hip.

"Comfortable?" Emily asked quietly.

"Very," Declan responded quietly into her hair.

Emily took his hand from her hip and pulled it to her chest, their fingers intertwined. "So am I, now."

It had been a month since Freeman had been killed. At the transport pod, the men would harvest fish and then spend the majority of the night beating and raping the women. While the men were gone harvesting fish, the women would spend that time tending each other's cuts and contusions.

It was daylight and the men had gone downstream. Kimberly

and Heather were doing their best to bring Phylicia back to consciousness after an unusually brutal night. Kimberly was trying to rinse some of the cuts on Phylicia's face. She could see that Phylicia's eyes were swollen shut and the bruises on her cheeks were a deep purple.

"We have to do something about the situation," Kimberly said to Heather. "I don't think Phylicia can take much more of this." She could see Heather's bruises and knew her own were probably just as bad.

"What can we do?" Heather asked with a disheartened tone. "Phylicia brings it on herself. She needs to keep her mouth shut and let them do as they please. Her talking back is what angers Palmer."

"It's the only way she has of resisting," Kimberly explained.

"Maybe, but Palmer will either break her or kill her," Heather said. "Maybe both," she resumed after looking sadly at Phylicia's damaged face.

"We have to do something," Kimberly insisted.

"I'm open to suggestions," Heather retorted. "We can't carry her, and I see no way of escaping. The men don't leave us alone long enough to even let us recover. So, I see no way."

"It'll probably be worse if one of us is out of commission," Kimberly said resignedly.

While on their way home, Murdock telepathically relayed to Mei Lee what Beron had told him about the Elder Oomah. He felt her sadness as if it were his own.

"*We have to be ready to go to the rite at a moment's notice,*" Mei Lee responded telepathically. "*Any insight on what the rite entails?*"

"*I got no hints from Beron on the subject,*" Murdock replied. "*Did Bridget say anything to you about it?*"

"Not a word," Mei Lee responded. *"Our only alternative, as I see it, is to be ready for anything."*

The rest of the trip home was uneventful. Once at the cabin, Mei Lee, with the help of the older children, got the younger ones bathed and in bed while Murdock emptied the cart and brought in enough wood for the night. Mei Lee fixed Murdock and herself something to eat while the older children went to bed, since they had bathed with their younger siblings. After eating, the couple bathed and went to bed.

"Have you given any thought to Annie or Declan?" Mei Lee asked her husband as they lay in the darkened cabin. "I liked Annie and was getting used to having her around."

"Not recently, I haven't. Beron is keeping an eye on Declan, to make sure he doesn't get himself killed. Personally, I was thinking about making the rounds to all the newcomers to make sure they are getting settled and preparing for winter," Murdock said quietly. He re-situated himself to look at the top of her head. "Are you missing people being around?"

"I sometimes wonder if we're too isolated from others," Mei Lee responded after some thought. "We do have children that will have to interact with other people, at some point."

"I'm not worried about having others around, for myself, but I do see your point about the kids," Murdock responded.

"We do have quite a few deer skins," Mei Lee said after a brief pause. "Maybe the others would be willing to trade something for them. They are, after all, going to need them."

"Are you saying this should be a family trip?" Murdock asked.

"I would like it to be," Mei Lee responded, "but I will acquiesce to your judgment on the matter."

Murdock smiled. "Mei, I have never known anyone like you!"

Mei Lee rolled over to look him in the face. "Nor I anyone like you, my husband," she replied as she kissed him.

~

Emily awoke and found that Declan hadn't moved at all during the night. She was still holding his hand and clutching it to her chest and found that she seemed to be more rested than usual. She disengaged her fingers from his slowly so as not to disturb him.

"How did you sleep?" Declan asked quietly as she was starting to get up.

"How long have you been awake?" she asked quietly. "I slept better than I thought I would." She had rolled over to face him. He was shorter than she liked and thinner than she preferred, but he was, in her opinion, handsome. She knew he probably wouldn't have any trouble finding a permanent mate amongst the other females, but the thought of that possibility made her a little jealous and she wondered at that.

"Not long. I probably woke up just before you did," Declan answered smiling at her. "I used to be a sound sleeper, but not so much anymore. That's what sleeping out in the open will do to you."

Emily put her hand on his stomach as she rested her head in her other hand.

"You didn't move at all during the night," she said. She could hear the others starting their daily routine. "We should get up so we can get the day started."

Without a word, Declan pulled her to him and kissed her deeply. Emily didn't resist, at first. After a few seconds, she gently pushed him away.

"Don't do that unless you mean it," she warned sternly. "I'm not one to be trifled with!"

"I didn't think you were," Declan said in all seriousness. "I'm sorry you didn't enjoy it!"

"I didn't say it wasn't enjoyable or unwanted," Emily responded seriously. "If I kiss someone that way, it means something to me!"

"It meant something to me, and it was meant to be taken seriously," Declan said.

"Excuse me, Emily," Keith Roger's voice came from outside the room. "We have a major issue that needs to be attended to!"

"Be there in a minute," Emily yelled back. "We'll discuss this later!" she said sternly, but quietly, to Declan. It wasn't long before she was up, rearranged her clothes, and out the doorway of the room.

Declan got up after he heard Emily's voice retreat from the doorway. As he got up and stretched, he straightened his own clothes before emerging. He did get a few strange looks from others as he made his way to the upper level. As he walked toward the cave entrance, he caught a few strange looks from more of the people. By the time he reached the entrance, he was quite self-conscious. When he was about one hundred feet from the entrance, he saw a man talking to Emily. The man was a little older, of a larger build, and was a little shorter than he. Declan recognized him, Keith Rogers. As Declan was passing, Rogers gripped his upper arm and guided him toward Emily so he would be engaged in the discussion.

"Is the hunting party back, yet?" Emily asked Rogers as Declan joined the conversation. To Declan, "Declan, this is Keith Rogers, my second-in-command."

"We've met," Declan said as he offered Keith his hand.

"No, they aren't back yet," Keith responded to Emily. He looked at Declan with a glare and didn't take Declan's offered hand.

"Careful, Keith," Emily warned, catching Rogers' glare and feeling the tension between the two men. "Declan has done nothing, so you be nice to him!"

"What's this all about?" Declan asked.

"Quite a few people have their nose out of joint over you being here," Keith said tersely.

Declan looked sadly at Emily. "You told me I was voted in," he said, and Emily could see he was disconcerted.

"That isn't what I said," Emily defended. "The people you've been helping have said lots of good things about you, and I did make the decision to allow you into our group."

"There is a faction, led by Raymond Tutt, looking for a reason to take away the leadership from Emily," Keith explained.

"For me, he can have it," Emily retorted. "I've asked for very little and given a lot to this group!"

"I know, Em," Keith replied trying to calm her, "but Tutt having the leadership, at this point, would be a major disaster!"

"Who is this Ray Tutt?" Declan asked. "That name doesn't sound familiar to me."

"He was the contractor for the community building at the pod," Keith said to Declan, "and he blames you for two weeks of nightmares. I think he's being a superstitious ass."

Declan blanched at hearing about the nightmares. "I had nothing to do with his nightmares!"

"I know," Keith said. "It's ridiculous to think anyone can give someone else nightmares!"

"If it will help, I'll leave and go back to camping under the trees," Declan said to Emily. Keith was about to say something and became silent and turned to look at him. Emily's mouth was agape.

"That sounds like a good idea," Emily said excitedly, smiling. "I'll join you!"

"Now, wait," Keith said pleading, "will both of you calm down a little? I need a second or two to think. Em, tell me you weren't serious!"

"As serious as a heart attack," Emily said sternly. "Keith, why don't you gather everyone together that gave the go-ahead for Declan and persuade them to twist some arms, or break a few heads, or whatever it is you do, and when you get it all handled, let me know. I'll be with Declan."

Emily stormed toward the cave entrance with Keith in her wake trying to plead with her not to go. Those who saw her coming quickly got out of her way. Declan followed along behind them. He could see that she had a good mad going on, about what exactly he couldn't be sure, and she wasn't about to have it dowsed quite so easily. Emily didn't slow down until she was back at Declan's campsite. Keith almost ran into her when she stopped suddenly. Declan had followed, but was back far enough that any sudden stops would be avoided easily.

"You can just march your ass back to that ungrateful bunch and tell them I resign," Emily yelled when she stopped walking and turned on Keith.

"Now, Em, calm down! Let me see if I can get the others calmed down. Are you going to stay here?" Keith asked. Declan could see that Keith was panicked at the thought that Emily would quit.

"Are we?" Emily asked Declan sweetly. Declan noticed the marked change in her tone when she spoke to him. So did Keith.

"I'm not planning on moving any time soon," Declan responded. After a short pause he added, "Unless, of course, Emily decides she wants to move somewhere else." He managed a sheepish grin at Keith and a quick wink to Emily. He saw Emily grin a tiny bit.

"Declan, in all the excitement, I forgot to ask if you wanted company," Emily said sweetly. "I'm truly sorry for assuming or imposing."

"I didn't take it that way," Declan responded softly. "As I have told you so many times before, you are always welcome."

"In that case, what do you think of moving the camp?" Emily asked.

"I don't know," Declan said, playing to her remarks, "I was starting to be comfortable here. Honestly hadn't thought about it much."

Keith first looked to Declan and then to Emily, trying to figure out if either was serious. All he got back was grins, the kind that gave him an unsettled feeling in his stomach. Without another word, he turned and went back to the cave.

Emily was having trouble holding in the laughter long enough to let Keith get out of earshot. Once she was sure, she started laughing, heartily. She was laughing so hard that Declan had a hard time not laughing.

"Serves him right," Emily said as her laughter wound down. "I took the job of leading that…that mob, on his suggestion." Emily started to storm around. "I took the job because I was truly trying to help as many as I could. I was trying to make things better for everyone." She started flapping her arms around in wild gestures. "You have no idea how many hours of sleep I lost worrying about the job. How many times I made sure everyone had eaten and drank before I had any!" Declan could hear her voice start to tremble a little. Her storming had slowed to pacing. Suddenly she stopped. "I'm sorry if I got your hopes up about joining the group, Declan!" She crumpled to the ground where she was standing and started sobbing.

"It's okay, Em," Declan said softly as he came over and sat next to her to comfort her. "I understand, more than most might think." He touched her shoulder gently. It was then that she threw herself into his lap and started sobbing uncontrollably. All Declan could think to do was to just be there and let her get it out of her system.

16

A s Murdock was packing the cart for the family trip to the other encampments, he had the idea of loading a couple of axes along with the extra deer hides and a hindquarter of smoked venison. He had also packed Rose's machetes and waterskin, as a gift for Declan. Beron had kept him apprised of Declan's situation, and he had seen the mental vision of Declan, and some woman, sleeping under a tree, away from others, for the past couple of nights. He didn't know if Declan had any tools, but Murdock wasn't opposed to loaning him some.

Beron had also shown him where all the other newcomers were located, and it pleased him to see that the group he had helped were still off the first ridge. That meant that Annie Cooper and Doctor Harris would probably be where he had left them. Once the cart was loaded, Mei Lee and all the children took up their positions for traveling. As they left, Murdock pulled the cart while the two older children took up point. The two younger children rode in the cart and Mei Lee either walked or rode as it suited her. He had opted for a more leisurely pace, at least to start off. This allowed him to communicate with Mei Lee telepathically and impart to her all that Beron had shown him.

"It's nice that Declan has a woman interested in him," she replied telepathically after the information was imparted to her.

"I'm interested in seeing if Declan has dealt with his issues," Murdock replied.

"If he hasn't, any relationship will be fraught with problems," Mei Lee finished his thought.

"To say the least," Murdock added.

After several hours, they had reached the river crossing. After a short rest, Murdock levitated everyone and the cart over the river.

"On!" he shouted, and Mei Lee and the two older children climbed aboard the cart. They were settled in seconds and Murdock started his ground-covering trot. They were at the top of the ridge in short order.

After checking for possible observers, Murdock levitated the cart, while Mei Lee levitated the older children and herself, down from the ridge. Once at the bottom, everyone resumed their positions on the cart and, once everyone was settled, Murdock resumed his trot. A few hours later, the Murdock family reached the top of the second ridge and, same as before, descended after checking for observers and finding none. At the base of the ridge, Murdock and Mei Lee set up a midday camp.

As he walked back to the caves, Keith Rogers wasn't pleased. It was about midday of the third day of Emily's resignation and he had refused to tell the others that she had resigned. He liked the perks of being the power behind the throne and wasn't about to give them up easily. He felt that Emily was being unreasonable, and he blamed Declan for turning her head. Until Declan had come, he had Emily under some control. Now, things were a mess and he deplored political messes.

As he approached the encampment, he saw Raymond Tutt and fifty of his followers packing up equipment.

"Where are you going?" Keith asked Tutt as he approached.

"Anywhere but here," Tutt said sharply.

"Is there anything I can say or do to change your mind?" Keith asked, trying not to seem like he was pleading.

"As long as Declan is around, we won't be," Tutt yelled. "No one here wants to experience those nightmares again and no one had them before he came around!"

"That notion is ridiculous," Keith said vehemently. "No one can give you nightmares. That isn't possible!"

"You haven't talked to the others that were on that ridge with Declan and me, so how would you know?" Tutt snapped back at the smaller man. "We have warned you and everyone else that keeping him around is dangerous!"

"I agree you have disturbed a lot of people with your suspicions, but they have no basis in reality," Keith explained. "Since you've made up your minds, how can we contact you?"

"Once we decide on a place, we'll send someone back with that information," Tutt explained irately, "until then you're on your own!"

"Dammit," Keith said, more to himself than anyone else, as he stood there watching the procession of heavily laden people headed away from the camp and away from the river.

Declan watched as Emily paced back and forth, ranting. He had listened to Keith while he tried to convince or cajole Emily back to the caves and the leadership. It was the same arguments he had heard four times a day for the last three days. At one point, yesterday, he had seen Emily get so angry that she grabbed Keith by the front of his shirt and lifted him off the ground, one handed. Seeing the feat had impressed him. He knew he couldn't have accomplished it.

"Em, let's go for a walk," Declan said finally, with an upbeat tone. He knew that she had a lot of nervous energy that needed to be burned off.

"Why would I do that?" Emily snapped at him without thinking.

"Because you need to get away from the pressure Keith is applying and he won't follow us if we go to the river," Declan explained calmly. "Besides, I want to go for a walk with you!"

Emily was about to protest, but thought better of it. She held out her hand for him to take it as she smiled. Declan took her hand and led her to the river at an angle that would put them at the river by the ridge. Most of the people that went to the river went by a path that would lead them a fair distance downriver from the ridge. He had no idea why he went that way. His intent was just to walk with Emily, hand-in-hand. He liked the feeling he got whenever he held her hand or kissed her and felt the need for more of it.

It wasn't long before he heard children laughing at the river ahead of them. He stopped suddenly and Emily saw him blanch.

"What is it?" she asked concerned.

"I think Murdock is at the river," Declan said to her quietly.

"How do you know it's Murdock?" Emily asked quietly.

"I hear children laughing and Murdock has the only children here, so far," Declan explained.

"Is that a problem?" Emily asked. "I would like to meet him and his family."

"I'm not sure that would be a good idea," Declan said haltingly.

"Oh, sure it is," Emily exclaimed while pulling him along.

Declan managed to stop Emily from dragging him just before they cleared the cover of the trees close to the bank.

"You don't understand, Em," Declan protested. "You don't know how dangerous Murdock is. I'd try, but I'm not sure I could defend you if Murdock decided to —"

"If Murdock decided to...what?" came Murdock's voice behind Declan and Emily.

They both jumped and spun around to face him. Emily had her machete out and ready.

"You won't need that," Murdock said calmly, looking between the pair. "Hello, Declan. Who is this?" Murdock asked, indicating Emily.

"Emily Brooks," Emily said with a wry grin. She sized up the much smaller man in front of her, didn't see that he was any threat, put away her machete, and extended her hand with a smile.

"Kevin Murdock," Murdock said as he took her large hand and shook it, firmly. "Nice firm grip you have there, Mizz Brooks!"

"Everything okay?" a female voice came from behind Declan and Emily.

Declan closed his eyes as if he were in pain, tilted his head slightly back, and slumped his shoulders. Emily turned slowly to see a very small and petite-looking Asian female with a bow at full draw. To Emily, the arrow looked huge, mainly because she was looking at it from the business end.

"Hello, Mei Lee," Declan said, without turning.

"Mizz Brooks, this is my wife, Mei Lee," Murdock said. "It's okay, Mei," he said to Mei Lee, who slowly let off on the bow and replaced the arrow in her quiver and slung the bow over her shoulder.

"Mizz Brooks? Mei Lee Murdock," Mei Lee said as she walked forward to the bigger woman.

"Em or Emily, please," Emily said as she stuck out her hand for the much smaller woman.

"Em," Mei Lee said with a smile taking the huge hand of the amazon.

"How have you been Declan?" Murdock asked jovially, clapping the man firmly on his shoulder almost knocking Declan to the ground. "Hey, I like her! She has good reflexes and good instincts!"

"We were about to have something to eat," Mei Lee said to

Emily with a friendly smile. "We'd like it if you two would join us." She turned and started toward the river, assuming Emily and Declan would follow.

Emily and Declan followed Mei Lee into their campsite and were met by the two older children, machetes drawn.

"It's okay, children," Mei Lee said as she entered. Emily saw the children put their machetes away.

Emily had the impression that she and Declan at no time had the upper hand in this encounter and was glad it went as it did. She and Declan walked over to a log close to the fire and sat.

"What was that argument all about?" Murdock asked after they were seated and given a skewer of hot meat.

Emily's mouth dropped open. "I wasn't aware we were being observed," Emily said, after a pause and maintaining her friendly grin. "How long had you been there?"

"Awhile," Murdock answered cryptically, "long enough to know that it had something to do with the leadership of a group, and long enough to see that Declan was concerned."

"I didn't see you there," Emily responded.

"You weren't supposed to," Murdock stated flatly. "So, Declan, tell us how things are going."

While the group ate, Declan informed Murdock and Mei Lee of his life since he'd left. Emily added in her role in the recent events and of her assuming the leadership of a group of one hundred people that had left the transport pod after the fall of Phylicia. Murdock and Mei Lee sat and listened intently while the couple talked. By the time they had finished eating, all the information was revealed.

Murdock sat in silence for some time. "Do you really want the leadership, Emily?" he asked finally.

"I don't know," Emily responded honestly. "I do like helping others, when I can, but I don't like the expectation of not having a life away from the leadership position."

"Do you understand that you can't please everyone?" Murdock asked pointedly.

"Of course, I also know that I can't hold people together when they don't really want to stay together," Emily explained.

"Well, then, you have your answer," Murdock explained.

"I don't get it," Declan said.

"He means that I can either lead or stay out of it, but each has its price," Emily said. Murdock grinned coyly.

"In my opinion, you don't need to lead everyone by the nose," Murdock expounded. "If they can't figure out that they need to get water to drink and want someone to tell them to go get it, then the leader needs to step back until they figure it out. You aren't doing them any favors by doing their thinking for them. That would allow you to have a life other than being the leader all the time."

Emily nodded, seeing the wisdom in Murdock's statement. "Do you think I have been doing too much of the thinking for everyone?" she asked finally.

"I don't know," Murdock answered. "Only you can decide if you're hampering them by doing too much for them."

Mei Lee had been seeing to the children, allowing the three adults to talk without interruption. She had noticed that it was getting close to sundown and had sent the older children to gather firewood and fill waterskins. She also reminded her husband telepathically of the lateness of the day.

"You two can stay here tonight, if you want to," Murdock offered. He arose and motioned to Declan to follow him to the back of the cart. Once there, Murdock dug out Rose's machetes, waterskin, and hatchet. "These belonged to your sister and I think she would want you to have them," He told Declan as he handed them to him. "Do you have feelings for this woman?" he asked as he burdened Declan with the weapons.

"Yes, I do," Declan stated.

"Then stay with her. Don't let anyone or anything get in the way of that. Do all you can to make sure she feels how important she is to you. Just some free advice," Murdock said as he shrugged.

"Thank you for the weapons," Declan said quietly, "and the advice. It's much appreciated!"

"What have you been sleeping on?" Murdock asked.

"The ground, it's all we have, right now," Declan responded sheepishly.

"I thought so," Murdock said as he dug out several hides and gave them to Declan. "You can make a quick shelter with a couple of them and lay on some and cover yourself with the rest. There are five hides, so that should work for a while."

"Thanks! I'll make sure to clean them up before returning them," Declan said, expressing his appreciation.

"No need," Murdock said seriously. "Consider them a wedding present!"

"But we aren't married," Declan corrected.

"Really? If you love her with everything you have within you and she returns it, then you're married. That is the way it was with me and your sister." Declan heard Murdock's voice break a little at the thought of Rose. "Marriage is more than a piece of paper. A piece of paper can't keep you together and you have a very long wait for anything resembling an Earth-style marriage. By the way, you sleep with the fur side against you."

While Murdock and Declan were at the cart talking, Mei Lee took the opportunity to talk privately with Emily.

"Do you care for Declan?" Mei Lee asked.

"Very much," Emily responded. "He listens when I talk and really cares about me. Something I haven't had before."

"He hasn't had it either, I suspect," Mei Lee informed. "From what I know, he's had a very hard life, before coming here, and it made him tougher than he thinks. He has some issues, but then, who doesn't? Did he tell you why he left us?"

"Yes, he did. He said he was angry with others and himself," Emily said. She saw Mei Lee's eyebrows rise.

"Then he's learned to be honest with himself," Mei Lee remarked.

∼

It had taken Murdock and Declan no time at all to set up a low tent and lay out the hides for sleeping. Murdock, Mei Lee, and all the children slept under the cart, with a hide tented from one side, while Declan and Emily slept in their tent, a short distance from the fire. Declan and Emily cuddled together under the hides.

"The Murdocks seem nice," Emily said quietly.

"It's funny. I didn't think they were the last time I was with them," Declan responded.

"You were angry the last time you were around them. You're not that way, now." Emily snuggled her back into Declan. "These hides sure make it cozy!"

"You make it cozy," Declan said. Emily could hear he was smiling by the sound of his whisper and responded by patting his hand, which was on her hip.

"Is that where your hand goes?" Emily asked, whispering. She gently took his hand and placed it between her breasts, fingers interlocked, hugging it to her. "Better?" she asked quietly.

"No," Declan whispered. Declan started to sit up a little and Emily rolled over to look at him. As she rolled towards him, he kissed her, deeply, passionately, and she kissed him back the same way. "That's better!" he said when the kiss was finished.

Emily gently pushed him back as she rose up. She laid her head on his chest and he stroked her head gently. "I love you, Declan," she whispered, putting as much immediacy into the statement as you can when whispering. "You make me feel like I belong!"

"You do, my dear. You belong with me," Declan whispered.

He fell asleep with Emily's head on his chest, stroking her head lovingly.

The next morning, Emily was up before Declan. She wandered around gathering firewood. She was joined by Murdock's eldest son. He had startled her by coming into her line of sight and she hadn't heard a sound.

"Good morning," Emily cheerfully greeted him. "I'm Emily."

"Andrew," the boy said quietly; so quietly that Emily had to strain to hear him. "So, you're my new aunt?"

That made Emily blush a little. "I'm hoping to be," she said cheerfully.

"You are, or so I am given to assume," the boy said with a chuckle. "What do I call you?" he asked seriously.

"Emily works for me," Emily said, a bit taken aback. She saw his head pop back a little and turn a little.

"Mother and Father are awake," Andrew said without turning toward the camp.

Emily said nothing. This boy was a puzzle. In fact, to her, the entire family was a puzzle. She was chagrined that Kevin had surprised her and Declan on the trail, the previous day, and neither had heard Mei Lee come from behind. To add to it, here was a boy not more than four asking adult questions and carrying on an adult conversation. He was also armed. It hadn't registered, the previous day, the two older children were armed and ready when the adults entered the camp and they seemed to walk around unsupervised and comfortable in the wild. Also, the boy had heard his parents in the camp at a distance he shouldn't have been able to hear anything, but he had heard it above her talking to him. She had gathered an armload of wood and took it to the campsite.

"Morning, Em," Murdock said cheerfully as she entered the camp. "It looks like you were up early!"

"Not really," Emily replied. "I woke up and wanted to do something to help out."

"It's appreciated," Murdock replied, "but that's Andy's and Chun's job."

"Sorry, I wasn't aware," Emily apologized.

"It's okay. I'm sure they won't hold it against you for too long," Murdock chuckled.

"Please don't punish them on my account," Emily pleaded.

"Punish them? Why would I do that?" Murdock asked, shocked.

"I was doing part of their chores. I thought—" Emily realized that she had made an assumption about Murdock that was unwarranted.

"You think I punish my kids? I may instruct them, but never punish them." Murdock explained. "Can I ask you something personal?" Murdock continued after an uncomfortable pause in the conversation.

"Sure, but I reserve the right to not answer." Emily looked at him, dreading an embarrassing question.

"How tall are you?"

"Six-four, the last time I checked."

Murdock got up, went to the cart, and got out his bow. Emily had followed him.

"Can you draw that?" he asked, handing her his bow.

Emily grasped the bow and tried to pull it back. She managed only a couple of inches of deflection. She tried again and managed a three-inch deflection.

"I'm impressed," Murdock said. "Most people can't pull it at all!"

"What's going on?" Declan asked as he joined Murdock and Emily.

"Nothing much," Emily responded.

"Just seeing if Emily could pull my bow," Murdock answered. He then handed Mei Lee's bow to Declan. "Can you pull that?" he asked Declan.

Declan grasped the bow and pulled it back almost to full draw before he started shaking a little. He let it down and returned it to Murdock.

"Have you decided what to do about the leadership position?" Murdock asked the couple.

"I think I'll keep it, if I can have it on my terms," Emily said.

"What do you think, Declan?" Murdock asked.

"I think Emily can take it if she wants. I'll support her decision." Emily smiled at Declan.

"What's the problem the members of your group have with Declan?" Murdock asked.

"From what I understand, some think he had something to do with giving people nightmares," Emily answered.

"You mean recently?" Murdock quipped.

"No, when he was working on the community building at the pod," Emily explained.

"That would be impossible for Declan to do," Murdock said.

"I know that. Too bad I can't get the rest to see it that way," Emily said.

"So, what are you going to do?" Murdock asked. "I take it you two want to be together and they don't want Declan around, correct?"

"Essentially," Emily said. "I was hoping to live with Declan in the cave. It has enough room and it has a spa for bathing. We spent a lot of time securing it and it would be a shame to do without the amenities, but if we must, we must."

"You didn't answer my question," Murdock said good-naturedly.

Emily looked to Declan who looked to Emily. Neither spoke up. "I guess we don't know," Emily said finally.

"Why don't me and Declan escort you back and make your decision final," Murdock said, "while we see what is available for you two. If nothing else, we can start a cabin, after breakfast, of course!"

"That sounds like a good idea," Mei Lee piped in, handing

everyone a skewer of hot meat. She was up and about for some time and Murdock was the only one who noticed.

∼

Unbeknown to the others, Murdock had been communicating with Beron since the night before to see if there was a smaller cave closer to the river with a spa inside it for Declan and Emily. He was told that there would be, in a day or two and where it would be located. He had toyed with the idea of taking the couple to his cabin, but was unsure of Declan and Emily.

∼

"Why did you want me to draw Mei Lee's bow?" Declan asked while they ate.

"Wanted to see if you were strong enough to draw it," Murdock explained. "Living out here is not going to be easy and you need to hunt deer for food, clothing, and anything else you may need." He looked at how Declan and Emily were dressed and was not too dismayed. They both, at least, wore jeans, athletic shoes, and a kind of denim shirt. All of which would be fine for summer, but when winter came, they'd have to have something warmer. "Have you learned to hunt deer?" he asked either of the pair. Both shook their head to indicate the negative. "You'll both have to learn. I'm not opposed to teaching you. Mei Lee can help as well. She has become quite a good leather worker."

Emily looked at Mei Lee's buckskin dress. "Who made your dress?"

"It was a group effort," Mei Lee explained. "Rose, Kevin, and I all worked on it. Kevin made my boots. He also made the bows, quivers, and all the arrows."

"Impressive," Emily said in awe. "Where do you two live?"

"They have a very nice cabin," Declan said excitedly. "If

Kevin would help me with a cabin, I'm sure it would be just as nice!"

"We shall see what we find," Murdock explained. "If we have to help build a cabin, I'll need to go home and bring back a few tools."

"Did you build the cart?" Emily asked. "I'm sure we'll need something similar."

"When I was the leader of the first group," Mei Lee explained, "I had a few people work out how to build one with materials available."

"If either of you want to try to copy it, feel free," Murdock said.

After eating breakfast, Murdock prepared himself for escorting Emily to her group. As he did so, he was pleased to see Declan trying to outfit himself with Rose's equipment. Emily sported two twelve-inch machetes and a filled waterskin.

"You're starting to look like you belong here," Murdock said to Declan with a grin and slight chuckle, handing him one of the extra spears.

"Am I really going to need this?" Declan asked as he looked at the spear.

"The important thing you need to remember is, if you need something, it's nice to have it," Murdock explained. "There are beasties out there that would love to have you for lunch. Having that may deter them from that notion. Besides, having something and not needing it is not an issue."

As they were about to leave, Murdock kissed Mei Lee and kids good-bye and admonished the children to mind their mother. Murdock took point as the three people entered the cover of the trees.

"Training may as well start now," Murdock said quietly.

"Both of you watch where you step and try to be as quiet as possible. That means no talking, as well."

As the three moved toward the location of the group, Murdock was watching all around. Every time one of the newbies would step on a twig and make it snap, or their foot would slide on a rock, or drag their foot while stepping, a cringe would go through him. He knew he had to be patient, but found it difficult.

Once at Declan's campsite, Emily proceeded toward the caves while Murdock and Declan looked around the campsite.

"Why do you insist on quiet when we travel?" Declan asked.

"It was practice. If you can move quietly, the game won't know you're there. If they don't perceive any danger, it's easier to take one," Murdock explained. "Most people can't shoot a primitive bow accurately much past twenty yards, and that takes lots of practice. That means you have to get close. The key to getting close is—"

"Quiet," Declan finished nodding and grinning.

"You also have to be mindful of smells, humans and others, wind direction, predators, a thousand things. When you become proficient, all that will be processed automatically. It's called experience."

"Can I ask you something?" Declan asked haltingly.

"Sure."

"Are we still family?"

Murdock turned to look at Declan with a questioning look. "Why wouldn't we be?"

"I thought maybe I would be disowned, or something, because I was being an ass."

"More accurately, you were acting like a spoiled child. So, how can you disown family? I never understood that."

"True, I was, and I'm truly sorry for acting that way. So, we're good?" Declan asked offering his hand to Murdock.

Murdock looked at Declan's face and could see how contrite

he was. He took the offered hand and gave a firm handshake. "Yeah, we're good!"

~

When Emily got to the perimeter of the encampment, she was met by one of the guards barring her way.

"You're not authorized to pass beyond this point," the guard said coldly.

"Good. Can you retrieve Keith Rogers or someone in charge?" she responded just as coldly as the guard had been.

The guard called out for his supervisor and the two had a tense discussion outside Emily's hearing. He returned once they were finished.

"No one is available at this time," the guard said coldly.

"Okay, no problem," Emily replied, obviously miffed, and turned to go.

"Those machetes are to remain here," the guard said before she took a step.

"And why would I do that?" Emily asked, turning to glare at the guard. She had her fists on her hips and was looking defiant.

"They belong to the group. They were just a loan. You know that," the guard said impatiently.

"And if I refuse?" Emily asked stubbornly.

The guard started approaching with disdain for her disobedience evident on his face. Before he was three steps from her, Emily had drawn a machete.

"Stay back," she warned as she stepped back a little.

The guard paid no attention to her threat and reached for her arm. Emily quickly brought the machete into play and sliced the guard's forearm.

"You bitch!" he yelled as he grabbed his arm and stepped back.

Emily used the guard's shock to her advantage. She turned and started walking toward Declan and Murdock. She did her best to refrain from running, even though she wanted to. She didn't want to give the guard, or anyone, the idea that she was intimidated. As she strode away, she heard the guard calling to his supervisor.

Once she was out of sight of the guard, Emily started to trot toward Declan's campsite.

Just as Declan and Murdock had finished shaking hands, Emily came trotting up to them. She ran to Declan and started crying into his shoulder. It took Declan a few minutes to get her calmed down enough to tell them what had happened. She had just started when six guards came into the campsite.

"There she is! Disarm her," the guard leader yelled and then noticed Murdock and Declan, both of them armed. "Disarm them all!"

Murdock stepped in front of the advancing guards and was walking forward. He heard Declan pull his own twelve-inch machete and smiled to himself. As the closer guards attempted to split around Murdock, a few quick strikes to the legs caused the first two to fall hard. Another step and the guard directly in front of Murdock got his head knocked with the butt end of his spear. Even though he was focused on the guards in front of him, he could hear Declan and Emily defending themselves behind him. Another two steps, a quick jab, with the butt end of his spear to the next guard, he fell down. When he reached the last two, one of which Murdock assumed was the head guard because he hung back, one decided to run far around Murdock. Without taking his eyes off the last guard, Murdock tossed his spear in such a way that the one running tripped on the spear's shaft and fell face first to the ground. As soon as Murdock let his spear fly, he pulled his own twelve-inch machete and proceeded forward. The last guard in front of Murdock had a panicked look on his face.

"Hold," Murdock yelled.

"Hold," the head guard yelled. The fighting stopped.

"Are we going to dance?" Murdock asked with a grin. "No need for everyone to get hurt when you and I can settle it." The head guard licked his lips several times before putting away his machete. Murdock did the same.

"Get everyone picked up and get back to the compound!" the head guard yelled. "We need to have your weapons," the guard said to Murdock. He was almost apologetic.

"Forget it," Murdock said sternly while he put his hand on the handle of his machete again. "I want your weapons!"

"Forget it," the head guard said just as sternly.

"Well, there you go. No one is going to give up anything. Apparently, we have to try to kill each other to get what we want. Is that what you want?"

"No."

"Neither do I, so why don't you call it a day?"

The man thought for a second and decided that Murdock was correct and turned to follow his men back to the compound. Once the guards were gone, Murdock turned to see Emily, standing at the ready, and Declan still holding onto his machete despite the fact that he had blood dripping from his right arm.

"You two okay?" Murdock asked.

"Fine," Emily replied.

"Not so much," Declan said. "I'm…feeling a little…woozy."

Emily caught him before he hit the ground and eased him down. She took his machete and replaced it at his side. She was rolling up Declan's shirt sleeve when Murdock came up.

"Is he okay?" Murdock asked concerned.

"He should be, if I can get this cut cleaned out and stop the bleeding."

"Use your waterskin and let it bleed. Open it up a little to see how bad it is," Murdock told her as he trotted over to retrieve his spear and return. "How bad is it? Any pulsing blood?" he asked as he dug in the grass to get to the dirt. Once at the dirt, he used his waterskin to mix with the dirt.

"No pulsing blood, but it is deep," Emily told him as he scooped up the mud and put it over the cut, patting it lightly to help seal it to the skin.

"We need to move before they come back with more help," Murdock said emphatically. "You are family, now, so I expect total discretion," he said looking at her directly so she would know he was extremely serious.

"You have it. Just, please, help him," Emily replied, close to tears.

M urdock telepathically told Mei Lee to pack the camp and meet them at the cave Beron had made for Declan.

"I want you to walk back toward the river the same way we came and keep your eyes forward and don't look back, got it?" Murdock instructed.

Emily got to her feet as she nodded her assent. She started walking at a good clip in the direction that Murdock had instructed. Once Emily was a few yards ahead, Murdock levitated a limp, ashen Declan and followed her.

It didn't take long before Murdock saw the entrance to the cave ahead of them. It was about ten feet off the ground and was well hidden behind the branches of the nearby trees. If he didn't know its location, he wouldn't have found it. Once in position, he told Emily to stop and he levitated himself, Emily, and Declan through the entrance. Once inside the cave, he located the path that led down, told Emily which direction to go, and followed. The familiar structure curved slightly down to a small anteroom. He quickly appraised the anteroom and found the way into the main room. He directed Emily into the main room, and he followed. Once inside the main room, he set Declan down gently on a small area of sand.

"Keep his arm out of the sand, but stay with him. He looks like he's lost a lot of blood," Murdock instructed Emily as he left the room.

Murdock made his way to the entrance just as Mei Lee and the children entered. Murdock levitated the cart into the cave entrance. While he picked up a few deer hides, he instructed the elder children to stand lookout at the entrance. Mei Lee grabbed the younger children and followed her husband down to the main room. Once there, he spread out a hide for Mei Lee and the younger children and then spread one out for Declan. Once the hide was placed, he levitated Declan onto it and then covered him with the remaining hide. Murdock left the room to get more supplies from the cart.

"How did he do that?" Emily asked Mei Lee after Murdock had left the room.

"That's something you'll need to ask him, but I would accept what he says without further questioning. Just accept it." Mei Lee advised. "How's Declan?"

"He has a nasty cut on his arm and has lost a lot of blood. We did what we could to get the bleeding stopped," Emily informed her without taking her eyes from Declan's pale face.

Murdock returned with the rest of the hides and the meat and, after finding a place to put the meat, to keep the sand off it, spread a hide and put the meat on it. He then set the extra deer hides off to the side until he decided where to bed down his family. It was then that Murdock came over to Declan and Emily.

"How is he?" he asked.

"I don't know. He is breathing, but shallowly and he is still unconscious," Emily said, concerned.

"I think he'll be okay, for now anyway. I need to get some wood and get a fire started."

Once Murdock was outside the cave, he cast around, looking for sign of their passage. As he collected firewood, he obscured whatever sign he found. Any wood or rocks, to be used, he levitated into the entrance of the cave. The elder children carried it all to the main room where Mei Lee and the children set the fire-ring and got a fire started.

Once the fire was started, the cave was well-lit. Mei Lee looked around and noticed that it was a smaller version of the cave at the Oomah hive mountain by Rose's grave. Emily looked around in awe. She left Declan only long enough to get a better look of her surroundings.

"I thought the cave we found was one-of-a-kind, but I can see that I was wrong," she said as she wandered around the cave.

"These caves are more abundant than you think," Mei Lee said emotionlessly, not wanting to say too much.

"Did you know this cave was here?" Emily asked.

"We haven't explored everywhere," Mei Lee stated.

"What happened? How did he get cut?" Murdock asked.

"One of the guards recovered enough to slash out with his machete and Declan instinctively put his arm up. After he was cut, he punched the guard to knock him out and then drew his machete. I was busy with one of the guards as well," Emily explained.

"Well, there's nothing to do but wait. What happened when you went back to the compound to give whomever your decision?" Murdock asked.

"I didn't get far," Emily explained. "The guard stopped me and refused to let me pass. When I asked to see Keith Rogers, he wasn't available. Then the guard wanted my weapons and I refused. He grabbed me and I cut his arm. Then I came back to Declan's camp."

Murdock sat and listened to Emily's explanation of events with only a few nods to indicate he was listening. When she had finished, he sat there running the attack over in his mind.

"What are you thinking?" Mei Lee asked her husband.

"I'm thinking that this Keith Rogers needs to be a little more sociable. He should have allowed Emily a chance to tell him where to stick the leadership position," Murdock responded, more to himself than anyone in the cave. "I'm also thinking that Declan may need Annie."

Mei Lee just nodded.

"Who's Annie?" Emily asked.

"The nurse that helped Mei Lee deliver Huo Jin," Murdock answered. "Tell me more about this Keith Rogers."

Keith Rogers had been walking down the catwalks and ladders when the six guards returned from their encounter with Emily. He was fairly certain that they would have no trouble disarming Declan and her, if he was with her, as he had hoped. Without a single weapon, how long could they survive? With those two out of the picture, then he stood a better chance of convincing Tutt to bring back his group.

As he reached the top of the last ladder before he hit the ground, he saw the guards and they appeared to have had a battle. As he got to the ground, he called them to him.

"What the hell happened to you?" Keith asked the head guard before he could get too far.

"Murdock was there," the man answered angrily.

"Did you get all their weapons?" Keith asked figuring they should have gotten some, if not all of them.

"No, Murdock stuck his nose into it, so we got nothing!"

"Not a single weapon?" Keith asked in shocked anger. "Six against three and you come up empty?"

"Not exactly. Murdock, alone, easily kicked the hell out of us. We think one of them was injured, but we're not sure!" the head guard answered with surliness.

Keith Rogers' face turned a deep red, his anger evident. "Get your asses out there and finish the job I gave you," he shouted.

"Do it yourself," the head guard snapped back. "It wasn't

worth it to die for a couple of machetes! Besides, Murdock had his own weapons and Declan had more than a twelve-inch machete!"

"Where did Declan get more weapons?"

"Let me think! Um, maybe he got them from Murdock, dumb ass. Use your head for something besides keeping your ears from banging together!"

Keith was speechless, from the insult of the head guard and anger at the guards' failure. He was under the impression that Declan was *on the outs* with Murdock, so someone was lying. However, if true, then they were all in big trouble. Keith had decided to stay close to the cave entrance for a while; just until someone found out if they were going to be attacked. He turned and went back into the cave.

While Murdock, Emily, and Mei Lee were talking, Declan moaned. Emily rushed to his side and offered him some water.

"How are you doing?" Murdock asked as he came over to Declan.

"Weak," Declan said and tried to chuckle. "I guess I screwed up!"

"Why would you say that?" Murdock asked, concerned.

"I should have blocked that guard's attack with something other than my arm," Declan said weakly with a grin. "How bad is it?"

"Don't know yet," Murdock said. "I think we should get Annie or Doctor Harris to look at it."

"There's a doctor here?" Emily asked, shocked. "I had no idea!"

"Yes, there is, but she's had a hard time of it," Murdock explained. "Feel like eating?" Murdock asked Declan. Declan nodded weakly. "Give him all he can eat," Murdock told Emily.

While Mei Lee fed Huo Jin, Emily cut some meat for everyone and started roasting it over the fire. After the venison was cooked, Murdock selected some for him, Mei Lee, and the kids and gave it to them. Emily picked up enough for herself and Declan and started to feed some to Declan.

"Will we be safe here?" Emily asked as she fed Declan.

"As safe here as anywhere," Murdock said. "The problem, as I see it, is remaining hidden. With Declan down, it would be exceedingly hard for you to care for him here. If the others came looking for you, they'd find you, probably when you went out for wood."

"So, what are we to do?" Emily asked, concerned.

"You'll come home with us," Murdock said flatly. "After Declan is capable, and you desire to, you can go where you want."

"I don't want to impose," Emily protested politely.

"If you were imposing, would I have invited you?" Murdock asked good-naturedly.

When Declan had eaten his fill, Emily joined Murdock and Mei Lee at the fire. As she sat, she got a better look at the cave interior. "This looks to be a smaller version of the cave we found and established as our home."

"There are many such caves," Murdock said as he poked the fire a bit, refusing to look Emily in the eye. "What was the one you found like?"

"It was a grand cave with many smaller rooms off the two main rooms. It had two main rooms, one above the other with a spiral ramp, and, what we called, a bathing room with a spa! It was quite a stroke of luck to find it!"

"I'm sure it was," Murdock responded, wondering if it was luck or leading.

"When are we leaving here?" Emily asked.

"Early tomorrow morning, I'm thinking before sunup," Murdock informed.

"Will Declan be well enough to travel by then?" Emily asked.

"He's already strong enough. We'll put him on the cart, but you'll have to walk," Murdock informed her. He saw Emily nod that she understood. "As for me, I'm going to soak," he said as he got to his feet.

Without any instruction, that Emily could hear, Mei Lee got the children ready to bathe as well as herself, once they were all at the side of the spa pool. Murdock had stripped and, once in the water, helped the children and Mei Lee into it. Emily, after thinking about it for a minute, came over to the pool.

"May I join you?" she asked quietly.

"Suit yourself," Murdock said as he made room for her. While Emily stripped, Murdock got a good look at her body. She was a big woman and looked like a weightlifter.

"I hope Declan never makes her angry," Murdock told Mei Lee telepathically, *"she'll snap him like a twig, if he does."*

Mei Lee had a hard time hiding the fact that she had thought the same thing.

"Can I ask how you managed to get Declan and me into the cave?" Emily asked, looking at Murdock.

"I levitated you," he said with a smirk.

"If you didn't want to answer, you could've said so. You didn't need to poke fun at me," Emily snapped. Murdock just shrugged.

"What do you suggest for your old charges?" Murdock asked Emily after a short pause.

"Leave them! I'm well shut of them," Emily responded angrily. "I think Declan would say the same thing, but he's free to answer for himself, once he's up and about!" She laid back, her head against the edge of the pool and closed her eyes. She resented the offhand way Murdock had refused to answer a valid question.

When Emily was awakened by Mei Lee, she found that she was still upset at Murdock's seemingly flippant response to her question. After the cart was packed with all the gear, with Declan, who was in and out of consciousness, and the two younger children, everyone was assembled at the mouth of the cave. After a brief wait, she was instructed to close her eyes. She complied, but after she felt the morning breeze on her cheek, she opened them and became a little disoriented and her stomach became queasy. The movement of the group and the cart without a physical conveyance was disconcerting to her.

By sunup, the Murdock tribe, for that is how Murdock himself looked at them, was a mile away from the ridge edge. They were well on their way toward the group that housed Annie and Doctor Harris. Murdock had decided to save some time by bypassing the river crossing to avoid being seen by anyone.

Emily was amazed at how they all knew what their travel positions were and how they assumed them without being told. The silence of their passage also impressed her. All she could hear were her own footfalls. After an hour of the quick pace, one set by the elder children who lead the way, Emily chastised herself for being upset at Murdock's seemingly flippant response to her question of the night before.

Murdock's tribe didn't stop until around midday. As everyone drank, Murdock came around to each giving them some of the small pieces of smoked venison. When he got to Emily, he handed her more than the rest.

"Give some to Declan," Murdock explained quietly. "Are you holding up okay?"

"It isn't easy, but I'm managing," Emily said as she chewed on some of the venison.

"With any luck, we should be able to camp somewhere close to the group just before dark," Murdock said quietly. Emily just nodded that she understood as she tended to Declan, giving him some water and a few pieces of venison.

When everyone was rested, the tribe pressed on. They traveled at a slightly faster pace. As they traveled, Emily could see the ridge drawing closer with each passing hour. It was close to sunset when they all stopped inside a large, dense group of trees. Emily could smell wood burning and knew they were close to the group that was Murdock's target. After setting the cart down and drinking some water, Murdock headed toward the group's encampment while the rest of his tribe made camp.

When Murdock returned, he had Annie Cooper and Elizabeth Reyes with him. Everyone greeted Annie with hugs and handshakes as she made her way to the cart where Declan lay semi-conscious. Annie and Emily washed off the mud to allow Annie a good look at the cut on Declan's arm. Emily and Mei Lee were helping by holding up brands they had picked up from the fire built while waiting for Murdock to return.

Murdock and Reyes were off by themselves talking out of earshot of the others. However, Murdock was allowing Mei Lee to hear everything that was being said and Mei Lee was returning the favor by letting him watch and listen to Annie while she worked.

"Let it breathe for a while," Annie said to Emily after a good look at the cut.

"Is he going to be okay?" Emily asked, deeply concerned.

"He should be, if he takes it easy for a while," Annie answered as she walked toward the fire.

Murdock and Reyes joined her at the fire, as did Emily and Mei Lee. Murdock made the introductions all around.

"I need to talk to you, Murdock," Annie said and then added, "Privately."

Murdock nodded and started walking away from the fire, and Annie followed. Once they were out of earshot, Murdock turned to her. "What's on your mind?" he asked.

"What's your plan for Declan and…Emily, was it?" Annie asked quietly.

"I was taking them to my place," Murdock informed her.

"They can't go back where they were and they can't stay here, because of Declan's arm, and they don't know enough to survive on their own." Annie was nodding as he spoke.

"That makes sense. When did Declan get cut?"

"Yesterday, late morning. Why?"

"When I inspected the cut, I noticed it was already healing. I would have guessed the cut was a week old, at least. What did you do to make it heal like that?" Annie was looking at him skeptically.

"Just mixed up the mud and applied it after Emily washed the wound and got it to bleed pretty well. He has been unconscious a lot of the time since it happened. Fed him, gave him water, and made him rest," Murdock explained.

"Well, I've not seen anything heal like that before. If that was all you did, then I'm at a loss to explain it. I could see that he's lost a lot of blood from it, but there was no permanent damage. The reason I asked to talk to you privately is because of Irene."

"Doctor Harris? What's happened?" Murdock asked.

"She's as alright as she's likely to be," Annie tapped her head with a finger. "She's too skittish to be around the group and things have gotten kind of heated with the others. They all say she should be turned out to fend for herself. None of them liked her before she came here, and most are holding a grudge. I was thinking she could go with you. At least she would feel safer with you."

"Why would she feel safer with us?" Murdock asked. "She doesn't know us, and we don't really know her."

"She remembers you and Mei Lee did what you could for her after her escape from the pod. She gets panicked by the looks some of the other men are giving her. What I think she needs is a quiet, loving home environment," Annie explained. "And time, of course," she added after a brief pause.

Murdock hung his head a little to think. "Is she rational enough to function as a doctor?"

"She should be. I think it's a case of her expecting to be

attacked again and caring for Declan would give her something useful to do," Annie explained. "Our group has more men than women and I have caught a few of them leering at her."

"Any other reasons?" Murdock asked skeptically.

"Frankly," Annie took a deep breath and let it out, "I've been by her side since we brought her here and I'm tired. Reyes has requested that I speak to you about taking her. She had originally thought that having Irene in our group would be an asset, since Irene is the only doctor on the planet, but for now, Irene is a liability."

"I don't know what we can do for her, but she can come with us," Murdock said. "I hope she is ambulatory, though. We have no room on the cart to transport her."

"She has been outside of the cave quite a few times and can walk," Annie explained, "until she gets panicked."

"Have her here tomorrow morning and we'll take her with us," Murdock said. He had already asked Mei Lee telepathically and gotten an affirmative answer. "What should we do for Declan's arm?" he asked.

"If he's going to be active, I'd put some mud on it to keep it from reopening. Otherwise, let the air to it. It'll help to keep it dryer," Annie explained, "but Irene will know how to treat it."

With that, Murdock and Annie headed back to the fire. Once there, Annie socialized a bit with Mei Lee and Emily. Reyes had been socializing while Annie and Murdock talked. It wasn't long before they bid their good-byes and Reyes and Annie left the camp.

The next morning, Annie brought Irene Harris to Murdock while they were packing the cart. Declan seemed to be getting better, though he was still weak and pale. After introductions were made, they all bid farewell to Annie and headed further upriver. At the ridge, Murdock made no effort to hide his ability to levitate from his tribe. He just levitated them and then refused to talk about it with Doctor Harris or Emily. Just before sunset, they reached Murdock's cabin.

~

Declan found Murdock sitting on a pile of logs sharpening the ax. It had been several weeks since he had arrived and his arm was healed, even though he had a bright, red scar on it. He knew he would always have the scar. They had been working on a sleeping room with a small fireplace to give Emily and him some privacy. It was freestanding but close to the main cabin entrance.

"Can I ask you a question?" Declan asked quietly. He had begun to understand that talking quietly was less unnerving for the others.

"Of course, what's on your mind?" Murdock asked. He stopped his sharpening to listen to Declan.

"Did you kill any of those men that attacked me and Emily?" Declan looked grave. That was how Murdock knew a straight answer was what he required.

"No, I didn't," Murdock answered.

"Why not? I was injured and Emily could have been killed," Declan said heatedly. "At least one of them should have died!"

"Really? Is that what you really think or are you saying it because you're angry?" Murdock asked.

"Both, I guess. How are they going to learn to not attack people who have done them no harm?"

"How does a dead man *learn* anything?" Murdock asked. "How do you *teach* a dead man anything? Isn't it a waste of time and effort to teach someone something just to kill them a minute later?" Murdock resumed sharpening for a few seconds then stopped again. "Ever kill anyone?" he asked, and Declan shook his head, to indicate the negative. "It's not that easy to do. Nor should it be." Murdock tossed Declan the sharpening stone. He caught it deftly and began sharpening his hatchet.

"Have you ever killed anyone?" Declan asked after they had been working for several hours.

"You mean today? Not yet, but the day's young so I remain hopeful," Murdock quipped, and Declan looked at him with the look that said *be serious* without actually saying the words. "I have, but I didn't like it. It was just something that needed to be done, like killing a rabid animal."

"That seems to be a cold-blooded attitude, to me," Declan observed.

"Why? It wasn't something I undertook without a lot of reflection and consideration and I did try to reason with them. It's been my experience that those who attacked you and Em will probably be crushed when the *karmic wheel* gets back to them," Murdock responded seriously.

Both men resumed working.

Emily and Irene were trying to learn how to make rope from the tall grass by watching Mei Lee.

"How is Declan doing?" Mei Lee asked as she worked.

"His arm is scarred," Irene Harris responded without looking up from her work, "but he'll live. I'm still trying to figure out how the cut healed so quickly."

"He hasn't lost any use or any sensation, either," Emily added.

"Adding to my confusion is the fact that I'm still trying to get my head around this *tribe* thing you mentioned," Irene stated while she continued working.

"There's nothing hard to understand," Mei Lee said. "It's just a gathering of people who come together for their own betterment. A member of the tribe may or may not be family, but we'd all share the things that would ensure survival. As an example, Kevin and Declan go hunting, but Kevin is the only one to bag the game. We'd all share in that. Another example would be if we were confronted by Ben Palmer, Kevin would do the talking and we would all back him."

"And what if Kevin did or said something we didn't like or didn't agree with?" Emily asked.

"It would depend on the situation," Mei Lee explained. "If there was an immediate danger, everyone would be expected to do as Kevin instructs until the danger passes. If we are all alone, no strangers around, we can discuss it, but Kevin would have the final decision and we'd have to back him."

"Why should we do as Murdock says?" Irene questioned.

"Do you think Kevin has an agenda other than survival and taking care of all of us?" Mei Lee asked with an accusing glare to the other two women. "Is anyone else more qualified for survival here?"

Irene looked shocked. "I was asking because I don't know what to expect from him," she said sheepishly. "I didn't mean to offend!"

"What you can expect is Kevin continuing to act like he has since I've known him," Mei Lee snapped. Why do you think he brought you here?"

"Declan needed a doctor," Irene Harris said with a shrug.

"And how much doctoring have you done since you've been here? Was there something so critical that we couldn't have managed without you? Or maybe there was another reason?" Mei Lee asked, apparently still miffed.

"Will Kevin accept the leadership?" Emily asked trying to divert Mei Lee's anger from Irene.

"As long as we don't expect him to be a shepherd, he should be fine with it, especially if we don't tell him," Mei Lee said seriously.

Emily smiled at her remark. "How do we pull that off?" she asked.

"Easy. If something comes up, we just defer to his judgment, unless we have something useful to say. That would be something he'd want to hear anyway," Mei Lee explained.

"You make it sound so easy," Emily said with a chuckle and shaking her head a little.

"I found it works well enough. I've been doing it for close to five years, now," Mei Lee grinned a little. "To be clear," Mei Lee continued as she shifted her gaze to Irene, "Kevin wouldn't stop you, if you wanted to leave. I brought it up so you two can feel like you belong here. I know what it's like to be uncertain about belonging."

Irene looked embarrassed. "Since the rape, I have a hard time trusting, especially a man," she said quietly.

"Yes, you suffered a major trauma, but you can either live the rest of your life as a victim, or you can do something about it," Mei Lee said somewhat harshly.

"You don't understand," Irene retorted, trying to elicit sympathy from the other two women.

"Is that what you think?" Mei Lee scolded. "All the women from the first ship were beaten and raped, some multiple times. So, don't tell me I don't understand. As I said, when you decide to quit being a victim, maybe then you can do something about it, but you have to decide." The other two women looked at Mei Lee, mouths agape.

"No! Absolutely not! I refuse," Murdock yelled. Everyone had finished eating and the children were put down for the night. The adults had gone outside to enjoy the evening while the pile of brush finished burning.

Declan had sympathy for Murdock's plight. Mei Lee had sprung her idea of leadership of their little tribe on him.

"But why?" Mei Lee asked quietly.

"I don't want it," Murdock snapped back.

"From my point of view, you don't really have a choice," Mei Lee responded sedately. "You have been the leader for as long as I've known you. All we're saying is that you continue as you have been. You have served us all quite well and we wish that to continue. Consider it a vote of confidence!"

"I've only done what I thought best for my family," Murdock countered.

"Exactly, you've been a wonderful husband and provider and we all wish that to continue." Mei Lee said emphatically. "All we're saying is we are here to help you any way we can and to support your decisions!"

"But I don't want the responsibility for everyone else," Murdock argued.

"Maybe," Emily chimed in sweetly, "that is exactly why we want you to be *Leader*. We know what your agenda is, and we have no fear of you becoming another Palmer."

"No one here is more qualified to ensure our survival," Declan added calmly. "Did you let Emily starve because I was unable to provide for her? Did you do what you could for Irene even though she was unable to care for herself? Did you leave her out in the wild after her rape? Or did you do the best you could for her?"

Murdock had been looking at the dying flames as they all had their say. When he looked up, he saw them all looking at him respectfully. "I did what I had to do to be able to live with myself, that's all," he said defensively.

"Kevin, are you the head of our family?" Mei Lee asked.

"I wouldn't classify myself that way," Murdock defended. "But I would have to say yes."

"And who is included in that family?" Mei Lee asked.

It seemed, to Mei Lee, that everyone held their breath waiting for Murdock to answer. They all thought they were included, but what if Murdock had decided otherwise?

"Everyone here," Murdock relented.

Everyone sighed in relief.

"And so, you still are," Mei Lee agreed. "Nothing changes. We'll continue on as we have been. Taking direction, where you feel direction is required, and expressing our concerns." Mei Lee having broached the subject ended the discussion with, "And that's all there is to it!" She got to her feet and walked over to him, putting out her hand. "Let's go take a bath and go to bed," she said sweetly to Murdock.

Murdock said nothing. He did smile as he took her hand and let himself be led.

"Is your bath private?" Emily asked as the couple headed toward the spa.

"It's as private as the rest of you want to make it," Mei Lee said over her shoulder as she led Murdock to the back of the cabin.

"You two go ahead, if you want," Irene said as she got to her feet. "I'm going to bed."

Declan and Emily looked at each other and then got to their feet and followed Murdock and Mei Lee.

In short order, Murdock, Mei Lee, Declan, and Emily were soaking in their spa, relaxing.

"I hope you've learned something, Declan, from our little discussion," Murdock said after a few minutes of silence.

"What would that be, Kevin?" Declan asked, unwilling to blindly enter any verbal traps set by Murdock.

"From the day I fell for your sister, I have yet to win an argument," Murdock stated.

"Maybe not, Kevin, but part of the reason that's true is we don't argue," Mei Lee stated. She moved to sit in Murdock's lap facing him. "We discuss things until such time as you come around to my way of thinking," she finished sarcastically with a smirk.

"I wouldn't be a bit surprised," Murdock responded as he kissed her.

"It's time I made the rounds to ensure the others are getting ready for winter," Murdock said the next day at breakfast.

Mei Lee, who was nursing Huo Jin, stepped outside the cabin and sniffed the morning air.

"Seems a little early in the year for that," she said as she reentered the cabin. "Maybe in a few weeks, but not much longer than that."

"Mei has a nose for these things," Murdock explained conspiratorially to the other adults and chuckled.

Everyone else chuckled as well, even Mei Lee. Emily was looking at Murdock and saw his expression change suddenly.

"What's wrong?" Emily asked, concerned at Murdock's expression.

"*Is time,*" came to Murdock and Mei Lee's minds. They both knew it was from Beron.

"We need you three to watch the kids," Mei Lee explained. "There's something Kevin and I need to do. It's important!"

"You kids behave and mind your Aunts and Uncle," Murdock said seriously as he got to his feet and started putting his traveling gear together. "I'm leaving the cart, in case you need it," he said to Declan.

Mei Lee was also getting her traveling gear together, including her sling for the baby. "Huo Jin is coming with us, as we don't know how long we'll be gone."

Declan, Emily, and Irene were watching the two adults rush around gathering what they needed. All three looked dumbfounded.

"Where are you going and how long will you be gone?" Emily asked as Murdock gathered a couple of hides for sleeping.

"We need to go somewhere and do things none of you know about, yet," Mei Lee said as she tied the hides that Murdock had rolled tightly. She had used a very long thong so Murdock could carry the hides behind him with the thong going across the front of his body.

"We're sorry for being vague, it is unavoidable. Just do what you can and watch the kids. We'll explain it later," Murdock said as he slung his quiver and grabbed his bow.

When they were ready, Mei Lee and Murdock left the cabin, shutting the door behind them. Declan had gotten up and gone to the door and opened it. He could see no sign of them.

"Huh! That's the damnedest thing," Declan said as he shut the door. "They're gone already!"

18

A s soon as Murdock and Mei Lee exited the cabin, Murdock had sent a telepathic message to Beron that they were on their way. Beron levitated the couple from the cabin to the meadow that was used for the "Springtime Rite", as Murdock called it. It seemed to take no time at all for the couple to arrive. Upon arrival, Mei Lee was led away from the gathering of the males. Murdock, on the other hand, was placed close to the old Oomah that was Beron's father.

"Important you observe," the old Oomah sent to Murdock's mind. *"Important to me."*

Murdock gave a sad smile as he looked down at the old Oomah and gently stroked his head. He had become quite fond of him over the years. *"I'm here,"* Murdock said telepathically. *"Important for me as well."*

As Murdock looked around, he saw Beron looking rather large and very stoic. He hadn't contacted Murdock's mind since his arrival, but he didn't recognize anyone else. The rest of the male Oomah, in the immediate vicinity, all looked like younger versions of Beron, so he assumed they were all related. He hadn't been there long when his perception changed dramatically. At first, it shocked Murdock. He was apparently seeing the actual world with one eye and the *sharing state* world, as Murdock called it, with the other eye.

With one eye, he saw a white smoke come from the old bear. The other eye saw a thin, dark form that he had come to know as the Oomah in the *sharing state* world, rise up from the body of the old one and float to the first row of younger Oomah. It seemed to select one and Murdock saw the dark form step into the younger and disappear. His hand, which was still on the head of the old bear, could feel the body grow cold. He didn't know how he knew, but he seemed to know that when he saw the smoke/dark form leave the body of the old one it had died and nothing he would know was left behind.

"Transference complete," Beron sent telepathically to all present.

The body of the old Oomah was levitated, Murdock assumed by Beron, and all the males followed slowly behind. The body slowly drifted toward the falls and, as they all watched, followed the water over the falls. The body had remained inches above the water all the way down the falls. Murdock then saw it float toward trees in the middle of a grassy area. Just as the body disappeared, Murdock remembered that area as the *dread feeling* area he had found within days of being on this planet.

All the males dispersed as soon as the body was out of sight.

"This for males only," Beron sternly warned Murdock as the body disappeared. *"Take care not share with mate or females."*

"Understood," Murdock responded. *"Questions?"* he asked after a brief pause and received a slight nod from Beron. *"Was that the old one's entity that entered the younger Oomah?"* Another slight nod from Beron. *"Confusion."*

"Share…later/not now…and explain," came to Murdock's mind as he followed Beron over to the females, along with all the other males that were present.

"Is the old one gone?" Mei Lee asked quietly and reverently as Murdock approached.

"Yes," was all Murdock could think to say. He knew the

entity that had lived in the shell of the old one was still around, but he wasn't sure what he could tell Mei Lee and what was forbidden. He wasn't about to jeopardize his standing with the Oomah over saying too much.

Beron and Bridget led Murdock and Mei Lee down the mountain to the chamber that Murdock and Rose had occupied and left them there. They had been strangely silent the entire trip.

"What were you doing while I was witnessing?" Murdock asked Mei Lee once they were alone and settling in.

"Just communed with Bridget about Huo Jin and the rest of our brood," she replied. "You do know that what you witnessed was meant for *family* only?"

"I didn't know," Murdock exclaimed.

"I gather it is a high honor to be requested," she explained.

"I'm wondering if I'll be requested with all the other Oomah that had declared me *kin* after Rose's death," Murdock speculated.

"Doubtful," Mei Lee said. "The ones that declared you 'kin' are far too young to pass anytime in your lifetime. You might if any of them become mortally wounded or fatally ill, but that doesn't happen often."

After eating and Huo Jin's needs being met, Murdock and Mei Lee got into the spa pool to relax.

"I'm wondering who the new *Elder* of the Oomah is," Mei Lee asked as she relaxed, with eyes closed, in the hot water.

"I'm not sure," Murdock responded as he lounged, "but I think Beron is. He was acting like he was *in charge*."

"That's what I was thinking as well," Mei Lee responded. "What do you have in mind for Declan, Emily, and Irene?"

"I was going to ask them what their plans were," Murdock responded, "making it clear that they could stay with us if they wanted. I don't know if we want to include them into the *Oomah connection*, yet. I wanted to get your and Beron's input before making that decision."

"For myself, I'd say let them all the way in. It would have made our sudden departure less odd, to them, if they were already aware of the Oomah," Mei Lee responded.

"Do you think it would help Irene?" Murdock asked as he pulled his wife to him. He held her on his lap while he caressed her.

"It could," Mei Lee responded as she relaxed to her husband's ministrations.

Since the day that Freeman was killed, Ben Palmer had been having everything his own way. He had finally gotten Phylicia to be subservient to him, so the beatings had reduced greatly, to his dismay. He had enjoyed beating all the women, until they quit fighting him. Wagner, Osterlund, and Hornsby had become quite excellent bootlickers and he only had to cuff them periodically to keep them cowed.

It had been weeks since Murdock had issued his edicts about the range from the pod they could travel, so Palmer felt that it was time to test those limits. He had sent Wagner and Hornsby to the river several times, in the past two weeks, and they had returned without incident.

"Get everyone together," Palmer commanded, without turning around, as he heard someone coming toward him from behind. "We're all going to the river!"

"What about Murdock?" Osterlund asked as the others were gathering.

"What about him?" Palmer scoffed. "We aren't going to let him tell us what to do!"

"He did make it plain that we are not to leave the pod area," Hornsby said as he was picking up a staff and a couple of the waterskins.

"We need water and fish. He can't deny us," Palmer stated loudly. "He is only one man, after all!"

"He did make short work of all the guards the last time we tangled with him," Wagner stated as he armed himself.

"That stream can't support us all!" Palmer chided. "What's wrong with all of you? Are you all cowards? Grow a spine, for Christ sake!"

Wagner, Osterlund, and Hornsby quit complaining and herded the women in front of them as all of them headed toward the river.

Hours later, when they could all see the river, they stopped to see if anyone else was there. All of them had become more nervous the closer they got to the river. Seeing no one else around, they all proceeded to the riverbank. After reaching the bank, the women filled the waterskins as the men kept watch. Once everyone had filled waterskins, Palmer started a small fire while Osterlund and Wagner tried their hand at catching the larger fish. After catching a couple, they cleaned and cooked them.

"I wonder what is on the other side of that river," Palmer asked aloud, to no one in particular.

"I remember seeing some of the others head this way, so they could be over there," Wagner said quietly. He noticed Jax Hornsby rubbing his hand where Murdock's wife had shot him. "Hand bothering you, or are you remembering?" he asked quietly.

"A little of both," Hornsby replied after making the conscious effort to stop rubbing his hand. "Hurt like hell the first time, so I'm not looking for a repeat."

"Don't blame you there," Wagner agreed.

Wagner and Hornsby had done a lot of thinking about the last time they had tangled with Murdock. Both were nervous about running into him again, even though neither discussed it aloud. Neither man expected to survive another encounter with an angry Murdock.

As they ate, they heard three splashes in the river. All the men scrambled to their feet and ran to the riverbank. They

306

arrived in time to see the three women hobble into the trees on the far bank.

"After them," Palmer commanded. "Don't let them escape!"

Wagner, Osterlund, and Hornsby tentatively crossed the river, unsure of what they would find, and leaving Palmer alone at the river while the rest searched.

It wasn't something they'd planned. It was an opportunity that had presented itself. Usually, on the rare occasion Phylicia, Kimberly, and Heather were allowed close to the river, they had been hobbled with rope around their ankles. This time, however, Palmer, being certain he had control of the women, had allowed them to be untethered. It wasn't long after they'd reached the trees that they heard Palmer yell and the men enter the river in pursuit.

All three women ran as fast as they could, but Phylicia was too exhausted to go far. Kimberly and Heather picked her up by draping Phylicia's arms over their shoulders and each trying to keep her on her feet with their arms around her waist.

"Keep her up and moving," Kimberly said breathlessly to Heather. "We can't let them catch us!"

"I'm trying," Heather replied. "Come on, Phylicia, keep going!"

Both women were panicked hearing the men in pursuit. They couldn't be sure, but they seemed to be gaining on them. The women turned and headed for the cliff that was upriver from their entry point. As they ran, they did their best to be as quiet as possible. It wasn't long before they saw a path leading to their right, but as they turned to take the path, they were grabbed by men that they weren't familiar with. After a brief tussle, all three were tied and gagged.

Bass Heartly had heard the commotion and had led his men toward the river to investigate. Since Murdock had shown them the advantages of moving stealthily, Bass had been training his men on stalking. He thought it would make them better hunters. He had no idea it would come in handy for catching interlopers. After subduing the fleeing females, he communicated, with hand signals of his own devising, that his men should remain hidden and quiet. He heard the men that were pursuing the women and they seemed to be getting closer. Bass slowly raised his hand and three of his men prepared to fire their bows. *I doubt these men could hit the ground with their hat,* he thought, *let alone a moving target. I'm hoping that the sight of three bows, aimed at their general direction, will change their minds, and send them packing.*

As the pursuing men turned to enter the path that the women had taken, they all skidded to a halt. They were looking at seven men with machetes drawn and three with bows ready to fire. The shock made them all beat a hasty retreat to the river.

"Remove the gag of one of the prisoners," Bass commanded quietly after the pursuers had left the area. "The blonde!"

"Oh, thank God you found us!" Heather said breathlessly after her gag was removed.

As he looked at the woman, he failed to recognize her, or any of them. Their features were lost in bruises, dirt, and swelling. "Go get Reyes and Annie Cooper!" he ordered one of his men.

"How did this happen?" Palmer asked, pacing the bank of the river while the other three men were catching their breath after their retreat. "Why weren't those bitches hobbled?" His mind was racing. The last thing he wanted was Murdock showing up for retribution. He paused in his ranting for someone to answer. "Why didn't you retrieve our property?" he asked when no one spoke up.

"There were too many of them," Ted Wagner yelled back at

Palmer. "Some had bows. It's a wonder we managed to get away!"

"Catch some more fish for later!" Palmer commanded. "I'm heading back!" He turned and walked in the direction of the transport pod.

Bass Heartly was having trouble with a couple of his men murmuring amongst themselves when one or two had recognized the three fugitives. He was pacing and hoping Reyes would show before things got out of hand. To reduce the chance of more violence, he had sent a few of his men toward the river to alert them if the interlopers returned. He finally breathed a sigh of relief when he caught sight of Reyes and Annie.

"What happened?" Reyes asked. Annie had gone to the three women to assess their condition.

"We were hunting and these three ran into us," Bass replied.

"Untie them," Annie demanded.

"Leave them tied and gagged," Reyes commanded. "Assess them as they are until we figure out what to do with them!"

"They were being pursued," Bass continued, "by three men, but we managed to scare them off. I have men watching the river for further incursions."

"Keep me apprised, Bass," Reyes said as she dismissed the man. "How are they, in your opinion?" Reyes asked Annie after Bass had left.

"I can't be certain," Annie replied, concerned. "All three have massive bruising and they could have internal injuries. I'd say we need Doctor Harris to look at them."

While Murdock was waking, he became disoriented. He thought he'd heard soft footsteps, but he knew Mei Lee was still cuddled to him. The last thing he remembered was sleeping in the residence cave, with Mei Lee, after the passing of the elder Oomah. He sat up immediately when he heard more soft footsteps.

"Sorry," Emily said quietly after being startled. "I didn't mean to wake you."

Murdock looked around expecting stone walls, but seeing log walls. Mei Lee had been immediately awake when Murdock had sat up. Both were confused.

"You must have gotten in late," Emily said quietly. "I didn't hear you come in. I was going to add a log to the fire when I noticed you."

Murdock and Mei Lee looked at her, still confused.

"How did we get here?" Murdock asked his wife telepathically.

"Hell if I know," Mei Lee replied in kind. *"The last thing I remember is falling asleep at the cave."*

At breakfast, Murdock asked Declan, Emily, and Irene what they planned to do.

"I thought we were welcome to stay here?" Emily asked testily.

"You are *all* welcome to stay here," Murdock reassured, "but I don't want you to think you aren't free to leave, if you choose. If you stay, it should be because you really want to be here. It shouldn't be because you feel trapped or have no other choices."

"I, for one," Declan said, "am learning a lot and have no plans of interrupting my education or my training."

"Where my husband is," Emily responded, "there I'll be also."

Everyone looked at Irene, expectantly. "I'm not going to *give* an answer until I *get* some answers," Irene Harris stated. "I want to know where you and Mei Lee went, for starters."

"I hesitate to tell you," Murdock said after thinking about the question for a second or two. "First, I'm not sure you'd believe me. Second, there are responsibilities that come with that knowledge. Mei Lee and I have come to the conclusion that you need to know. Humans are not the apex predators on this planet." Murdock waited for the impact of his statement to hit the others.

"What is?" Declan asked. Emily sat silently, waiting, and listening.

"So, there is something else out there that we should fear?" Harris asked with a shocked look on her face.

"Not fear," Murdock stated, "respect. There are entities, here, called the *Oomah* that you *must* respect. They made this planet for themselves and require privacy."

"And why should we respect them?" Harris asked somewhat petulantly.

"Well, I'd recommend you do, as they can wipe every human from the face of this planet," Murdock blurted harsher than he intended. He waited for a reaction.

"Are they hideous? Why haven't we seen them before?" Emily asked.

"You may not have seen them, but you have profited from them," Murdock responded. "I don't think they're hideous, but that would be a subjective judgment."

"Do they appear as bears?" Declan asked, turning pale.

"Why do you ask that?" Murdock asked.

"During my beatings and recovery at the pod, I had mental visions of Rose," Declan started, "but she seemed to flip quickly from human to bear. I thought I was losing my mind, for a while, then, after a while, I just didn't seem to notice."

Harris was looking at Declan in disbelief. "You said your sister was telling you about Murdock coming for you. I thought you were just—"

"Crazy?" Declan asked with a slight chuckle, completing Harris' thought. "At the time, I thought I was totally around the bend!"

"That was the one Mei Lee knows as Bridget," Murdock stated. "She was doing what she could to give you some hope. Right now, the Oomah guard our borders. They are the ones that caused the workmen to pass out when they trespassed. They are the ones that made the caves, you know which ones I mean," Murdock said this last to the question on Declan's and Emily's faces.

"They gave the workmen the nightmares!" Harris said excitedly.

"And they informed all the others of Phylicia's treachery," Murdock said nodding his head. "The one I named Beron is who dispatched Whittier," Murdock said sadly. He saw Declan nod his head in understanding.

"Are we going to be able to see them?" Harris asked, being curious.

"Be careful what you ask for," Murdock responded, "you just might get it. They'll show themselves when they're ready. No one can force it, and no one can stop them, either." Murdock saw the impact of his statement on everyone's face.

"Are they that powerful?" Harris asked in hushed tones.

"I know they could pull an asteroid from space and have it hit the transport pod, if they had a mind to," Murdock explained. "That would be something easy for them. I think they could change the orbit of this planet. I suspect that would require a little more effort, but I'm not certain. Can any of us do the same? I know I can't!"

"Are they friend or foe?" Emily asked.

"To me, they have always been a friend," Murdock answered guardedly, "but then, I make a concerted effort to *be* a friend to them."

I'm sorry I gave you such a hard time when you levitated me and Declan, Emily thought while Murdock was talking.

"It's okay. Don't worry about it, Em." Emily heard inside her head in Murdock's voice. *"Keep this to yourself."* Emily sat in shocked silence.

"What's your take on them?" Harris asked after a long pause.

"From what we know, they are more sophisticated than the humans have been," Mei Lee responded. "At least they aren't cruel. If they were to wipe humans off their planet, I doubt we would know. It would be quick and merciful."

"But they're animals," Harris spouted. "How can animals be sophisticated?"

"You aren't listening, Irene," Murdock chastised softly. "They have the *form* of bears, or what passes for bears here. From what I understand, when we humans first landed here, they debated if we would be allowed to stay, or killed outright. They responded thoughtfully rather than instinctively. And I've yet to see one of them beat and torture one of their own, for no other reason than because they can."

"That sounds pretty civilized to me," Mei Lee interjected.

"To me as well," Declan added as he remembered the pain of the beating Palmer had given him. *I would like to meet Bridget and thank her for all she did for me,* Declan thought.

"That won't happen anytime soon. They do have customs and protocols," popped into Declan's mind, in Murdock's voice. Declan's mouth hung open as he stared at Murdock.

"You shouldn't stare, Declan. It's considered rude," popped into Declan's mind with Mei Lee's voice. This caused him to jerk his head and stare at her, mouth agape.

313

"Well, I, for one, will have to be convinced," Harris said resolutely. "How do you communicate with these *Oomah*? Bears can't talk!"

"Telepathically," Murdock said sincerely. Harris immediately started laughing.

"That's ridiculous," Harris said when her laughing slowed enough to let her speak. "There's no such thing as telepathy!"

"*Oh, yes there is!*" flashed to Murdock's mind from Declan and Emily simultaneously. This caused him to smirk a little.

"How are you planning to get Harris here to assess them?" Reyes asked. "I know we sent her to Murdock's, but we have no way of contacting him."

"I don't know," Annie responded. "All I know, is I have to try!"

"Well, what do you suggest doing with them until you can get to Murdock?" Reyes asked skeptically. "I'm not comfortable with these three knowing anything about our compound."

"So, you were going to just leave them here?" Annie asked, incredulous.

"No, I was going to ask Bass to leave a few of his men here until they get strong enough to leave on their own," Reyes explained.

"Even if that took months?" Annie asked. She knew Reyes to be fair, but she could also be quite hard.

"Of course not," Reyes replied, shocked. "I was thinking more like a few days."

Murdock! I wish you could hear me. Annie thought to herself as she checked on the three refugees. *I could sure use Harris' help.*

As everyone in the cabin looked at Harris, contempt for the notion of telepathy obvious, they saw her face change to one of grave concern.

"What is it, Irene?" Murdock asked.

"There is something wrong," Harris replied adamantly. She was on her feet, pacing. "I don't know how, but I have the feeling Annie Cooper needs my help. It's something serious!"

"I wonder how that could be possible," Murdock asked flippantly. "No one can come here without me knowing and no one has been here. No postal carriers. No pony express. No stagecoaches."

"You're mocking me," Harris accused. "I don't know how I know; I just do. It's just...a feeling!"

"I wasn't mocking you...exactly," Murdock responded. "I was trying to get you to challenge your own belief system. You may want to be more open-minded. Well, Declan," Murdock started as he got to his feet, "Irene feels the need to go see Annie. Are you up for escorting her?" Murdock asked.

"By myself?" Declan asked, disbelievingly.

"You don't feel up to it?" Murdock asked while he telepathically conferred with his wife.

"Sure, I can escort her," Declan tried to sound convincing and braver than he felt, "but if you wanted to walk along, I wouldn't complain."

"You know, I could use a good stretch of the legs," Murdock replied trying to keep from snickering and receiving a mental chastisement from Mei Lee.

Murdock and Declan outfitted themselves with bows, machetes, and waterskins. Irene Harris outfitted herself with her own machete and two waterskins. Murdock prepared the cart with his spear, deer skins, and a partial front quarter of venison. After Murdock kissed Mei Lee and Declan kissed Emily, the three headed toward the cliff, with Declan pulling the cart and Irene and Murdock walking alongside.

~

Palmer, Wagner, Osterlund, and Hornsby were all gathered together under the transport pod watching the fish cook. All were silent and pensive. All knew that Murdock would, most likely, come looking for them. None wanted to face Murdock's retribution. Not alone and not as a group. Wagner jumped up, machete at the ready, and scanned the prairie for any movement.

"What are you doing, Wagner?" Palmer asked. "Getting jumpy?" Osterlund and Hornsby chuckled quietly. "What are you two laughing at?" Palmer asked them sternly. "I don't see you two being particularly brave. We all know what's coming, so let's try to relax and be ready. Murdock is, after all, just one man!"

"I don't recall you having to fight him!" Wagner retorted.

"I fought him before anyone else did," Palmer replied quietly.

"And?" Wagner questioned.

"It went about as well as all the encounters we've had with him," Palmer replied calmly. "What do we know about him?"

"Not much!" Osterlund added.

"I know his wife is a dead shot," Hornsby chimed in, unconsciously rubbing his hand.

"Which tells me that Murdock is also damn good with a bow, a staff, his hands, and feet, but what about a knife?" Palmer asked.

"If you can't take him barehanded, what makes you think you can take him in a knife fight?" Osterlund asked snippily.

"Nothing, I'm just trying to figure a way for us to survive," Palmer said, obviously irritated.

"I say we cook all the fish, fill the waterskins, and lock ourselves inside the transport pod!" Wagner insisted.

"Do you really think that's a solution?" Palmer asked rhetorically. "We'd be better off trying to find more of the others. I doubt they're all located in one spot." No one offered a rebuttal.

"I think we may prolong things if we leave here and try to locate another camp. What could it hurt?"

Annie Cooper was keeping an eye on the three women trying to make them more comfortable and still trying to ascertain the extent of their injuries.

"How are they doing?" Bass Heartly asked on one of his rounds.

"Hell, I don't know," Annie replied, frustrated. "I think Phylicia has dislocated her hip and has some broken ribs, but I can't be sure. Heather and Kimberly seem to be better off, but not by much. All of them are severely dehydrated and starving!"

"We don't have enough food for everyone," Bass replied, "but you can give them some water." Bass handed her his waterskin, which she took.

"Thanks," Annie replied and then drank deeply. When she had enough, she tossed the waterskin to Kimberly, who drank her fill before passing the waterskin to Heather.

"I have patrols out, so we should know if Palmer and crew try to cross the river," Bass said to Annie. He made it obvious that he didn't want to look at the women.

"Is there a way we can untie them?" Annie asked. "I doubt Phylicia can move very fast in her condition, and the other two won't leave her behind."

Bass thought about it for a minute. "I suppose you can, but you'll have to be responsible for them. I can't spare any men to retrieve them, should they make a break."

Annie looked at the three refugees. "Where would we go?" Heather asked her resignedly.

After several hours, Heather and Kimberly were finally up and walking around, but Phylicia was still unable to get to her feet. As Annie was watching the women, she saw a man run up to Bass.

317

"Murdock and Harris are approaching with someone else," the man reported to Bass.

"Bring them all here," Annie commanded. Bass bristled at her giving orders. But he nodded to the man, who ran off towards the river.

As she watched the approach from the river, Annie breathed a sigh of relief when she saw Harris, Murdock, and Declan. Harris hurried over to Annie to get an update of the patients. Declan went to the patients and started stringing hides to give the women privacy. Murdock went to Reyes, mainly to keep her and Bass, out of the way.

As Harris and Annie entered the enclosure, Declan took up position outside to help keep the other men away.

"How are you feeling?" Harris asked the women.

"Kimberly and I are fine. Sure, we're a little beat up, but our concern is Phylicia. She was having a hard time moving and we had to carry her quite some distance when we escaped," Heather Stevens answered.

Harris tried to get Phylicia's legs to straighten without causing too much pain. As she continued her examination, periodically Phylicia would wince or cry out. When she was finished, Harris left the enclosure.

When Murdock saw Harris exit the makeshift enclosure, he went to her.

"What's the damage, Doc?" he asked.

"Heather Stevens and Kimberly Grey have massive bruising over fifty percent of their bodies. Most of the bruising seems to be centered on their sinus cavities, legs, ribs, hips, and arms. Phylicia looks to have a lot of damage to both her hip labrum, as well as extensive bruising. I can't tell more because there is no x-ray machine on this planet," she stated and then exhaled deeply, exasperated.

"What do they need?" Murdock asked as Reyes came up behind him.

"All three need rest, food, water, and, for Phylicia, minimal walking. No running or heavy lifting."

"So, what are we supposed to do with them?" Reyes whispered impatiently.

Murdock held up his hand to stop all conversation, as he noticed that the others were being overly curious.

"Declan, watch over them for a few minutes," Murdock said as he led Reyes and Harris away from the rest.

"So, you're now Murdock's lapdog?" one of the staff-wielding guards asked Declan a few minutes after Murdock, Harris, and Reyes were out of earshot. Declan remained watchful and silent. "That bitch had you beaten and now you're protecting her?" the man continued. A few more of the guards, who were hearing and agreeing with the speaker, were starting to gather around the enclosure. Declan remained silent and continued to watch.

As one of the men was reaching for one of the hides at a spot that was out of his reach, Declan noticed that another guard carrying a staff wasn't holding on to it securely. As quick as he could, Declan reached out and snatched the staff from the man and brought it down on the other man's wrist, causing the man to grab his wrist in pain.

"What do you think you're doing?" the guard who had just lost his staff asked.

"I think you're way out of your league, Declan!" another guard added. More of the guards came in closer menacingly.

As a different guard took a swing with a staff, one that was aimed at Declan's head, Declan blocked the strike with his borrowed staff and countered by sliding the staff toward the man's body and raked across fingers. A sharp upper strike with the lower part of the staff smacking the guard's wrist caused the staff to fly into the air. Declan managed to catch it before it hit the ground. It was then that Annie Cooper came out of the enclosure, Declan handed her the extra staff, and the two of them prepared to make their stand.

~

"I thought you were one of us, Annie," Bass Heartly said as he rubbed his wrist. "And you, Declan, have gained a few skills."

"Bass, what's going on?" Reyes asked. During the scuffle, Murdock, Reyes, and Harris had returned from their discussions, unnoticed by the rest.

"These two are protecting those three bitches. You know how much we all suffered because of them," Bass said harshly.

"They're doing what I expected them to do," Murdock said. His tone was calm, but menacing. "They would do the same for you."

"You have a point, Bass, but they are our *guests*," Reyes said.

"Maybe, but now I require satisfaction. I've been humiliated in front of my men," Bass replied with venom.

"He does have a point, Murdock," Reyes said.

"What form does this *satisfaction* take?" Murdock asked. "He's already disarmed two of you and stopped a third from gaining access to Phylicia. That should tell you something, Bass."

"I wasn't ready, and he caught me by surprise," Bass pleaded. "If he beats me in a fair fight, I guess I can live with that!"

"What do you think, Declan?" Murdock asked. Declan still said nothing. He stood ready and stared at Bass. "*Qui tacet consentiret*, 'he who is silent is taken to agree' it is, then. Okay, Annie, give Bass your staff. The rest of you back away so they have some room."

Annie tossed the staff to Bass and retreated a little toward the enclosure. Murdock gave his spear to Harris and then walked in between the two men.

320

"So, just to be clear, if you lose, Bass, that will be the end of it?" Murdock asked as he faced Heartly.

"As far as I'm concerned, it will," Heartly agreed.

"Since you qualified the statement, if anyone else wants to take up this argument at a later time, they'll take it up with me!" Murdock turned to Declan. "Be calm and remember your training," he said calmly and quietly, so Declan was the only one to hear him. "This will be staffs only, so no other weapons are permitted." After a short pause, he said, "Begin!"

Declan moved in cautiously, watching Bass for any possible openings. Bass gave ground a little and seemed uncertain. There were a few testing strikes by both men. When Bass finally decided to strike, he swung the staff like a baseball bat, in a downward motion, trying to hit Declan in the head. Declan brought his own staff up to meet Bass' as perpendicular as he could, parrying the blow. He then turned his back toward Bass and stepped backward as he slid his staff backward and caught Bass in the *solar plexus*. The strike was sharp enough that Bass, having the wind knocked out of him, dropped his staff. Declan stopped and backed away, still ready and watching.

19
___

A fter making sure that Bass wasn't going to get up right away, Declan went over to help the man up.

"Are you okay?" he asked, concerned.

"I...suppose...so," Bass managed while trying to catch his breath.

As Declan helped Bass to his feet, Murdock came over and motioned for Bass' men to help him.

"I never would have thought you would defend Phylicia," Reyes said as she walked up beside Murdock as Bass was being helped. "I had thought you'd want her head on a pike after all the damage she's caused. And to get Declan to help you defend her is staggering, to me."

"What are we doing here?" Murdock asked Reyes. "Are we just trying to survive, or are we trying to build a civilization? Are we no better than a pack of wolves? Is that all you want, or do you want more?"

Reyes stopped to look at Murdock.

"It's just something for you to think about," Murdock said as Reyes left.

"What's the verdict?" Annie asked after Reyes and the seven men left the area.

"It's obvious. They don't want Heather, Phylicia, or Kimberly here," Declan said, "and I don't think they are too happy with us right now, either."

"Phylicia will be laid up for a while," Harris said, "but the other two should be okay to take care of her. The problem is where? They have no shelter and they don't know how to fend for themselves."

Declan, Harris, and Annie looked to Murdock for a response, but he just stood there, eyes closed and not moving or even indicating that he'd heard them.

"I have a way to get them some shelter, and we have some food for them," Murdock said after a minute. "It'll mean that either Annie, or Irene, stays with them for the medical treatment Phylicia is going to need."

"I, for one would rather go home," Irene said.

"I need to check in with Reyes. I may be out of a place after what she said," Annie said.

"Annie, you go do what you feel you need to, but know I'll see to it that you'll have a place," Murdock said earnestly. "Do you need me to escort you?"

"Maybe you should. I'm unsure what kind of reception either of us is likely to receive," Annie said guardedly. "I, for one, would appreciate the company."

"Declan, use my spear. You and Irene watch over our charges," Murdock said. "I shouldn't be gone long."

When Murdock and Annie reached the perimeter of Reyes' encampment, they were challenged by the guards and Reyes was summoned.

"What do you want, now?" Reyes asked, testily, once she was out of earshot of the guards.

"Did you think about what I said?" Murdock asked.

"I have and I'm not certain where we're going, as humans,

since our disembarkation. More than a few of us have turned into animals, but when you keep wolves for protection, you do need to give them some red meat once in a while," Reyes said wryly.

"Am I allowed back in?" Annie blurted finally.

"After you've shown us where your loyalties lie?" Reyes responded incredulously. "I'd say no. And, frankly, I'm surprised you'd even ask!"

Annie looked at Murdock, who was clenching and unclenching his teeth, as evidenced by his jaw muscles flexing.

"I'm going to set up Harris and Annie with housing," Murdock said after a long pause. "I expect them to be unmolested by any of your people."

"Expect all you want. I'm not going to guarantee their safety. Come to think of it, I can't guarantee your safety, Murdock!"

"You better think about that one for a bit. Your men are no match for me, and you know it," Murdock warned.

As Murdock finished having his say, he saw Reyes move a little and heard the distinctive twang of a bowstring. He reached out and grabbed the arrow just before it struck Annie in the chest. Murdock moved Annie behind him and walked calmly over to Reyes, being sure there was no clear shot at either of them.

"Would you like me to return this to its owner?" Murdock asked menacingly while waggling the arrow between his fingers. Murdock saw Reyes blanch. "I think I'll do it later, when you least expect it!"

As Murdock started to back away from Reyes' compound, Annie, taking the hint that she should turn and go back the way they'd come, did so, quickly. Murdock backed away as casually as he could. He knew better than to turn his back on Reyes' compound, especially since they'd demonstrated their intentions. He stopped when he was fifty yards out from the compound and leisurely removed his bow and nocked the arrow. He saw Reyes casually walk inside her compound.

When the pair returned, Declan was keeping a vigilant watch and Harris was checking on Phylicia's condition.

"What's the plan?" Annie asked as they joined the others.

"After we rest a little, we're going to the pod," Murdock said.

"What about Palmer and crew?" Annie asked. "I'm sure they'll have something to say about that."

"Right now, they aren't there," Murdock explained. "It is the quickest way to give you, Harris, Phylicia, Heather, and Kimberly shelter. It's the best way to ensure that Phylicia has time to recover." Murdock motioned to Declan to follow him as he moved toward Reyes' encampment a little to talk privately. "How do you feel after your duel with Bass?" he asked after they reached a point so as not to be overheard.

"I'm okay, now," Declan said quietly. "I was scared to death during the fight, though."

"It was a good move you made, though. It ended the fight quickly and didn't permanently damage Bass."

"That was luck," Declan confessed with a slight chuckle. "I was trying for his stomach, but I guess I was too close, or not close enough, and accidentally struck him in the *solar plexus*."

"That's how things usually go," Murdock chuckled. "I was impressed with the fact you didn't allow them to bait you into anything and you stood your ground. Also, you backed off when Bass went down and didn't drop your guard. Plus, you helped him up afterward. That displayed a degree of honorability that Bass will always remember. So will the others."

"On another issue, we will be leaving for the pod shortly. I want you to hang on to my spear and bring up the rear," Murdock instructed.

"Why there?" Declan asked after he raised an eyebrow. "I heard you say that Palmer and his men have left, but what if they come back? And why did you defend Phylicia?"

"Why did you?" Murdock asked.

"Yes, she's evil and manipulative, and she did have Palmer beat me mercilessly, but it didn't seem right to let Reyes' people vent their rage on her. From what I've seen, Heather, Kimberly, and Phylicia have all suffered greatly and will continue to suffer from their injuries."

Murdock chuckled a little. "You're learning," he said as he walked back to the others. "Get Phylicia loaded onto the cart and repack it with everything we brought," Murdock whispered. "When we leave, I want Heather and Kimberly pulling the cart while Annie and Irene walk on either side of it. Declan will bring up the rear."

"We aren't your slaves," Heather fumed. The back of her head was immediately cuffed by Annie.

"You need to drop the attitude," Annie chastised. "We just saved your asses, or are you so clueless that you don't realize it? Reyes' people were going to take their anger out on you three and torture you all. I got shot at for trying to help and defending my patients!"

"Nobody asked you to," Kimberly jeered.

"We can fix that quick enough," Irene Harris said angrily. "Come on, Annie, we'll just leave these three out here for wolves or other animals to prey upon. They don't appreciate what we're trying to do, so they can all stay here!"

"Why should we pull the cart?" Heather asked. "Why can't one of the men do it?" This time it was Harris who cuffed her.

"Because, you brainless twit, there are only two of them and they're going to be busy making sure we women-folk are protected. Show some appreciation by shutting your pie-hole and doing what you're told to do!"

"Okay, that's enough," Murdock interrupted. "I'm telling you because you can't shoot my bow and don't know the way."

"I know the way better than you do and who says I can't shoot your bow?" Heather challenged.

Murdock smirked. "Okay, those are fair points. I'll tell you what. You pull my bow to full draw and I'll pull the cart myself. If you can't, you'll do as you're instructed without any more sass. Deal?"

Heather looked around to the others while she thought about it. She saw Annie and Harris cover their grins while Declan was chuckling openly. Phylicia looked at her dubiously. Only Kimberly was giving her any encouragement. "Deal!" she said after a few seconds.

Murdock handed his bow to Heather and watched as she fumbled with it, trying to get it into a shooting position. Once in a shooting position, Heather grabbed the bowstring and started to pull. When it didn't move, she put all the power her slight frame could generate and still it didn't move. Finally, she put the bow on the ground, stood on the riser, and pulled up on the bowstring for all she was worth. Still, there was no deflection of bowstring or limbs.

"That's not fair," Heather complained after giving up. "That's a trick bow or something. Nobody could pull it!"

Without a word, Murdock walked over, picked up the bow, and drew it to full-draw with ease. After holding it for a few seconds, he let it down.

"Sometimes, it's just easier to do what you're asked," Declan said softly behind Heather. "It's definitely a lot less embarrassing. I may be taller than Murdock, but I can't pull his bow either. I'm suspecting that he's the only one who can."

Heather stomped to her position to pull the cart, since it was now loaded. Kimberly was at the rear of the cart to push. When Murdock gave the signal, everyone moved toward the river.

After several hours of walking and numerous stops to rest, the small group, led by Murdock, finally reached the transport pod. The sun had gone down many hours before. As Murdock, Declan, and Annie looked, they saw no fires or any sign that anyone was around.

"Stay here, while I check it out," Murdock said quietly.

As he approached the pod, Murdock's senses were on high

alert. His night-vision showed no signs of the recent inhabitants. As he reached the underside of the pod, he saw that the ramp was down. He climbed it slowly and as stealthily as he could. He quickly checked every compartment inside the pod and found nothing.

"*Bring them in,*" Murdock flashed to Declan and received an affirmative signal from Declan. "*Bring everything and everyone inside the pod,*" he instructed telepathically.

It wasn't long before everyone was up the ramp, including the cart, and Murdock closed the ramp.

"Irene, you and Annie get Phylicia settled where you want her," he said. "Declan, secure the cart so it doesn't move."

After Phylicia was secured inside the infirmary, the compartment that had housed Declan, everyone else was complaining that they were hungry.

"We'll eat in a bit," Murdock said. "Everyone should find a place to sit. I'm going outside. Declan, after I leave, close the ramp and secure yourself."

Once he was outside the pod, he heard the ramp close. He stood there and started to concentrate. It wasn't long before the pod was levitated and moving toward the cliffs that he had levitated the pod down last spring. As he approached the cliff-face, Murdock levitated the pod and himself in a smooth, upward angle. He was doing his best to not jostle those inside. Once at the top of the cliff-face, Murdock let himself down and turned the pod toward the river.

After a few hours of traveling, he let the pod down close to the river crossing that he had used so often over the years. Once the pod was back on the ground, he signaled Declan to open the ramp.

"I was starting to wonder what was going on," Declan said as he started down the ramp. "What the hell? The stream is in the wrong place."

"That's not the stream, Declan, that's the river!" Annie

exclaimed as she descended the ramp. "This place does look familiar to me. I thought I felt movement."

"You two get a fire started under the pod and away from the ramp," Murdock said as he entered the pod and retrieved the cart.

It didn't take long to get the fire going and some venison cooking. Everyone was moved outside and sat around the fire, waiting for the venison.

"This is a safe enough place," Murdock said as he tended the venison. "Your only worries are the animals with more than two legs."

"Where are we?" Irene Harris asked.

"You've been here before and so has Annie and Declan," Murdock said. "I'm leaving after we eat to bring Emily here and bring some tools."

"What's the plan, Murdock?" Declan asked.

"This place is secure from any human that doesn't belong here. I'm going to bring Emily to help with Phylicia, Heather, and Kimberly, mainly because I don't trust them."

"And why is that? Kimberly asked snidely.

"I don't trust you because none of you have given me a reason to. Quite the contrary you've given me every reason not to trust you. To prevent you three from harming anyone else, you will be restricted to the pod and the immediate area. Annie and Harris can either tend to Phylicia or they can instruct Heather and yourself in her treatment. I would prefer you to be trained.

"I'll be in and out of here until Phylicia is able to fend for herself. There is no need to worry about food or water, I'll provide the food and will leave enough waterskins so you can get your own water. Whoever stays here, are to make you three fend for yourselves as much as possible. Heather, Kimberly, and Phylicia, you have until Phylicia is able to fend for herself to figure out what you're going to do after that."

"This pod is more ours than it is yours!" Phylicia retorted.

"True enough, but I have need of it to house you and get you back on your feet. No one else was using it, so—"

"A case could be made that where this pod rests is rightfully ours," Phylicia taunted.

"Good luck with that," Murdock chuckled. "That attitude could be one of the reasons people have a problem with you. But, if you or anyone else wants to leave, please, feel free. I doubt anyone who knows you will shed a tear when you end up inside a wolf or something worse. I have enough to worry about already to be overly concerned with you. I know I've done what I can to offer you a chance to live."

Everyone sat in silence while the meat cooked. When it was done, everyone took a portion and separated to enjoy, either alone or with preferred company. Murdock had found a spot away from Phylicia and was joined by Declan, Irene, and Annie.

"What are you going to do, Annie, when this chore is done?" Murdock asked between bites.

"I don't know. I haven't given it much thought, until now," Annie replied.

"Declan, Emily, and I have been enjoying the teachings of Kevin and Mei Lee," Irene offered. "I think you'd be welcome with us."

"Thanks, Irene, but Kevin made that offer to me some time ago," Annie replied. "I chose to stay with Reyes and her group. Now, that has gone by the wayside. It looks like life with Kevin has helped you. And Declan, I'm glad you finally gave up all the anger."

"I'm feeling useful, which is a big part of my being angry," Declan responded between bites. "What happened when Annie went back to Reyes' group?"

"I got shot at," Annie answered, "and if it weren't for Kevin, I'd at least have a nasty wound, or be dead. I'm sorry, Kevin, for causing you a problem with Reyes."

"You didn't cause any problems, Annie," Murdock responded. "It's human nature to want revenge after you've been hurt by someone. It's that need for revenge that caused the rift, not you."

"It helps to know you don't blame me," Annie replied.

"Why would he blame you?" Irene asked. "You did what you're supposed to do. You protected your patient over the wishes of those in political power. I did the same for Declan."

Murdock grinned a little at the other three sitting with him. "Sometimes, it's enough to be understood and I appreciate you three for trying. As far as our guests go, I would suggest closing the ramp when I leave, and Declan sleeps close to it to prevent the others from venturing out on their own. I'd also suggest that you three take turns watching through the night. Don't trust them and don't underestimate them. I'll be back by dawn with Emily and more meat."

"Don't you get tired of looking out for everyone else?" Annie asked. "I, for one, owe you a lot!"

"All I've ever asked is for people to learn something and quit making the same mistakes," Murdock said. His exhaustion was evident in his voice. Without prompting, Irene got up and gave him a hug before returning to the guests and trying to get them inside the pod. Taking a hint from Irene's action, Annie got to her feet, hugged him, and helped with the guests. Declan got to his feet and so did Murdock. "Look after Annie and Irene, Declan. They're special."

"I know," Declan said as he stuck out his hand.

Murdock shook his hand, took the cart, and disappeared into the darkness.

When Declan awoke, he opened the ramp. Emily and Murdock were sitting close to the fire. They had restarted it and were sitting and waiting. Declan bounded down the ramp and greeted his wife with a big hug and a passionate kiss. He was followed, a few minutes later, by Irene and Annie.

"Em, this is Annie Cooper," Declan said.

"We've met," Emily said as she extended her hand to the much smaller woman.

"A pleasure to see you again, Emily," Annie said as she took the Amazon's hand. As she watched Emily's hand close over hers, her hand seemed to disappear.

"Nice to see you, too, Annie, and you can call me either Em or Emily," Emily replied.

Irene came over and gave Emily a hug. "How are you, Em? How're our kids...err, umm, Murdock's kids?"

"There just as healthy as can be," Emily responded.

"And just as exasperating as usual, too, I bet," Irene said good-naturedly.

"Well, they *are* Murdock's kids," Emily joked.

"Very true," Irene responded with a big smile.

"How are our guests?" Murdock interjected.

"Quiet," Declan reported. "No problems at all."

"Phylicia is about the same, physically," Irene reported.

"Is it going to work having Heather and Kimberly treating her under your tutelage?" Murdock asked.

"Who knows?" Irene responded. "It's only been a day. Ask me again in a week. I did tell them that they had to take care of Phylicia. I told them neither I nor Annie is going to do it. I'll add Emily to that list as soon as possible."

"Have you given any more thought to what we discussed at the cabin?" Murdock asked.

"I have and I'm in," Irene stated. "With everything going on and with everything that has happened, I like the idea of belonging."

"Good, I'm glad to hear it," Murdock said with a small grin. "Right now, I need to go to where the pod was to see if they left anything behind that we can use." Murdock waved Declan over to him. "I need you to stay here and get things organized," he told Declan once he was in earshot.

"Do you need me to go with you?" Declan asked. "I know Mei Lee would kill me if anything happened to you."

"No, I need you here," Murdock said with a chuckle, "but I do appreciate the offer."

"Oh, my freakin' God!" Phylicia's voice sounded from the ramp. "Who is this walking mountain of flesh? You need to go on a diet, dearie!"

Emily got to her feet and turned to face Phylicia. "Was that directed at me?" she asked with a scowl.

"She's too dumb to know who we're talking about!" Phylicia snickered. Heather and Kimberly laughed openly.

Irene, Annie, and Declan ran over to Emily to try to restrain her, but Emily was dragging Annie and Irene, who had each grabbed one of Emily's arms, and Declan was being slid backward as his wife pushed forward. Phylicia had a panicked look on her face, as did Heather and Kimberly.

"You two better keep her under control," Murdock warned as he hung a quarter of venison from one of the landing struts. "Talk like that is rude and unacceptable. As you can see, we are trying to keep Emily from snapping Phylicia in half," Murdock said gravely, "but I'm afraid they're losing ground."

"Do something, Murdock!" Heather yelled.

"Like what?" Murdock asked. "I guess I could gag Phylicia until she learns to keep a civil tongue in her head. Or you two can."

While Murdock hung the second quarter, Emily threw off Annie and back-handed Declan's shoulder, knocking him to the ground and out of her way. Irene couldn't restrain her alone and let go.

"Murdock!" Kimberly screamed as Emily grabbed Phylicia by the front of what was left of her shirt and straight-armed the much smaller woman. Kimberly and Heather had grabbed onto Emily's arm so that all three women were hanging free of the ground.

"From what I understand, I'm here to see to it that you three behave," Emily yelled to be heard over the screams of the three small women hanging from her right arm. "Apparently, I have to teach you three some common courtesy as well!"

Murdock started chuckling. "Glad to see that you women will work it all out."

"Em, don't break anything important," Irene pleaded as she came up to Emily after helping Annie and Declan to their feet.

"My husband and my friends felt that you were worth saving," Emily said through clenched teeth, giving them all a good shake. "They risked their lives and all they get in return is insults, sass, and back-talk. I, for one, will not tolerate it! Prove to me that you're worth the cost or I'll throw you all over the cliff myself!" With that, she dropped Phylicia and the other two released their grip on the big woman's arm.

"I protest this—" Phylicia started.

"I don't care what you protest you're going to learn to be civilized, even if it kills you!" Emily boomed cutting off Phylicia's protest.

"I'd listen to her if I were you," Murdock cautioned, with a chuckle, as he left the pod area.

Once Emily had boomed, there were no more protests and all three guests were silent.

"Now then, my name is Emily, but you can call me Misses Griffen. You haven't earned the right to call me by my first name. We're going to start with morning clean-up, so get your skinny asses to the river and bathe!" All three women walked fearfully to the river with Emily close on their heels.

"Impressive, isn't she?" Declan asked Annie and added a deep sigh afterward.

"Was she mad?" Annie asked sheepishly.

"Oh, no, she was just a little irritated at the rudeness," Declan explained. "If she would have been mad, you would know!"

"I've only seen her as very sweet and lovable. I hope I'm never the focus of her anger," Irene said while shaking her head slightly.

~

By the time Palmer, Jax Hornsby, Ted Wagner, and Nels Osterlund reached the cliff downriver from their plateau, it was only hours before sundown. As Palmer stood by the edge, he could see no movement below, but he could see what appeared to be paths on the other side of the river and into woods. He suspected that the paths led to the others. From his vantage point, he could see the zig-zag path down the cliff and knew it was going to take a while to navigate the cliff.

"We have some careful climbing to do to get off the cliff," Palmer said aloud. "I don't want to be on that treacherous path after dark, so move it along!"

By the time the four men had managed the cliff-face, it was after sunset and getting dark quickly. Working together, they managed to get firewood collected, a fire started, and a couple of fish caught. While the fish were cooking, Palmer could see an old campsite on the other side of the river and figured the others were close by.

"I think the others went into the woods on the other side of the river," Palmer said as all four men sat to eat by the fire. "Tomorrow, we'll see if we can find them."

"What kind of reception can we expect?" Osterlund asked.

"I'm more worried about being safe out here through the night," Hornsby said.

"You three can rotate a watch to keep the fire going and to wake the others if needed," Palmer said around a bite of fish. "I'm sure we'll have a frosty reception, but maybe we can wheedle a place somewhere. We should keep an eye out for possible campsites, though, just in case."

The night passed quickly and without incident for the four men. At daylight, they started packing and cleaning their campsite. When that was finished, they walked downriver to find a place that would be easier to cross.

"If we run into anyone, let me do the talking and just agree with me," Palmer told the other three.

It wasn't long before they found the same place that those who had crossed the river had used. After crossing, they headed upriver because Palmer wanted to investigate the campsite he'd seen the night before.

"What are you doing here?" a stern voice asked from inside the tree-line when they had traveled half the distance back upriver. They all reflexively grabbed for their twelve-inch machetes.

"We're looking for that bitch, Phylicia," Palmer responded cordially. "Have you seen her? The last time we saw her, she was traveling with those other two twits, Heather and Kimberly."

"They're not here. Like you, they wouldn't be welcomed here!" the voice said with anger. "You need to leave. Go back the way you came and don't ever return!"

Palmer shrugged and turned to leave the way they'd come. After they'd all left and crossed the river, they stopped. They had decided to eat before continuing on downriver. When they got to the next cliff-face, they could see that the trees were fewer and they saw a small encampment close to the cliff and on their side of the river.

"What do we do now?" Osterlund asked standing at the edge. "If we descend the cliff-face, we'll be inside their encampment."

"I'd suggest we move toward the stream and see if it comes this far downriver," Hornsby added. "It may afford a safer way down the cliff, if you still want to head downriver."

"Or we could recross the river and see if there is a way down on the other side," Palmer offered. "It wouldn't delay us as much."

"What about being told to leave?" Wagner asked. "If they catch us on the other side of the river, they could kill us outright."

"Based on where the river was crossed, back there, I'd say

that the group that crossed it is located against the cliff upriver. I doubt they patrol this far downriver," Palmer posited. "I think we'd be better off gathering more information on them before making a decision about moving on. I doubt they patrol at all. We ran into that guy because he was probably going to catch some fish. I didn't hear or see anyone else with him."

"Doesn't mean there weren't others with him," Hornsby speculated. "They could have just been waiting for us because they saw us heading downriver."

"Since you seem to be so skeptical, Hornsby, I think you should scout the area across the river first," Palmer said. "You'd be the quieter of us," he said after Hornsby blanched, "and less likely to get caught. Just go over and be stealthy. See if there's anyone else over there. You don't need to go far."

When Murdock reached the spot that had once been occupied by the pod, he scrutinized the ground looking for anything that was left behind. The few things he did find, he placed inside the incomplete log building and started to levitate the structure and move it closer to the pod. As he proceeded, he found it to be effortless to levitate. In short order, he had the partial structure within a mile of the pod.

"Declan, get the guests inside the pod," he flashed to Declan.

"Will do," he received the telepathic response. A short time later came, *"Done."*

As Murdock came within sight of the transport pod, he could see Declan, Irene, and Annie watching his approach. One hundred feet above him was the common house that the others had started and abandoned, floating. He could see their mouths agape. After setting the building down gently a short distance from the pod, they all came over to him.

"How did you do that?" Annie asked.

"Can you teach us to do that?" Declan asked.

"That's impossible!" Irene stated her disbelief evident on her face.

"We can discuss this later, when we're alone," Murdock said. "It's one of those things that stay within the family. Since we have outsiders, we need to be aware of what we say and who is around to hear it." Annie, Declan, Irene, and Emily nodded their head in agreement. "You can let the others out."

Declan went over to the pod and dropped the ramp. "You can come out now, if you want," he shouted into the interior and returned to the campfire.

"Thieves!" Phylicia shouted as she slowly made her way down the ramp shortly after Declan opened it. "Robbers! Larcenous scoundrels!"

"What is your problem, now?" Murdock asked Phylicia in all seriousness and with irritation. "Nothing has been taken!"

"You had no right to steal the hard work of the others who built the Meeting Hall!" Phylicia fumed.

"It's an unfinished building with no one to finish it. No one was working on it and there are some here that are going to need it," Murdock defended. "Now, you three," Murdock said looking to Heather, paused, then to Kimberly, paused, and then to Phylicia, "need to understand a few things. Phylicia, you are here because you've been injured to the point that you need to be taken care of, for the time being. Your escape to Reyes' domain has left you vulnerable. Her security people were going to either kill you, or have their way with you, and then leave you to die in the wilderness, all with Reyes' blessing.

"Kimberly and Heather, since you chose to back Phylicia, you were a target for their wrath as well. Your purpose here is to care for Phylicia under Doctor Harris', or Annie's, tutelage. There is no other reason for you to be here.

"While you three are here, you are to conduct yourselves in a civilized manner. You are to treat everyone with respect and appreciation. In other words, continue to disrespect us and make yourselves major pains in our asses, then you can't expect us to treat you with respect. Too much of it and I'll put all three of you right back where you landed.

"To me, none of you have any standing whatsoever. Declan, Annie, Irene, and Emily have all earned my respect and appreciation. If you want respect or appreciation, you have to earn it."

"I neither need nor want respect from any of you," Phylicia fired back. If Heather and Kimberly are to care for me, why do I need Declan and that...that Amazon?"

"Declan and Emily are here for security," Murdock explained.

"Who do we need protection from?" Phylicia asked snidely.

Murdock chuckled. "They aren't here as security *for* you. They are here for security *from* you." Murdock could see Emily's wicked grin starting to form and he saw Phylicia blanch as his words sunk in.

20

On one of his return trips to the pod, seven days later, Murdock called Declan, Irene, Annie, and Emily together for a private conversation.

"How's Phylicia?" he asked as the other four trickled in toward the fire.

"She'll recover most of the function in her hips," Irene stated. "It'll be some time before I'd say she has recovered it all."

"Heather, Kimberly, and Phylicia have been secretive since you laid down the law," Declan said as Emily came over.

"They may be planning something," Emily reported. "In fact, I think it likely. None has given us any grief, though. I think it was a combination of you setting them straight and me not taking their crap."

"I don't know if you've noticed, but it's close to the end of summer," Murdock informed them. "The weather is going to keep getting colder and wetter from here on out."

"Are we keeping *them* any longer?" Annie asked. "Phylicia can walk pretty well. Maybe not perfect, but better than when we brought her here. I, for one, would like them gone."

"I'll bow to you and Irene's recommendations," Murdock answered. "What concerns me is the winter and who will be staying in this building?" he asked looking over the unfinished meeting hall. "I don't want to waste the effort if none of you is going to stay in it."

"Speaking as someone who started it, this thing is going to be too big for just a few people," Declan explained. "It was designed to be both offices and meeting hall for the three council members and to function as a place for everyone else in case of emergency or group meetings. It was supposed to be two stories tall."

"If it's only one story tall," Murdock started, "it can still be used as a *longhouse* for everyone on this side of the border. All we need to make it suitable is a couple more courses and then roof it. To preserve it, we'll have to roof it anyway. I'm open to thoughts and suggestions."

"Do we have the time?" Annie asked. "If we do, I'd say stay in the longhouse this winter. I think it will be warmer and cozier than the pod."

"I agree with Annie," Irene said. "I'll stay here if she will. I wouldn't want to be here all alone."

Emily had been sitting and apparently thinking, as she hadn't added her ideas to the discussion. "What do you think, Em?" Murdock asked finally.

"Well, from my point of view," Emily started finally, "the pod is being used, right now, as a way to control the petulant children. It gives us a way to lock them in. I, for one, don't like the idea of being without a bath all winter, or not having the company of my family for as long as you say winter lasts. If it were up to me, I'd put it in the pasture downriver from the house and finish it there. It would make things a lot easier and it will make everyone available to help with the stocking up for winter. It would mean that only one person is needed to watch the spoiled brats instead of four."

"I agree with Em," Declan piped in. "It would also allow room for projects that are too big to be enclosed in the house or the transport pod."

"What kind of projects are you thinking about?" Murdock asked.

"As an example, making some crockery," Declan responded. "We'll all need some, but now, we'd have to do it outside. When it's nice outside, we don't have time to work on them and in the winter, the weather would become an issue."

"You know how to work clay?" Murdock asked Declan, clearly surprised.

"I'm not an expert and the firing process would be a challenge," Declan responded, "but I think I could figure something out."

"I, for one," Irene started, "feel, as medical personnel, we need to stay out of the political machinations. Personal issues with the Leaders of the other factions shouldn't make a difference when it comes to giving care. Annie's treatment by Reyes' group, to me, was unacceptable.

"That being said, we, as humans, have a deep-seated need for friends and family. That doesn't mean we all have to live in the same house. I think Murdock, Mei Lee, and their kids need to have their house back. Moving the meeting hall and finishing it would allow the rest of us an alternative to our imposing on them further. It would also have the effect of helping the four of us to be more self-reliant."

Murdock sat and listened to all input from the others, nodding his head periodically.

"Annie, can you check on our charges?" Murdock asked finally. Annie nodded and went to check on Phylicia. "What do you think of letting Annie into our little group?" he asked after she left.

"That is up to her, of course," Irene said. "I have no problem with her, and she has proven her worth many times."

"I agree with Irene," Declan piped up. "She has helped tremendously. I'd welcome it!"

"I don't know her," Emily added, "so I have no opinion one

way or the other and so will accept what the rest of you suggest."

"Mei Lee and I have had this discussion and have accepted her into our family," Murdock said. He saw Annie approaching and motioned for her to join them. "Just so you know, we have been discussing you," he said once she was in earshot.

"What about me?" Annie asked guardedly.

"If you're interested, we would like you to join our little group," Murdock said. "It does come with some restrictions, though, that you need to be aware of."

"What kind of restrictions?" Annie asked.

"By us accepting you, it means that we think you are trustworthy," Murdock answered. "The restrictions are that things you learn or see stay within the group and are not to be discussed with outsiders or in their presence or hearing."

"So, nothing different from what I've been doing already," Annie responded good-naturedly.

In the eight days that Palmer, Hornsby, Osterlund, and Wagner had been lurking — they called it exploring — around the area of the second terrace, they had managed to surreptitiously observe all three groups that lived there.

One group, the one furthest from the river, seemed to them to be the more isolated and had fewer occupants.

The four men had managed to find a roughly triangular depression that they were using for shelter, close to the edge of the third terrace.

"It appears," Palmer said as he looked around at the viewable scenery, "that the mountains retreat at a steep angle on the next terrace down." He wasn't talking to anyone, in particular, just voicing his thoughts.

"It appears so," Jax Hornsby observed. "I've noticed that this group doesn't go to the river, so there has to be a water source close by, maybe a stream from the melting mountain snow."

"Well, short of making contact with them," Palmer observed, "we aren't going to know. What are the chances of one of us being accepted?" He saw the other three men blanch at the thought.

"You want us to approach them?" Wagner asked with apprehension. "What if they recognize us?"

"No," Palmer responded, "I want *you* to approach them. Did you recognize anyone there?"

"No, but they may recognize me," Wagner responded.

"I doubt it," Palmer stated. "Frankly, Wagner, you aren't that memorable."

"I agree," Annie replied.

"There are creatures, here, called the Oomah," Murdock explained. Declan, Irene, and Emily nodded and patiently waited for Murdock to say something they hadn't heard before. "If you saw one, you'd think they are bears, but that is how we perceive them. They have helped us in innumerable ways for more than five years."

"Were they responsible for my memory block and being transported during the night?" Annie asked.

"Partially, I did the transporting, but they did help with making you unconscious," Murdock explained.

As he was talking, Annie was looking behind Murdock and saw two huge bears headed their way.

"Do they look like that?" Annie asked as she pointed behind Murdock.

Everyone turned to see two bears meandering toward them.

"Don't anyone panic. They are friends and won't hurt you," Murdock instructed.

As they all watched, the smaller one had stopped some

distance away and the bigger one proceeded toward them. Their mouths began to drop open as the huge bear came up to Murdock and was towering over him.

"This is Beron," Murdock said as he reached out to touch the huge bear's fur without turning to look where his hand was. "He is the current leader of the Oomah, as well as my dear friend. The other one is Bridget and she is a mate of Beron's." Murdock saw everyone, mouth agape, clustering together to gain some strength from each other. "Respect him and you'll be alright."

"Glad see you better, Dee Clan," Declan, Emily, and Murdock heard it clearly as it flashed through their minds. Irene heard something, but was refusing to believe what was happening.

"Nice to meet you, Beron," Declan answered aloud. *"Many thanks to you and your mate for your help."* Declan flashed telepathically to the huge bear.

They all were stunned when the huge bear gave the slightest of nods.

"Beron has come to help you all...understand," Murdock told them. "He does this by *sharing*. It's a mixing of your memories with his. He uses it to get to know you and determine if he can trust you. It isn't something forced, and you do have some control over what is shown him. You just have to trust him and don't hide anything from him."

"I'm game," Declan said enthusiastically.

"I'm in as well," Emily responded.

"I don't believe it, but I'll try it and see what happens," Irene said.

Murdock could see Annie chewing her bottom lip. "You've done this?" she asked, her voice trembling a little.

"Mei Lee and I have done this many times. We've done this between each other even more often," Murdock explained. "It is also a way for Beron to communicate with you personally."

"So, Beron gets to see all the intimate details of our lives, but what do we get out of it?" Annie asked.

STEPHEN DRAKE

"A side benefit of the *sharing* is a better connection with the rest of us for telepathic communications and increased ability in telekinesis. It has something to do with a minor realignment, a fine-tuning, if you will, of the brainwaves, I think," Murdock explained. "You also get to see some things about the Oomah. No one is forcing you to do this. You're free to decline."

"Okay, I'll trust you, Murdock. How do we start?" Annie asked finally.

"Find a piece of turf and get comfortable," Murdock instructed as he lay down.

Several hours later, they all started to wake from the *sharing*. Murdock was on his feet first and went around to each and helped them up. Each one was, in Murdock's opinion, much more at peace.

"Is that really what happened to the first transport pod?" Emily asked.

"It is. That was from my perspective merged with Rose's perspective and Mei Lee's perspective. I don't think you'll get anything more accurate," Murdock said. He was looking around at the rest and noticed Declan crying. "You okay, Declan?"

"Yes, I'm fine. It was hard seeing my sister battered like that, but I did get to see her happy," Declan said.

"What did you think of the experience, Irene?" Murdock asked. "You were the skeptic, but I do value your opinion."

"It was...different," Harris started. "At least I figured out what my issues were and became able to let them go, well, some of them, anyway. I do feel better about things and myself."

"So, any of you have any regrets about the *sharing*?" Murdock asked. No one spoke. "How about you, Annie, do you have any thoughts on it?"

"I feel closer to all of you than I thought possible. I'm glad I did it," Annie said. "I do know, now, where your authority

346

comes from. I was always wondering why you thought you had the authority to lay down the law to Phylicia and the others. Now, I know."

"Can I talk to Bridget?" Declan asked.

"You'd have to ask Beron or talk to her through him. I think it is forbidden for her to talk directly to a male," Murdock explained with a shrug. "It's a cultural thing."

"Welcome to the family," flashed to everyone's mind and they all knew it was from Mei Lee.

Ted Wagner was standing in front of Raymond Tutt. He had been working with the group for fourteen days doing odd jobs and was expecting to be admitted.

"Well, Wagner, everyone says you work well and keep to yourself. Why is that?" Tutt asked.

"I prefer to not be a bother to anyone," Wagner shrugged. "It's just the way I am, I guess."

"What we need are bowmen. We have very few bows and few enough arrows, but we need someone who can hit what they're aiming at. Is that you?"

"I don't know, Tutt, but I'm willing to try."

"If I give you a bow, am I going to have to worry about you shooting me with it?" Tutt asked as he narrowed his eyes.

"As long as you don't stand in front of me, you should be safe. It's been a very long time since I shot a bow, so I can't promise anything, but I would think you'd be okay," Wagner answered.

"I mean are you loyal? I need loyalty above all else. Can I trust you?" Tutt asked.

"All I'm asking is a chance to prove myself. If you find, after a reasonable time, that I can't be trusted, then remove me." Wagner was hoping that his past work and his arguments were enough for the skeptical leader.

"Okay, I'll take a chance on you, but if you can't prove to me that I can trust you, you'll find a hatchet in your skull. Is that clear enough?" Tutt asked with a rough tone.

"Crystal clear, sir," Wagner said with a grin of excitement. This was more than he had been told to accomplish, by Palmer, but it was something he wanted. He knew that Palmer was going to start a war between the different factions, hoping to come to the rescue of the survivors. Wagner hadn't decided, yet, which side he was on. He was starting to believe that he would be safe here, safe from Murdock's wrath.

Wagner's instructions from Palmer had been to keep a low profile, watch, look, and report back. It had been fourteen days and he had watched and investigated, but he had yet to report back. He wasn't sure he wanted to. He knew what Palmer would most likely use the information for, and he wasn't sure he was willing to do that.

One of the craftsmen had developed a bow and a few arrows. Tutt had gathered all the men in their group for an archery competition to see who had any skill or aptitude. No one hit the target and he had gotten closest. He knew he wasn't the best of the best. *It's more like I was best of the worst*, he thought. *At least, now, I can practice and maybe earn my way as a hunter for the group.*

It was a few days after Murdock's tribe increased that Murdock received a flash.

"*Harvest hides?*" Beron flashed.

"*Yes, thank you.*" Murdock flashed to Beron. He started loading the cart with what he might need. "*Hides need harvesting,*" he flashed to Mei Lee and Declan.

Mei Lee immediately informed all the female tribal members.

"*What does that entail for us?*" flashed to his mind from Emily.

"*It means that we will be able to outfit you, Declan, Irene, and Annie with some clothing. It also means that Declan and I will be away for a while,"* Murdock responded, *"with a lot of work for all of us to process the hides."*

"Where are we going?" Declan asked aloud as he came up to Murdock.

"We're going to be in the vicinity of your sister's tomb, so we can take a minute to pay our respects before getting on with our work. You need to get outfitted like I am," Murdock responded as he finished loading the cart. Mei Lee brought the kids out and they all bid their father good-bye, waving as he and Declan levitated across the river. They hadn't gone far when Murdock stopped.

"Why are we stopping?" Declan asked.

"We need to get there faster, so you need to get on the cart," Murdock said. As he picked up the handles of the cart, Murdock started off at an easy lope. After they had been traveling an hour or so, Murdock stopped next to Rose's tomb.

"That was a quick trip," Declan exclaimed. "You must have been doing thirty or forty miles an hour!"

Murdock ignored the quip and went to Rose's tomb. After standing there quietly for a few minutes, he ritualistically kissed his fingers and touched them to the tomb. "Your turn," he said to Declan as he returned to the cart. He watched as Declan approached the tomb, looking over his shoulder sheepishly. The thought struck Murdock that Declan may not know what to do, in this situation and it caused Murdock to chuckle to himself a little.

When the two men had finished, they proceeded at a normal pace downstream a few miles. They knew they were in the right spot when they came upon twenty deer corpses.

Murdock stripped off his leather shirt and waited for Declan to do the same.

"Watch and learn," Murdock said to Declan as he pulled his six-inch knife and started skinning the first deer. "It isn't too hard," he said as he scored the hide around the neck, close to the deer's head. "The skill comes in cutting just the hide." Declan watched carefully as Murdock scored the hide around all four legs and then started the long cut down the underside of the neck to the back legs in a straight line. He then cut the hide on the inside of each leg up to the center cut.

"Now, comes the hard part," Murdock said. "Grab a leg and pull the deer onto its back." As soon as Declan managed to roll the heavy animal onto its back, Murdock deftly started peeling the hide as he cut the membrane holding it. It seemed to take little time to trim the hide off half the carcass. "Your turn, Declan, just do what I did," Murdock said.

Declan took his own six-inch knife and tried his best to copy Murdock's movements, while Murdock was holding the carcass. It only took Declan three times longer than it took Murdock. When they were finished skinning the first one, Declan stacked the hide on the cart, with the head attached, and the back-strap tendon on the inside of the hide.

After the first one, they each took a deer and skinned it. It continued for several hours and the hides were stacking up.

"Time comes for long sleep. You need meat?" Beron flashed to Murdock.

"Yes, we could use some," Murdock responded.

"Take what need," flashed back to Murdock from Beron.

"We are taking two of the deer home, so we need to quarter them before we're done," Murdock said to Declan. "Do you know how to do that?"

"I wasn't much of a hunter before I came here," Declan responded sheepishly.

"The more you do something, the easier it is to do," Murdock said with a smile.

Murdock was standing in the transport pod the day after he and Declan had returned with a heavily loaded cart. He had already hung the deer quarters in the smokehouse and had left the cart with all the hides at his cabin.

"I haven't decided what I should do with you," Murdock said to Phylicia, Heather, and Kimberly.

"Why are we being held captive?" Phylicia asked haughtily. "We've done nothing to warrant being incarcerated!"

"Since you three have been here, you've done nothing to contribute to the rest of us," Murdock said ignoring Phylicia's questions. "Consequently, we're not inclined to allow you to be here. You were brought here to allow Phylicia to heal from her injuries and for your own safety. Now, you'll be allowed to fend for yourselves, but not here. You're going to be put back where the pod landed."

"But we'll die," Heather shrieked. "We don't know how to survive here!"

"You're handing us a death warrant," Kimberly said hotly.

"No use in appealing to his better nature, girls," Phylicia responded condescendingly. "He is without any empathy and is unduly cruel. That's just what I'd expect from a *murderer*!"

Murdock chuckled: "You're back on that again? Like I told you, I didn't murder anyone. Your cousin made his own choices and died because of them. The only ones I killed, from the first pod, were two of your cousin's henchmen and that was done because of their raping and trying to kill two women and a man. I caught them in the act, and they were given a chance. It was a trial by combat, and I was unarmed. They were armed. The rest died from starvation or at the hand of your cousin."

"My cousin would never hurt anyone," Phylicia raged.

"He killed five people, with his own hand! One was a baby, his own child!"

"I refuse to believe anything you say," Phylicia said through a clenched jaw.

"You can believe what you like," Murdock said quietly. "I really don't care what you choose to believe or how you wish to delude yourself." Murdock shifted his gaze to Heather and Kimberly. "Are any of you pregnant?"

"That is none of your business," Phylicia raged.

Heather and Kimberly both looked shocked and started to blush. "Yes," Heather said with downcast eyes. Kimberly just looked at the ground and nodded.

Murdock sighed. "That complicates things."

"Why should that be a complication for you?" Phylicia asked angrily. "It's our problem and we'll deal with it!"

"Irene, I need a doctor's opinion," Murdock flashed to the doctor. *"Heather and Kimberly need an examination,"*

"An examination...for what?" flashed to his mind from the doctor.

"Would you both consent to being examined by Doctor Harris?" Murdock asked quietly.

"Pregnancy," Murdock flashed to Harris after the two women nodded their consent.

Shortly after Palmer had sent Wagner to the group furthest away from the river, he sent Jax Hornsby to the group that was closer to the river and Nels Osterlund to the group located below the terrace they were currently on. They, like Wagner, were to observe and report back. While they were gone, Palmer had managed to roll a few logs and cut a few limbs and was well into the process of making a makeshift shelter.

It had been close to twenty-one days since he had sent Wagner and a fortnight since he'd sent the other two and none had returned to report. He was beginning to doubt any of them would return. Every few days, Palmer would trek to the river, harvest a fish, and refill his waterskin. On one of the return trips, he followed the edge of the terrace closely, looking for an easier way down. Finding none, he returned to his shelter and cooked the fish.

As he sat enjoying his meal, he thought about getting off the terrace. He had no idea what was below the terrace, but he knew it would be less crowded than the current one and, he hoped, there would be better shelter than he currently had. He had been feeling the weather getting colder, especially in the mornings, and knew his makeshift shelter wasn't going to afford him much in the way of protection from the weather.

After finishing his meal, he walked to the edge of the terrace and continued to follow it in the direction of the mountains. After he'd gone a little over a mile, he saw a huge tree growing close to the terrace edge. As he looked at it, he figured it was only five or six feet out from the edge and had plenty of heavy limbs close into the trunk. He knew it was a huge risk, but he felt if he got a run, he could jump over to the heavier limbs and then climb down. *If I miss, it will be a long drop through the tree*, he thought, wishing he had enough rope to climb down, not that he had any rope at all. The others had made sure to take it all when they deserted the council.

As he contemplated his jumping to the tree, he sat on the edge of the terrace and looked over. *It looks like the edge overhangs a few feet, so sliding down on my butt is out of the question*, he thought. *Sliding would work only for the first few feet and then I'd be dropped straight down. A fifty-foot drop would be exceedingly painful. And what happens if I hit a small tree that I can't see or a rock. No, the jump would be better, and I could climb down. If I miss my target, then…what? No one would know where I am or where I went.*

As he got to his feet, he had decided to consider it another day, but he would sharpen some small limbs to act as arrows to point the way to this spot on his way back to his camp. When he arrived at his camp, he collected firewood and made sure the fire was going. He had no sooner accomplished this than it started to rain.

As he huddled inside his leaking shelter, he was trying to keep from shivering while putting more wood on the fire. *This is going to be a miserable night*, he thought.

~

When Irene Harris arrived, being escorted by Emily, she removed her weapons and both women went into the pod. On their entry, Murdock left to wait outside the pod. He spent his time gathering more wood and keeping the small fire going.

When Irene and Emily entered the pod, she escorted Kimberly back to the room she had been using as a sickbay. Emily waited in the main room with Phylicia and Heather.

"What are *you* doing here?" Phylicia asked dourly.

"I'm here to keep the peace," Emily said matter-of-factly, "and to ensure Irene's safety."

"Can't the doctor take care of herself?" Phylicia asked disrespectfully. "Am I that much of a threat?"

"To Irene, you might be," Emily responded dismissively. "To me, you're no threat at all."

After a few minutes, Irene and Kimberly exited the room and Heather followed the doctor back.

"So, what's the verdict?" Phylicia asked. She didn't look angry, but her voice said she was.

"Probably am," Kimberly responded quietly.

"That was smart," Phylicia chided. "You just had to get yourself knocked up, didn't you?"

"That is enough, Phylicia," Emily commanded. "Leave her alone."

A few minutes later, Doctor Harris and Heather came out of the sickbay and Irene and Emily exited the pod.

"What did you find out?" Murdock asked as he handed the doctor her weapons.

"Since we don't have the means to do a proper pregnancy test, I can't say definitively that they are pregnant," Irene said. "However, given the time they spent with Palmer and his goons and given all the external symptoms, I'd say that it is likely that both are pregnant."

"That changes things," Murdock said pensively. "I was going

to put them back at the original pod site so we wouldn't have to worry about them attacking us. Now, I can't do that. The pod needs to be used for their shelter here and they need to be checked on periodically."

"Would moving the pod closer to the cabin help?" Emily asked.

"It would make checking on them during their pregnancy easier," Irene said.

"Yes, it would," Murdock said, "but it would make it easier for them to attack us. It would endanger the kids and the rest of us and that is an unacceptable option, to me. I could put the pod across the river, but then they might see things I don't want them to see."

"So, what are you going to do?" Emily asked.

After a few minutes, Murdock went into the pod.

"You three are to stay here," he told the inhabitants. "You're not going to be guarded or restricted. While Heather and Kimberly are pregnant, you will be given venison and you can get your own fish, water, and wood. It will be up to the three of you as to how well you are taken care of. Doctor Harris will come around periodically to check on your pregnancy progression."

"Can we leave?" Phylicia asked haughtily.

"I wouldn't recommend that as you could be attacked by wolves or other wild animals, but if you really want to, knock yourselves out."

"Where are you going to be?" Heather asked.

"That knowledge is on a need to know basis and, frankly, you don't need to know."

"So, what are we supposed to do?" Kimberly asked with a slight tremor in her voice.

"I don't care what you do or where you go. Kill each other off, if that's what you want, but be advised that winter is coming soon, and it will get bitterly cold. You don't have the clothing to survive the exposure for long. Also, be warned! If you come around our camp, you could be shot as intruders." With that, Murdock turned and left the pod.

Just as Murdock, Harris, and Emily left, it was starting to rain and the three wasted no time getting back to their camp.

By the time daybreak came, Palmer was soaked, cold, and miserable. He hadn't slept well after he ran out of firewood. He had resigned himself to get off the ridge and find a more suitable shelter. He got to his feet, gathered his waterskin and twelve-inch machete, and left the makeshift shelter for what he thought would be the last time.

As he retraced his path back to the edge of the terrace, he was finally warming up with the exercise. It didn't take long before he was at the edge of the terrace with his target tree five or six feet out, he guessed. He took several reappraisals of the situation, partly to gather his nerve. Finally, he walked straight away from the tree and turned. After several deep breaths, he started running as fast as he could toward the terrace-edge. He'd figured he had hit his top speed about the time he reached the edge and launched himself into the open air, arms out and hands open to grab the first limb he made contact with. He had fixed his eyes on a particular limb and had kept them fixed on his target. *Shit*, he thought as his feet left the ground. *What have I done!*

As he flew through the air, he noticed that his target limb was moving up. *I'm going to miss it*, he thought just before he impacted the limb below his target. His hand grabbed the limb, but as his body swung under, he felt his hands slipping off the rain-soaked bark and then felt extreme pain in his left shoulder. From that point on it was a series of bouncing and tumbling off limb after limb as his body fell. He felt his ribs, on the left side, crack when they impacted a limb. He felt excruciating pain in his right thigh as it impacted another limb and he knew he'd broken it. His fall through the tree seemed to go on forever. When he finally hit the ground, he felt more pain as his left hip impacted a rock and he passed out.

When he finally started to regain consciousness, he became aware that breathing was difficult, and his chest hurt. He kept his eyes closed as he tried to assess the damage. He could move the toes on his left foot, but his hip hurt so bad that he couldn't move his leg. It was then that he felt rock under his right hand, and he could hear something that sounded like purring. He felt something sharp biting his nose. He opened his eyes to see a blue-tinted buckskin color with bluish-white spots. And he saw very sharp, white, bloodstained teeth.

"Hey!" he yelled as he tried to move something, anything to fend off the animal.

Startled by his voice, the animal moved away, a little, and looked at him. When it did, he saw what looked to be a cougar, a kitten by the looks of it. It was then that he became aware of excruciating pain in the area of his right thigh. He couldn't move to look at it, but he could feel something tearing his right pant-leg and then gnawing on his right thigh. He heard the grinding of teeth on bone coming from that general vicinity. It was then that he realized what was happening. He was lying in a cougar's den and the cougar had cubs and he, being paralyzed, was dinner. It was then that Ben Palmer finally realized how stupid his actions had been.

21

T ed Wagner had been with his assigned group for some
time before he returned to the depression that Palmer was
attempting to use for shelter. For him, this was the first
opportunity he'd gotten to return and report to Palmer without
someone from his new group following and watching him. It
had taken him some time to decide if he wanted to give Palmer
any intelligence on the group he'd joined. He had decided to tell
Palmer that he was not giving him anything.

As he wandered around the campsite, he noticed that there
was no sign that anyone had been there for some time. The fire-
ring was stone cold and the bows that Palmer had placed for
protection against the elements were in need of repair. As he was
looking for tracks, Jax Hornsby and Nels Osterlund were
striding across the open ground towards him.

"Where's Palmer?" Osterlund asked as he came to the fire-
ring.

"I have no idea," Wagner responded. "I was expecting him to
still be here, but I can find no sign of him."

"Well, he had to build this shelter," Hornsby said. "It didn't
build itself. Where did you get the bow, Wagner?"

"The leader of my group gave it to me," Wagner responded.

"They needed hunters and since I had some minor skill with a bow, I was appointed. I've been trying to do some hunting for game."

"Any luck?" Osterlund asked.

"None, yet," Wagner answered.

"So, now what do we do?" Hornsby asked.

"Well, we could try to leave a message carved into the log of the shelter," Wagner said. "If we put it on the outside face, I'm sure he'll see it." Wagner pulled out his twelve-inch machete and started carving on the log. "Are you two coming back here to report?"

"I don't know," Osterlund said. "I'm pretty sure that I won't be able to get back here until spring. I was lucky to get away this time."

"I don't know either," Hornsby responded. "I'm not being watched too closely, at present, but I'm not in the group, yet. They mentioned Declan Griffen and keep asking if I'm going to disrupt their lives as he did."

"What does that mean?" Osterlund asked.

"They won't tell me the details," Hornsby said, "so I'm hoping, at some point, they will. Right now, I'm just an outsider doing work for them before they allow me into the group. Who knows, I could be back here at any time because they rejected me."

"I, for one, will not be back, if I can help it," Wagner said as he continued to carve on the log-face. "Palmer was going to try to start a war with all the different groups and he wanted information on the groups to be used to instigate it."

"Yeah, we know," Osterlund said, "and I don't like that idea. It could get us killed if we're caught trying to be agitators. I happen to like most of the people in my group."

"That's the way I feel about it," Wagner said as he finished the roughly carved message, "which is why I won't be back unless I absolutely have to. That should do it."

All three men stood for a minute looking at the message

before they broke away and headed back to their respective groups.

~

Murdock, Emily, and Declan had just left Reyes' compound and were heading toward the ridge further downriver.

"I'm not sure I like this idea," Emily said from her position beside the cart.

"Why is that?" Murdock asked.

"The last time we were there, we didn't exactly make many friends," Emily responded. "I'm not sure it will be worth the effort. Rogers, Tutt, and whoever is in charge of Carter's group should know that winter is coming soon and should be making their final preparations for a long winter."

"I don't want it said I didn't try to warn them," Murdock said as he pulled the cart.

"I think you're being a lot nicer to them than they've been to you," Declan said as he walked beside Murdock on the opposite side of the cart from Emily. "I don't think most are worth a warning!"

Murdock chuckled: "If Mei Lee heard you say that, she'd say that I'd corrupted you."

"Well, being inside your mind on our last *sharing* was an eye-opener," Declan responded. "I guess I'd been sheltered too much. I never knew people could be so cruel. I was raised to be nice."

"So, what happened?" Murdock asked chuckling. "If you put people under stress, civility goes right out the window."

"I don't understand Reyes," Emily joined in. "I thought you'd been quite respectful with her prior to that last meeting."

"You ever take a toy away from a child?" Murdock asked. "Reyes and her guards were all keyed up to take out some of their frustrations on Phylicia, Heather, and Kimberly. I was the key player in stopping it and Declan didn't help by besting Bass Heartly so easily. Add to that the arrow I caught when someone shot at Annie."

Emily and Declan nodded their understanding.

A few hours before sundown, Murdock, Declan, and Emily were making camp inside the cave that Beron had made for them.

"This place looks somewhat familiar," Declan said as they entered.

"I'm surprised," Murdock said as he deposited his load of wood beside the fire-ring in the center of the main room. "You were pretty well out of it the last time you were here."

"Yeah, you were pretty bad off," Emily added as she got a fire going.

Murdock left to levitate the cart into the cave entrance and get more firewood. When he returned a short time later, he laid the wood close to the fire-ring. Emily and Declan had done their part by getting some venison cooking. When it was cooked, they all sat around the fire enjoying the hot meat after their long trek.

"What kind of reception are you expecting from the rest of the groups?" Declan asked as he chewed.

"I'm expecting a chillier reception from the remaining three groups than we got from Reyes," Murdock said after he'd swallowed what he was chewing on.

"That would be rather arctic. Do you always expect the worse?" Emily asked.

"When dealing with people, I expect the worse, but I hope for the best," Murdock answered.

"That seems kind of negative, to me," Emily stated.

"If I expect the best and it doesn't happen, I'll be at a disadvantage. My way I get to be pleasantly surprised if I'm wrong."

"And how many times have you been wrong?" Declan asked.

"Far too seldom," Murdock said.

∾

Within a couple of hours of finishing breakfast, Murdock, Declan, and Emily were just outside the guard post of Emily's old group's site. They had managed to stop one of the men going to the river for fish and had requested to talk to Keith Rogers, or whoever was in charge. When the man left to return to the campsite, they had followed and were promptly stopped by the guard.

"You're not welcome here," the guard said to Emily and Declan.

"We aren't here to impose on your hospitality," Murdock said interposing himself between the guard and Emily after dropping the handles of the cart. "*Pick up the cart and make ready to leave in a hurry if things go badly,*" Murdock flashed to Declan.

Declan responded by taking up the cart and had pulled Emily's arm a little to get her to back away from the guard.

The guard scowled and looked Murdock up and down a few times. "I remember *you*," the guard said curtly. "You nearly broke my leg with that spear of yours!"

"Well, I didn't, obviously, else you'd be nursing it," Murdock replied bluntly. "Pick up your feet next time. I can tell it didn't improve your manners." Murdock could see the guard's jaw muscles tense and loosen rhythmically and saw his hand drift to his twelve-inch machete hanging on his belt. Murdock's hand drifted to his own machete.

"You have caused enough problems," the guard started, "and I don't know why I should bother to grant your request."

"I don't see that our business with the man in charge is any of your concern," Murdock responded coolly. "What I have to say to...Rogers is it? What I have to say to him he might be interested in hearing."

"Tell me, and I'll make sure it gets to him," the guard suggested with a surly tone.

"I've come too far to put up with a surly lackey who places himself higher than he should," Murdock responded sternly. "If you want to pull that machete, then do so. You're likely to get a big surprise." By the expression on his face, Murdock could tell the guard was thinking about it. Slowly the guard's hand moved away from his machete and Murdock matched his action.

"What the hell is going on here," a thirty-something man yelled as he came up to the guard post.

"Keith Rogers, this is Murdock," Emily said over the top of Murdock's head.

Both men looked each other up and down a few times.

"What do *you* want?" Rogers asked with derision.

"Don't worry," Murdock replied, "We're not here to impose. We've come to inform you that winter is coming."

"I'd already figured that out," Rogers quipped.

"Good! That tells me you're not as clueless as I first thought," Murdock retorted. "If true, then you are already aware that it will be bitter cold and the river will freeze, leaving your people without that food source."

"I'm sure you're exaggerating," Rogers replied condescendingly. "It would have to get pretty cold to stop the river flow."

"Ah, so you're into ice fishing," Murdock said sarcastically. "I'm sure your people will appreciate that about you when they're all standing on the frozen river trying to catch something with the clothes they have available. Freezing to death is *much more* pleasant than starvation!"

"Our needs will be met," Rogers said dismissively. "Besides, it isn't your problem, is it?"

"We'll be back after the spring thaw, if for no other reason than to bury you. You might want to consider working with someone outside your group, or are you not interested in being something more than a pack of wolves." *"We're leaving. Head downriver,"* Murdock flashed to Declan and Emily as he turned away.

～

"Quiet, for a while," Murdock flashed to the pair as he brought up the rear of their little column. *"Be on alert. We may be attacked."*

"That is likely," flashed to his mind from Declan.

"Watching," flashed to him from Emily.

Murdock was moving quickly and quietly up behind the pair with the cart and only cringed a few times when they made too much noise. *At least they're learning,* he thought.

～

A few hours later, Murdock, Declan, and Emily had cleared the trees. Murdock had spotted three people walking away from a point in the distance. One was heading away from the river. Another was heading toward the river, and the third was heading in their general direction.

"We have three individuals in the distance," Murdock reported.

Declan was blocking the sun with both hands while scanning the distance. "I don't see anything," he said after a short time.

"Nevertheless, they are there. One is heading in this general direction."

"Who are they?" Emily asked straining to see into the distance.

"They're too far away to see who they are," Murdock reported. "Move a little towards the river and we should intercept the one heading this way. I want to know who they are and what they're doing out here."

～

"It's the guard Mei Lee shot when we were helping the doctor after her rape," Murdock piped in after an hour or more of walking in the direction of the river. Declan and Emily jumped a little after so long a time of being quiet and straining to hear anything moving close at hand.

"You two wait here," Murdock said as he began to trot toward the person heading their way.

A few minutes later, Murdock was standing in front of the man he'd recognized, scowling. He didn't know his name, but he did remember his actions.

"What do you want, Murdock?" the man asked dismissively.

"How's the hand?" Murdock asked snappishly. "I want to know who you are and what you're doing out here?"

"Jax Hornsby. My hand is fine. None of your business," Hornsby responded blankly.

"That tells me that you are up to no good," Murdock said continuing to glare at the man. "Who were the other two you met with?"

"I'm busy," Hornsby said derisively and tried to push past Murdock.

Murdock grabbed the offending wrist and had Hornsby's arm in an arm-bar and Hornsby face down on the tall, dry grass.

"All right, all right," Hornsby said anxiously. "No need to break my arm!"

"Out here, in these miles and miles of miles and miles, you shouldn't shove someone aside," Murdock chided. "Now then, one more time. Who were you meeting and for what purpose?"

"Ted Wagner and Nels Osterlund," Hornsby said begrudgingly.

"For what purpose?" Murdock asked as he applied a little more pressure to Hornsby's elbow. Hornsby grunted a little, but was silent.

"Palmer," Hornsby yelled finally once the pain in his elbow convinced him to talk. "Palmer told us to!"

"So, Palmer told you to meet him, for what reason?"

Murdock asked again and applied pressure on Hornsby's elbow until the man screamed in pain.

"Okay, I'll tell you everything. Just let me up," Hornsby finally capitulated. "Some time ago," Hornsby started as Murdock let loose of the arm-bar and he got to his feet, "we were sent to the three groups in this area. We were supposed to watch and keep a low profile and report back. We all came back and couldn't find Palmer."

"Did you have a specified time to come back?" Murdock asked.

"No, we didn't."

"So, you think it's just a coincidence that all three of you show up at the same time and I happen to come along as well?"

"I really hadn't thought about it," Hornsby said with a shrug.

"Well, I think we need to investigate it and you're coming along," Murdock said sternly. "You can come quietly, or you can come restrained, either way, you're coming."

Hornsby hung his head as he walked in front of Murdock taking his directions.

"I'm heading to the cliff edge with Hornsby," Murdock flashed to Declan and Emily. *"You two can proceed and we'll intercept you. Just keep your eyes open and be careful. If something comes up, let me know."*

Murdock and Hornsby intercepted Declan and Emily, sometime later, not far from the triangular depression that Palmer had chosen for his shelter. Murdock had called for a halt on the side of the makeshift shelter that was furthest away from the terrace edge. He then began to look around the shelter. He inspected everything, sometimes using his twelve-inch machete to lift things up. Declan, Emily, and Hornsby were at a loss as to the whys and wherefores of Murdock's actions. As they watched, they saw Murdock walk out of the depression and follow some trail away from the river. Murdock suddenly stopped and motioned for the others to join him.

"Did you look this far from the shelter?" Murdock asked Hornsby once the three had reached him.

"No. Well, *I* didn't. I don't know what Wagner did. He had gotten to the shelter before we did," Hornsby explained.

"Did you find anything?" Emily asked. She had been watching Hornsby, suspiciously, ever since he joined their little expedition.

"I think you're wasting your time," Hornsby said derisively. "You can't tell anything from looking at the ground!"

"I can tell Palmer had a hard night when it last rained. At that time, he had finished off the remains of a fish he'd caught and had made more than one trip this way," Murdock pointed away from the river, "and he wanted to be able to find something after his first trip."

"How do you know all that?" Hornsby asked. "I think you're just making it all up," he scoffed.

"I found fish bones," Murdock explained, "with no meat on them. No animal eats fish that way. I found a few fish intestines away from the shelter with feathers from the scavenger birds, which wouldn't come around unless someone left the area for a period of time. I saw the mud under the shelter, where he had lain, that showed signs of someone rolling from side to side with some puddles caused by rain dropping inside the shelter. I also found tracks of someone walking along the edge. Two sets going away and one returning, all made by the same person. Add to that," Murdock bent to pick up a sharpened stick, "I found this pointing this way," he indicated the direction he was walking.

Hornsby stood there listening to Murdock's explanation with his mouth hanging open.

"Amazing what you can learn by opening your eyes," Murdock chided.

"So, where do we go, now?" Declan asked.

"We go where he went," Murdock responded.

"And if he went nowhere?" Emily asked.

"I don't know where that is," Murdock responded with a grin. "Everywhere is somewhere."

Murdock continued to follow the sharpened sticks to the cliff edge with the tall tree. Once there, he leaned over the edge some and studied the tree from where he was.

"Take Hornsby back to the shelter," Murdock told Declan and Emily. "I'll be along in a bit."

Once Emily, Declan, and Hornsby left by the same path they had followed, Murdock levitated himself over to the tree and inspected the first few branches. He found the one that Palmer had grabbed by the scraped bark. As he looked down, he saw a lot of broken limbs and followed them to the ground. Once on the ground, he kicked a few of the limbs out of the way where Palmer had impacted the ground and the buried rock. He found a few tracks of a large cat of some kind. By his estimation, the cat had dragged Palmer's body off, and Murdock was determined to find it.

As he tracked the drag marks, Murdock began getting feelings that he could only interpret as "hunger, cubs, food coming". They were odd and alien to his mind. After all the years of sharing with Beron, he had no idea of any other animals capable of telepathy, but the fact remained that is what was happening. As he rounded a corner of the cliff, he was suddenly levitating about thirty feet from the cliff and thirty feet off the ground. He knew something had startled his subconscious mind and it responded automatically by levitating him out of harm's way.

When he looked down, he saw the cougar and it yowled loud and deep. Its ears were back and its tail twitching nervously. He was startled to see such a big cat. He had seen plenty of cougars before coming here, but they were usually three feet high at the shoulder and weighed no more than two hundred twenty pounds. This one was the size of a Bengal tiger. He guessed its weight at about four hundred pounds. As he floated there, the huge cat jumped at his feet, presumably to drag him down and it was falling short, but not by a lot.

As he looked around, he found a cave fifteen feet, or so, off the ground in the ridge. He projected his astral self into the cave and found three cubs gnawing on something. By the cloth that was still attached, he knew it was Palmer. With some effort, he levitated Palmer's body away from the cats and up to the top of the cliff. As he floated away, he saw the mother cougar jump into the cave easily.

Once he was back on the terrace where Declan and Emily were, he started his long trek to the shelter with Palmer's body floating behind. By the time he'd reached the shelter, it was dark, and Emily and Declan had a fire going and were cooking some venison.

"Bring a brand over towards the path we took to the tree," Murdock flashed to Declan.

"I think Murdock found Palmer," Declan said as he picked up a brand from the fire and headed towards the path away from the river. Emily and Hornsby followed.

They hadn't gone far when they saw Murdock standing next to a body.

Hornsby took one look and headed away from the rest. Everyone could hear him retching in the dark.

"What happened to him?" Emily asked after seeing what was left.

"The best I can tell," Murdock started, "he jumped for the tree. He caught a limb, but it was slick from the rain and his hands slipped, fell through the tree limbs, and hit the ground hard. Broke lots of bones on the trip through the tree and probably passed out when he hit the ground. A cougar carried him off to feed her cubs, but I think he was alive during their dinner."

"That's pretty harsh, even for him," Declan said in a low voice.

"After what I've seen of your treatment by him, I'd say it was appropriate," Emily replied harshly.

"Maybe, but that's still one hell of a way to go," Murdock added as he slowly shook his head.

Hornsby had finished emptying the contents of his stomach and had rejoined the rest.

"Palmer, you mean sumbitch. You went and got yourself kill'd," he said softly.

Murdock clapped him on the shoulder and whispered, "You get to bury him tomorrow."

A few days after they'd found Palmer, Murdock, Declan, and Emily had returned home. After a few hours rest and a good soak in the tub for all three, they were mentally ready to give the report to the rest of the group.

"Palmer is dead and buried," Murdock started his report to the others who were gathered inside his cabin, "and the rest have told us to bugger off."

"How did he die?" Irene Harris asked eyes closed and speaking softly.

"Best I can figure," Murdock said, "he was dinner for a family of cougars. It appeared that they didn't kill him right away."

"Cougars?" Mei Lee asked quietly, her head snapping in his direction. Her expression was that of grave concern.

Murdock flashed the images of the cougars he'd seen. All those present nodded as they received the images.

"How big?" Declan asked quietly.

"Bigger than a Bengal tiger," Murdock explained. "On Earth, cougars are all over and are the largest cat in North America, three feet tall at the shoulder and two hundred twenty pounds for males. The one I saw was female, four hundred pounds at least and I'd say was five feet tall at the shoulder. Other than its size, it looked just like any cougar you'd likely see back on Earth."

"How big of a threat are they?" Mei Lee asked.

"Big enough that I'm concerned," Murdock responded. "They're larger and can jump higher than one would expect. A lot depends on how far they've come this way and why haven't we seen them before? We did stop and tell the leaders of the groups that they could be a threat. Speaking of the other leaders, Emily?"

Emily stood and cleared her throat a little. "The leaders of the other groups have basically decided to go it alone. Yes, they all knew winter was coming and we shouldn't worry about them was the nicest response we got."

"Any potential allies?" Annie asked.

"As the groups go, no, there may be some individuals, though," Emily responded.

"Anything else you feel the need to report?" Mei Lee asked. She paused long enough to allow someone, who had anything to add, to speak. "Thoughts?" she asked to open the informal discussion.

"I, for one," Irene Harris started, "would like to see a more centralized medical facility."

"We all would," Murdock responded with a chuckle to himself, "but that would mean an agreement, of some sort, to see to it that the medical personnel would be safe and secure."

"Right now," Emily said, "none of the leaders trust anyone else enough to make that a possibility."

"With winter coming on, how safe are we going to be here?" Annie asked.

"Winter here," Mei Lee offered, "is lots of snow and bitter cold. High winds tend to drive the snow, making visibility close to zero and close to impossible to travel. Kevin and I can, but with great difficulty."

"From what I was able to see," Murdock said, "the rest haven't gathered enough hides to make the clothing needed to venture far in the snow and cold. I think they're going to try to hunker down and wait it out."

"What are we going to do?" Declan asked.

"We will hunker down as well," Murdock responded. "It won't be easy, but we have the advantage of more than a single cabin and we can venture out some."

"We have all sorts of things to help pass the time," Mei Lee added. "We can all do our part by keeping busy. We have plenty of hides to work into clothing and materials for making weapons."

"Not to mention training," Murdock interjected with a smile, "lots of training. But before we get snowed in, we need to get the longhouse completed."

For the next few weeks, Murdock and Declan worked on the longhouse, while the rest worked on finishing the hides. It hadn't taken the men long to get the building ready for the chimney and hearth. Murdock had decided on slabs of granite, from the nearby mountains, for the chimney and firebox.

"How are you milling the granite?" Declan asked. "It all looks smooth and cut precisely."

"I utilize my telekinetic abilities to remove the microscopic grains along a line. It effectively cuts the granite leaving a sharp, square edge," Murdock explained. "Square edges and flat surfaces make building something a lot easier. The roofing timbers and the weight of the slabs will hold the chimney in place."

With everyone working on the hides and finishing the longhouse, no one saw Heather Stevens watching them from across the river. She had been watching for some time as she had taken it upon herself to walk upriver from the pod. She had been thinking about the long winter and wishing she had more people around than Phylicia and Kimberly.

"Anything I can do for you?" Murdock's voice sounded from behind her. She had been too focused on the flurry of activity to notice she, too, was being observed. She turned, startled, to see Murdock scowling at her.

"No, I was just watching," she replied as steadily as she could manage. Her voice still had a quivering quality to it.

"Why were you watching?" Murdock glared. "See anything of interest? What did you see?"

"I was just watching," she responded shyly. "It's nice to see so many people cooperating and getting along." Heather's voice seemed to trail off as her thoughts went on of their own accord. "They all look like they belong," she said pensively.

"They appear to belong because they *do* belong," Murdock scolded. "Did Phylicia send you?" he asked roughly.

"No, no one sent me," she dropped her gaze to the ground in front of Murdock. A tear had started, and she closed her eyes to get it to stop.

"We have an intruder," she heard Murdock's voice.

"Where did *she* come from?" Emily asked.

Hearing Emily's voice startled Heather a little and she snapped her eyes open to find that she was across the river and standing in the middle of the group. She became panicked and started to look for a means of escape.

"Running will do you no good," Murdock's voice boomed.

"Would you quit terrorizing her?" Mei Lee scolded her husband as she walked over to Heather. "Look at me," she commanded sweetly of the frightened intruder. "What are you doing here?" Mei Lee asked softly after Heather had calmed down somewhat and was focusing on her.

"I...I don't know," Heather started. "I just wanted to get away from Phylicia and Kimberly," she said as she shrugged her shoulders. "Honestly, I couldn't tell you why I came upriver. I had no idea what I would find."

"You do know you could've been killed?" Mei Lee asked in her quiet manner.

"I know," Heather responded quietly. "Is there something I can do to help?" she blurted.

Everyone was dumbfounded. "Why," Mei Lee asked finally, "would you do that? We aren't doing anything to help Phylicia directly, so I'm puzzled."

Heather swallowed hard and breathed deeply to try to calm herself. "Frankly, Phylicia's constant haranguing on Murdock and the rest of you, has become...tiresome," she said finally. "I'm sick to death of the sound of her voice."

"Why should we trust you?" Mei Lee asked. "None of us know you well enough to vouch for you, as you have spent most of your time here in close proximity to Phylicia. We have too much to lose to trust blindly."

"I can understand that," Heather said quietly. "I don't know what else to do. I can't survive alone, and the rest of the people aren't likely to last long. How did the rest of you come to be in a position of trust?"

"Everyone here is trusted and has earned their way into that position," Mei Lee stated coldly.

"What are you willing to do to earn our trust?" Declan asked.

"I'll do whatever I can to remain here," Heather responded.

"That is a broad statement," Murdock observed.

"I mean it," Heather said emphatically.

"What is Phylicia planning?" Emily asked suspiciously.

"Currently, she is planning on being a burden to you," Heather responded. "As much a burden as is possible so she can play the victim. Her long-term goals are the same as they were since day one. Take control of everyone and kill Murdock and his family. It has something to do with avenging her cousin, not that I know what that's all about."

"The last time I was inside the pod," Emily asked, "I saw you three whispering and you stopped when I got too close. What was that all about?"

"Has it been bothering you?" Heather asked with a slight chuckle.

"Yes, it has," Emily responded hotly.

"Phylicia had noticed that you were being too curious as to what we were doing. It was one of her games to make you wonder what was being said. I don't agree with it, but it is, obviously, effective."

"To be frank, Heather," Declan began, "you never struck me as being overly intelligent. Now, however, you seem to be a lot smarter than I originally thought. Why is that?"

"Look at me," Heather stated. "All my life people see my blonde hair, blue eyes, and my figure and think I'm a *dumb blonde*. Men think that and so do a lot of women. Sometimes, it's easier to find out what I want to know by letting those types of people think they know me, when they don't." Heather shrugged a little. "I let people think what they want and don't waste a lot of time trying to convince them otherwise. Similar to what Murdock does."

"What does that mean?" Murdock asked, shocked that his name had come up.

"Please! You're shorter than any man on the pod and were probably in that category on your own pod. I'm not foolish enough to underestimate you again, but I think you welcome others to. Am I wrong?" Heather was looking straight at Murdock. Murdock shrugged and gave a slight grin.

"Are you willing to stay with Phylicia and Kimberly to keep us apprised of their plans?" Mei Lee asked.

"I would as long as there is a time limit on it," Heather stated. "I came here to get away from all the bickering and complaining. If I must stay where I am, then so be it, but there is a limit to my patience."

"I'd say stay where you are for the time being," Murdock inserted. "It would allow us to know of any impending attack and it would give us a chance to think about your request."

"Fair enough," Heather added, "as long as you remember that my nerves are frayed because of Phylicia and Kimberly."

"We'll keep that in mind," Murdock said as he motioned to

Emily. "Emily will escort you back, with some venison. It will give the impression that you were intercepted by Emily before getting too far or seeing too much. Just keep your eyes and ears open."

Emily turned Heather around as she stopped long enough to grab a front-quarter of venison from the longhouse.

"Don't mistake Murdock's forbearance for weakness," Emily warned as they strolled toward the pod. "He is most capable!"

22

Seven days after Heather was escorted back to the pod, it started to snow. Phylicia, Kimberly, and Heather were sitting outside the pod cooking some venison when the air became frigid and the rain that had been falling, turned to huge, blue-white flakes.

"Well, that's just great," Phylicia raged. "How are we supposed to get fish now?"

"We?" Heather questioned with a sideways glance. "Do you have a mouse in your pocket?"

"What is that supposed to mean?" Phylicia asked glaring at Heather.

"It means," she started hotly, "that you don't get fish or water or wood. Kimberly and I do it. You do nothing but complain!"

Kimberly intruded: "I don't think this is the time to be having this conversation."

"Sure it is, Kimberly," Phylicia responded hotly, "I want to hear whatever Heather has to say. So, you're saying I do nothing?"

"Oh, you do something," Heather piped up, her anger becoming apparent. "You bitch, you moan and groan, and you complain! That is the extent of what you do, and, frankly, I'm tired of it! You need to get off your ass and help!"

"I've carried wood!" Phylicia defended.

"You carry wood when Emily, or one of the others, are around. The rest of the time, you leave it for me and Kimberly. Would it kill you to carry the waterskins to the river and fill them once in a while?"

"I'm not going to listen to this anymore," Phylicia said as she tried to get to her feet. She suddenly inhaled sharply and grabbed for her hip. She started for the ramp, limping, and dragging her foot a little. Kimberly ran to her to help her into the pod.

"Let her do it herself, Kimber," Heather scolded. "Her hip wasn't bothering her a minute ago!"

"What are you doing?" Kimberly asked when she returned from escorting Phylicia into the pod.

"I'm tired of Phylicia and her games," Heather said angrily. "You and I may be pregnant. Who is going to take care of us when we can't walk anymore? If we count on Phylicia, we'll be without wood, water, and food long before we deliver."

"Phylicia has always been there for us," Kimberly defended. "She'll be there when we need her."

"I wish I had your optimism. I'm hoping that Doctor Harris or Annie Cooper come around often before we deliver. The only thing we can count on with Phylicia is that we can't count on her." Heather clutched the hide closer to her as she sat looking into the fire. "I think the snow is going to get deep."

Twenty-one days after the first snow, Murdock called for a meeting in the longhouse. He, Mei Lee, and their children had walked the one hundred yards to the longhouse and entered. Murdock was carrying a bunch of hides and placed them close to the huge hearth in the center of the building.

As each member came to the hearth and found a place on the log benches, they were all murmuring expectantly.

"I called you all together for some announcements and for some unfinished business," Murdock said loudly. "First of all, are there any pregnancies to announce?" Murdock's question wasn't directed to anyone in particular. It was clear that anyone could answer.

Declan cleared his throat a few times: "Emily and I are excited to report that we are expecting."

A loud cheer went up from everyone.

"Mei Lee is also expecting," Murdock reported.

Another loud cheer filled the longhouse.

"Is there anyone else?" Murdock asked when things had quieted down.

Everyone looked around expectantly.

"No one else? Okay," Murdock resumed, "there are a few unfinished business items to dispense with. Emily Brooks-Griffen, please come forward."

Emily, puzzled, stood, and came to Murdock, who handed her a bundle of hide.

"Annette Cooper, please come forward."

Annie, looking puzzled, came to Murdock and was handed her own bundle of hide. By this time, Emily had unfolded her bundle and screamed in excitement and ran to the other side of the longhouse. She was back in no time wearing a buckskin dress and shoes that made her look like a larger version of Mei Lee. All of the women, once they were presented, retired to put on their new dresses. All were very excited.

"What about Declan?" Emily asked. "Shouldn't he have a set?"

"Do you think he deserves a set?" Murdock asked. "Hmmm...I didn't think he wanted a dress." Murdock had a sly smile. "Declan, come here."

Declan got to his feet and came to Murdock who presented him with his own bundle of hide.

"This, to some, would seem silly, but I take it seriously," Murdock stated after handing Declan his own bundle. "From this point forward, you all belong to our tribe, and by wearing these clothes, you are showing your pride in it. It is our tribe because we all make it what we think it should be. We all belong to each other and that is a serious obligation."

Shortly after Murdock sat down, he looked at each of the tribal members with pride. All were dressed as he was, or as Mei Lee was, and it made him feel the way he did when Beron had made him part of the Oomah. He was filled with a sense of pride and obligation to something greater.

Seven days after the presentation, another meeting was called to discuss Heather Stevens.

"When was the last time someone checked on the pod?" Murdock asked.

"Annie and I checked on everyone at the pod, yesterday," Emily replied. "All seemed well, to a point. Heather seemed to be angry with Kimberly and Phylicia, about what I have no idea, but there was a definite tension in the air."

"Physically, Kimberly and Heather are proceeding with their pregnancies as I would expect," Annie Cooper reported. "Phylicia is feigning hip discomfort when she is around Heather and I suspect it is to garner sympathy."

"Their food situation," Emily continued, "is acceptable. They have enough venison for seven more days and enough fish for two or three more. The water situation is a different matter. The river has frozen solid enough that water will run out and no more fish can be harvested. The wood situation is also dire, for without the proper clothing they are unable to gather the wood they need."

"Suggestions?" Murdock inquired. No one spoke. They just

looked at each other or looked into the hearth and the flames. "No one has any suggestions?"

"I do, but I don't think you'll like it," Annie piped in.

"So, tell me," Murdock said. "I have an idea, but I want to know if the rest of you have a better one."

Annie took a deep breath and let it out slowly: "I suggest you move the pod closer to the longhouse."

Everyone waited to see how the suggestion would be taken. Murdock was tapping his knife on the bench he was sitting on with his head down.

"Would it be easier to bring them here individually?" Murdock asked finally.

"No, it would be easier to bring the pod with them inside," Emily said. "That way if they get to be too much, they have somewhere else to go to give us a break from dealing with them."

"They would have a way to preserve their privacy," Declan offered, "as would we."

"It would be more convenient for Irene and me," Annie stated. "Not so much of a trek to see the patients."

"I had already come to the same conclusions as the rest of you," Murdock said quietly. "I'll admit that I'm reluctant to force someone who is clueless to choose between starving and freezing. The first winter here, those in the first pod had to face that decision. Mei Lee, Rose, and I didn't. Has Heather been true to her word about letting us know what Phylicia is planning?"

"She said that she hasn't been privy to that information for some time," Emily said.

"If we allow Heather and Kimberly into the longhouse, we'll have to treat them as guests," Murdock reminded. "They are to remain ignorant of our ways and our skills. Also, Phylicia will not be allowed into the longhouse. Anyone disagree?"

"At this point," Declan piped in, "we agree with you, but we are also aware that the situation is likely to change."

~

Two days later, Heather descended the ramp and was met with a snow-covered longhouse just to the right of the pod. One hundred yards past the longhouse was a snow-covered cabin and a frozen river was to her left, which was the wrong side. She stood on the ramp, mouth agape as it dawned on her that the pod had been moved while they slept.

Currently, the snow had stopped, and the wind was calm, but it was quite cold. As she looked around for firewood, Emily came out of the longhouse dressed all in hides.

"No need to build a fire out here," Emily said with a smile. "Just knock on the door and someone will open it up. We have a nice hearth that is usually warm and cozy."

"Water?" Heather asked.

"Inside, just ask. We have some venison cooking currently."

Heather was looking around in shock: "Why?"

"We've decided to remove the choice of starving or freezing from you. Is Kimberly up and moving?"

"Are you two going to stay there so the rest of us freeze?" Kimberly yelled down from the top of the ramp.

Heather and Emily hurried off the ramp toward the door of the longhouse and they heard the ramp close. At the door, Heather hesitated, but Emily indicated the door for her to knock on. She rapped the door four times with her knuckles and Irene Harris opened the door. A blast of warm air hit her through the open doorway.

"Come in," Harris smiled her greeting and turned away. "We're not heating the outside, so shut the door behind you!"

Heather closed the door behind her and turned to look at what had been an unfinished meeting house a few weeks before. It was now a functioning longhouse for those who needed it. She was looking all around in admiration as she made her way to the hearth.

"Sit and be comfortable," Irene said as she sat on the log bench by the hearth.

"This is more than I expected," Heather said as she sat on the crudely made bench.

"It is very nice," Harris said excitedly.

"That is a nice dress! Looks warmer than what I have on," Heather said while subconsciously gathering her torn denim shirt about her, "is it new?"

"Yes, it's newly acquired," Harris chuckled a little.

Heather looked around and noticed there were two doors, each at opposite ends of the longhouse. It was then that Murdock entered wearing a heavy, deerskin parka. He came over to her after shucking it off and hanging it from a peg behind the door.

"Mind if I join you?" he asked looking down at her and putting his hands toward the flames to warm them. She shrugged and he took that as an invitation.

"We decided to help you out this winter," Murdock said. "As you can see, it does get pretty cold and snowy."

"What do you want for allowing us to be here?" Heather asked skeptically.

"If you feel the need to add something to the group, feel free. We don't particularly like strangers and we like watching someone freeze or starve even less."

"Well, other than you, no one seems to have the clothing required to do anything outside. If I went to gather wood, I'd not last long."

"Wood is stacked on the other side of that wall," Murdock said as he indicated a wall away from the side where the pod was placed. "There is a door over there and the way the wood is stacked, you should be protected long enough to get some wood in. Usually, one of the others will stack a bunch inside the door and then carry it over to the hearth. I'm sure it would be a help if someone took it from the door to the hearth."

"I still don't know why we're here," Heather said

suspiciously. "I'm enjoying the warmth and the company, but I'm just not sure what the price is." Murdock looked like he didn't understand her. "What do you want from me, Kimberly, and Phylicia? I understand that you're being generous, and I want to know what your expectations are."

Emily and Kimberly entered by the door closest to the pod. Emily made a quick scan of the room and started guiding Kimberly over to the hearth.

"Here's the pair of 'em," Emily said to Murdock as she indicated where Kimberly should sit. "I've already told *Her Majesty* that she will not be allowed entry. I need to take her some venison and water, though. Are they going to be okay here?"

"They're fine. I'm certain they won't be any trouble. After all, who would be foolish enough to give people cause to kick them out of a nice warm place? How did Phylicia take it?"

"She's madder'n a wet hen, but what can she do?" Emily chuckled as she walked off with something wrapped in a leaf and a waterskin.

"Why isn't Phylicia allowed in here?" Kimberly began to rage. "She should be allowed in! I'm not staying here if Phylicia isn't allowed in!"

"This is not an inn or a tavern, it's someone's home. They were generous to allow you to be here and, as such, expect you to be respectful. If you don't like it, there's the door," Murdock said quietly.

"You bet I'll go! Don't think for a moment I won't!" Kimberly yelled. Emily had stopped, at Kimberly's yelling, and returned so Kimberly ran into the bigger woman as soon as she'd turned to leave.

"Have it your way," Emily said as she handed the bundle and the waterskin to Kimberly and took her by the upper arm to the door.

"She'll be back," Heather said sadly after the ruckus had subsided. "The pod may be built to withstand the heat of reentry, but in cold like this, it'll suck the life, and heat, right out of a person."

"You look terrible, Heather," Murdock observed.

"Gee, thanks," she responded with a small chuckle. "Between the cold and being alone, I haven't slept in a while. I had to feed the fire just to stay somewhat warm. Now, all I want to do is sleep."

Elizabeth Reyes was hunkered down inside the cave that they had found on their first trip to this encampment. She had two deer hides draped over her back and head to help hold in her body heat and was putting the last of the wood on the fire. She glanced up when Bass Heartly came into the cave with an armload of wood.

"This should help take the chill off," he said as he dropped the wood near the fire-ring.

"It would help if we could figure a way to block the entrance," Reyes observed. "How's everyone else holding up?"

"Everyone has someplace to go to try to get out of the cold. The guard posts at the entrance have quite a few people huddled together for warmth and they have fires in the lower levels. If it doesn't snow for a while, we should be okay."

"Water and food?" Reyes asked through chattering teeth.

"With the river and the small stream frozen, we're going to chip away at the ice and try to melt enough for drinking. We have some fish and quite a bit of venison in the smokehouse."

"Will it be enough?" Reyes asked.

"I have no idea," Heartly said in a low voice, warming his hands in the fire. "I'm hoping so, but if it gets colder or snows more, we could be in a bad way."

"I wonder sometimes if it would have been better to break up into smaller groups. Say, no more than ten people in a group. They could all answer to a local leader and all the leaders answer to me. It would help to ensure some of our people would survive."

"We can plan it and try to implement it in the spring. I'm going for more wood, it's one of the few things we have plenty of," Bass chuckled as he tried to stick his hands into his armpits to keep them warm. "You may want to see about some food for us," he said as he left the cave.

～

Keith Rogers was standing at the main entrance of the cave complex. The huge door, it was more of a drawbridge than a door, had been opened to allow others to carry in more wood for the cooking fires.

I hope you're happy, Emily, he thought as he pulled the deer hide closer. He had been trying to gather the hide to him to preserve some body heat, but had been largely unsuccessful. *You deserted us when we needed you the most.* As these thoughts ran through his head, he saw Jackson, *"just call me Jax"*, Hornsby returning with his arms loaded with wood.

Hornsby had been a late addition, having been admitted just before the first snow, to the rest of Roger's charges. To Keith, the man looked familiar, but he couldn't place him. He had resolved to keep an eye on Hornsby until he was satisfied as to his intentions.

"Are you done, yet?" Rogers asked Hornsby as he passed him to deposit the wood in one of the first small rooms inside the cave entrance. The first four rooms had been too cold for anyone to sleep in, two on either side of the main entrance, and Rogers had determined it should be used to hold wood. Until their population increased significantly, they would just be empty anyway. "I'm cold and want to get below!"

"So, go," Hornsby responded somewhat testily. Rogers could tell by his tone that Hornsby knew he was being watched closely and Hornsby didn't like it. "I need to do two more trips for wood before I can call it quits for outside work, but then, you knew that. You assigned the job to me," Hornsby said with a bit of a scowl.

If I ever see you, Declan, I'm going to enjoy seeing you suffer. It's what you deserve for disrupting our little community, Rogers thought. Of late, thoughts of revenge against Declan, Emily, and, of course, the ever-accursed Murdock, had given him some comfort as he huddled in his room.

"When you're finished, find Carpenter and he'll assign a new job," Rogers told Hornsby as he passed him on his way to the lower levels.

"Mister Rogers," Cliff Reed interrupted once he was on the lower level. "We need to have a discussion about the food situation."

"Follow me," Rogers said without slowing his pace toward his room at the other end of the huge cave. "What is the situation?" Rogers asked once he had arrived at his room and placed the hide he had been wrapped in on the floor.

"Based on current consumption rates, it's getting dire," Reed reported. "By my estimates, we have enough for maybe twenty days."

"Have you heard back from the runner we'd sent to Ray Tutt?"

"Yes, and he reports that Tutt is unwilling to help. His exact words were 'stick it'."

"So, that could mean that he can't help, which is more positive than he won't help. Send the runner back with the offer of a few of the women for food. We have more women then we need, and he has few. It would serve both our needs to normalize the ratio between the sexes."

"The difference isn't more than eight and some of our men like having more than one woman," Reed reminded.

"If those men don't like it, then they could be on the menu. Remind them of that. Send another runner to Carter's camp with the same offer. Maybe we can get the two camps to bid against each other. If I could have, I would have normalized the situation a long time ago. You'd think that out of one hundred forty, the sexes would have been more even."

"We don't have anyone available to run to Carter's camp," Reed said quietly.

"Send Hornsby, once he's done with the wood for the day."

Jackson Hornsby had just finished stacking the wood from his three trips outside when Reed came over to him.

"We have a job for you," Reed said as Hornsby was exiting the wood storage room.

"I was told by Rogers to look for Carpenter," Hornsby rebutted.

"That was before I talked to Rogers," Reed said dismissively. "This has top priority."

"Sounds important," Hornsby said.

"It is. We need you to carry a message to the leader of the camp just off this terrace by the river. Do you know where it is?"

"I've seen it from a distance," Hornsby replied guardedly. "Who is the leader?"

"We have no idea who their leader is," Reed responded.

"So, give me the message," Hornsby held out his hand expectantly.

Reed looked down at Hornsby's grubby hand: "It's not a written message, have you seen anything resembling paper here? You are to ask the leader to meet with Rogers here."

"You know he's gonna ask why and for what purpose," Hornsby responded.

Reed took in an exasperated breath: "It's a rather delicate matter, concerning women, and we would prefer to discuss it in person, here. He will be allowed one other, from his camp, and no more. You will leave tomorrow, before sunup, and will be expected back by sundown. Failure to return by sundown will mean you'll be spending the night outside. You understand?"

"Yes," Hornsby responded, "I understand. What you fail to understand is that it is a fair distance, even without the snow and cold. If they come with me, they'll slow me down, so, by not letting me in when I get back, you won't know what the answer is. I doubt I can survive outside after dark in the cold and snow."

"Fine, I'll leave word to let you in whenever you return," Reed capitulated.

Kimberly was finally cold and hungry enough to lower the ramp and knock on the door to the longhouse. It was immediately opened by Declan and was closed behind her as she hurried in.

"Where's Heather?" Kimberly demanded after the door was closed.

"She's lying down over by the hearth, but I think she is sleeping so leave her alone," Declan said.

"You forced her to sleep on the floor like a dog?" Kimberly asked louder than normal. "She's no dog to be kicked to the floor and refused anything resembling acceptable human treatment!" Declan was holding up his hand to try to get her to quiet down and to interrupt her tirade.

"No one forced her to lie on the floor," Declan said. "She chose to lay there. The floor in front of the hearth is quite warm and, with a deer hide, can be quite cozy. I do it myself sometimes." Declan could see that Kimberly didn't have an argument in mind to continue her rant. "What is it that you wanted?" he asked.

"I came to appeal to your sense of decency. You need to allow Phylicia inside to stay warm," Kimberly argued, "that's assuming, of course, that you have anything resembling a sense of decency."

"That isn't up to me," Declan said. "The decision to ban her was made by everyone and can only be rescinded by everyone. You and Heather were allowed in because we all agreed."

Kimberly looked around to see who was inside the longhouse. She noticed that Doctor Harris and Emily weren't around. Neither was Murdock. "Can I request a hearing to plead Phylicia's case with those that voted not to allow her inside?" she asked with an increasing disrespect.

"You can ask," Declan stated and then waited with a smirk.

"Well?" Kimberly asked frustrated by Declan's silence. "Who do I have to ask?"

"You can ask me or anyone that lives here," Declan responded. "So far, all I've heard are demands."

"I just did, you brainless twit," Kimberly raged.

"That is enough," Annie said as she'd joined in because of the loudness. "Declan can only make a request when we have a meeting and if he chooses, you churlish, clay-brained harpy. You're quickly wearing out your welcome!"

"*Harpy* is a bit harsh," Murdock chuckled as he entered from the door opposite the one Kimberly had come through. "*Waterfly* might be closer to the truth." Kimberly paled and turned to face him.

"Speak of the devil—," Kimberly started.

"And he'll appear?" Murdock finished with a smirk. "Well, if I'm the devil then shame me by telling the truth. What is it you want? I know you want us to relent and allow Phylicia entry, but why? Is it to salve your own conscience for wanting to stay inside where it's warm?"

Kimberly's complexion paled and then flushed of its own accord before she could give an answer.

"First of all, you need to apologize to Declan for coming into his home and making demands," Murdock stated. "I find you to be rude and I wouldn't blame him for putting you out permanently. Then, you need to apologize to Annie for the same thing and for raising a ruckus. If you don't have the common courtesy to do that, then we have nothing to discuss."

Murdock stood there glaring at her and waiting for her to comply.

"I don't see why I should," Kimberly said with disdain. "If it weren't for Phylicia, you wouldn't have this building. You stole it from us!" Kimberly crossed her arms in defiance.

"You need to apologize, Kimberly," Heather demanded from where she lay near the fire. "You and I were going to die if these people hadn't helped by bringing the pod closer. They didn't steal anything. Declan helped plan and build this building and with Murdock's help, finished it and made it useable. Declan, Annie, Doctor Harris, me, and Emily have a claim on the building, as it was unfinished and unused."

"Murdock has no right to demand anything of anyone inside this building," Kimberly raged as she kept her arms crossed and refused to look at anyone.

"I don't know the particulars," Heather started, "but I'd guess that the building is currently on his property, property that has been homesteaded by him long before we got here. So far, everyone here has been accommodating and civil to you, me, and Phylicia. It's you that's been rude!"

Kimberly remained obstinate and stomped her foot a little and made a harumph while holding her crossed arms tighter. The door that Murdock had entered through banged open and everyone jumped and turned to stare at Emily, who looked incensed.

Kimberly started retreating through the door closest to her as Emily was quickly crossing the room. She had managed to start the ramp cycling, and waited for it to open, as Emily reached the door and exited. Kimberly didn't take two steps up the ramp before Emily lifted her feet free of the surface. Kimberly immediately began screaming and ineffectually kicking to try to gain freedom from Emily's grasp.

An hour later, Murdock was banging on a bench with a piece of firewood to get the others to be quiet. Kimberly and Phylicia were gagged, their hands tied behind their backs and their feet tied together with the legs of the bench. Heather was sitting quietly and was preparing her arguments mentally.

"We are called...again...to try to resolve this issue with Phylicia and Kimberly," Murdock announced. "Heather has agreed to act as a spokesperson between us and them, even if she doesn't fully understand our position."

"Are the gags necessary?" Annie asked without standing.

"They wouldn't be if we could count on civility and some sort of order from Phylicia and Kimberly," Murdock answered. "Since we *can* count on them to disrupt and confuse the situation as much as possible, the gags stay on."

"My friends," Doctor Harris said as she stood, "I'm sorry to say that I agree with Murdock. These two are the epitome of *chaos*. I move we dismiss the hearing and just put them out to fend for themselves." Everyone looked to the doctor with shock. "I know you're shocked that someone dedicated to life would make such a statement. There is a point, in the growth of an organism, that one or two members of that organism will endanger the survival of the entire organism. Cancer is a good analogy. These two are a cancer, a detriment to our survival. Putting them on some other group would just be infecting that group with chaos and passing the problem onto someone else." Irene Harris sat.

"First," Murdock said as he got to his feet, "I would like it clearly understood that I have not decided what to do with these two. Also, this is not a legal process. We came together to form our own tribe, for the purpose of having others around us that we can trust and depend on to work toward the continued survival of our tribe and the children born into it. Being a member of our tribe means we all have a say and we all have to take responsibility for the actions of the tribe." Murdock resumed his seat. The others, seated, made some murmuring noises as they nodded agreement.

"Members of this tribe," Heather said as she stood, "I have no defense for the actions of these two. All those that witnessed the apprehension of Kimberly by Emily already know I have tried to argue your point and for whatever reason, these two fail to grasp the simplest concepts of appropriate behavior. They show no tendency toward civility or manners of any sort. I can only conclude that they were not trained as children to have manners or know what it means to be civil or the accepted protocols that we all use and interpret as manners." Heather resumed her seat. Kimberly started becoming animated and tried to stand, even though she knew she couldn't. Phylicia just sat and glared at everyone else.

"Are we going to allow them to speak for themselves?" Declan asked without standing. Everyone groaned.

"Do we have to?" Annie asked, looking to Declan and then to Murdock. "I have heard more than enough from these two. Listening to them is irritating."

"I have a question for them," Murdock said as he stood. "Do you two understand that we are considering putting you in the pod and removing the pod from our influence so you two can live or die by your own skills and tenacity? Just a nod of your head would be a sufficient answer." Murdock was watching the two women for some sort of signal that they understood what was going on. Heather was also watching them.

"They have not shown any sign, that I can detect, that they don't understand," Heather said as she stood. "I'm of the belief that they do understand and that they don't recognize your authority to do anything to punish them in any way. If I'm wrong," she said to Kimberly and Phylicia directly, "just let me know." She stood there looking closely at the other two women, concern traced out on her face. After more than a few minutes, her gaze met only contempt and silence, she sat and turned toward the members and shrugged.

"Emily, remove these two so we may deliberate," Murdock said without standing. "Put them inside the pod and untie them. Block the ramp to keep them inside."

"Well, what are we to do with them?" Murdock asked after

Emily had escorted the pair of women out of the longhouse door.

"I have no idea," Heather said with concern and exasperation. "I've tried to get through to them, but it seems to do no good. I'm at a loss!"

"It's like you said, they act as if no one has ever taught them any manners at all," Irene Harris said. "What kind of parents would do that to their child?"

"I think Kimberly knows better," Heather said, "but she sees Phylicia getting away with it and is emulating her."

Declan broke into the room from outside. "They have escaped! They knocked Emily off the ramp and escaped."

23

_____

There was a flurry of activity, inside the longhouse, as Annie, Doctor Harris, and Declan ran out to see how Emily was. Finding her unconscious, they did whatever was necessary to get her inside.

Murdock had donned his parka and went out the other door to search for the two fugitives on his way to his cabin, his concern being for his wife and children. He had no idea how much of a head start they had, and it worried him.

"*Get the kids inside and bolt the doors,*" Murdock flashed to Mei Lee. "*Phylicia and Kimberly have escaped, and Emily is injured.*" Murdock took a few more steps and got no response from Mei Lee. His steps quickened. Before he could reach the steps to his porch, he received images from Mei Lee.

"*You need to calm down and release Andy, Phylicia,*" flashed to him from Mei Lee.

Mei Lee was standing in the middle of the cabin with her arms out. "Kimberly, please don't hurt my babies," she pleaded. She knew Kevin was outside and she had opened a telepathic connection to him so he could see and listen in. "Phylicia let my son go. We have done nothing to you."

"They're both in there, armed?" flashed to Mei Lee.

"Yes, Phylicia has Andy and Kimberly has Huo Jin and Rosa," she flashed back.

"You've done plenty," Phylicia yelled. "You've abetted the killer of my cousin!"

Murdock could see the situation through Mei Lee's eyes. Kimberly was cradling Hou Jin with a six-inch knife close to his throat and was holding little Rosa Lea with her knife hand, in such a way that any struggling on anyone's part could result in both being killed by a single slashing movement. Phylicia had a good grasp on Andy's neck with one hand and a six-inch knife in the other and was holding it at Andy's throat.

Murdock moved around to the back door of the cabin. From the positions Phylicia and Kimberly were in, that would be the least visible point of entry. When he was ready and could hear Phylicia yelling something, Murdock slid his twelve-inch machete from its sheath and slid the bolt on the door back. He crept in as quietly and as quickly as he could and closed and bolted the door as quietly as he could. He was hoping he had done so quickly enough that the two assailants hadn't noticed the momentary drop in temperature inside the cabin.

He could see the women clearly as he was peeking out from behind the deerskin partition for Chun Hua's sleeping area. As he crouched there, a tiny hand reached out to touch his. He jumped a little, initially, but gave Chun Hua a quick smile. He didn't know if she could see him, but it made him feel better that the child knew he would do what he could. He stood up straight and readied himself.

In a sudden burst of energy, Murdock was running around the inside of the cabin. To him, everyone seemed to be either not moving or moving so slowly it was hard to tell which. As he passed Phylicia, he grabbed the wrist holding the knife and yanked it straight away from Andy's throat. The tip of his twelve-incher found the hollow of her throat and didn't stop until it severed her spine.

He stopped running in an instant, twisted, and threw his machete at Kimberly's head. Just as it was about to stick, Murdock saw Rosa Lea being tossed toward Mei Lee, the six-inch knife in Kimberly's hand slit the throat of his infant son and the knife being tossed toward Mei Lee, all in a single motion. Mei Lee was falling forward. Kimberly's head snapped back violently as the machete slammed into her skull, the blade buried deep into her brain.

Rosa Lea had rolled with the impact on the floor and was being held by Andy to keep her safe and out of the way. Chun Hua had come out, her own six-inch knife drawn, and was standing next to her brother and sister ready to attack anyone else who would harm them. Murdock bent over and rolled Mei Lee over to see the six-inch knife sticking in her lower abdomen.

"Irene, I need you at the cabin, quickly!" Murdock flashed.

He saw the blood starting to seep into and stain Mei Lee's leather dress and he knew the doctor would be there as soon as she could, he was hoping it would be in time. "Chun, open the door and see that the doctor comes in here," he told his daughter and she did as he asked. "Andy, are you and Rosa okay?"

"We are uninjured, father," Andy said stoically.

"Sorry, daddy," Rosa said with tears, "but that woman was trying to hurt us. When I saw you, I bit her arm as hard as I could."

"That's okay, Rosa, you did just fine," Murdock tried to console her without leaving Mei Lee's side.

"Andy, get the table cleared away. Rosa, go to your sleeping area, please."

"What's happened?" Doctor Harris said as she entered the room through the main door with Chun Hua in her wake.

Chun started helping her brother to quickly clear the table. "When the table is cleared, I need her on it. Be careful not to pull or push the knife at all." Murdock nodded that he understood.

"Table's cleared," Andy said, and they moved out of the way.

Murdock carefully levitated Mei Lee onto the table. The Doctor took the moment to check on Huo Jin, who hadn't moved nor cried since the melee started.

"I'm so sorry Kevin." Irene placed her hand gently on Murdock's back as he laid his wife on the table. Her soft tone revealing what he already knew to be true. *My son is dead.* The Doctor immediately started working on Mei Lee. "I'm going to need more light and something to soak up all the blood. I'm also going to need a needle of some kind and something to use to sew her up on the inside."

Murdock passed the doctor's requests to Annie telepathically and tried to maintain his composure for Mei Lee's sake. A tear, however, managed to leak from his eyes for his dead son.

Annie came in shortly after he'd sent for her with everything the doctor had requested. With her arrival, Murdock gathered the three children and headed toward the longhouse. He was worried about Mei Lee, but he felt that he should leave so they could do what they needed without kids and husbands underfoot.

Just as he got to the door, it was opened by Declan: "Come on in. *Mi casa su casa.*"

Murdock had carried Rosa and Chun Hua. "You three go find a corner to sleep in," he said as he put the girls down. They immediately did as their father had told them.

"Mei Lee okay?" Declan asked.

"Unknown, at this time," Murdock responded coldly, his voice cracking a little. "Irene and Annie are working on her now."

"Huo Jin?" Emily asked trying to get her head to stop bleeding.

Murdock said nothing. He just looked grim and shook his head slowly.

"What happened to you, Em?" Murdock asked after a while, to break the uncomfortable silence.

"It was my own fault, really. I took my eyes off them for a second and they pushed me into the edge that the ramp seals to. I must've been stunned because before I knew it, I was on the snow looking up at the pod and my head was spinning. Then nothing until Declan roused me."

"How are Phylicia and Kimberly?" Heather asked in a concerned, quiet voice.

"Dead," Murdock responded coldly, "along with my infant son and maybe my wife." Murdock didn't speak harshly, nor did he turn toward her to answer. It struck Heather that his reactions were oddly cold. *He's either uncaring or he cares so much he's afraid to let out how much,* she thought. With what little she knew of him, she decided it was the latter. *He may act cold and distant, but he isn't.*

Murdock had no idea how much time had passed, as he had dozed off, when he received a telepathic message to come to his cabin. He knew it was from Doctor Harris, but there were no details.

"Keep an eye on them?" Murdock flashed Declan as he got to his feet.

"Always! They're no trouble," Declan flashed.

It didn't take Murdock long to reach his cabin. It was very cold outside, and he could see the signs that the sun would be up soon. As he got to his front door, it opened.

"You need to be calm," Doctor Harris started as he entered and the door was shut behind him, "I did what I could, given the primitive conditions. You said Mei Lee was pregnant earlier?"

"Yes, I did."

Irene Harris took a deep breath and exhaled it in exasperation: "The damage she suffered from the knife was extensive, I did the best I could, but the baby didn't survive." the doctor answered his unspoken question, with a comforting hand on his shoulder. "When Mei Lee fell, the tip nicked one of her ovaries. I sutured it as best as I could, along with all the bleeders, and scraped her uterus, since the baby was already gone."

"Will Mei Lee live?" Murdock asked quietly.

"I think so, but I'd like to wait a while to see if there are any complications to be sure. Huo Jin had exsanguinated, before I got here, with a clean, deep slice to his jugular."

"Does Mei Lee know all this?" he asked as the tears started down his face.

"No, she passed out some time ago from the pain of the surgery. We are monitoring her, but she hasn't awakened, yet."

"Don't tell the kids the details, Doc?"

"I won't. I will if you ask me to, at some later time. I'll get Emily up here to help with the clean-up. You just stay with Mei."

It was sometime after breakfast that Emily and Heather trekked to Murdock's cabin.

"Does the sight of blood bother you?" Emily asked Heather.

"It does if it's mine, other than that, not that I've noticed," Heather responded, "why do you ask?"

"You do know what happened last night?" Emily asked incredulously of the other woman's ignorance.

"I don't know the details, but I know Murdock killed Phylicia and Kimberly. He did say something about his son being killed and maybe his wife."

"Well, the inside of the cabin is going to be a mess, probably look like a slaughterhouse. There'll be blood all over the place from the arterial spray. We need to get three bodies out and get as much blood cleaned up as we can. If it were up to me, I'd have Mei Lee moved to the longhouse to recuperate. It would give us longer to get it cleaned up for her, Murdock, and the kids."

When the two women got to the cabin door, Murdock opened it and glared at Heather.

"I'm going to need help, Kevin, and Heather is willing to help," Emily said trying to turn away his anger. "I'll take responsibility for her, if it will make you feel better."

"I would feel better if I'd dispatched those two before this all happened," Murdock said.

"Wouldn't we all," Emily responded sadly.

It took the two women days to get the bodies moved to Murdock's cart and to try to get all the blood cleaned from the wooden floors and table. All of the bodies were wrapped in deer hides and tied until the weather changed so they could be buried.

When Emily and Heather had gotten as much blood as possible off of the floor and table, Murdock tried to remove more by removing the wood fibers that were stained using the same principle he used to cut stone. It had the effect of planing the wood. The table looked new when it was finished, and so did the floors, even though they were missing a few millimeters in thickness.

Fourteen days after the attack, Mei Lee wasn't getting better, so Doctor Harris was called in.

"I think I need to go in and remove your ovary," she told Mei Lee, in Murdock's presence, after her examination. "I tried to sew it up, but it appears that the fix isn't going to work."

"If you do, can I still get pregnant?" Mei Lee asked.

"You should be able to, as long as there are no other complications," Harris said. "I just wish there was something I could give you to knock you out."

"I'll be fine," Mei Lee tried to reassure her friend. "I just need to go into the *sharing state.*"

"I think we'll do it in the pod," Doctor Harris added. "It is metal and a lot easier to clean and sterilize, easier than your cabin, anyway."

～

After helping to clean Murdock's cabin of the carnage, Heather remained and had been helping out with Murdock's children. She felt she was doing it out of a sense of guilt for what Phylicia and Kimberly had done. *After all, I knew what happened was possible and likely,* she thought. *I knew them better than the rest did and should have said something sooner. Maybe the children would still be alive if I had.*

Murdock and Mei Lee had accepted Heather's help only after long hours of denials, on their part for the need, and questioning of her motives. Her job had been to help with meals and to watch over the children. She also tended to Mei Lee while she was recovering from her injuries.

Murdock had been angry after the attack, with Phylicia and Kimberly, certainly, but also with himself. *I should've been faster,* he thought. *Maybe I should have learned to crush their skulls or how to pinch off an artery. Maybe that would have been better and preserved two of his children and saved Mei Lee such pain and suffering.* His thoughts caused him to growl at most people, even though he hadn't meant to. It had gotten bad enough that the remaining three children referred to him as "the Bear". "Is the Bear up?" or "Isn't it early in the year for the Bear to be awandering?" were some of the more common things that were said.

On the day of Mei Lee's second procedure, Murdock had gotten her to the pod and lay her on a table, helped her to achieve the *sharing state,* and left to wait in the longhouse for word.

"Looks like the Bear is out and about," Declan flashed to Emily's mind.

"Behave yourself, husband," Emily flashed back to Declan.

"Can I get you anything?" Emily asked Murdock.

"No, I just don't want to wait inside the pod," he responded in a sharp tone. Emily sat next to him, with some difficulty, and was studying his face.

"I know you're concerned," she said after a few minutes, "but you need to talk to someone about what you're feeling. You need to do it before it eats you up inside."

"I know," Murdock answered chagrinned. "You look content, though."

"I look fat," Emily stated with a chuckle, "but pregnancy tends to do that. I am quite content, though."

"When are you due?" Murdock asked.

"We'd figured sometime in late spring or early summer."

"Come up with a name, yet?"

"I want to name her Emily," Declan said as he came over and joined the conversation, "but this one ain't havin' it."

"That would be too confusing," Emily argued. "I like Krystal, if it's a girl. I like Deacon or Derek if it's a boy."

"Dustin was my father's name," Declan piped in, "but people used to call him Dusty for short. Not sure I'd like my son called that. Dixon is nice."

"That would be Dix, for short," Emily said with a smirk.

"Hmmm...I guess that would also preclude Richard for the same reason." Declan chuckled. "Gordon is a nice strong name for a boy."

As much as Murdock hated to admit it, the banter that went on between Declan and Emily usually made him chuckle and would, most times, bring him out of his funk, but not this time. He was worried about Mei Lee and had just had his home invaded and two children killed. The loss of the children was the worst feeling he'd had since Rose died. He was certain Mei Lee felt the same way.

The weather wasn't cooperating with them. At least, that's what Reyes was thinking. The nights were bitterly cold, and the days were usually snow and wind. Sometimes, the snow and wind happened at night, which made it even colder in the cave. She was hunkered down with quite a few of the others that had moved from the guard posts once the winds kicked up. As it turned out, the enclosed area under the guard posts wasn't chinked correctly and the wind would whistle through the logs.

They had been using a few pots to melt snow and ice to drink. Most of the time, they made soup to make the venison stretch as far as it could. *Yesterday, we found three of our company frozen to death,* she thought. *We had no place to put the bodies, except under one of the guard posts.* A few of the men had tried to harvest a deer, but they couldn't find any.

"Things are going to get worse before they get better," Reyes said to Heartly. "That is what you're saying?"

"Unless we get some protein, very few of us are going to survive until spring," Bass answered. "Those that survive may not be strong enough to recover sufficiently, once we can fish."

"So, what are you suggesting?" Reyes asked. She already had an idea of what he was going to say and the thought of it turned her stomach.

"We have some protein under the guard post —" Heartly started.

"Absolutely not," Reyes yelled before Heartly could finish.

"They aren't going to need anything anymore and it could mean the rest of us survive," Heartly pleaded. "We've already been eating soup to make the venison stretch, I doubt anyone would know."

"I'd know," Reyes countered.

"If it means we make it through the winter, don't you think we should consider it?"

∾

That was one of the best ideas we ever had, Keith Rogers thought as he stood looking at the ramp that was blocking the main entrance to the caves. It looked similar to a picture of a drawbridge he had seen in a book and was keeping the majority of the howling wind out of the cave.

"Has Hornsby returned yet?" Rogers asked the guard stationed at the huge wooden door. "It's been four days. He should've been back by now."

"Hornsby isn't back, yet, I see," Cliff Reed said as he came over to Rogers.

"I'm not sure he will be back," Rogers said aloud. "If he hasn't found another group, he's probably dead someplace. I doubt he could survive four days out in weather like this." They heard something that sounded like rocks hitting the outside of the gate. "Lower the gate," Rogers commanded.

As the gate was dropped, the wind howled through the opening unhindered. Everyone gathered a hide closer to them to protect them from the bitter cold and rushed to the opening. They could see a lump on the landing across from the gate. They rushed over to see what it was. As Rogers arrived, his deer-hide flapping in the wind, the guard turned over the lump. It was Hornsby. He was covered in ice and snow, but everyone there recognized him, and he had a wolf carcass.

"Get Hornsby and his prize inside and get Roy White to see to him," Rogers commanded.

It was several hours before Roy White, the paramedic, would allow anyone to see his patient.

"How are you doing, Hornsby?" Reed asked as he entered the small cave that White was using as a sickroom.

"I'm still cold," Hornsby responded, his teeth chattering as he shivered.

"Has White let you soak in the hot water?" Reed asked as he

glanced at Hornsby's arm and the black patch that was covering part of his forearm and a few on his face.

"No, not hot, yet," Hornsby responded, "just the cooler water. He's trying to save what he can of the tissues under the skin, but they need to thaw first. I'm shivering so hard I feel like I'm wearing out my clothes from the inside."

"Did you find the camp?" Reed asked.

"I did, and they said they weren't interested," Hornsby responded through chattering teeth. "They also said that they weren't interested in anyone coming for visits or any other purpose."

"What is their problem?" Reed asked.

"Something about leaving them behind and failing to support Carter, whoever he is."

"He led us away from the transport pod, initially, but decided to go out exploring and left us all to fend for ourselves. They've got to be out of their minds, if they think that way." Reed was fidgeting a bit.

"I don't know nothin' I don't haf-ta," Hornsby said with a slight chuckle. "I steer clear of politics."

"Where did you get the wolf?" Reed asked.

"Not far from here, I actually ran across him and caught him off guard. Figured we could make soup out of him or some such. I want the hide, though."

"The hide will be distributed as needed," Reed said quietly, "as you well know. We share everything, and I do mean *everything*."

"Buck up, old son!" Declan said loudly and clapped Murdock on his shoulder. "You won your fight and did what you had to do. I doubt anyone would hold it against you that the attackers were women."

Murdock looked shocked: "That statement is wrong on so many levels!"

"In what way?" Declan asked, confused.

"Do you really think you can win a fight?" Murdock asked. He was waiting in the longhouse for Doctor Harris to finish her post-operative examination of Mei Lee.

"Sure," Declan said with a shrug. "Someone does something to you and you beat his ass. You win."

"Is that what you really believe?" Murdock asked. "If someone, say Bass Heartly, calls you out and you subdue him, you think you won. Bass goes about his business, but the loss wears on him because he can't let it go. You run across him again, this time you're alone and he has a couple of his cohorts and challenges you again. Did you win anything the first time? No one wins an altercation. You can only hope to survive it, and its repercussions."

Declan looked at his brother-in-law, shocked. "What else was wrong with my statement?"

"You implied that women aren't as dangerous as men," Murdock stated, "and that simply isn't true. Women can be, and often are, more dangerous than men. They hide their animosity better and are far more patient. You are what, six-foot-two and come in at over two hundred pounds?"

"Something like that," Declan answered.

"The next time we spar, I'll put you against Mei Lee. She's five foot nothing and just over a hundred pounds and I'd bet she'd take you apart."

"Well, yeah," Declan started, "she's had a lot more training."

"That is a factor, but she'd win because you see the size difference and the fact she is a woman, and so you'll take it easy with her. That is a big mistake! She's going against a much larger opponent and so will have nothing to lose by going all out and won't go easy on you."

"Hmmm...I'm beginning to see what you mean," Declan responded. "So, how traumatized are Andy and Rosa Lea?"

"They aren't traumatized," Murdock responded. "They are aware of what happened and are thankful things didn't get any worse. They are more aware, now, though. Like me, they had become complacent, thinking that their isolation, or living with me and Mei Lee, kept them safe. They understand that they are as safe as they can be, but that doesn't guarantee anything."

"I'm sure they already knew that, knowing you," Declan said.

"They did, as it concerns wild animals. They hadn't thought people were a threat. Now, they know to be more alert and to take some responsibility for their own safety."

"How can you say that?" Declan asked, shocked. "Andy is only four! What can he do to protect himself?"

"More than you think," Murdock said, "and he's almost five, or is five, it's hard to say when exactly his birthday is. Anyway, he admits to feeling less on his guard, around people. He and Chun both carry six-inchers and keep them razor sharp. They can do plenty of damage with them. They were just complacent, this time, with strangers."

"*I need to see you in the pod,*" flashed to Murdock and he got up to leave.

"I'll be back in a few," he said to Declan.

"Mei Lee should be fine, in time," Doctor Harris was explaining to Murdock and his wife with her best professional expression. "I did end up removing one of her ovaries, but she should be able to conceive. It may be a little more difficult, but it should be possible."

"Any other restrictions we should know about?" Murdock asked.

"No lifting and nothing too strenuous for a few more weeks," Doctor Harris said. "You did just have your stitches out, so be careful. I don't want anything to open up. Do you have any questions?" Both shook their heads to indicate the negative. "If you notice anything unusual, anything at all, let me know immediately."

"I'm sorry, Mei," Murdock said as they lay in their bed.

"What do you have to be sorry about?" Mei Lee asked as she snuggled closer to her husband.

"I should have been faster, or done something different. Something to make sure you didn't get hurt and to keep Huo Jin alive."

"There was nothing you could have done," Mei Lee said, voice wavering. "I know you did your best, as always. I don't blame you. I should have been more aware before opening the door." Mei Lee sobbed. "I thought it was you or one of the others. I set my knife down to open the door." Her tears flowed freely.

"It wasn't your fault, Mei," Murdock said as he pulled her closer, his own voice cracking.

It had been a long winter, so far, for Ted Wagner. He spent most of his time hunting for something edible for the rest of the residents of the cave. He had tried for a deer just before the first snowfall and managed it, but since, there had been nothing. He managed to drop a couple of wolves, though, but most of the people had not liked it. Most, including Ted, felt they were eating someone's dog

"Eat it or not, it's all there is," Raymond Tutt said to the complainers. "Better yet, you can go out and find something else. Ted is doing his best."

The followers of Raymond Tutt had been those who had followed Emily Brooks and Keith Rogers to the huge cave a couple of miles from the river. They were also the majority of the metal workers. They had brought most of the smelting and metal working tools with them when they left. Tutt, remembering the nightmares from violating Murdock's edict, had convinced the rest that Declan had caused the nightmares that still plagued him, from time to time. He had warned everyone that associating with Declan could cause them to live through the hell of horrific nightmares every night.

Wagner didn't buy into Tutt's nightmare theory. He had steered clear whenever Tutt went into one of his many rants. Wagner figured that the nightmares were the by-product of a guilty conscience and were not attributable to someone else. He couldn't even imagine someone being able to — through sheer concentration or force of will — cause someone else to have a nightmare. To him, the notion was laughable.

The tunnels that Tutt's crew found were deep, and in the frigid cold of winter, very warm. They had found plenty of iron ore, coal, copper, silver, nickel, and gold. In fact, the bow he carried out on hunting trips had wooden limbs attached to a metal riser and was one of the first things they manufactured. They were also trying to perfect large copper kettles and a pan that resembled a wok. *I think someone is going to try to build a still, with the copper kettles, in the next year,* he thought. *I know I could use a stiff drink.*

Some of the deep tunnels emptied into great pools of melted snow and was warmed by the heat generated far below the surface. These pools had a large fish species that tasted like cod or tilapia. There were hot pools in some of the lowest chambers and everyone made use of them as often as possible. *I just wish there were more free females,* he thought whenever he thought of the pools and bathing. *There's nothing better than a wet, naked female for scenery.* This thought caused him to chuckle to himself.

Wagner's current task was hunting for something other than fish, as the residents were tired of it. It was frigid and Wagner had to be mindful of the cold before he was frostbitten. *We have no medicos, if something happens,* he thought, *so, easy does it.* He was currently crouched behind some of the bare bushes close to the path leading to the mine entrance, looking out across the open plain. He noticed that the clouds were coming in and would probably snow more before day's end. *We really need a deer,* he wished. *There aren't that many of us and we can't have that much of winter left.* As he watched, an older buck was meandering toward his position.

He had seen deer wander toward this particular spot before, but before they got into his range, something would startle them, and they would run off. He had selected his current position because it was the only hidden position anywhere close to the mine entrance and he wasn't dressed for prolonged exposure. As the deer came closer, Wagner noticed the brief gusts of wind were hitting his face, making his ears and cheeks burn from the cold. Periodically, the buck would look around. On one of the buck's scans for threats, Wagner pulled out and nocked an arrow. As he held the bow and arrow, his fingers seemed to be going numb from contact with the metal. *Just keep coming. A little further.*

As the buck took a few more steps toward him, he suddenly stopped to look around. Seeing nothing, he pawed the ground looking for something to eat. While the buck's head was down, Wagner pulled the bow back and let the arrow fly. *Please hit. Please hit. Please —* the arrow missed, hitting the ground between the buck's front and back legs, and Wagner's confidence was crushed.

24

M urdock, Mei Lee, Declan, Emily, Doctor Harris, and
Annie were all sitting in the longhouse. They had all
just returned from the spring rite that Murdock and Mei Lee had
attended since their arrival. The first-timers were still excited at
observing the Oomah and their acceptance, by the Oomah, by
being associated with Murdock as being part of his family.

"I have a question," Emily piped up. "What about Heather?
How long will we leave her on the outside?" She was frowning
as she was rubbing her swollen belly.

"Are you okay, Em?" Declan quietly asked, seeing his wife's
discomfort.

"I'll be fine," Emily said to her husband and then to the
others: "Heather helped clean up the mess in Murdock's cabin.
She helped with the kids while Mei was recovering, and she has
gone out of her way to help us all anyway she can. I think we
need to vote her in."

Everyone looked to Murdock and waited for his response.

"It isn't quite that easy," Murdock said looking at everyone
present. "Yes, she's earned a place with us, but is that what *she*
wants? She really hasn't had a choice, so far. Don't you think we
need to find out if that's something she'd be interested in?"

412

"I'm voting for her to be included," Declan said, raising his hand.

"So, who's going to talk to her to find out if she wants to be one of us?" Murdock asked.

～

Elizabeth Reyes was standing in one of the guard towers watching the rest of her charges bury the dead from the long winter. Her clothes hung on her. She had lost considerably more weight than she had intended. *Everyone is close to starving*, she thought as she watched the others. *Thank god we caught quite a number of fish since the thaw. It'll take a little time to get us built back up.* "What was our final count?" Reyes asked without turning around.

"Thirteen," Bass Heartly responded behind her. "It could've been worse."

"It could've been better, too. If it wasn't for Murdock, the insufferable, maybe more would've survived. He should've helped!"

"But he did ask before winter and we told him where to stick it."

"He should have come to check on us more often! Once, in all the months of winter, is not enough!"

"But he did bring us half a deer and it did see us through. At least we didn't have to resort to the *other* alternative."

"Maybe so, but now we have to deal with him lording it over us, that he saved us. Do you think he'll let us forget that we survived because he helped? I don't think so. This year, I want to prevent anything like that ever happening. I want multi-family structures built, properly chinked this time. We need smokehouses and before next winter we need to have plenty of food stored. I don't want us to be caught short again."

"We have all that and planting some crops we brought and trying to find other foods we need," Heartly added absentmindedly. "That is a lot to do in only the few months we have before winter comes again."

"Let's get to it, then. Get everyone working on something, right after they're finished with the burials."

Keith Rogers, the newly elected leader of the group that lived in the big cave close to the river, was standing just inside the cave entrance taking in the fresh air that was gently wafting up from the forest floor. He could smell damp dirt and some pollen from the grasses and trees. There were no wildflowers, yet, but the promise was there.

"How many winter casualties did we have?" he asked as Clifford Reed came up behind him.

"We had no casualties from exposure, but we did have one from the fight that broke out," Reed reported.

"Cabin fever can really get to some people. How are you feeling, Cliff?" Rogers asked as he looked down and toward his back.

"I'm glad it's spring and let's leave it at that."

"How's Hornsby doing?"

"He has some scars from his winter trek, but overall he seems to be okay."

"We need to have a meeting with him and a few of the other men. We made it through the winter, but something else needs to be done, before long, so we can be better prepared for the next one. Do we have any farmers?"

"Not many. Most of them went with those that are waiting for Carter to return."

"Get Clem Adams to locate volunteers to help the farmers get what they need to be done. Has there been anything new from our weapons development group?"

"Nothing, yet. None of them are engineers, by any stretch of the imagination. Maybe we need to talk to Tutt's people and work something out for weapons and tools?"

Rogers turned with a dour look: "Do you really think that superstitious baboon would help us?"

"What can it hurt to talk to him?" Reed asked with a shrug. "We aren't out anything by trying and who knows, he might help us if we had something they wanted or needed."

"I already know we do. Not many of the women wanted to go with them, so they'll want women." Rogers exhaled loudly.

"When was the last time you were outside the cave?" Reed asked.

"I haven't been outside since the altercation with Emily, Declan, and Murdock," Rogers responded quietly. "Why do you ask?"

"I'm thinking that you could use the fresh air. You could take three or four guards and go visit Tutt. Maybe you two could work something out for weapons and who knows what else."

Alvin Jones sat in the corner of one of the community huts, feeding a small fire to warm his hands. He had followed the largest group here after helping Palmer take care of Freeman and after threatening Phylicia. *It was wrong to threaten the women that way*, he thought. *And the way Palmer took out Freeman.* His head shook side-to-side subconsciously. *Murder is murder, no matter how you try to dress it up as something else.*

He was accepted into the group without questions. He had always been a loner, and, for whatever reason, most people failed to see him or acknowledge him. He walked in, did his work with the farmers harvesting the wild barley-like grain, and kept to himself.

When Osterlund showed up, just before winter, it caused him to panic a little. He went to great lengths to be elsewhere most of the time until winter forced them all indoors. It was then that he went out of his way to make sure he wasn't in the same hut as Osterlund.

By the time Hornsby had come to the camp, it had initially caused him some concern, but it passed when it became obvious that Hornsby hadn't remembered him. Early in the winter, he had taken to shaving off his beard, with a sharp six-incher, and keeping his head shaved, from forehead to ears in the front, and letting the rest grow long so he could braid it in the back. He had hoped to have changed his appearance enough so no one would recognize him.

During the long winter, everyone had survived by fishing as much as they could until the freeze and laying in a lot of grain. They were all served a little fish with a large portion of grain. It did get them through the winter, but Alvin had decided that they needed venison. He was sick of fish and barley soup.

During the first big meeting, after the ground had started to thaw, a lot of ideas were bandied about. They had decided that they needed a mill, of some kind, to grind whatever grain they collected; they needed draft animals, and they needed other food sources and a means of preserving it all. *That is too much for this small group*, he thought. *It would be nice, but it is a bit too ambitious. Do we have a plow, or a means for making one? I don't know how to make one, but maybe they do. From what I'm hearing, we're going to need some support from the other groups.*

Heather was waiting outside Murdock's cabin. She had been told that she was to report there, but wasn't told the reason. She got to her feet when she saw Mei Lee coming toward her.

"Hello, Heather. How are you doing today?" Mei Lee greeted her with a smile.

"Fine, Ma'am," Heather responded. *Ma'am? Where did that come from? These people weren't formal*, she thought. *I'd heard Murdock refer to Declan as 'Hey You'.*

"Mei Lee is fine. We aren't that formal," Mei Lee responded with a slight chuckle. "You have been a great help to all of us here. Have you given any thought as to what you'd like to do or where you'd like to go?" she asked as she sat on a log close to the burn pit. She patted the log to indicate that Heather should sit.

"What do you mean? I was of the impression that I wasn't allowed to go anywhere else," Heather said as she sat.

"Not by us. It's our opinion that you can go anywhere you like. Our concern is that the others may remember you... in a bad light and try to take out their frustrations on you. Like Reyes and some of her group did. Because of the...altercation and because winter is a time for hunkering down, you didn't have much of a choice. It is spring and we want you to feel free to leave, if that is what you want, or you can stay."

While Mei Lee spoke, Heather had been listening and swinging her legs nervously.

"Mei Lee, to be honest, I don't know what I'd find away from here. I've felt safe and wanted here, but it has been lonely."

"I understand. I know Kevin is planning on going to check on the others tomorrow. It may turn into a burial detail, though. You're free to accompany him to see what you can find, if you feel up to it since your miscarriage."

"Who will be going with him?" Heather asked.

"Annie will probably be going, to aid those who need it. You've been trained to defend yourself since coming here, but you still need to be careful."

"I would've thought Declan would accompany him."

"Under normal circumstances, he would, but Emily is very close to her time and he needs to be here. I would go, but I have children to look after as well."

"I understand and I would like to accompany Kevin and Annie," Heather said. Mei Lee had been studying her facial expressions and noticed there was something Heather wanted to say, but, so far, hadn't found the words.

"Was there something else you wanted to say?" Mei Lee asked.

"Not to offend or imply anything," Heather started hesitantly, "but did you know there may be a lot of things here that would help with our dietary needs?"

"Such as?" Mei Lee asked, genuinely curious.

"I'm not certain, but there appears to be a grain, of some sort, across the river. I'd be willing to bet there are more things, like carrots, potatoes, and onions growing wild over there, too. If we cultivated them more, they would help get us through the winters better, maybe?"

Mei Lee grinned at Heather's noncommittal attitude. "Yes, those things would be a great help. If you return, you can explore those possibilities. I was never a gardener, and neither was Kevin, obviously. He is more of a hunter than a gatherer," Mei Lee chuckled.

Early the next morning, Murdock, Heather, and Annie left the encampment and charted a course downriver. Murdock, pulling the cart loaded with hides, tools they thought they'd need, and venison. Heather walked alongside with Annie. All three had their own waterskin, twelve-inch machete, and a six-inch skinning knife.

"How are your levitation skills?" Murdock flashed to Annie.

"I don't know, for certain," Annie answered. *"I can manage myself, I think, in the transition to the bottom of the terrace coming up. Why do you ask?"*

"I was asking because of Heather," Murdock flashed. *"Should we allow her to see? Or should we trust her to keep her eyes closed?"*

"I'd say the latter. If she keeps her eyes closed, it will go a long way to being able to trust her more fully."

"I agree. When we stop, you explain it to her," Murdock flashed

with a grin. "Annie, grab a spear and take the lead," he said aloud.

"We aren't going to cross the river, so go straight when you get to the river crossing," Murdock flashed to Annie after several hours of walking in silence.

"Where are we going to transition?" Annie flashed back.

"We aren't, just yet. I want to head in the general direction of Reye's camp, but stay up here."

"Any particular reason why?"

"I'm not going to place us in harm's way unnecessarily. I've been thinking of a means to talk to her without her guards."

"So, you're going to levitate her up the terrace to us? Is Beron going to knock her out?"

"That would be the plan. Besides, I've wanted to explore that area anyway. We do have to be aware of wolves, though."

"Rest here," Murdock said aloud when he could see the edge of the terrace in the distance.

"How long are we going to be here?" Heather asked.

"Not long," Murdock said. "We'll eat later, unless either of you can't wait." Murdock took a big draw on the waterskin. As he replaced it, he took up his bow and quiver of arrows from the cart. "I want Heather to pull the cart and Annie to bring up the rear. We'll be going into an area that I've not been in, but I know there are wolves, so everyone needs to be aware and ready."

Neither of the women said anything. Both nodded that they understood. As Murdock strode off, Heather took up the cart and followed him. Annie took up her spear and followed. After several hours, the mountains seemed to push them toward the terrace edge. It wasn't long before they found their path blocked by rock, but Murdock could hear the falls. He crept up close to the edge of the terrace so he could see over it. Below him was Reye's camp.

∾

It was late in the day when Liz Reyes left the cave that was her office and living area. Looking up at the sky, as she stretched her back muscles, she could tell the sun would go down soon. It was then that she became very dizzy and felt herself falling backward. She waited to impact the ground, but it didn't happen, for some reason.

When she felt the ground, her hand was touching moist grass. It was then that she knew she wasn't in the canyon. She sat up, startled.

"Have a nice nap?" Murdock asked her with a toothy grin.

"Where the hell am I?" Reyes demanded hotly. "How did you manage to kidnap me from inside the compound?" As Reyes looked around, she saw Annie Cooper and another strange female tending a fire. There were tents, made of skins, close by and she could smell the venison roasting, causing her to salivate.

"I *invited* you to our camp to have a discussion," Murdock said pleasantly.

"About what?" Reyes snapped.

"About the future of humans on this planet. Have you given any further thought to what I said before winter? About a civilized mindset versus a pack mentality?"

"What about it?" Reyes snapped again.

"From what I've seen, the people on this last transport pod have divided themselves by skillset, more or less. You have very few, if any, farmers or metal workers and the group downriver has lots of farmers, but few metal workers, as an example. You'd think there could be something traded to the benefit of both."

"And who would be determining who trades what?" Reyes questioned.

"Not me. It would be up to the leaders of all the groups to figure things like that out. You all need to cooperate, the harsh winter should have taught you that."

"It taught me to get tough and get organized. It taught me to gather as many resources as possible to prepare for the next year. It also taught me not to rely on *you!*"

"And I should have shown you that your compound isn't as safe as you think it is." Murdock motioned and Heather came over with venison for himself and Reyes.

"I see you have a slave, now," Reyes said as she bit into the hot venison.

"I have no slaves," Murdock corrected stoically. "What we do have is cooperation. Take Heather there," Murdock said indicating Heather. "She is one of those that you wanted Bass to exact your revenge on. She can't hunt or track, yet, but she is quite good at fires, cooking, and helping. She is unafraid of trying something new. For that, she is well treated and well fed. If you noticed, she has put on some weight, all of it muscle, since you last saw her, while you, Liz, have lost considerable mass."

Reyes became caustic: "And what of her two *companions*? As I recall, there were three of them. Where are they?"

"They murdered innocents and were executed," Heather said stoically.

"There are no *innocents*," Reyes smirked.

"Okay, how about a newborn and a to-be-born," Heather said.

"Serves you right," Reyes said as she glared at Murdock. "That's what you get for interfering!"

"Are you finished with your beratement?" Murdock asked speaking softly. "You were brought here to try to get you to see reason—"

"I'll never be reasonable with you," Reyes spat. "I lost thirteen good people because of you, so I'm done!" She stood and intentionally dumped her venison into the fire. As she walked toward the terrace edge, she dropped to the ground. Then she was levitated to the ground below the terrace.

"I was wondering how long you were going to take her guff," Heather asked with her back to Murdock, trying to fish the meat out of the fire.

"What now?" Annie flashed to Murdock as they all sat close to the fire.

"We proceed to the last group and work our way back," Murdock responded.

"What are you trying to accomplish?" Heather asked after sitting in silence for some time.

"I'm trying to get the others out of their pack mentality and to think about being more civilized," Murdock said quietly. "Right now, they're all attacking anyone outside their small groups, like a pack of wolves. I'm trying to get them to act civilly with everyone and to cooperate with each other."

Heather looked puzzled for a long time and then said, "I don't know if you're naïve, ignorant, or undauntedly optimistic. I'm sure your pod gave you a briefing when you arrived?"

"It did," Murdock responded quietly.

"As of the time I was taken, the Earth was overrun with arrogant, self-serving, egocentric individuals. No one helped anyone unless they were compensated, in some way. Everyone thought they were right, especially if they weren't. People never got along for more than a few minutes and you had to watch what you said and who was around to hear it. Islamophobia ran rampant. The term micro-aggression was thrown at everyone for everything you thought, said, or did, and no one took responsibility for their actions."

"I know. I was there. What's your point?" Murdock asked impatiently.

"My point is those people were pulled from that environment and dropped here. They've had no time to unlearn anything or lose their biases. They haven't experienced how wrong their own prejudices are. They went to sleep there and awoke here. Do you really expect them to act any differently?"

"I'm just trying to get them to build a human civilization here," Murdock said after some thought.

"Personally, even though that is a lofty and admirable goal, I don't think it's attainable. In the entire history of mankind, there has been no 'civilization' to speak of. Just new and different ways to steal, kill, and enslave one another." Heather sat quietly after she had run down and tended the fire.

"So, you're saying that we aren't civilized?" Annie asked after a long, thoughtful pause.

"As individuals, yes, we can *act* civilized, from time to time, but taken as a whole, humans are hairless apes that are scared, most of the time, and destroy everything that comes their way," Heather stated.

"That seems rather negative," Annie said.

"Can you name me a single instance of that not being the case?" Heather asked.

"Why don't we see what we can do to change that," Murdock added.

Three days later, Murdock, Annie, and Heather were sitting around a fire with the people below the third terrace downriver. They had arrived earlier in the day. Murdock had helped them by harvesting a few fish.

Heather had done her part by helping the women grind some of the grain they had left-over from the long winter.

"Is this wheat?" Heather asked as she squinted at the handful of kernels in her hand. "Or is it barley?"

"It doesn't look like either, that we're used to," Kathy Watkins answered. "Once it's ground and cooked, it tastes like a mixture of the two."

As Heather watched, Kathy picked up a rock that was roughly pan-shaped with a slight ridge running around the outside and placed it across her legs and put a few handfuls of grain on the rock and, picking up a roughly rounded rock, began to crush and grind the grain. She would periodically stop and pick out husks from the crushed grain. It took Kathy some time to work it into a powdery consistency.

"You don't pound the grain," Kathy explained as she put more on the rock with the powder. "It's more of a rolling, grinding action."

"Mind if I try?" Heather asked. Kathy nodded and passed the grinding rocks to her. As she began grinding the grain, she started to get a feeling for doing it. To her, it had initially looked easy, but it wasn't long before she could appreciate how much hard work went into this simple, and ancient, chore.

Annie had spent her daylight hours tending to a few people who had minor injuries.

"So, how did your group fare during the winter?" Murdock asked aloud to no one in particular. He had noticed the sod huts built against the ridge wall.

"We did okay," Markus Lantz answered. Murdock had been informed that he was the temporary leader while they waited for Jeffery Carter. "We had planned for the cold and snow and had a lot of the wild grain stored."

"You're coming up on a year being here," Murdock informed all in the range of his voice. "I bring it up because you lasted a year and the higher chances of death through misfortune come in the first year. As long as you all keep your eyes open and your wits about you, it's unlikely that many of you will die by accident."

"We'd figured that out already," Lantz condescended.

"Have any of you been on the other side of the river?" Murdock asked, more than a bit put out with Lantz's attitude.

"A few of us have," Lantz replied, "for wood and possible game."

"I'd be very careful going over there, if I were you," Murdock stated. "Palmer was killed, just before winter, by a huge cougar across the river. It had cubs, so a word to the wise."

"How big was it?" Lantz asked as his eyes widened with surprise and curiosity.

"I'd guess four hundred pounds, about the size of a Bengal tiger."

"We'd heard he was dead, no loss, but we didn't know how he died. Who found him?"

"I did. The cougar almost got me, too. It looked like it let the cubs feed on him while he was alive."

"That sounds ghastly!"

"Ghastly?" Murdock paused. "Ghastly. Yes, I'd say that was exactly what it was, ghastly. Anyway, we came to see how you all fared and to see if you needed anything or if there was something we could do for you."

"We are mostly farmers, here, so I'd like to know how to deal with the cougars or any other pests," Lantz said.

"Pests? Huh. You do have wolves and cougars to worry about," Murdock responded. "I doubt they could be classified as pests, though. As always, you don't venture out too far from the majority of the group and have effective weapons."

Heather brought over a plate of food for Murdock as he was talking. When he looked at it, he was surprised to see some kind of bread with some hot grain meal and hot venison. He tasted the bread and his eyes went wide.

"What happened to Phylicia and that group?" Lantz asked as he ate as well.

"I already told you about Palmer. Phylicia and Kimberly had a hard time of it before they died. Other than that, I don't know who you'd want to know about," Murdock said between bites. He was watching Lantz as the two men ate.

"At the time we left, there were quite a number of other people that were left behind, as I recall. What happened to them?"

"I've already told you of the ones that are dead, that I know of. Where the others are," Murdock shook his head slightly. "Who can say? You are our second stop, so far, so there could be much I'm unaware of."

Lantz nodded slightly. "We managed to only lose seven to exposure this last winter. We are planning on being better prepared this coming winter. Where can we get a few bows and arrows?"

"You can either make them yourself or try to find someone to trade you some," Murdock stated flatly.

Lantz looked at him oddly: "That seems rather obvious, so I'm not sure if you're serious or not."

"If I were joking, you'd know. Out here, a ranged weapon is highly prized. If you have some artisans, I can let them inspect my bow and arrows or spears. If not, then you could be in for more difficulty."

"Do you know where the other groups are?" Lantz asked.

"Of course, I made the rounds before winter to all the groups."

"There used to be a number of metal workers in the group at the landing pod, but I have no idea where they went. Do you?"

"You go up the terrace and cross the river. When you get to the mountains, I'm sure they'll let you know," Murdock said with a slight chuckle.

Lantz sat staring into the flames and nodded for a while. "You've been here a while. Have you domesticated the deer for draft animals?" he asked finally.

"No, I don't seem to have the time," Murdock chuckled. "By the looks of your clothes, you're all going to need to make some leather clothes and probably could use the venison. That may be an enterprise for someone to try."

"Catching one is going to be the problem. We tried trapping a few in a coral type of enclosure."

"What happened?" Murdock asked.

"It wasn't high enough and they jumped over the enclosure walls."

"They can be quite slippery to trap. Ever seen one get a good run before jumping?" Lantz answered by simply shaking his head. "They are very fast, very strong, and can jump higher and further than you'd think. If someone tries to trap one, I'd have medical personnel handy. They're going to need it!"

On the day that Murdock, Annie, and Heather left Lantz's group, Keith Rogers, Gary Carpenter, and Jackson Hornsby set out to find Raymond Tutt and the group of miners that had gone with him. Gary Carpenter appeared to have come through the winter unscathed. Rogers appeared sallow from his long, self-imposed, incarceration.

From what Carpenter could see, the black patches on Hornsby's face were replaced by scars of pale skin mostly on his cheek and forehead.

"Is something bothering you?" Hornsby asked testily when he caught Carpenter scrutinizing him.

"You seem to have come through your winter ordeal with minimal damage," Carpenter stated as he looked away.

"You don't get the right to say anything like that to me," Hornsby snapped. "My feet still hurt!"

Rogers put a hand on Hornsby's chest to interpose himself between the two men. "Jax lost a few toes to the frostbite," he said quietly to Carpenter. "Let's try to be respectful of each other for the duration of this trip, shall we?"

"Sorry, to hear that, Jax," Carpenter apologized. "I didn't know."

All three men were outfitted similarly with fish, two machetes — a twelve-inch and an eighteen-inch—, a six-inch knife, and a waterskin. Hornsby had fashioned himself a seven-foot walking stick to help with his balance.

"Do we know where we're going?" Jax asked with some impatience.

"All I know is Tutt headed off toward the mountains," Rogers responded. "Don't know if he found them or not."

"He did," Hornsby responded reflexively.

"How would you know that?" Carpenter asked as he looked at Hornsby suspiciously.

"I'd like to know that as well," Rogers said.

"I know someone who found Tutt and told me a little about it," Hornsby said. "That was before I was admitted to your group."

"So, what do you know?" Carpenter asked.

"I told you. That is all I know."

"So, where are they located? Do they have weapons? If so, what kind?" Carpenter asked in a rapid-fire manner.

"I have no idea. As I said, I knew someone who went there. They didn't tell me all the little details."

"So, what did you think?" Murdock asked after they had gained the top of the terrace and had taken a rest at the river.

"About what?" Heather asked.

"About the farmer group. Was it somewhere you'd like to stay?" Annie asked.

"Honestly, it was a little creepy," Heather responded.

"In what way?" Murdock asked as he prepared to push on.

"I was half-expecting them to jump us for our weapons," Heather said. "The way Lantz was eyeballing us and our equipment, I could see he coveted them, and it gave me a creepy feeling."

Murdock came over to Heather. "I need you to trust me and to keep your eyes closed," he said in a reassuring tone. Heather immediately complied without question. "Okay, open them," Murdock said a few seconds later.

Heather looked around a little and seemed to be indifferent

to the fact that the river that was in front of her, was now behind her.

"Nothing to say?" Murdock asked.

"About being levitated over the river? Why would that surprise me?" Heather asked with a shrug.

"What makes you so sure that's what happened?" Murdock asked in disbelief.

"How else? You moved the transport pod, the base of the longhouse, and me, several times. You did that all by yourself, so you are either a god or you can levitate. Knowing you, I vote for the latter," Heather explained.

"You never cease to amaze me," Murdock said to Heather with a chuckle and a grin. "I can see that you perceive more than most people would think."

"Did you see how that bread was made?" Annie asked

"Yes, and I ground some of the grain," Heather answered, "so I know what the grain looks like raw and what it takes to prepare it. I do remember seeing a picture of someone grinding grain on a small grinding wheel, once. It was two smaller stones together and one turned around on the other with a handle sticking up on the top stone. The top stone also had a hole to put the grain into."

"Well, try to remember any details you can, and we'll see about making our own when we get home," Murdock said. "The bread was good, even if it was unleavened."

"It would make the meat go further and give us some grain in our diet," Annie offered, "but I'm more of a nurse than a farmer."

"That could change," Murdock chuckled.

After several hours of walking in silence, Murdock, Annie, and Heather decided to make camp. They were well past the terrace edge where Palmer was buried, but Murdock could see they had some distance to go to reach the mountains.

∿

After a day of walking, Rogers, Carpenter, and Hornsby decided to make camp for the night. They had no protection from creatures or the elements and seemed blissfully unaware as they sat around their fire.

Raymond Tutt had arrived at the overlook, per Ted Wagner's request. "What did you want?" he asked as he came up behind Wagner.

"We have company coming," he said without turning around. He pointed in two different directions. "You can see their fires from here."

Tutt looked out over the flat plain and clearly saw two bright lights where Wagner had indicated. "I want you to intercept them before they get too close," Tutt ordered. "Take what armed men you think you'll need."

"Okay. They'll be here sometime tomorrow," Wagner said.

25

_____

After breaking camp the next morning, Murdock, Annie, and Heather continued the trek toward the mountains. Murdock was out in front with his bow, leading the two women by fifty yards. Heather was pulling the cart, and Annie, carrying a spear, was watching for threats from the rear.

As they walked, Heather began to worry. With every step, she felt that something was wrong and there was trouble close at hand. With each step, she turned her head from side-to-side looking for anything. *I know what to do, in case of an attack,* Heather thought. *I am to drop the cart and get under it with my twelve-inch machete drawn to defend myself. I am to use the solid wooden wheels for cover and a place to strike from with my machete.* That was all she had to worry about. She was told, repeatedly, that Murdock and Annie had their own procedures and she wasn't to worry about theirs. Two arrows stuck in the ground around the cart and a giant unseen hand grabbed her and placed her under the cart. Annie followed quickly behind her as an arrow struck the cargo area of the cart and penetrated the wood, causing the two to yelp in surprise and Annie to inhale through her teeth as the arrowhead penetrated her thigh.

As Heather glanced around from under the cart, she saw and

heard several arrows hit the ground around the cart and one or
two bounce off its edges.

"Push up with your back a little to raise the front of the cart and
turn it sideways," Annie explained to Heather.

Heather, with Annie's help, managed to get the cart turned
sideways to their direction of travel.

Murdock ran back and ducked behind the wheel that placed
the cart between him and whoever was firing at them, his bow at
the ready.

"I can't see who's shooting at us, but by the trajectory, they
have to be a fair distance away," Murdock said aloud to the
women.

"*One of the arrows came through the cart bed,*" Annie flashed,
"*and it hit me in the thigh. It appears to be a metal arrow.*"

Ted Wagner watched as the first volley was fired at the first of
the intruders.

"Keep them pinned down," he said to his men as he made his
way down from cover. *I wonder who they are. The cart looks familiar
so it could be Murdock, or it could be anyone,* he thought. *I'm glad we
practiced this before we needed it.* He cautiously made his way
toward the cart. When he was about one hundred fifty yards, an
arrow hit his bow knocking it out of his hand. Immediately, a
shower of arrows rained down on the intruders. Wagner gave
the signal to cease fire and the shower stopped. *That return shot
was too well-placed to be luck and I'm standing out here in the open.*
As he watched, he saw a man stand and begin walking toward
him, from one hundred fifty yards away, unafraid of the possible
lethal rain of shafts. Wagner blinked and the man was less than
fifteen feet from him.

"One more arrow comes close to me or my people and you'll be the first to go," Murdock warned.

"What are you doing here?" Wagner asked derisively. "You weren't invited, and you're not wanted."

"Are you in charge?" Murdock asked.

"No, Raymond Tutt leads us."

"Then go fetch him, but before you do, signal your men to stop firing and lay down their bows."

"And if I don't?" Wagner derided.

"You see your man up there at about two hundred yards? Would you like me to stick him?"

"That's not poss—." Murdock took what appeared to be a quick shot, one that wasn't, in Wagner's opinion, aimed, "—ible?" As Wagner was finishing the last syllable, he saw the man Murdock had indicated go down from an arrow to his shoulder.

The other archers prepared for another volley. *He has taken two shots and has hit what he was aiming at both times. We've fired two volleys, each with multiple arrows, and are preparing for a third and have yet to hit him.* Wagner signaled the cease-fire immediately. "You've injured one of my men," Wagner stated as he turned toward Murdock.

"He could have been dead rather than injured," Murdock retorted. "I needed to get your attention."

"You got it! What do you want to talk to Tutt about?"

"That is something he and I need to discuss. Just tell him I'm here and need to talk to him, out here." Wagner turned to go. "If you bring down your man, we might be able to give him medical attention."

Wagner nodded that he understood and left to climb up to the vantage point that he had selected. One of the archers had been tending their injured comrade.

"I need one of you to give me a hand taking this one down to the cart. I need another man to get Tutt here to talk to Murdock. The rest of you keep them covered. If they try to approach or retreat, fire. Otherwise, hold your fire. If we become prisoners, then open fire." All the archers nodded that they understood and one of them disappeared, presumably to get Tutt.

Wagner and the archer lifted their injured comrade and headed down to Murdock's cart.

"You two can come out," Murdock flashed to Annie. *"Grab your kit. They're bringing down an injured man."*

"It's clear for us to come out. Get my kit, so I can fix my leg," Annie instructed Heather as they both were crawling out from under the cart.

"What kind of an injury?" Annie flashed.

"Arrow to the shoulder," Murdock smirked as he came close to Annie.

"I see you couldn't help yourself," Annie smirked.

"How bad is your injury?" Murdock asked seeing the small blood stain on her leather dress.

"The arrow that penetrated the deck of the cart nicked my thigh. Only went in a half-inch or so. I'll be fine."

"Heather, make camp here. Use the cart for cover. I don't trust these bastards," Murdock said to Heather quietly. Heather nodded that she understood and moved to comply. Murdock grabbed a couple of hides and headed toward the men carrying the injured man. Annie followed Murdock and stopped when he did.

It took several hours, but Annie managed to remove the arrow from the wounded man and treat the injury before Raymond Tutt, who was intentionally stalling, approached the wounded man. Wagner, standing close by, watched everything carefully.

Murdock spent his time watching Wagner and the armed men hidden in the rocks halfway up the hill.

"What was it you wanted?" Tutt asked testily.

"I wanted a private conversation with you," Murdock responded. "I didn't come for any other purpose and was then attacked, without provocation, I might add. If you're claiming an area, put up some signage so someone knows they are entering a killing zone."

"You and yours seem to have managed unscathed," Tutt said with a slight chuckle. "And you've injured one of my men and gotten me out here without informing me of your intentions." Tutt crossed his arms over his barrel chest, waiting.

"One of mine was minorly injured. I came here to give you a rundown, of sorts, of the rest of your fellow newcomers." Murdock waited.

"Well, then, give it," Tutt ordered impatiently when Murdock's pause had gone beyond long enough.

"I'm not sure I should," Murdock responded. "You have attacked me and mine and I have yet to hear an apology."

Tutt and Wagner started to laugh uproariously. When the two men opened their eyes, Tutt had a very close view of a flint arrowhead being aimed at his chest. Without being noticed, Murdock had managed to meander around so that Tutt and Wagner were lined up directly in front of Murdock. Neither man laughed.

"So, go ahead and shoot," Tutt said to Murdock. "You can't get both of us and my men will cut you to ribbons."

"This arrow passes through deer. It'll easily go through both of you, at this range," Murdock countered. "Give the signal to open fire. Let's see what happens."

Tutt gave the signal. When nothing happened for several minutes, he gave it again.

"Huh. Nothing happened. I wonder why?" Murdock taunted. He could see the two men blanch.

∾

Rogers, Hornsby, and Carpenter had been walking for more than a day when the mountains forced them downriver. When it was close to sundown, the three men came across two men sitting back-to-back and arguing with each other. Rogers recognized Tutt as one of the men. Hornsby recognized Wagner and blanched.

"Untie me," Tutt bellowed. "This is totally unacceptable!"

Rogers started to walk toward the two men when Carpenter stopped him. "How did you two get in this predicament?" he asked distrustfully.

"Murdock! He's around here, somewhere. Hope you have lots of guards," Tutt said.

"It's just the three of us," Rogers offered.

"That's interesting," Murdock said from their right. All three were startled and turned to see Murdock standing less than ten yards from them with an arrow aimed in their midst. "I think you three should disarm and go over by your friends."

"To whom do I lodge a protest?" Rogers asked loudly. He and Tutt had been arguing for some time.

"I wish to lodge one as well," Tutt stubbornly raised his voice, as an afterthought. "I wish to protest this torture!"

"Torture? What torture?" Rogers asked incredulously. "I'm the one that has to put up with your bellowing! You sound like a distressed water buffalo!"

Carpenter, Hornsby, and Wagner had been sitting. They had listened and refrained from making any remarks that might antagonize the situation, but found it difficult to remain impassive.

"Complain all you want," Murdock said loudly. "I don't care if it takes a month, but when we leave here, there's going to be an understanding between you two!" Rogers made a nervous laugh.

"I may bellow like a water buffalo, but you, Rogers, laugh like a hyena," Tutt retorted.

Carpenter, Hornsby, and Wagner all nodded agreement at that remark.

"I fail to see what is so difficult," Murdock yelled in frustration. "Currently, you are both acting like spoiled children. If Rogers has someone who works in clay, but has no idea how to fire it and Tutt has someone that knows how to build a kiln, but has no idea how to form clay, what's the harm in sharing? As leaders, you two should have been doing that from day one!"

"This *imbecile* let Declan into the cave," Tutt accused loudly.

"This *superstitious ass* thinks someone can give someone else nightmares," Rogers retorted just as loudly.

"Stop," Murdock insisted with raised hands, "Declan had nothing to do with anyone's nightmares!"

Tutt pursed his lips and glared at Rogers: "It just means I can't trust him," he said to Murdock.

"And I can't trust you, either," Rogers said in a high-pitched voice.

Murdock spent a lot of time looking from one man to the other. "Maybe, your groups need new leadership!" Both Tutt and Rogers glared at Murdock.

"What's *that* supposed to mean?" Rogers asked.

"It means he's looking to take over," Tutt said indignantly.

"Arghh," Murdock yelled in frustration as he threw his hands into the air and walked off toward the cart.

"Mind if I try?" Heather asked. "You've been at it for hours and, apparently, gotten nowhere."

"Be my guest!"

"Who *do* you trust, other than yourself?" Heather asked Tutt.

"I trust Wagner," Tutt said after some thought.

"And who do *you* trust?" she asked Rogers.

"Cliff Reed," Rogers answered after some thought.

"There's your problem," Heather said to Murdock after turning to face him. "You're talking to the wrong people!"

After many threats and much cajoling and badgering, Murdock had secured a promise from Tutt and Rogers to abide by any agreements that Reed and Wagner made for the benefit of the others in their respective camps. Murdock had promised to escort Wagner to a meeting with Reed and to return him unharmed. *I can see what Murdock is trying to do,* Wagner thought, *and I agree with him, we need to come together.*

Hornsby and Carpenter were released and sent back to their camp, Rogers being hostage, to prepare Reed for a meeting with Wagner.

Wagner walked Tutt up the hill to their fortified position to fetch his bow and arrows.

"I trust you to not give away our camp," Tutt said jokingly as they walked.

"I'll do my best," Wagner chuckled.

"Can you trust Murdock?" Tutt asked.

"By rights, he could have killed us all for ambushing him. He's a much better shot than anyone in our camp. I don't understand why our men didn't shoot."

"I think I found out why," Tutt said as he entered the concealed firing position. All of the men present were unconscious; sleeping peacefully. Shortly after they reached them, some of the archers were awakening.

"I don't know how he did it, but something tells me that Murdock knows more about this than he's willing to admit," Wagner stated.

"You need to be watchful of him and his strange ways," Tutt said, nodding agreement to Wagner's statement.

Another archer, disarmed, accompanied Wagner back down to Murdock's makeshift camp to help the wounded man back into the mines. Wagner waited patiently while Murdock, Annie, and Heather broke their camp.

Keith Rogers wasn't happy with the situation, but had decided that since he couldn't change it, it might be better to go along.

"I haven't heard anyone mention Emily. Tell me she's okay?" Rogers asked after a long while of walking in silence beside Wagner and Murdock.

"Why would we give you any information about a family member?" Annie asked, with a derisive tone, from her position on the cart next to Heather.

"I was just asking. Trying to make conversation to pass the time," Rogers explained.

"Why don't you pass the time in quiet contemplation," Murdock suggested.

Wagner chuckled: "He means shut-the-hell-up, Rogers. I'm starting to appreciate Murdock more all the time."

"What's that supposed to mean?" Rogers asked with a bit of petulance and a sideways glance at Wagner.

"He can't be all bad," Wagner observed. "He doesn't like you. And some think Murdock has no taste."

Do I tell Murdock, or do I keep it to myself? Heather asked herself. She had noticed Wagner and knew he was one of Palmer's henchmen. *I know I probably should have said something to Murdock, but I don't want to ruin anything for someone trying to make a life here.* She had also spotted Jackson Hornsby, in Rogers' entourage, and Nels Osterlund and Alvin Jones in with the group of farmers. It had taken her a while to piece together all the players, but now that she had, she was torn. *Murdock does have a right to know who these people are, or were, if he doesn't already.*

"Time for a break," Murdock said after several hours of pulling the cart. "I need some water and a breather." Heather dismounted when he set the cart down and handed him a waterskin. "You okay?" he asked Heather after taking a long pull on the waterskin.

"Not really, no," Heather said quietly.

"What's bothering you? Anything you can tell me?" Murdock asked.

"Wagner used to be one of Palmer's henchmen," she said under her breath and turned away from the others. "So did Hornsby and others."

Murdock winked at her and put an index finger beside his nose. "I know," he said very softly. "We'll talk later."

The rest were sitting wherever they could find a place.

"I'll be glad to get home," Rogers said aloud to anyone that would listen.

"How far is it to your area?" Murdock asked.

"It's a fair piece yet," Rogers said. "I'd say we'll be close when we stop for the night."

"We'll be stopping for the night when it is close to sundown," Murdock informed, "unless someone needs to stop sooner." With that, the waterskins were stowed and Heather walked behind the cart being pulled by Murdock. Annie climbed down from the cart before it started to move.

"What was the tense conversation with Murdock?" Annie asked Heather as they both walked behind the cart. All the men were walking in front of the cart and ignored the women.

"I recognized Wagner and Hornsby," Heather said quietly. "That caused me to remember where I'd seen two others that were with the farmers."

"Why did that bother you?" Annie asked.

"I thought Murdock needed to know that I recognized them as Palmer's henchmen. I feel I owe him."

"You're acting like you're still bothered by it, are you?" Annie asked.

440

"To me, Murdock is not acting cautiously enough around them. I felt he needed to be warned. At the same time, I didn't want to jeopardize anyone's chances for self-redemption. I know I'm not perfect and have made plenty of mistakes. I'm not sure I'd appreciate someone else reminding me of them when I'm trying to redeem myself."

"Well, you've done all you can," Annie said. "It's up to Murdock to do what he thinks best with the information." Annie noticed that Heather seemed to perk up a little.

It was several hours before Murdock called for a halt and nodded assent when Heather asked about setting up camp.

"Are we stopping for the night?" Rogers asked no one in particular. "It is hours before sundown. We should keep going."

"You want to keep going, then, by all means, do so!" Murdock said sarcastically. "The rest of us could use a rest and something to eat, but far be it for me to hold you back when you, obviously, have something else more important to do."

Rogers took a few more steps and then stopped. He turned to look at the rest of his traveling companions and saw that they weren't following him. He watched for a few minutes as the women were setting up a campsite and Wagner was gathering wood for the fire.

"Aren't you afraid I'll run off?" he asked as he slowly returned to the group.

"I'm concerned that wolves or cougars might get you and put a kybosh on any potential arrangements we might come to," Murdock responded, "but hey, if you want to go so bad, then I'm sure I can explain it to your man, when and if he arrives."

"Maybe I am being a bit too overanxious for my own good," Rogers said as he sheepishly returned.

"Don't come back empty-handed," Murdock scolded. "Give Wagner a hand with firewood."

~

It was just sundown when the camp was set, and everyone sat around the fire cooking their own piece of venison.

"So, Murdock, what do you get out of any agreements we make?" Rogers asked while he checked his cooking meat for the third time.

"Hmm…not a lot. Maybe a peaceful walk in the woods without worrying about getting shot is enough," Murdock responded with a sideways glance to Wagner.

"Sorry about that," Wagner said as he checked his own piece of venison. "You seemed to turn that situation around soon enough, though."

"I should've turned it around sooner than I did and spared Annie a wound," Murdock replied, "but that wouldn't have been friendly."

Rogers gave Wagner a puzzled look. "A group of men, under my command, opened fire on Murdock and the two women when they entered our lands," Wagner explained, clearly uncomfortable with the explanation.

"So, what happened?" Rogers asked after waiting a long time for Wagner to continue.

"Murdock…explained that we were not being very friendly."

Annie snickered loudly.

"You fired…twenty arrows? Or was it thirty?" Murdock asked.

"Twenty," Wagner corrected chagrinned.

"And how many did Murdock fire?" Rogers asked. The sparse facts had piqued his interest in the tale. He was looking around the fire at the faces. The two women smirked, Wagner scowled, and Murdock remained stoic.

"Two," Wagner said quietly, sheepishly.

"What?" Rogers asked. "I didn't hear you. Can you speak up a little?"

"Two!" Wagner shouted as he stood and started to pace.

"Two, alright? We fired twenty he fired two! He demonstrated his clear superiority and I quit antagonizing him!"

"Wagner," Murdock said as he stood and gave his venison to Heather to finish cooking. "Sit and calm yourself." Murdock took up his spear and walked into the dark.

"Where is *he* going?" Rogers asked aloud.

"We find it healthier to refrain from asking such things," Annie said as she bit off a chunk of venison.

A few minutes later, they all heard "Ouch!" and "Stop!" and "We surrender!" along with several scuffle sounds from several men in the dark. A few minutes after that, they all saw Murdock prodding three other men into the firelight.

"Nice of you to join us, Mister Hornsby, Mister Carpenter, and Mister Reed," Rogers said as he ate his venison.

Wagner had started to eat after he had calmed down. As he chewed, he watched the three men enter the camp, not too badly bruised or battered.

"You men really need to learn the proper way to enter someone's camp," Murdock chastised. "You don't do it by sneaking around in the dark!"

"We weren't sneakin'…exactly," Hornsby said sheepishly.

"Yes, we were," Carpenter said calmly. "We had to be sure it was safe, and I, for one, don't know the proper way to announce myself in the wild. I apologize, Mister Murdock."

A stout man, not much taller than Murdock, pushed his way forward.

"I'm Cliff Reed, Mister Murdock," the man said with some confidence as he stuck out his hand to Murdock. "These men were doing as I asked and as seemed prudent to me. If there has been any offense given, I trust you will exempt them, as they were following my orders." As he spoke, he glanced several times to his offered hand.

Murdock just looked at the hand and then back to the man.

"I trust you've been treated well, sir?" Reed asked Rogers without turning away from Murdock.

"Very well, thank you," Rogers responded. "Murdock, do you mind if I have a word alone with Cliff?"

"Not at all," Murdock said indicating that they should move out of earshot from the fire. "Take Carpenter with you."

"I want a word with you two," Murdock said to Wagner and Hornsby after Reed, Rogers, and Carpenter left for their private conversation. "I know who you are. Heather knows who you are, as well. We have…concerns."

"Okay, so you know who we are," Wagner said, distressed. "We used to follow Palmer, but I quit that a while back. I'm trying to make a fresh start with Tutt."

"And I'm doing pretty okay with Rogers and their group. I mean okay by them as well as myself," Hornsby said, chagrinned.

"Does Rogers and Tutt know about your prior allegiances?" Murdock asked.

"Rogers knows very little," Hornsby said, "and I'd prefer it to stay that way."

"Tutt knows nothing of my involvement with Palmer," Wagner said. "I've been loyal to him since joining him and have made a small place for myself with his group. I didn't offer the information and he didn't ask."

Hornsby was nodding his agreement with Wagner while he spoke.

"I'm not going to intrude on your lives," Murdock assured them. "I'm all about redeeming yourself and turning your life around. This little chat was more for information, than anything else."

With that settled, everyone sat at the fire.

"Tell me of Reed," Murdock said as he picked up his now cooked and cold piece of venison and sat next to Heather and Annie. "Can his word be trusted?"

"He's a good egg," Hornsby said as he struggled to sit. "If he gives his word, you can count on it. He does tend to speak plainly and carefully, though."

"You'll be leaving to escort Rogers to the cave you call home, Hornsby. Can I trust you to take him there without doubling back on us?" Murdock asked.

"Yes, sir, I'll see him home and only there," Hornsby assured as Reed, Rogers, and Carpenter were returning.

"Well, gentlemen, you have settled your business, I trust?" Murdock asked as he ate.

"I've given my instructions to Reed," Rogers stated, "if that's what you're referring to."

"Mister Reed, this is your counterpart, Mister Wagner," Murdock introduced.

Wagner got to his feet and offered his hand to the smaller man, "Ted, please."

"Nice to meet you, Ted," Reed said shaking the offered hand.

"So, Rogers, you're leaving tomorrow, with Hornsby and Carpenter, I assume," Murdock stated.

"I wasn't going to," Rogers said. "I thought I'd hang around and see how things go for a couple of days. It would give me a chance to get the lowdown on Emily."

"You misunderstood me," Murdock said sternly. "It wasn't a question."

"That seems rude," Reed said, concerned.

"Not really," Murdock said. "You and Wagner will be busy hammering out an agreement. I'll be busy trying to keep you two from killing each other and won't have time to protect what I need to protect. It would be safer, for all concerned, if Rogers went home."

"I'm going to need Carpenter," Reed said.

"For what purpose?" Murdock questioned between bites.

"When I'm finished, I'll require help getting home," Reed replied

"When I set this up, it was going to be just the two of you," Murdock stated. "Now, you want an extra man. Wagner agreed to come alone. Is he the bigger man? He doesn't need anyone's help for anything and appears to be able to take care of himself.

What does that say about you?" Murdock waited for a response from Reed. "It tells me," he continued when Reed didn't respond, "that you want to have things weighted in your favor. Do you really need an entourage? I can understand Rogers needing one, but you?"

"What's *that* supposed to mean?" Rogers asked.

"It means," Murdock responded, "that it's my considered opinion that you'd have difficulty locating your ass with both hands. You're a hindrance to most everything that needs to be done and I think you enjoy being one."

Gary Carpenter interposed himself between Murdock and Rogers and glared down at Murdock. Murdock slowly got to his feet.

"I'll give you a choice," Murdock said, to the bigger man, with a sardonic grin, "you can walk home or be carried, assuming, of course, you can find someone to carry you."

"Hold on," Rogers intervened. "We don't want any trouble. All we want to do is support and protect Reed."

"I told Wagner that I'd see to his safety. Do you think I would do any less for Reed?" Murdock asked without taking his eyes off Carpenter, as neither man had backed down.

"Carpenter, stand down," Rogers commanded. "Carpen—," Rogers started when Carpenter seemed to be ignoring his command.

Murdock saw Carpenter's hand reach for his twelve-inch machete and responded with a stiffened thumb upward to the larger man's solar plexus. Carpenter, gasping for air, stumbled back a few steps before catching his heel on a rock and falling backward to the ground. Rogers did what he could to catch the larger man, but ended up under him.

"That was uncalled for," Reed yelled.

Murdock quickly turned to face the rotund man. Faster than Reed could blink, Murdock had his twelve-inch machete out and twirled it, by the hilt, on his finger a few times. "Would you have preferred this?" he asked holding the machete in his outstretched hand. "He reached for his own machete and I... handled it."

Reed backed away from Murdock and the small pile that was Rogers and Carpenter. "Is this the kind of treatment I'm to expect?" he asked, concerned.

"Murdock is his own man," Annie interjected. "It isn't wise to threaten him in any way. Speaking from experience, I can assure you that he is...restraining himself."

"Well, then," Reed started as he relaxed a little, "let us hope he is more successful at his restraint. Very well, Murdock, I'll trust that you are a man of your word and will see me safely home. Hornsby, see to Carpenter and Rogers and the three of you can leave in the morning."

The next morning, Murdock, who hadn't slept the night before, saw to it that Wagner and Reed had their own area to discuss their agreement. It was a smallish clearing not far from Murdock's camp. Murdock had stationed himself within sight and was armed with his bow. Reed and Wagner were both unarmed.

"*How is it going?*" Annie flashed.

"*About as expected,*" Murdock flashed back. "*You have any thoughts on Heather?*"

"*She'd make a good addition. She told you of the recognition of Palmer's crew out of a sense of loyalty, loyalty to you,*" Annie flashed.

"*Congratulate me,*" Declan intruded excitedly. "*I'm a new father!*"

"*Congratulations!*" Murdock replied, grinning

"*What did Emily have?*" Annie asked, grinning.

"*I'll introduce the two of you to Maureen Emeline Griffen when you return,*" Declan responded. "*She's quite the beauty, if I do say so myself...and I do. Emily is doing fine. I haven't decided how I'm doing, yet.*"

Murdock chuckled to himself and shook his head slightly. His concentration was disrupted by Reed storming away from Wagner.

"Trouble in paradise," Murdock remarked.

"Already?" Annie injected.

It was sundown as Murdock, Wagner, and Reed sat in front of the campfire eating.

"For the last three days, I've been listening to you two hammer away at each other," Murdock said. "And I watched as you two gestured and threatened each other for three days before that. Please tell me that you are getting close to some sort of an agreement."

"This *towhead* is being unreasonable," Reed said with disdain.

"I'm being unreasonable?" Wagner disputed. "I've been *most* reasonable! We only have one major request — not a requirement, a request — and you say I'm being unreasonable! And what does my hair color have to do with anything? Is there some sort of Nordic bias here?"

"Our group refuses to be involved in human trafficking," Reed vehemently stated.

"Who is asking you to engage in something like that? All we want is for you to allow your women to consider our group as an option," Wagner defended. "What could possibly be wrong with that?"

"Wait. That is your only request?" Murdock asked. "What about Reed's weapons request?"

"We're willing to make the weapons they need and give them some training on their use," Wagner stated.

"And what about the payment for the weapons?" Murdock asked.

"At this point, we require deer hides for clothing and protection when working with metal. We understand that deer hides are very difficult to obtain without the weapons we're offering. Consequently, we're willing to turn over the weapons and wait for the payments until the fall."

Murdock turned to look at Reed. "What would it take for a woman to leave your group?" he asked skeptically.

"That would depend on the circumstances," Reed replied. "Our group dynamic is different than Tutt's. To us, every individual has a specific place and specific tasks that the rest of the group has come to rely on. Everyone in our group is currently engaged in polyamorous relationships. So, should a woman want to leave, it would be up to others as to what would be an equitable remuneration for any and all services rendered by that individual, in whole or in part, to the rest of the community."

Even though Reed had stopped talking, Murdock continued to look at him, mouth agape. "What if," he began, after some thought. "A woman was outside gathering fish or water or something and ran across Wagner here. They speak and she finds him attractive and wants to continue to get to know him. Some time passes and she decides that she needs to be with Wagner permanently. What would be the procedure?"

"Again," Reed started, "that would depend."

"On what, exactly?" Murdock asked.

"Hypothetically speaking, if she were a layabout and refused to help anyone in the colony with anything, it would fall to Rogers to determine if she were valuable enough to warrant, for lack of a better term, a dowry. Other considerations could be, but not limited to, where she was planning on going, ancillary people she would likely interact with, and other skills she had and if the removal of those skills would negatively impact the group as a whole.

"Given your scenario, if she wanted to leave to go to Tutt's, she'd be incarcerated for a period of time until it was determined that she wasn't impaired mentally. The same thing would happen if she went to your group, or any other group, or no group."

Murdock scowled, and Reed could see he was getting angry. "So, to break it down for us non-politicians, they are slaves, or they are delusional, if they wanted to leave your perfect society? Is that what you're saying?"

"If you think about it," Reed started with a serious contemplative look, "you'd have to be crazy to want to leave perfection. As far as being a slave, it might appear that way to the uninitiated, but actually, we have only our fellow community member's best interest at heart."

"Can you explain to me why the animosity toward Emily when she left?" Murdock asked.

"Emily, by way of being elected to the leadership, had given up her right to choose what was best for her. She was precluded from leaving and depriving the rest of the community of her leadership. The only way for her to give up the leadership was to be voted out, but that wouldn't have allowed her to just pick up and leave. Her skills were needed by the rest of the community in an emergency situation. So, we will be exerting our claim on her, should she show herself to our members."

Everyone heard what Reed had said and everyone was shocked into silence.

26

M urdock sat at the fire thinking. All of them had escorted Reed to the general area of his cave having immediately concluded their negotiations. When they left, they set a course for the ridge straight downriver from Rogers' group. Everyone was still in shock of what they heard from Reed.

"Now what do we do?" Heather asked. "Do we escort Wagner home, or do you have something else in mind?"

"I've checked all the waterskins and we are in dire need of water," Wagner said as he came in close to the fire. "Sorry, things didn't go as you planned. I was hopeful, but that's how it goes sometimes."

"Can I ask what your group needs?" Murdock asked.

"We barely made it through the winter," Wagner explained. "I like to froze to death trying to take a deer just before the end of winter. Food wise, we have fish, a white fish that reminds me of tilapia or cod, only tasteless. Water is no problem and it's warm in the mines, sometimes too warm.

"Most of us would like to have something else to eat, venison and river fish being the only other meat available, that we know of, and we need hides for making the leather clothes, and tools we need in the mines. Since most of us are men, not too many women followed Tutt when he left *'Paradise'*, most of us would like some female companionship."

"Is that all?" Murdock asked with a small chuckle.

"That's pretty much it," Wagner said. "Why?"

"The group of farmers needs metal tools, plows and such, to start with, but they have access to large amounts of the wild grain. I'm fairly certain they'd barter some grain for what they need," Murdock suggested.

"That would help," Wagner said. "Personally, I would like some training in hunting, but I understand if you're reticent."

"Hunting isn't a mystical art. It's just knowing your prey and being aware of what's going on," Murdock answered offhandedly. "I think our camp would be well-served if we had a large cooking pot and a wok. Do your people make anything like that?"

"As a matter of fact, we do," Wagner said.

"Well, I'd be willing to trade some hides for a large cooking pot and a wok. What about some arrow points that would fit onto wooden shafts?"

"I'm reasonably sure our people could figure something out. Especially if you provide a shaft of the size you use. We use metal arrows."

"We noticed," Annie glared as she passed by the men.

"They may work for you now, but wood or aluminum would be lighter and allow the arrow to be faster."

"Not to change the subject, but where are we?" Wagner asked.

"We can't go any further downriver from where we are right now. The ridge is close by. I want to head toward the river, tomorrow. It would allow us to refill our waterskins and I could introduce you to the temporary leader of the farmers."

"Are you going to escort me back to Tutt's?"

"I wasn't going to. It *is* a simple matter to find your way on your own."

"I'm afraid I'm going to have to insist," Wagner responded.

"You guaranteed my safe return and traipsing through Rogers' area — I'm assuming they are claiming everything from their camp to the ridge — isn't all that safe. Besides, it would give us a chance to work out our trade deal and for you to talk to our designers about your arrow points."

"I was just curious about the kettle and the wok. I'd prefer to talk to my wife, or have her decide the sizes she'd like. The arrow points are something I'm going to have to think about before I place any kind of an order, again, being curious about your people's expertise."

Murdock eyed Wagner curiously. *What are you up to?* he asked himself.

After walking most of the next day, the group reached the river close by the ridgetop. The women, upon arrival, went to fill waterskins and bathe. Murdock had gathered rocks for the fire-ring and was in the process of lighting the fire. It was on his second strike of the machete's spine on a piece of flint that he saw a brilliant spark touch off the tinder and his lights went out.

As he started to regain consciousness, his head was pounding and something warm flowed over his face. A bit went into his mouth. Unconsciously, his tongue touched it and he knew it was blood, probably his own. His brain seemed fuzzy and he felt like he was being rolled, legs and arms bound. Then, he had a falling sensation followed by extreme pain in his ribs and the crashing sound of tree limbs. *This is surreal*, he thought as he lost consciousness again.

Annie and Heather, sporting wet hair, were walking back, with large grins and filled waterskins. They weren't far from the intended campsite when they were greeted by Wagner headed toward the river. Annie eyed him suspiciously as he passed and relaxed a little once he had passed.

Suddenly, she felt a punch to the base of her skull. The blow stunned her and before she could protest, she was knocked to the ground, rolled onto her stomach and hands tied behind her.

Heather screamed and ran toward the camp. Just as she entered, she heard Wagner behind her.

"Drop the knife!" he said sternly.

When she turned to face him, she saw that Wagner was holding a knife to Annie's throat, her hands bound, her mouth gagged. It was then that she looked down and saw her twelve-inch machete was in her hand, even though she didn't remember drawing it. She willed her hand to open and she heard the machete hit the ground.

Wagner punched Annie again and dropped her. He rushed to Heather and seemed about to pick up her dropped machete when he rose quickly and struck the side of her head with his elbow and upper arm. She was distantly aware of her body hitting the ground.

Not long afterward, Heather remembered to open her eyes and saw Annie lying beside her, bound and gagged. It was then that she felt her own restraints cut into her ankles and wrists. She heard the cart moving and knew they were both on the bed of the cart.

"Is Murdock on the cart?" she whispered to Annie. She saw Annie close her eyes slowly and reopened them slowly, which seemed to her to be a sad motion, and saw her shrug slightly.

"Murdock is hurt or dead and Heather and I are prisoners. Wagner attacked us," Annie broadcasted. *I hope someone hears me,* ran through her mind. *"Murdock is hurt or dead and Heather and I are prisoners. Wagner attacked us,"* Annie repeated telepathically.

Maybe Beron would hear, she thought. *Surely, he will hear her call and respond. Is there anything beyond Beron's capabilities?*

～

Mei Lee jumped when the cabin door slammed open. She rushed to it and saw Beron and Bridget standing in the yard.

"Mate hurt!" she heard in her mind. She jerked her head toward Bridget. *"Not! You mate!"*

Mei Lee rushed through the cabin throwing things she didn't want and telling, loudly, Andy and Chun Hua to head to Declan's with Rosa. She had grabbed what she needed and left, slamming the cabin door closed.

"Irene, we have an emergency!" she flashed. *"Get ready to leave!"*

"Declan, I've sent the children to your place. There is an emergency with Murdock," she flashed. *"I'll let you know more when I do."*

By the time Mei Lee, riding Beron, and Bridget reached Declan's cabin, Doctor Harris was waiting outside with her medical kit.

"Whoa!" Harris yelled as she was levitated to Bridget's back to settle at the base of the huge female's neck. Mei Lee saw Harris' white knuckles as the two huge bears traveled thirty feet above the trees.

"Murdock!" Mei Lee flashed as they gained altitude. *"Annie, where are you!"*

"Murdock, Annie, where are you!" she flashed again as they passed over the first ridge and again after passing over the second ridge some time later.

"We are relatively unharmed, for now," a response flashed to her. *"We were attacked by the river and the top of the ridge above the farmers. Make sure he's okay and then come for us."*

Before Mei Lee could tell Beron anything, he was adjusting his course accordingly.

Mei Lee estimated that it was a couple of hours before dawn by the time the search party had landed. It was too dark for her to see anything. Beron had found the ring of stones that were intended to be a fire-ring. Mei Lee touched the huge bear as he was searching with his nose to the ground. *Beron seems to be a little frantic,* she thought as she was being led. *He doesn't seem to be as calm as he usually is.*

"*Murdock over edge here,*" Beron flashed to the rest at dawn.

"*I can't see anything down there,*" Mei Lee responded when she looked over the edge. "Irene, stay with Bridget." Mei Lee pulled her own twelve-inch machete and slowly levitated herself over the edge.

As she slowly floated down the ridge-face, she saw plenty of rocks for a body to bounce off of as well as tree branches growing to the rock face.

"*Found!*" Beron flashed.

Not long after, Murdock was laying on the ground being tended by Doctor Harris. Mei Lee, Bridget, and Beron close at hand.

"Well?" Mei Lee asked as Harris rose to her feet.

"I wish I had an x-ray of Murdock's skull," she started with a concerned expression. "I'd be willing to bet his skull is thicker than Declan's, probably thicker than any other human. He was hit hard on the right side of his skull, with a rock probably. It should've killed him. He has several broken ribs on his left side, which should've killed him.

"He is alive, but he needs to be kept still and closely observed until we can get him home and I give him a proper exam. The broken ribs can puncture his lungs if we're not careful. I'm surprised they haven't already."

Mei Lee looked around for signs of the struggle and for any clues.

"Find anything?" Harris asked.

"The cart is missing, as well as all of Murdock's personal weapons. I did find a good-sized rock with blood on it over there," Mei Lee indicated the general region of the fire-ring."

"Probably the rock used. Anything else?" Harris asked.

"No, it's what I didn't find. I haven't found any sign of a struggle from Heather or Annie."

"Knowing Heather, she'd go quietly if Murdock was injured and Annie was threatened," Harris added.

"*Annie, are you okay?*" Mei Lee flashed. "*We found Murdock and he is badly injured,*" she continued when no response came. "*We're taking him home and then we'll be coming for you and Heather.*" I really didn't expect an answer, but I was hoping, she thought.

It was late in the day when Mei Lee, Doctor Harris, Bridget, and Beron, levitating Murdock, returned to the camp.

"Put him in here," Declan offered, holding the door open.

"*No. Take to cave,*" Beron insisted. "*Heal faster.*"

"*Irene needs to monitor him closely,*" Mei Lee tried to explain.

"*Doc Tor go with,*" Bridget flashed to her friend.

"Is there anything you need for Murdock's treatment that needs to be done here?" Mei Lee asked.

"We aren't much past the 'stone knives and animal skins' stage, so it doesn't matter much, to me, where. It might matter to Murdock, though," Doctor Harris responded. "Why did you ask?"

"Beron is insisting that Murdock would heal faster at the cave," Mei Lee said trying to keep the peevishness out of her voice. *He is my husband, dammit!*

"I have no idea…wait, *the* cave?" Harris asked. "Whatever for? Unless there is an x-ray machine, ultrasound equipment, and a good MRI, he'd be better off here."

"*Meaning?*" Beron asked Harris.

"*Those are machines that would allow me to see inside Murdock's body, to see that everything is where it should be,"* Harris tried to explain. *"An x-ray would allow me to see any broken bones, if he has any, which I think he does. Ultrasound and MRI would allow me to see the soft tissues inside without cutting him open."* Harris had decided to try to keep things simple for the animal.

"Share?" Beron asked.

Harris shrugged and lay down. She was soon in the sharing state.

In the sharing state world, she saw Murdock standing in front of her. He didn't appear to be lucid and as she watched, she saw the flesh dissolve leaving only the skeleton. As she looked, Doctor Harris could clearly see the broken ribs and the multiple skull fractures radiating from the impact point.

"Can you add in some of the internal organs around the ribs, please?" she asked somewhat sheepishly.

As she watched, intestines, lungs, kidneys, and liver were all added in. Harris could clearly see his lungs were in danger of being punctured.

"Can you stabilize the ribs, otherwise there may be a problem when we move him," she suggested. *I know this is all taking place inside my mind, but damn! If this was real, I'd love to learn how it's done!*

"It is all real, Irene," she heard from somewhere behind her. "Your denial of a reality doesn't make it any less real for your patient."

Harris turned to look toward the voice, but there was no one there. *Huh ...that sounded just like Doctor Prescott from my days in medical school. I don't ever recall him saying those words to me, but that was his voice.*

The sharing ended.

"We're going to the cave," Harris said emphatically to Mei Lee. "He needs it!"

Mei Lee stared in disbelief at the doctor's sudden change in opinion.

A week after Murdock was taken to the cave, Mei Lee helped him to his feet and Irene Harris helped walk him around a little.

"How are the kids?" Murdock asked weakly.

"They're fine," Mei Lee reassured him. "They're with Declan and Emily."

"So, they're being spoiled," Murdock responded with a slight chuckle and cringed at the pain it caused.

"What happened?" Mei Lee asked.

"The meeting was a bust," Murdock explained. "Didn't you see it in the sharing while I was unconscious?"

"I did, but you were hurt pretty bad and I thought you were hallucinating."

"I wasn't. That is what happened. Then I made a fatal error in giving Wagner a little trust and now Annie and Heather have been paying for it."

"Well, I don't think Annie is doing any of the paying," Harris interjected. "Last communication I had with her, she was fine and so was Heather, Tutt's men, not so much. She said she'd have them all softened up for you by the time you're better."

From the time of her abduction, Heather was frightened of what could happen. She wasn't in fear for her safety. She feared what Murdock, or any of the others, would do to Wagner. She had enjoyed talking to him and flirting with him on the journey through the hinterlands.

For months, she had been lonely and in need of a male companion and for that purpose, Wagner would suffice. Now, though, he had done the unthinkable. He had killed Murdock and stolen herself and Annie. *I'm certain someone is going to be coming to exact retribution,* she thought.

~

"You've really screwed the pooch this time, Wagner," Annie taunted still bound, but not gagged in the back of the cart. "Why don't you let us go before things get out of hand?"

Wagner was struggling with the cart. For Murdock, the cart rolled easily, but since his appropriation of Murdock's property, the cart didn't seem to roll very well.

"What the hell is going on?" Wagner cursed, dropping the handles of the cart, and walking to the rear. As he looked behind him, he could clearly see a dark trail where one of the wheels wasn't turning. "Have I been dragging this the whole way?" he asked.

"Maybe you left the brake on," Annie taunted. "What is your plan for us? I'm sure you had some sort of a plan before you bashed in Murdock's head."

"Like I told Murdock, we needed leather and women. Now we have both."

"Is that what you really think? Do you think we're your property? You could have had more leather than you could use, if you would have dealt fairly with Murdock."

When Wagner looked at Annie, he frowned, and his face reddened seeing her smug smile and hearing the condescension in her voice.

"You want to be gagged again?" he asked angrily.

He started looking under the cart to see if there was something preventing the wheel from turning. Seeing nothing wrong, he tried to stand and banged his head hard on the underside edge of the cart bed. He grabbed the top of his head, sucking air through his teeth indicating his injury, seeing stars as he stepped out from under the cart. He then felt something grab his neck from behind and drive his head into the solid, wooden wheel.

A few minutes later, he came to, lying on the ground and his head felt like it was splitting.

Heather, watching the scene, felt sorry for Wagner. She suspected that Annie was causing his problems. *We haven't even gone halfway, yet,* she thought. *How far was it to Tutt's camp? Fifty or sixty miles? I'm not sure of the distance, but I'm sure Wagner is going to feel every inch of it.*

"What do you know about Murdock?" Annie asked rhetorically. "Do you know how loved and respected he is among his people? What do you think they're going to do to you when they come for us?"

"What makes you think that you're worth coming for? Whoever tries is going to die!" Wagner snapped.

"Did you kill Murdock?" Annie asked.

"Yeah, I did! I hit him in the head with a rock as hard as I possibly could. Then I rolled him off the cliff, for good measure."

"Are you a Doctor or have you had any sort of medical training?"

"No, but he was dead!"

"Huh…What do you think is going to happen if you failed to kill him?"

Seven days after Wagner stole the cart, Heather, and Annie, he finally reached the entrance to the mines. Raymond Tutt had come to the entrance as soon as word reached him of Wagner's return.

"You look terrible," Tutt said to the younger man. "What happened?" He made a point to not mention the dark line that ran from the mine into the distance.

"I have no idea," Wagner said, exasperated. "I've got to be

the clumsiest person alive. First, one wheel wouldn't turn, then the other one. I checked several times, but there was no reason for it. Every time I looked under to check, I'd hit my head getting out from under. I ran into the wheels with my forehead so many times I lost count. I couldn't seem to take more than two steps without tripping on something or tripping on nothing."

"That sounds bad," Tutt sympathized. "How long have you been doing that?"

"Since we left the river seven days ago."

"It took you seven days to make a trip that should have only taken two or three days?"

"That's why I look this way."

"How did you get the cart from Murdock?" Tutt asked.

"I killed him. Bashed in his head and then rolled him off a cliff."

"Are you certain he's dead?" Tutt asked, disbelievingly.

"Yes, I'm certain!" Wagner snapped. "Why is everyone so surprised that I killed him? Do you think that's something I would make up?"

"I don't doubt that you *think* you've killed him, Ted. It's just that it's been tried before."

A week after Wagner's return, the earthquakes started. People raised the alarm throughout the mine. Evacuations began in the lowest levels and worked their way up, everyone rushing to avoid chunks of falling ceiling. No one stopped when they reached ground-level, but exited the mine and were promptly escorted to an area that was "out of the way" by Murdock, Mei Lee, Harris, and Declan.

When Annie and Heather exited, they were escorted behind Murdock's people.

When Tutt and Wagner exited, finally, they were slammed against the wall inside the mine, by forces unseen.

"I have questions for you," Murdock stated to Tutt after everyone else was evacuated from the mine. "Were you aware of Wagner's duplicity before it occurred?"

"That would depend on what you're referring to," Tutt answered. "You don't intimidate me, Murdock. I lived through the nightmares brought on by Declan so I can withstand anything you can come up with. Besides, if you wanted me dead, I would be, so you want something and that is what is staying your hand."

"Did you know," Murdock restated, "that his plan was to try to kill me and steal everything he could?"

"If you aren't strong enough to protect your stuff, then you deserve to lose it," Wagner yelled defiantly.

"No, I didn't know," Tutt said with a smirk.

"And do you condone it?" Murdock asked quietly.

"It is my opinion," Tutt began, "that you are the biggest impediment to humans smoothly conquering this world and making it our own. Any actions that remove the impediment are welcomed, by me."

"So, you're saying that you sanction Wagner's actions?"

"Yes, that's what I said."

"You all heard what your leaders said," Murdock said to the crowd of Tutt's followers. "Tutt, either knowingly or unknowingly sanctioned Wagner's actions. Those actions were an attempt on my life, and theft of my property, and the kidnapping of Annie and Heather. I require a solution, from the rest of you, to fix this." Murdock returned to his own group and said nothing else.

"What are you expecting?" Declan flashed.

"I'm expecting them to come to a solution that they can live with," Murdock responded.

"Even if that solution isn't what you want?" Declan flashed.

Murdock looked at him blankly. *"And what is it that I want, exactly?"*

"You mean you don't want revenge?" Declan flashed, incredulous.

"I want to be done with this whole affair. I want to be left alone to live as I prefer. That is what I want," Murdock responded.

～

It took those following Tutt some time to come to a solution. They were all standing outside the mine entrance facing Murdock and his people.

"We have decided," the chosen spokesman started, "that we agree with Tutt and Wagner." There was an air of contempt in the entire group.

"So, just to be clear," Murdock started as he walked toward them, "if I were to tell you all to get out of my mine, you'd leave?"

"Well, no," the leader said after thinking about it for a second or two.

"And why not? By your logic, none of you, either individually or as a group are strong enough to protect it. I can walk in and take it over and none of you can stop me. So, I'm entitled to it, correct?"

There was a lot of grumbling amongst the people in front of him.

Murdock spoke after letting them a stew little: "Just as a final vote, anyone who backs Tutt and Wagner, can join them in the mine entrance. If you don't agree, then form up outside the mine."

As he watched, Murdock saw roughly half the people divide and enter the mine. The rest milled around outside.

"Anyone else?" Murdock asked trying to prompt them into making the choices final. "Make your choices and be certain." A few changed their minds; some outside went in and some inside left. "Okay. That's it," Murdock said as he stuck two long spears into the ground on either side of the entrance. "As a fair warning, those inside the mine cannot leave. Those outside can enter, but the entrance is strictly one-way. This is only temporary, as I am planning a more permanent solution."

As he spoke, one of those individuals inside the mine tried to leave and fell, unconscious, half inside. His fellows dragged him back inside.

"What are we supposed to do?" a man asked with a look of panic on his face. "The mine has the only food source and water source in the area."

"The rest of you can go wherever you want. That way," Murdock indicated a direction toward the farmers, "are the farmers. I think they would be glad to have more individuals, especially those with metal working experience. Over that way," Murdock indicated a rough direction to the huge cave, "Keith Rogers' group may welcome you back, but I wouldn't count on it. Regardless, the mine is closed."

"But what about those left inside?" someone else asked.

"I can reopen the mine," Murdock responded. "All you need to do is go inside and kill everyone in there." He looked sternly to the rest. "Do that and I'll reopen it."

"You can't ask us to do that," someone said, shocked. "That would be murder!"

"Isn't that what you want me to do? You want me to 'take care of the problem' for you. I'm refusing, so you can take care of it yourself. I'll wait a little while for you to accomplish it, but not long. I'm heading home."

After waiting an hour, Murdock entered the mine alone. As he walked around, he collected all of his equipment, which was on his cart at the time it was stolen and reloaded it. As he made his way to the exit, he saw Tutt and Wagner.

"I'm missing several hides so, in exchange, I'm taking a wok and the biggest kettle I could find," he said to the two men. "Either of you have a problem with that?"

"I have a problem with *you*," Wagner seethed.

"Sorry to hear that," Murdock said with a slight smile and a glare.

As Murdock was staring at him, Wagner began to feel a pain in his chest and pressure around his heart.

What is this? I am young, too young to be having heart problems, he thought. *Is Murdock causing this? That's impossible!* The pain worsened and Wagner fell to the stone floor of the mine.

As suddenly as it started, the chest pain ended.

"A little something to remember me by," Murdock said, his expression unchanged, as he left the mine.

2 7

Before winter, in the year of Tutt's incarceration, Murdock erected a twenty-foot high block-wall of granite. The wall completely surrounded the mine holding Tutt, Wagner, et al. Murdock knew they would tunnel out eventually, but they would have to tunnel more to get out of the walled in area. In various places around the wall, he placed engraved stones. The stones were all the same and gave the warning: "Behind this wall are the most despicable people alive. Call them anything you want, but, to me, pirates, thieves, and murderers seems to fit the best. Leave them. Everyone else will be better off."

After enclosing the mine, Murdock refused to leave the "Oomah Plateau", as he called it, for anything except escorting one of his tribe, or helping Doctor Harris and Annie.

He had named the mountain that housed the Oomah warren as "Mount Oomah" and no one dissented. Also, he referred to the different plateaus as "the stairs of Mount Oomah". He thought it great fun, when at the farmers' group and heading home, to refer to it as "climbing the stairs of Mount Oomah". No one else seemed to think it funny or even amusing, but he was Murdock and, in their opinion, was entitled to call it whatever he wanted.

He hunted and fished with anyone and everyone, from his tribe, who wanted to go. He trained his tribal members in both woodcraft and martial arts, so those who chose to venture off the plateau would be able to handle any threat.

In the year before the next group of newcomers and being unaware of the means for determining the position to land, Murdock moved both previously landed pods to the stream on the same step as the medical facility. He spent the rest of the year wondering if it would do any good.

Annie and Doctor Harris had decided to build a medical "facility" at the base of the second step from Mount Oomah. Murdock and Declan had helped them design and build a stone building, roughly the size of Declan's home, which used to be the community building. They had decided to locate it at the site Murdock had camped when he first met Emily.

After two years of work, the complex consisted of a two-story block house of granite, on the roof of which was a filter system for a small portion of the river that was diverted for the medicos' use. Part of the house extended under the ridge face. This was surrounded by a twenty-foot-high granite wall with a small doorway that only allowed people to enter single-file, and thus made it defensible by a small force. The walled area was large enough to encircle the house and the yard, with a sizable garden inside it.

Roy White, the paramedic who had been living with the Rogers' group, had decided to join Harris and Annie. He brought with him all the medical supplies that Rogers had and, in turn, collected all the medical supplies from the farmers.

Heather chose not to join Murdock's tribe. She had decided, after spending another winter on the Plateau, to join the farmers. She had taken a shine to Alvin Jones and had decided to live with him on the outskirts of the farming community. They worked on taming a few deer for draft animals.

Most of those who had resided in the mine and didn't agree with Tutt's ideals, found their way to the farmers, and started a small metalworking operation to benefit them.

Reyes' group had chosen to be completely cut-off from the others. Murdock abided by their choice and avoided them and their territory. He also instructed his tribal members to do the same.

Either from damage to her ovaries, or melancholy over the loss of two of her children, or both, Mei Lee failed to conceive for three years and was plagued with despondency.

Declan and Emily had two more children before the next transport arrived: Roslynn, born a year after Maureen, and Gordon, born early in the spring before the next landing. Emily helped with the tending of the community garden with Mei Lee, Andy, and Chun Hua. Declan spent his time with Murdock or working on his pottery. He had managed to fire his own bricks and built a large functional kiln.

Declan Griffen was sitting at the table located on the roof of the "Harris Medical Facility". It was a nice morning and he had a pleasant trip from his home to visit his friends and fellow tribesmen.

"Have a nice trip, Declan?" Doctor Harris asked as she handed him a plate of venison, carrots, and onions with some barley-bread toast.

"I did! Thank you! And before you ask, everyone is fine," Declan responded as he pulled out his six-incher and wiped the blade on his leather pants-leg. "Em is as beautiful as ever and the girls are growing like weeds. Gordon will get there in the next six months." As he ate, he flashed mental pictures of his family to the doctor.

"How's Mei Lee doing?" Harris asked as she sat at the table with a plate of toast for herself. "Has she improved at all?"

Declan frowned while he chewed. *"Not really,"* he flashed as he took another bite. *"Murdock has said nothing and Beron won't comment, but I think their relationship is very strained."*

"I was thinking of visiting," Harris started, "just as a friend, and to use the spa. I worry about them. They've had a hard time of it."

"You know, this is pretty good, for hospital food," Declan said with a grin, trying to change the subject to something more pleasurable.

"Thanks," Harris said with a small chuckle and a slight grin. "Annie will be glad to hear you still like her cooking."

"I thought you made this," Declan said, shocked.

"Declan Griffen, you know I have difficulty boiling water! Annie and Roy do all the cooking. I do what I can in the garden."

"How are things going with him?" Declan asked.

"About like it was when Heather first came to our tribe. Annie and I try to make a point of vocalizing as much as possible, so he doesn't feel left out. We both tend to sub-vocalize when we communicate telepathically, so we try to not do it around him."

"Been working on your levitation?" Declan asked.

Harris chuckled. "When we first built this place, there was no need for stairs. Annie and I just levitated ourselves up to the second floor or the roof. Since Roy joined us, that has come to a halt. We actually had to relearn how to use steps."

"Well," Declan started after a few minutes of silence, "I'm here to inform you that the next pod is due any day now."

Harris looked shocked: "It's been five years already? I guess I'd lost track of time."

"Murdock has said he would send out a message to those of us who can communicate telepathically when the pod is on its way down. He did move the other pods towards the stream on this plateau. He's hoping it will help direct the next pod to land somewhere close to here and away from *Mount Oomah*."

"Hopefully, it'll work, and we can avoid any culture clash. Trying to explain the Oomah to outsiders is difficult at best. To newcomers, it's impossible."

"Yeah, you and I know all about that," Declan chuckled as the words triggered a memory.

Harris chuckled as she remembered her own skepticism. "Where are you off to next?"

"I have to check on a possible mount that Heather and Al are working on for us."

"I'd think Murdock would have taken care of that himself."

"The whole affair with Tutt and Wagner has soured him on strangers. Not that he was all that sociable, to begin with."

"Sociable is not how I'd describe Murdock even in the best of times," Harris chuckled. "Don't get me wrong, I love the guy, but he can be very...unyielding."

Declan became serious. "The funny thing is, I think of Kevin as my best friend, except for Em, of course. Murdock's best friend is Beron. I know that and accept it, but I don't think it's all that healthy. He needs more human interaction."

"Good luck convincing him of that," Harris responded seriously.

"I'm suspecting that Beron is teaching him things while he's in the 'sharing state'. Seven or eight days ago, I saw Murdock drop a deer from more than a hundred yards."

"That's nothing new. Murdock is a phenomenal shot with a bow."

"He didn't use a bow or arrow or even a spear."

"So, how did he do it?" Harris asked.

"I don't know. When I skinned it out, I saw nothing that would point to a cause of death. I think he just stopped the heart or pinched something off from the inside. It scared the hell out of me to see it all happen and Murdock was so...callous. I've seen him show more remorse before when hunting, but not now."

"So, you're thinking that all the sharing he's done with the Oomah has changed his mental make-up?"

"I don't know. I don't think humans were meant to have that kind of power. Who can stop him if he goes completely off the rails?"

"I think you're being overly dramatic," Harris said. "Murdock is one of the most level-headed people I've ever met. I think what you're witnessing is the stress of losing a child and what that can take from you on top of the stress of trying to set so many on the path of survival. Everyone has placed a heavy burden on him, and he feels it. Add to that, there are even more landing soon. My advice is to watch him and, if appropriate, question him about some of his actions and how it relates to his mental state."

"So, I'm overreacting?" Declan asked.

"I think you're someone concerned for a good friend, and that is a good thing." Harris grinned at him a little.

"Well, I have to push on. Be sure to tell Annie about the impending doom of 'newcomers'," Declan chuckled.

"Already have. Take care of yourself and your family," Harris said as she bid farewell to her friend.

He used to be a patient and now he is a dear friend, Irene thought.

Then a thought hit her and shocked her. *I've never had this many good and true friends. I don't think I had any, on Earth.*

Beron gave the notice to Murdock who, in turn, sent out the notice telepathically to everyone who could perceive his thoughts. The new arrivals were on their way.

Doctor Harris, Annie, and Roy were sitting out on the roof of the Medical facility when Irene and Annie received the message. They both stood and looked up at the quickly lightening predawn sky. Shading their eyes with a hand, they looked up at what appeared to be a hole in the sky; and it was getting larger.

Declan was saddling his new mount when the message came. He stopped and looked up seeing the huge hole in the sky and whistled to himself.

"Dancer, either that is one huge ship, or a meteor is coming," he said to his mount as he watched it descend.

Dear reader,

We hope you enjoyed reading *Civilization*. Please take a moment to leave a review in Amazon, even if it's a short one. Your opinion is important to us.

The story continues in *Resolutions*. To read the first chapter for free go to:

https://www.nextchapter.pub/books/resolutions

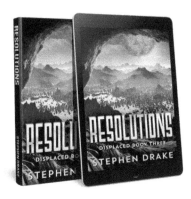

Discover more books by Stephen Drake at https://www.nextchapter.pub/authors/stephen-drake

Want to know when one of our books is free or discounted for Kindle? Join the newsletter at http://eepurl.com/bqqB3H

Best regards,

Stephen Drake and the Next Chapter Team

ABOUT THE AUTHOR

Stephen Drake, a retired computer programmer of 20+ years, is an American fantasy/sci-fi author. He is an avid Harley-Davidson Motorcycle enthusiast and versed in many survival skills such as martial arts and bow hunting. He is also an avid reader of sci-fi especially that by R.A. Heinlein and John Scalzi.

Although he has been a long-time resident of Washington State, he was born in Iowa and has lived in Wisconsin, Nebraska, Iowa, Montana, and Virginia. He draws on his experiences to create gripping and believable stories.

OTHER BOOKS BY THIS AUTHOR:

The Displaced series:

Displaced (book one)

Civilization (book two)

Resolutions (book three)

The Blackwing saga:

Blackwing (book 1)

Jessica Strange (book 2) (Work In Progress)

POST YOUR REVIEW

Now that you've finished reading, please take a moment to share your thoughts. Your review means a lot to the author and helps other readers!

Post your review on Goodreads or on Amazon.

Civilization
ISBN: 978-4-86747-050-3

Published by
Next Chapter
1-60-20 Minami-Otsuka
170-0005 Toshima-Ku, Tokyo
+818035793528

15th May 2021